VOICE OF THE SILENCED

VOICE OF THE SILENCED

FALLON DEMORNAY

Podium

All rights reserved. No part of this publication may be reproduced, stored in a retrieval system, or transmitted in any form or by any means electronic, mechanical, photocopying, recording, or otherwise without prior written permission from Podium Publishing.

This is a work of fiction. Names, characters, places, and incidents are either products of the author's imagination or used fictitiously. Any resemblance to actual events, locales, or persons, living, dead, or undead, is entirely coincidental.

Copyright © 2026 by Fallon MacLean

Cover design by M.S. Corley

ISBN: 978-1-0394-8285-2

Published in 2026 by Podium Publishing
www.podiumentertainment.com

My sister, Zory—I hope you are resting among the stars.

VOICE OF THE SILENCED

CHAPTER ONE

Vesper Crole didn't appreciate being summoned like a dog to heel, but when SIGA snapped their fingers, you either bent the neck or hung by it.

Rough hands yanked away her blackout visor without warning and Vesper blinked furiously as searing light cut across her corneas like a scalpel. Faces emerged from the canvas of hot white in little pinpoints of color that rapidly expanded into men and women gathered around a boardroom table shaped like a crescent moon.

Not holos. Live humans. *Politicians.* An easy guess, even if they weren't all dressed in the same crisp suits stamped with SIGA badges on their lapels. They'd all mastered the dour look of someone struggling to take a shit after five days of stony bowels as if it were a mandated part of their uniform.

"Sit," an almost robotic voice demanded.

Her captors nudged Vesper toward the single empty chair, high-backed and wrapped in buttery black leather. Refusing it, she continued to stand and scanned her surroundings.

The oval suite was dimly lit, with smooth glass walls tinted official SIGA blue—a stark, rich navy only government and STARs agents were allowed to wear. There were no windows. Not surprising, given she was standing less than eight feet away from the chairwoman and her board. Viewports were a security risk, and a blank room offered little insight as to where the SIGA base was situated.

One thing became immediately apparent. Although the board wanted to maintain the utmost secrecy, whatever they wanted from her was important enough for her to be faced with the most affluent members of government, including the chairwoman herself—in the flesh. Anyone else might've found themselves shocked, but as Vesper had grown up around the most affluential men and women of the Inner Circle, it would take more than a dozen elected officials to rattle her nerves. What did surprise her, however, was the woman seated to the immediate right of the chairwoman. A face she hadn't seen since walking out the doors of her family's palatial estate four years ago.

Tri-city senator Dameris Shinoda.

Her *mother*.

Approaching the table, Vesper removed her crossbody sack and dropped it on the pointed tip of the diamond-lacquered table. All eyes tracked the movement. Pleased by their curiosity, and always one to stir the pot for shits, Vesper deactivated the nanite-cover to reveal its contents. To her profound pleasure, a mixture of disbelief and stomach-churning disgust washed across their distinguished faces.

"Is that . . . ?" A balding director nearest to her pressed a hand to his mouth to stifle a whimper.

"De'Adrick Weaver," Vesper answered with a sharp grin. "Or what's left of him."

The head bobbed in the cylinder of glass filled with stabilizing fluid to preserve the soft tissue from decay. Another request from the woman who'd hired Vesper, as she planned to keep the abusive bastard displayed on a mantle in her chop-shop.

His mouth hung askance, courtesy of the broken jaw Vesper had given him when they went to blows in the streets of the lunar outpost before she'd finished him with a clean shot to his temple. De'Adrick ran her almost three months to the day, but the bounty she was due would be more than she'd made in the last two years. She'd have gotten more—much more—if she'd brought him in alive and allowed her client to have fun with him first.

But Vesper preferred it this way. The dead were easier to transport, and fortunately for her, she'd had him already bottled before the cybers had shown up to bring her in.

"Thank you for meeting with us." Seated at the middle of the crescent, Annelise Aramir folded her hands before her as if giving an address to the public. As the second woman ever elected as chair of the SIGA board and only a year away from running for a third term which, if she won, she'd be the longest-serving person to hold the title since the Inner Circle's inception.

United we circle, together we thrive!

Her campaign slogan echoed the dreams of their forefathers' vision before launching the centuries-long Zone Wars, seizing the best planets for themselves after the working class had done the heavy lift with terraforming.

"Not like I had a choice." Vesper gestured to the two cybers still standing guard at her back. The same ones who'd interrupted her afternoon and, after displaying their ordnance, gave her the choice to come in without incident, or face retaliation. Vesper was a skilled fighter but only a fool would dare take on a lone cyber, let alone two.

She was no fool.

Collapsing into the available chair, Vesper kicked her boots onto the pointed edge of the table next to De'Adrick's floating head, earning a scowl from her mother who sat with her shoulders drawn with military precision.

You could level a house by the line of her posture.

"What's all this about? Last I checked, I'm good on my annual levies."

"I'll cut to the chase. We have a job for you." The chairwoman shook away layers of blond hair cut to frame her impassive face, and while Vesper considered herself good at reading people, Annelise Aramir gave nothing she didn't already want to give. An admirable skill. One that wasn't easily attained, only earned.

"What kind of job?"

"One of extreme urgency. And discretion."

Vesper gave a bored shrug while examining her nails, cut short and well groomed—even as a bounty hunter she was adamant about hygiene and cleanliness. "Whatever it is will have to wait. I won't have an opening for at least a month. Maybe two."

"Given the priority of this matter, the board will be more than happy to increase your standard rate to an S3 mark and will reimburse whatever was issued in advance on your next contract—for the inconvenience, of course, to ensure we have your undivided attention."

That sparked Vesper's interest, at least enough to continue listening. An S3 was reserved for the highest payouts, and few if any made it to the open hunting boards. More interestingly, though, it was uncommon for SIGA to solicit a bounty hunter, given their vast arsenal of agents and cybers to draw from. Whatever the job, they wanted this kept as far from them as possible, not only for the sake of optics but to evade potential blowback, which added spice to her already simmering interests.

This mark was someone SIGA either deeply feared or who had made the mistake of pissing them off. No one hired Vesper unless *dead* was not only an acceptable outcome, but a guarantee.

"Before we go any further—Lennox Namsara is our chief legal counsel. Lennox, if you would, please." Chairwoman Aramir gave a summoning wiggle of her fingers, and a man tucked to the side of the wall stepped forward.

He rounded the lower curve of the crescent table, heading toward Vesper with a young man trailing briskly behind him, a junior lawyer or assistant, hugging a tablet against his chest like a shield. Lennox was tall, built almost like a retired athlete, broad-shouldered and narrow-hipped. He wore a charcoal suit cut to him like he'd been born into it, and which complemented his silver beard, perfectly groomed to enhance the proud line of his jaw.

He held a small, flat remote between them, about six inches away from her face. "Please state your full *legal* name. Not an alias or preferred moniker. State what is listed precisely on your government registered identity tags, along with your personal code."

Vesper bristled. "Why?"

"It's for the NDA implant, which is a requirement for anyone without official or military clearance, so that sensitive information can later be redacted, either at the end of your contract term or as soon as you walk out those doors, should you refuse the board's proposal."

Vesper's hand instinctively shot to the side of her neck, rubbing across muscles as her mind spun from the moment of confrontation with the cybers to the removal of the hood once entering the boardroom. At no point did she recall the sting of an injection. "When was I implanted?"

"Soon as you were hooded. It's new tech. Minimally invasive," Lennox answered. "You wouldn't have felt a thing."

NDA implants were commonly used in high-profile corporate meetings discussing sensitive financials, top-secret prototypes, or high-stakes mergers and acquisitions. Once encoded, the implanted party would leave the discussion with only a vague recollection of events, the details lost in a haze after she was scrubbed. Sort of like struggling to recall the night after a drunk bender.

She'd know something had happened, but the *what*, *how*, and *why* would be murky, at best. It wasn't dangerous, and only effective for short-term memories, but still—she wasn't fond of the idea of someone messing around inside her head.

"Your name." Lennox weighed the black remote—smooth and with only a single blinking button. "Otherwise we'll have to terminate the meeting and have you re-hooded and returned to Kilar Outpost."

Vesper gave in with a resolute sigh, citing her name and personal code for the record. The button on the remote flashed from blue to red as she spoke, the pulses timed in tandem with the cadence of her voice.

"Thank you." Lennox handed the remote to his lackey, who tapped it against his pad, the hologlass tinted with privacy biometrics so only his eyes could read whatever was on the screen. "I'm going to state a phrase," he continued. "And when I'm done, I want you to repeat it to me when asked to do so. We'll run through the process twice. Any questions or concerns?"

"No."

"Good. Now—"

Static rang in her ears, high-pitched and crackling. Vesper winced against the grating sound as something was roughly scrubbed from the folds of her brain. "I—wait, what was the thing? I missed it."

Lennox's smile hooked across the left side of his mouth as he turned toward Chairwoman Aramir. "Integration successful. She's ready."

"Thank you, Lennox. You and Mr. Cho can leave us, and take the cybers with you. We'd like to have the room cleared for the utmost confidentiality."

Lennox bowed with a stately nod. "Madam Chairwoman."

"If we're clearing the room, then Tri-Senator Shinoda should be removed as well," Vesper said with a lick of her tongue across the edge of her smile. "My life and my dealings are of no concern to her."

Chairwoman Aramir followed Vesper's piercing glare to Dameris and returned filled with uncertainty. "We thought it best to have her present for—"

"For what? *Encouragement?*" Vesper laughed openly, a wild and harsh bark that sent the first ripple of tension through her mother's shoulders as confusion circled the board. "I see." Vesper dabbed at the corner of her eyes, cleaning away amused tears. "Whatever this job entails, it's linked to her, and you called me in for the contract not because of my skill or reputation but because you all thought I'd leap at the chance to be the doting daughter, eager to serve the familial interests at all costs, that it?"

"Your mother assured—"

"Don't call her that." Vesper's smile cut as cold as the knife she kept sheathed in her left boot. "She lost that privilege four years ago."

"I'm disappointed in you, Senator." Annelise drummed clear-polished nails atop the diamond-lacquered mahogany and arched a chilling glare to Dameris. "When you petitioned this board with the assertion Vesper would be not only willing but *eager* to act on your behalf, but clearly you misrepresented your bond."

"She'll do it." Dameris rose abruptly, her unsteady hands sweeping the wrinkles from the folds of her steel-gray dress-suit. "I just need a moment to speak with her. Alone."

A flurry of discourse rose around the table but Annelise silenced it with a soft tilt of her head, her attention fixed on Vesper. "Ten minutes." She raised two fingers, and a privacy cloak descended like a blanket of liquid smoke, obscuring sight and sound.

Vesper yawned, popping her ears clear of the sudden rise in pressure.

"They can't hear us now. We can speak freely." Dameris's voice flattened in the air like it struck a wall and immediately collapsed into nothing. Everything they said within the cloak was muted from the other members in the room, now little more than subtle shadows shifting behind the smoke-wall.

"Are you not paying attention? I *have* been speaking freely." Vesper snorted. "Don't waste your breath, Senator. I don't care if it's ten minutes or forty—there's nothing you can say to sway me. I'd rather chew on glass than help you."

"Vesper, please." Hands clasped, Dameris's knuckles shone bone white. "If not for me, think of Yasmin and Chance."

Vesper halted at the names of her niece and nephew. Her mind flashed to a memory of the day Chance had been born merely hours before he was placed in her arms. Ashleen had labored hard with him before medtechs intervened, extracting the squalling infant. She remembered the baby's soft powdery smell, and the way his hand gripped the length of her finger with a strength that seemed impossible for an infant. She remembered Yasmin's bright laugh when she'd been told she finally had a brother, and how it sent light to skip through her eyes like the sunshine across the marble courtyard at dawn.

They'd be eight and six now.

Vesper angled her gaze over her shoulder with a stiff sigh. "What about them?"

"Stop with the games, Vesper, you know perfectly well." Dameris sighed and held a beat, waiting for some sort of reaction, but when Vesper showed none beyond an arched brow, her mouth parted slightly in surprise. "You really have no idea what's happened with your uncle and his arrest?"

"Should I?" One of the perks of the trade was falling so far off the grid at times she was surrounded by nothing but silence and stars. No banal chatter and glittering parties where she'd had to prance and perform like the prized Akhal-Teke horses Uncle Padryck owned. Reared from a carefully preserved cache of embryos derived from one of the proudest lineages dating back to Earth-Prior.

"I suppose not." Dameris blinked a few times in startled understanding. "You were far out of range for quite some time, and this all happened so suddenly—I suppose it stands to reason you would not have heard . . ."

Vesper listened, irritation quickly giving way to shock and disbelief as Dameris laid out the events surrounding the disgrace and arrest of her uncle, Cormack Shinoda, little more than week ago. A once-deified executive at the head of a quintillion net-worth empire so swiftly brought low, following his failed plot to murder all inhabitants on the RIM. All because of the discovery of a unique mineral that possessed more power per ounce than prime but none of its weaknesses.

"According to the investigation," Dameris continued, "Dorothy Dobrevnic, as the alleged associate acting on Cormack's orders, was in fact responsible for the destruction of the United Planetary Nations forum, triggering the staged bombs to implicate Captain Indira Roscoe for the crime, preventing her from releasing information about the discovery of elite to the UPN leaders. Thankfully, Dobrevnic was killed before she could be taken into custody by Admiral Wallace and her task force. Without her, prosecution is weakened regarding Cormack's motives and actions as the figurehead of the attempted genocide—but there is one other key witness still able to bury us with her testimony. A RIM-rat who somehow infiltrated our illustrious Academy as a cadet-turned-villainous-rogue."

Rage, something Vesper had never seen in her mother before now, trembled across the lines of Dameris's face—shattering her usually poised mask of demure elegance into a look that promised violence. It was unsettling, and almost uncanny. Vesper saw the same expression whenever she looked in the mirror, and it galled her to imagine that her mother, a woman who prided herself on absolute composure, might actually be the parent she'd inherited it from.

"Shortly after Cormack's arrest," Dameris continued, "this cadet was granted a boon of graduating in commendation for her efforts, but instead of accepting her badge, she fled the Inner Circle to become a pirate. SIGA now has come to doubt whether the conspiracy she uncovered is in fact an elaborate fabrication to exonerate her pirate grandmother. SIGA would like her brought forward so they can evaluate the veracity of her sworn testimony and ensure... alignment."

"Sounds a lot like witness tampering." Vesper snorted. *So much for good ol' democracy.* "What's the point? Even if SIGA convinced the supreme justice to toss the entire trial, it wouldn't make a dent in restoring stakeholder confidence. A scandal like this? Genocide? Terrorism? IESO is dead, and the Shinoda name is scorched."

That tempered some of the fire searing behind Dameris's eyes. "You're right. Our familial name is forever tarnished, for that there is no recovery. But his assets... SIGA has seized his accounts. All that I had was invested in IESO shares, and with the seizure our accounts are near to run dry. But Chairwoman Aramir has promised, for our cooperation in handling this matter expeditiously, that they will release forty percent of his estate to split across all surviving relatives. For our cooperation, twenty-eight percent of that will be allocated to our household. Three hundred and forty-seven trillion credits."

Vesper frowned. That was an incredible sum of money, and it raised an interesting bone for her to chew on. Why would SIGA offer a bounty this high for a mark? Sure, it was easy to hand out a fortune when they were keeping the larger slice, but the *why* was a fishbone she couldn't dislodge from the back of her throat no matter how hard she coughed.

"If you don't take this contract, I could stretch what we have across the next six months. Maybe a year if I really cinch our belts. But after that . . ." Dameris wrung her hands, a fitful gesture she only employed when she was well and truly afraid.

And it wasn't just the notion of poverty that terrified her, but her own kin. If her mother was surviving off steam, the others likely were as well, and Shinodas were not known for familial loyalty once the chips were down. They were warped from centuries of power and greed, always hungering for more with a thirst that couldn't be quenched.

The second it became common knowledge that SIGA had disbursed assets, and that she had received the largest share, blood would be in the water and men that once lived as gods would go feral over scraps.

Dozens of uncles, cousins, half siblings, and their children. It would be a war between kin. Suddenly her mother's fear made alarming sense. This wasn't just about money to survive, but protection from the axe swinging for their throats.

Groaning, Vesper pinched the bridge of her nose. Sighed. "I'd do anything for Chance and Yasmin, you know that. But this job doesn't smell right. If this is purely about money, the kids can have what Dad left me. All of it." A flicker of tension flashed across her mother's face before she'd managed to smother it, and a laugh whispered from Vesper, soft and dark as a falling shadow. "You've already emptied my accounts."

Not a question.

"Your accounts were the only thing that didn't fall under the same guillotine following Cormack's arrest." Dameris raised the firm line of her chin with remorseless defiance. "So yes, I took what was once yours. Why not? You forfeited everything the moment you chose to abandon not only me but our name. Ironically, it's that choice that has kept us afloat."

Resentment settled in Vesper's soul, dark as the cloak swirling around them. "I was never a Shinoda. My father was Vector Crole. I am a Crole."

Dameris's chin wavered at the mention of her late husband, and the sheen of fresh tears brightened clear blue eyes, once the same shade as her incarcerated uncle's—before his accident had robbed him of both.

"I don't want to fight with you. Complete this contract, Vesper, and not only can we get it all back—SIGA will provide new identity tags and credit sleeves for us. You included. A clean slate."

Vesper caught her breath. "All this for *one* mark?"

"There's more at play here, so much more. More than even I know of, but none of that matters beyond this." Dameris rushed forward, gripping Vesper's hands, and the proud tri-senator sank to her knees. "Only you can save us. I know your heart holds no love for me after . . . *after.*" She set her jaw. "I own that. I embrace that. I failed Ashleen, arguably I even failed you, but please, I am doing what I can for them. Help me."

Seeing her mother on her knees, begging like a hound for scraps, brought something wicked to the surface of Vesper's soul. Oh, how she'd imagined this moment. The ways she would break her for failing Ashleen.

Her older sister had always struggled with mental health, but it had spiraled into something much darker following postpartum. She'd attempted to take her life a year after Chance's birth and although the medbots had mended her good as new, the disease eroding her mind only continued to fester. When Ashleen had attempted a second time, floating in the bath and nearly blue before someone resuscitated her, it was Vesper on her knees, begging her mother to act. To *do* something. But pride and ego held sway.

With an empire as vast as Cormack's, and as his beloved favorite sister, Shinoda lived in a fishbowl. Every movement captured in the newscasts. Having a mentally unbalanced daughter attempting suicide twice was an insult not to be born, and certainly not one that she could risk exposing. *What would that do to your uncle's empire? One bad headline and shares could plummet. We could lose all we have!* So she'd caged Ashleen to their private estate—bolstering her with high-grade medication, when necessary, but that only masked the problem instead of resolving it. Until one day, Ashleen lost her grip on reality and leapt from a balcony on the fourteenth floor of their estate.

Chance was the first to find his mother splattered on the marble stones of the courtyard like finger paint. A nearly unrecognizable mess of blood and fragmented limbs—a gory scene gilded in the light of a waking sun that set the auburn in her strands of hair to blaze like autumn leaves. No one knew how long he'd stood there, only that he'd been rendered mute from the shock and hadn't spoken a word for nearly a week after.

Vesper was the second. A month later, she'd left home and never dared look back.

And while the need for revenge howled at the base of Vesper's skull, yearning for her to seize this opportunity to break her mother until she was as broken as Ashleen's skull, this was the closest she'd ever seen her great and proud mother come to acknowledgment or accountability for what happened. Added to that, there were greater stakes to consider. Revenge would soothe for a moment, but it wouldn't bring Ashleen back. And it wouldn't protect her children.

"Drop the cloak."

"But—"

"What I have to say, I'll say to them. Drop it." The cloak lifted and Vesper took position in the center of the room. "I have two conditions." She addressed the board, and Dameris's back tensed so sharply Vesper almost heard the blades of her shoulders snap together.

Chairwoman Annelise settled closer, hands folded before her. "And those would be?"

"You've promised forty percent of my uncle's assets to split across his relatives, twenty-eight percent of that going to my mother for procuring this arrangement. I want that upped to thirty, to be delivered in full the moment I surrender the mark into your custody."

"And the second?"

Vesper met her mother's uncertain gaze, her hand fisted at her belly and knuckles shining white. "My niece and nephew are named as beneficiaries to receive the funds, which will be held in trust for them until they reach the age of maturity. Until then their grandmother, Tri-Senator Dameris, will manage the accounts with a stipend not to exceed two million a year."

Her mother sputtered in disbelief. "How da—"

"Done," Annelise agreed. "As for your commission—"

"Keep it."

Annelise arched a perfect brow. "You don't want a *single* credit?"

"Aside from an unlimited allowance for expenditures," Vesper said, returning to her waiting seat. "No."

"I must admit, you do surprise me. Given all reports, you're not at all what I expected." Annelise tapped a fingernail to the glossy wood. "We have an agreement."

"Good." Vesper settled back into her chair and hooked an ankle over the bridge of her knee. "Who am I hunting?"

CHAPTER TWO

Death had a particular sound.
With Sigourney it had been a crackling, wet noise that amplified with every struggling breath. The memory of it crept up on Nimah Dabo-124 like a shadow at stretching sundown. Entombing her in a gurgling roar so loud Nimah could barely hear her own raw voice begging Sigourney to breathe.

"No. Not again." Tears poured down her cheeks, and Nimah cradled her friend's thrashing head as Sigourney's nails, filed to talon-like points, tore open her own throat. Desperate to draw air into lungs rapidly filling with blood. "Please, I can't watch you die again!"

But she was.

It was the same hell every single night.

Fitful spasms of suffocation racked Sigourney's body and red frantic bubbles frothed from her gasping lips. Then it all went quiet. So very quiet.

A stunted breath rattled through Nimah as Sigourney lay still as stone. Her silver and black hair stained viscous red from the puddle expanding around her head in a grisly halo. Nimah raised shaking hands, her palms glistening like red oil as it built inside of her.

Rage. So much helpless rage.

Nimah tossed back her head, screaming her fury into the void. Blood became fire, erupting the darkness of the void around her in a violent explosion. Sigourney's body melted in the inferno and Nimah hovered above the maelstrom.

The Inner Circle was on fire. Swallowed in crackling veins of molten light that split apart and shattered a thousand worlds. She watched them rupture, one after the other. Devastating shockwaves that cracked Nimah to the core like snapping bones, and somewhere above it all—she heard it. Whisper soft. Tethered to her very soul . . .

Laughter.

Seated in the dark, sweat cooling on her skin and the sheets on her bunk twisted around her legs, Nimah knuckled her eyes. Three months of this bullshit—since the day of Dobs's betrayal—and not only was she unable to shake the awful nightmares, they were getting worse.

Every night, Sigourney, and those gasping, final blood-soaked moments that stretched like years. Or Dobs, a charred cackling husk that reached for Nimah with raw, bony hands. But no matter how the nightmares started, they always—*always*—ended the same.

With the brutal destruction of the Inner Circle—a scorching ring to light up the void. And despite every effort to console herself, Nimah couldn't shake the awful feeling that not only was she somehow responsible for the chaos, it was more than a dream. It was a warning.

A prophecy.

"Stop being so damn foolish." Rising from her narrow bunk, Nimah tapped the square button on the side of the steel frame and the mustard-colored blanket and rough cotton bedding immediately snapped taut, wrapping around the foam mattress with military precision. She collapsed the frame to the shuttle wall and engaged the hooks to anchor it in place.

Alerted by her movements, the shuttle's sensors hummed into activity. Lights rose in a soft glow from the tracks woven across the ceiling and down the side wall when the comms tag behind her ear pulsed, indicating an incoming wave.

She cursed softly as her grandmother's tag flashed on her wristdeck. "Hey. I was just about to—"

"*It's been twelve hours,*" her grandmother cut through, never one to waste words. "*Why haven't you checked in?*"

Why? Maybe because she'd wanted a moment alone to finally breathe for once after being cooped aboard the *Stormchaser* like a prisoner. But rather than say that, Nimah reached for an excuse to spare herself another argument.

"Sorry, signal's been choppy out here. Cables popped from overload and it took most of the night for the comms crew to get them replaced."

Not entirely a lie. She'd seen a cable crew at work when she'd anchored at the dock. As to what they were doing, well, that came down to creative speculation.

"*You know we're tight on time,*" Ro continued after a few tense moments of silence. "*Did you make the trade or not?*"

Nimah scored her tongue across the edge of her teeth. "Not yet. I got in late, and the market was shuttered by patrol sentries. Kesh has been under curfew the last week after some iced-out kid knifed a member from a rival gang." A strict curfew had been set until inquiries into the assault were closed. Ordinarily the murder would have been treated as routine, except the governor happened to be touring during that time, so the crackdown was severe.

"Market should be open in the next hour," Nimah continued. "I'm getting ready to make my way there now."

Ro sighed. "*Get moving. I want you back on the* Stormchaser *in three hours.*"

"Sir, yes, sir." Nimah mimed a mocking salute.

"*I mean it. Don't disappoint me, Sparrow.*"

The wave ended, and Nimah's face tightened into a scowl. Apparently, that's all she'd been doing the last few weeks. Disappointing everyone. Groaning, she pressed her palms over her eyes, then dragged them down, her cheeks stretching beneath the points of her fingers like softened clay. Whatever. Time was ticking. Best to move unless she wanted to risk Captain Ro showing up on Kesh3 to fry Nimah like an overloaded wire.

Kesh3 housed one of the busiest markets in the Fringe, which encompassed basically anything that fell outside of the Inner Circle. Shaped in a square, stacked with forty-six open levels, and bearing tens of thousands of shops and stores, bars, and booths, it hawked everything from recycled clothing to tech to shelf-stable food. Naturally the shop she was seeking just had to be four levels from the top.

Drones and carts whizzed overhead, hauling purchases or stock from level to level, bursting through filmy holoverts, faded and grainy in color unlike the vivid neon of Inner Circle cities. Merchants out on the Fringe couldn't afford the levies for premium advertisements, and they stuttered every few seconds or lagged in frozen circles like petrified ghosts.

Careful to match the rush of bodies, Nimah dragged the black hood over her head of curls, now cut short and styled into twists capped with silver beads and a low fade on one side. The curled wisps of bangs hung in her eyes, and she blew them clear. Boomer had worked his magic with a pair of shears a few weeks ago, and at first it had been jarring to see herself so altered.

But Nimah had needed the change. Something to shock her away from the familiarity of Academy life, where she'd been regulated for so long to maintain her curls to shoulder-length, parted down the center, and slicked back in a severe bun, often drawn so tight it gave her wicked tension headaches by the end of the day. She wasn't a cadet anymore, or an agent. She was a pirate.

It still felt strange to call herself that. Like struggling to put on an ill-made shirt with one sleeve too long and buttons misaligned. It didn't sit right, no matter how hard she tried. But it was all she had now. This was the life she'd chosen. To join her grandmother's crew, leaving behind a corrupt system that allowed the RIMers to be screwed for too long.

It had to fit.

It *had* to.

Nimah followed the directional pulses of her wristdeck. The beats increased in frequency as she neared her destination. Adjusting the weight of the rucksack on her back, her skin went slick with the bloom of sweat and her gray t-shirt clung to the center of her shoulder blades in darkened patches. Another downside to life in Fringe quads, limited reserves of coolant meant it had to be prioritized for managing engine heat spikes rather than the comfort of the populace.

Suddenly the beats of the navigation pulses stopped, and Nimah swung around on the spot—twice—with a confused, "Huh?"

According to her directions, she was in the right place, but "shop" was too kind a word for the narrow, closet-sized hole in the wall she stood outside of, tucked in a corner so tight she wondered how anyone could get inside, let alone use it to house a storefront. She rapped her knuckles twice on the folding partition that served as a door, made from a sheet of rusted tin. It screamed open a moment later, and a man stood on the threshold—so tall and wide he ate up every available inch of the entryway.

"What?" he demanded, chewing on a twisted stick of dried artificial protein coated in a chemical-based seasoning that fooled the senses into believing it was beef instead of a synthetic substitute.

Nimah arched her head back as far as it would go and still had trouble taking him all in. "Groober?"

He answered with a nod and grunt, the girth of his belly straining against a stained white shirt and woven belt cinched on hips that should've been far too narrow to support a man of his size.

"I'm here to make a trade." She nodded toward the rucksack on her shoulder.

He assessed her with coal-black eyes before stepping back so she could enter, which was near impossible to do until he miraculously wedged himself behind a tiny counter. He snapped thick fingers and the folding door slid shut behind Nimah, nearly canceling out the heavy noise of market traffic.

Impressive tech for a hawker. His shop, though thin as a matchstick, ran close to three levels up, fitted with endless rows of shelving that bore everything from vintage to new-age—electronics, clothing, scraps of material and glassware, food reserves, and trinkets. He even displayed a few haggard plants in dusty pots, preserved in a layer of sealant to keep them alive but delay further growth. A dozen mechanical arms whizzed on tracks to move or retrieve items from the layers of shelving.

"What ya tradin'?" Groober planted beefy hands on the scarred plastic countertop he stood behind, a patchwork of recycled bits melted together into a thick, muddy sheet.

Nimah dropped the rucksack on the counter and fished out the array of gears and wireboards, extracted from the *Stormchaser*'s engine after Chu refitted it to run on the remnants of Nimah's elite sparrow instead of prime.

Groober pushed a thick finger through the pile of parts and grunted, dissatisfied. "Junk."

"Junk?" Nimah balked and gestured to the towering, stacked shelves around her. "Everything in here is *junk*."

Groober shrugged, unbothered by her insulting assessment. "Ain't interest'd."

Pinching the bridge of her nose, Nimah bit down on the curse searing the back of her throat. If she came back empty-handed, she'd *never* hear the end of it. "The parts may be . . . weathered, but they're made from good steel. Melted down it can fetch a decent price at any steelworks or recycling plant."

"Sure. But ain't got non' those round here. Closest is out by quad six'een zone for'y two. Ain't worth effort transportin' all that way f'chump."

Great. "I'll take half what it's worth," Nimah offered. "To mitigate the inconvenience."

Groober rolled the meat-stick between teeth studded with jade, and a tongue stained black from a compound most liked to chew on instead of smoke. It was called 'baccy in most quads. Tar in others, since its residue was a deep, stubborn black that stained for several weeks. Months if you were regular with it, which Nimah guessed Groober was.

"Ain't interest'd," Groober repeated. "Got anythin' else worth a trade?"

Sighing heavily, Nimah shook her head. No, that was the best they could scrounge together for enough credits to see them through the next month.

"Then we done."

"No . . . wait . . ." He halted at her soft words. "Do you carry heliosmoke? Or something like it."

Groober's brows, gray as the film coating the riveted walls of his narrow shop, lowered until they swallowed his half-moon eyes in scrutiny. "Y'don't look like a puffer?"

Nimah dropped her chin, suddenly embarrassed and ashamed. "I'm not. I just . . . I need something to help me sleep."

"Plenty a'otha stuff f' that."

"It's not just getting to sleep," Nimah answered. "I need . . . to stop dreaming."

He hunched forward, and the countertop groaned under his weight. "Puffin' ain't a good way to go. Minds crack f' this stuff."

"Are you a hawker, or a medbay tech?" Nimah snapped. "I'm paying for a product, not your sage advice."

Groober's thin lips flattened into an even thinner line, and the wisps of hair on his chin writhed with each hard exhale. "Gon' cost you fiddy."

Fifty? That was a steal. Almost too good a price, when anywhere else would ask for nearly three times that. Her grandmother had assured Nimah that while Groober might be difficult and hard to budge, he was a hawker with integrity.

But this was verging on a handout.

Nimah mouthed a silent *ah*. "You know who I am."

Groober met her gaze with a stiff bob of his head.

So that was it then. News of Shinoda's arrest had come full circle—pun intended—and now there wasn't a person alive who didn't know her name or what she'd done. Perhaps she should be grateful that word of Captain Indira's granddaughter, fleeing a promising career as a STARs agent to take up the mantle of second-in-command of the Valkyries, had only just now reached the Fringe, but she had hoped to fly under the radar at least a little while longer.

So much for the haircut.

Nimah slapped plastic chips on the counter, the last of her cadet stipend. While credit sleeves were more convenient, it was far safer to walk with chips instead of a sleeve in these parts. Bending over with a heaving groan, the weight of his body creaking like rickety stairs, Groober wrestled underneath his counter and emerged, red-faced and panting, with a thin vial of smoky liquid.

"That'll be enuff to hold ya for two weeks. And watch y'dosin." He wagged a cautioning finger, nail bitten to the quick. "If ya take t'much a' once, it won't turn ya off, it'll keep ya on. F'days. Maybe a week, if it don't flatten ya."

"By flatten—you mean kill me, yes?"

Groober grunted in affirmation. "If ya start t'smell color or hear smells—means ya need an emergency flush, but if ya hands go blue . . . too late." He scraped a hand behind his neck, covered in thick, coarse hair that stopped just above the curve of his large ears covered in several gold hoops. "So be on the sharp." He tapped a finger beneath one squinting eye. "Puffin' right will keep ya straight, but it gots a way of draggin' ya down if ya can't hold yuh head."

"Understood." Nimah pocketed the vial as he swept up the credits into his cupped palm, and she tried not to let her thoughts stumbled into a nervous spiral about the fact she'd never dosed anything beyond low-grade pain meds.

"An' one more," he called out as Nimah turned to exit the shop, drawing over the folded partition. "If she asks, tell her I did good on ya." Groober dipped his chin and arched a stern brown. "Tell 'er I warned ya. Clear?"

In other words, if Nimah found herself choking on her own vomit with seconds to live, make sure her grandmother knew that she'd been properly advised not to do what she was about to do.

"Clear." She patted her pocket.

"*Nimah.*" Maverick's voice shuddered through her comms as she exited Groober's shop, thick with gritty static. "*Where are you?*"

Nimah pressed the dial on her wristdeck and assessed the pixelated schematics for the market spacity, scanning for the clearest pathway back to the docks. "Just leaving Groober's. Near west forty-two and north eighty-seven. Why?"

"*Captain wants to know what's taking you so long?*"

Nimah winced, her mind spinning over what to share and what to withhold. "I have another hour and a half before I'm due back, what's the problem?"

"*There's been a change of plans. We're here to get you,*" he responded with a weathered sigh broken with static. "*Don't worry about the shuttle. Boomer is corralling it. You just focus on moving fast. Security gave us our departure window, and it's tight.*"

"Exactly how tight?" Nimah adjusted her rucksack, tightening the straps so it hugged her back.

"*Twenty minutes to burn, and your route back to us will eat up most if not all of that. So take the eighty-four down to thirty-two and catch the taxicarts over to twelve. I'll meet you with the chair.*"

"I can manage witho—"

"*It wasn't an offer, Nimah. If you're late, we'll be grounded for forty-eight hours.*"

If that happened they'd miss the parlay with Blackfyre and her grandmother would chew her alive.

Not that she wasn't going to already, once she realized that Nimah had failed to complete this basic task she'd practically had to beg for. A fact that shouldn't have mattered, as she'd hoped to use the next hour to haggle with a few of the other stalls and make a trade before flying the shuttle back to the *Stormchaser*. But instead, Captain Ro had deviated from the plan—coming to her—so now Nimah was out of time because her grandmother didn't like the notion of Nimah wandering in the open when the heat on Cormack was so fresh.

Head hung, Nimah kicked a furious toe against the curved edge of a vent shaft, sending a cascading echo rippling through its cavernous belly like a dull groan. "Okay. Making my way to you now."

"*Copy. And Nimah—turn your location back on,*" Maverick warned. "*I don't want to have to ask Mumbles to hack into the spacity mainframe just to keep eyes on you. Again.*"

The comms sliced off with a jarring snap of silence, leaving the heat of his words to ricochet inside of her like a throbbing tooth. So . . . he was still mad at her. Guess it was to be expected.

She had broken his heart less than forty-eight hours ago before diving into the shuttle and rocketing over to Kesh3 for this trade run. In truth, she just needed to put parsecs between her and everyone else so she could carve out space to breathe. To lose herself in the chaos of a crowd where no one knew her face or cared to ask questions.

What's wrong with you? Why are you so pale? When did you last eat?

Bracing against the rail, Nimah looked out across the market. The spacity was thrumming in full force, everyone crammed into the streets, eager to maximize business hours thanks to the governor-sanctioned curfew, which meant cutting through that crowd was not going to be easy.

She should get moving to where Maverick had directed her, but the weight of the rucksack held her rooted. Torn between failure and the ticking clock counting down over her head. What was worse? Grounding the crew, or coming back to them with nothing to show for it? She couldn't go back with nothing, and right now that's all she had.

That's when the crowd opened and fate chose to smile upon her.

A man, gleaming gold and dripping with all his importance and wealth, stuck out like a golden carp amid a sea of minnows. Growing up on the RIM, he'd have been what they called a power-suit. Kesh3 was the kind of slum where only those who lived on the Fringe could afford to barter and trade. Seeing someone like him in a place like this—it was a miracle he still had his credit sleeve on him by the time Nimah reached him.

Two minutes of trailing, then a swift bump against his knee to send him staggering into a burly cart monger led to tossed hands, raised voices, and just the kind of distraction she needed to swoop in and make her lift. Her palms were sweating with the rush of adrenaline, and all her senses went crisp as a fresh sheet of real paper.

She forgot how intoxicating it all could be.

The risk and the thrill. It was a stupid move, given the number of footmen on patrol after the recent stabbing, but one that was too tempting to ignore when the credits on this sleeve would be enough to absolve her of the many other mistakes she'd made in the last two months.

Life in the void required two important skills: you had to be quick with lies, or quicker on the draw. Essential skills that Nimah had once been proficient in as a child while struggling to survive on the outer RIM.

But apparently after fifteen years of STARs Academy training, she'd lost her touch. Because the tailored suit concealed a truth she should've sniffed out the second she clapped eyes on him. He wasn't a true Inner-Circle greenie setting foot into the slums but a seasoned right-hand— the kind of dangerous gang leader that clung like remoras to the bellies of pirates, feeding on their scraps. The kind of man who squeezed credits from desperate, bleeding throats.

He'd felt her lift a second after the sleeve broke contact with his skin. And now he was very, very *pissed*. Barely avoiding his punch and flaming curse, Nimah took off like a shot, and shouts followed close behind her as she tore through the crowd. Pulse hammering in her ears and eyes scanning for a way out of the mess she'd just stepped into, she cast off the rucksack, its weight slowing her down, and clutched the sleeve tight as she charged through stunned bodies and wove around swerving carts.

A banister loomed ahead.

"Fuck!" Nimah sprinted for it and leapt without thinking into the dizzying blur of drones and pixelated adverts.

Breathless, she fell. Eyes watering, Nimah counted in her head, covering two floors every second as her hands scrabbled and searched for a cable, a line—*something*!

A drone clipped her side, sending her careening into another whose whirling propellers struck her shoulder as it fought to correct itself. Nimah slammed into the viewport of a delivery cart and rolled across the hard top, barely managing to grip onto a mooring hook seconds before she slipped off its tapered back end.

The delivery cart bounced and struggled against the addition of her weight, too heavy for it to maintain flight. It descended in an emergency landing and Nimah held on as it veered for the ground. People shouted and screamed as the cart touched down so hard Nimah bounced off its back and landed face down in the walkway.

She wheezed, struggling to her knees and back into a run, fighting through the gathering throng of people just as the alarms in the market started to blare. Nimah drew away from the central market, turning corners until she reached a narrow alley. Taking a sharp right, she set her back to the wall and gulped in fast, greedy breaths. Pressed against grime-coated steel, Nimah closed her eyes and listened.

No stomping boots. No chirp of comms calling for sentries or backup in pursuit. Just the steady hum from the vent she was perched behind, sucking in air for the recyclers to scrub clean. Stepping cautiously back out into the corridor, Nimah whisked her gaze left then right before swiftly merging with the streaming flow of bodies.

The weight of the man's stolen credit sleeve slapped against the side of her thigh, hidden inside an inner pocket of her cargo pants. Fashioned of real leather and embedded with high-grade microchips for easy tapping for payment and exchange of information—whether it was contact details, correspondence, documents, or other files. His entire world was embedded into a chip the size of a rice grain.

Hitting the end of the walkway, she skidded to a rough stop at the sight of footmen weaving through the crowd and headed her way. Great. Her antics had them hard on the hunt, and there was no clear way through without pushing right past them.

A clatter beneath her feet pulled her gaze down to her toes and an unruly smile broke across her face as a pair of rats, the size of small pugs, scuttled down piping and disappeared into the electricity tunnels.

The only way out is through . . .

The tunnels followed the same grid as the streets, and in a spacity this poorly maintained, were also extremely unsafe due to ancient electricity rails and corroded wiring that channeled enough voltage to kill her instantly if she was foolish enough to bump into them. But aside from that, they'd be clear of people. And footmen. Perfect.

Squatting low, Nimah hooked her fingers into the grating and lifted with a grunt. The rusted hinges gave with a sharp whine, easily swallowed up in the roar of the passing market crowd as she leapt inside and hit the bottom at the end of a nine-foot drop.

Nimah rolled when she struck the walkway, using the momentum to disperse the shock of impact through her body instead of hammering into the joints of her ankles and knees. Dusting her hands on her thighs, she stood, shook away a loose curl from her eyes, and assessed her surroundings.

The tunnel was dimly lit with track lights that pulsed with a soft, golden glow, illuminating the tunnel with a steady flicker that was as sluggish as a dying heartbeat. Steady and slow and fading.

"Mumbles," Nimah whispered, after adjusting the comms channel to her crew cabin where Mumbles often spent hours tinkering on her gadgets as well as monitoring the *Stormchaser*'s system. Her ingenious inventions were so advanced they seemed almost like magic, even though a brutal head injury close to forty years ago left her with the mental capacity of a seven-year-old.

"You there?"

"Goody-hi," Mumble's voice rasped after a moment of brief static.

"I'm in the electricity tunnels on Kesh3. Can you access the schematics and light me a path to the *Stormchaser*? Use my live location as the start point. Should be on . . . now."

Mumbles answered with something between a gurgle and a sigh, the sort of sound she often made when deep in focus. Within a matter of moments, the track lights running in the walls of the tunnel came to a flickering pause before the pulse pattern shifted into a single, steady beam streaking toward her destination.

"Mumbles, you're the best. Making my way to you now." Nimah kicked into a jog. "Tell Maverick there's been a change of plans, and I'll meet him at the docks instead."

"Dock chaser. Mav-Mav. Okey-doosy."

Nimah reached the *Stormchaser* in five and only slowed in her run once she was across the hatch and inside the cargo hold.

"Got them knuckles tore up," Boomer commented as Nimah rushed onto the bridge just as Maverick eased the *Stormchaser* from the dock and fell into the burn queue. "Who you been fighting?"

Tall and broad-shouldered, Boomer filled a room before he even spoke, and moved with the easy confidence of someone who knew his strength and—more importantly—when to use it. Always loud and unapologetic, he favored weaponry almost as much as he did food, but after three short months together as crew, Nimah couldn't imagine anyone else she'd rather have at her back when the chips fell.

Nimah grinned. "Your mother."

"Jokes on you." Boomer wiggled the dial of the dual hearing aids implanted into either side of his shaved skull, and purple lights pulsed against dark brown skin. "I ain't got a momma, but best believe if I did, she'd stomp you."

Ro turned from the main console at the sound of their laughter, her arms crossed and face stern. Unlike most captains who displayed their status in gold and fine thread, Indira Roscoe preferred dark cargos and a fitted black shirt that clung to muscle which hadn't softened with age. Her wicked black hair was always tied into a long thick braid and threaded with a single sweep of silver that began at the temple, like foam cresting a midnight wave. Small, earned scars added severity to her presence, along with her shrewd eyes, more gold than brown, that could silence rooms with a single look.

"Good of you to finally join us. In two more minutes, we'd be grounded."

"You should've waited for me to come to you. As planned." The ship pitched and Nimah caught hold of the flight chair seconds before she toppled onto her ass.

Her grandmother, however, held her feet with ease. Leaning with the sway of the ship as if she knew which way it was going to roll before it happened. A unique language she and the rest of the crew spoke fluently. One that Nimah was still struggling to learn, evident in the infinite healing scrapes and bruises she'd acquired across the last three months. And a pirate without sea legs was as pathetic as a bird without wings.

"What's our take from the trade?"

"There was no trade." Fighting to hold herself stable, Nimah set her hands on her hips but a quick dip had her grasping for the flight chair again. "Groober wasn't in a bartering mood. Called it junk."

"Told ya!" A snicker wafted through the grating flooring from below. "Ain't much on this heap worth rubbing two chips together."

Quick to scowl instead of smile, Chu wasn't having a good day unless it was a bad one, but as the only engineer capable of keeping the *Stormchaser* voidborne, a patchwork vessel she'd welded together from scraps and sheer vitriol, her foul moods were tolerated.

"Fucking Groober." Ro stroked the wings of silver curtain bangs away from her stern face. "Where's our gear?"

"Had to toss it."

"Why?"

"Footmen." The weight of the vial of heliosmoke was heavy as an anvil in the pocket of her cargos.

Ro sniffed. "Is that why you smell like you crawled through a sewer?"

"Pretty much."

"So no trade, which means we have no credits to carry us the next few weeks, and now we've lost our parts. Fuck, Sparrow, I gave you a simple task."

Here we go. "I didn't come back empty-handed." Removing the credit sleeve from her pocket, she waved it for all to see. "This should have more than enough to cover our incidentals."

Ro scraped the leather with the edge of her thumbnail, gauging its grade. "This is real." Her dark amber eyes narrowed. "Who'd you steal it from?"

"Does it matter? I saw an opportunity, so I took it."

Ro set her teeth. "That was reckless, Sparrow."

Nimah's gut soured. Was nothing she did ever going to make her grandmother happy? "Well, it's done now." She crossed the bridge and handed the sleeve over to Mumbles, strapped in her chair and feet whisking in circles. "Go ahead and crack it."

Digging through the breast pocket of her tattered oversized gray coat, Mumbles raised a loupe and fit it against her eye. Gripped in place between a lowered brow and the mound of her cheek, she hunched over the sleeve and brought the glass lens so close she was almost inhaling leather.

"Well?" Boomer called out. "How much we got?"

Mumbles waited another moment before lowering the loupe then raised two fingers and wiggled them in rabbit ears.

"Two hundred?" Gertrude chuckled. Almost as broad in the shoulders as Boomer, although she had traded her bold wigs and gauzy silks for pirate black, Gertrude kept her shorn hair brightly dyed, nails polished, and face covered in a full beat of makeup like she was seconds from a stage instead of running navigation on a ship. "Darling, that's hardly a lift. Would've found more rattling in a tin cup over dice."

Disappointment bloomed in Nimah's chest. Given the cut of his suit, she had banked on at least ten times that amount.

"It'll cover the levies to Blackfyre's quad at least," Ro interjected. "Which is what matters most, right now. We parley in fourteen hours. Best pray it swings in our favor." Turning from her granddaughter to the crew, Ro moved with a low, unhurried kind of authority that didn't ask for permission to take up space. She simply expanded, until every crevice and corner strained against the commanding weight of her energy. "I know we've had a few lean months." Her voice carried, proud and strong. "And I know bellies are beginning to gripe for it."

"I'm saying." Boomer tapped his flat washboard abs, pouting like a kid being told dinner wasn't ready yet.

Behind him Maverick swung his pilot chair around—the flight path locked so he was able to let the navsystem take over—and scrapped a strong hand over his granite jaw, always shaded with stubble to conceal the hooked scar that cleaved around the side of his tattooed neck. A souvenir gained after surviving a wreck from a highspeed void chase against SIGA in his mid-teens that made him a criminal legend but also left him in a wheelchair. Penetrating green eyes that were almost too vivid to be real contrasted against his dark, bronzed skin were his second-best feature next to his charming smile that always made Nimah's heart skip to a stop before thundering wildly back to life.

"For those who are new to the *Stormchaser*, Blackfyre and I have history," Ro continued. "She presides over the largest territory of any pirate lord, and it's furthest from the Inner Circle. It'll be our best bet for drifting."

Sometimes, in the heat of a chase or threat of assault, cargo vessels released their trams so they could escape like a lizard dropping their tail when evading a predator. Drifting was one way pirates without quads earned a quick credit, hauling out into Fringe zones in search of abandoned cargo trams, or sunken ships to strip of micro-tech, prime cores, and anything else they could resell. They would pay levies on every credit they made, but it was a solution to their pressing problem of imminent starvation.

"If you and Blackfyre have history." Nimah frowned. "Then why aren't you sitting down with her instead of me."

"For one?" Ro set her jaw with a look on her face that told Nimah, as her second, she should already know the answer to this. "We have . . . history. For two, this ain't a boardroom, Sparrow. When executives do business—it's CEO to CEO. For pirates, captains send an ambassador. Sending me to the table is like a whipped dog giving up her belly."

"Right." Nimah nodded. "I just thought . . . never mind."

"So we drift," Gertrude chimed in, deflecting the tension with a shift back to the topic of importance. Money. "Cool our thrusters until the Shinoda trial goes quiet. But what happens next, Captain? Drifting gets us by for a while, but it's hardly a means for long-term survival."

"I agree. Which is why I've already drafted a petition to take before the council for a slice of a quad. Fifteen years ago, I had quite the territory, but that was carved up once I went off grid. If I can sway the council, then we got ourselves a proper foundation to build on. Until then, our hopes for survival depend on reaching terms with Blackfyre. Boomer, when we reach the Beak—you will hold the ship. Can't leave the *Stormchaser* without our best gunner on board this deep in the Fringe."

Boomer's sulk deepened but he didn't voice any complaint.

"Gertrude and Chu will take points around the tavern, high and low, as parlays are known to get a bit scanty—and the Beak will have some unsavories. I'll also be on the ground, floating through the periphery and keeping a weather eye." Amber eyes shot to Nimah. "In case things go sideways."

She doesn't think I can do it. A bitter realization Nimah struggled to keep from showing on her face, but a sentiment she knew that if she looked around would be reflected in more than one set of eyes. Nimah had assumed second-in-command less than three months ago, and steadily ever since, things had begun to unravel. Jobs were scarce and credits, much like the crew's morale, were running thin. This parlay with Blackfyre would either keep their heads above water or tow them under to drown.

"Is that all, Cap?" Chu tipped her brim so she could rake arthritic fingers through her roughly cut salt-and-pepper hair.

"For now." Ro nodded. "We got a fourteen-hour burn to the Beak, so take your rest. We reconvene in ten."

CHAPTER THREE

Nimah assessed her reflection in the full-length mirror in her cabin. Bleached cargos, with a button-up shirt tucked at the waist, knee-high boots, and the cutlass sheathed on her hip. The dark brown trench made of scarred leather, tailored to fit her like she was born into it, gave it the final flourish.

She looked like a pirate. And felt like a fraud.

But that was nothing new when she'd spent over a decade feeling like one at the Academy. And yet, Nimah reminded herself with a determined lift of her chin, she still managed to claw her way into the top ten percent of her year. To convince her professors, fellow cadets, and even senior leadership, that she was sharp, capable, and deserving of her spot. If she could do that, then she could more than handle herself at the negotiation table for an hour in a tavern surrounded by booze-soaked pirates.

She could do this.

At least her eyes, bloodshot and carved with blackened hollows of fatigue from too many nights lost to either insomnia or night terrors, gave her a bit of grit. Heliosmoke had bought her eight hours of dreamless sleep, which was an improvement but apparently far from enough to remove the heavy weight of fatigue that still clung to her. A weight that grew heavier by the day, and a clear warning that Nimah was in serious trouble if she didn't get proper rest soon, but that was a problem for another day.

Too nervous to sit in her cabin, and afraid of losing herself to the spiral of nerves and dark thoughts, Nimah went for a walk, weaving through the corridors of the *Stormchaser* that flowed in a figure eight on the main level—and stopped at the sight of Mumbles when she rounded the second corner. She stood, hugging one of the arched corridor beams with her eyes closed and lips pressed into a serene smile.

Hearing Nimah, she opened one watery eye and smirked, revealing four of her six remaining teeth. "Nimsy, Ma go thump-thump." Mumbles slapped the heel of her palm to the beam in a firm beat. "Thump-thump." Reaching for her, she guided Nimah's ear to the beam, urging her to listen. Listen deep.

Nimah indulged her, squeezing her eyes shut and letting the silence stretch, soft and still, and was about to draw away when she felt something. And settled in closer. Listening. Listening . . . *There*! A faint echo, like the throb of a vein pulsing in her neck or the soft *whoosh* of her heartbeat when she tossed against her pillows, unable to find peace.

Thump. Thump.

That steady rhythm pulled Nimah in—made her float from her skin. Drawing her into a trance. Spiraling deeper, Nimah swayed. Sighed.

Thump. Thu—

"Hey! Sparrow, you good?"

Nimah blinked twice in alarm as her grandmother's stern face stuttered into focus. Confused, disoriented, she took a bracing step back as her surroundings solidified from the corridor of the *Stormchaser* into a narrow lift, whizzing upward at breath-snatching speed.

Shit. Not again.

Another annoying and recent development, between lack of sleep and nightmares—time jumps. It started as sleepwalking two weeks ago, then expanded to her mind blanking out. Last time it was a solid fifteen minutes of her spinning circles in her cabin before the fog lifted. And now . . . how much time had she lost?

"Yeah. Yeah, I'm great." She adjusted the lapels of her coat, latching onto the sensation of rough leather beneath the pads of her fingers to draw her back into reality.

They were near to arriving at the Beak, and if it was just the two of them in the lift, then Chu and Gertrude were already positioned inside. So, if she had to guess between when she ran into Mumbles to now standing on the lift, that had to push close to at least thirty minutes of memory loss.

A chill of cold sweat kissed the back of her neck that not even the weight of the scarred leather jacket with its temperature-regulated inner lining could dispel. This was the kind of cold that went soul deep, icing her from the inside out like the vacuum of deep space hollowing out a body.

Apparently the nightmares weren't the only thing getting worse.

Ro caught Nimah's jaw in a vise grip, forcing their eyes to meet. "You look burnt." The line of her grandmother's brows eased from scrutiny into genuine concern. "Are you okay, Nimah? Is there something I need to know?"

Tell her. The urge seized in her chest like a searing and coiling knot, before plummeting back down into her bowels. Telling her the truth would only further dispel any hope of earning her grandmother's trust and confidence in Nimah as her second, let alone as part of the crew. So she shook her head. "No."

"Are you sure?" She let go of Nimah's face, gaze probing. "I don't know. For a moment there, I thought . . ." Ro started, but then shrugged off the rest. "We need this, Sparrow. If you're not on point to handle it, tell me now and I'll take the lead with Blackfyre."

Nimah's cold sweat was replaced with the immediate snap of temper. "I thought you said my role as second is to be your ambassador in a parlay?"

"It is." Ro arched her brow.

"Then trust me to do my job."

For the first time in a long time, the line of Ro's mouth lifted with the hint of a proud smile. "That's all I needed to hear."

When the lift doors parted, the din of the Beak slammed into them in a sudden burst of noise, thumping music, and energy. There had to be close to a hundred bodies packed into an establishment meant for half that number. Her grandmother cast her a final look before she vanished into the dense crowd like mist in a strong breeze. An impressive feat, given her size and stature.

The lift sealed shut at her back, and Nimah took in a slow, deep breath to center her energy and pull her mind back to focus.

The *Kraken's Beak* was a tavern tethered to a raft. One of a thousand establishments speckled across this zone, made from a fusion of junk crates and the bones of sunken ships, all patched with hull scraps and stolen gravity stabilizers. Neon holoverts ribboned around the perimeter to lure patrons in for libations or other debauchery.

Entering the swollen belly of the tavern, Nimah was met with hard glares and harder shoulders, knocking her from side to side, so that every other step had her ricocheting between bodies like a stone clattering down a well.

Fraud. Disgrace, those looks seemed to say. Every stony expression ripe with accusation. *You don't belong here. You don't deserve to carry that sword or call yourself pirate. Not after what you've done.*

It was hard not to remember the early years at the Academy, the way she'd been met with equal derision, and the weight of her leather coat suddenly felt enormous, like she was a child being swallowed up. Not even closing her hand around the hilt of the cutlass seemed to bolster her with the assurance of authority.

"She's at your eight, Sparrow." Captain Ro's voice spiked through Nimah's comms. "*Third table left of center from the support beam.*"

Nimah swung her gaze across, following her grandmother's instructions. Zensha Blackfyre sat alone at a center table with an open bottle and a lit cigar. Captain of the *Renegade Bloodmoon*, and presider over the eight quads between zones A27 and C64, she alone held one of the largest territories. And the credits that came with it.

Approaching with a purpose and conviction she did not feel, Nimah dragged out a chair, its legs scraping over the patchwork flooring of metal tiles, and plopped herself down.

Zensha assessed her with a cool sweep. Thin platinum braids and long waves of hair tumbled across one shoulder, the sides of her head shaved to skin, revealing intricate metallic tattoos that flowed from her temple down the sides of her neck and disappeared into the neckline of her white cotton shirt, unbuttoned to the navel so that her many gold chains were proudly displayed. A heavy ankh pendant hung at the center.

It was impossible to imagine anyone could sit across from the woman and not be transfixed. Under normal circumstances Nimah might have found herself equally mesmerized, were she not currently battling the throbbing pulse of adrenaline punching against her temples.

"Captain Blackfyre." Nimah clasped her hands in her lap and pushed back her shoulders.

Zensha blew out a stream of gray smoke from her cigar, a thick roll of dark tobacco spiced with rich notes of coffee, leather, and burnt almonds. "So, you're the one they call Sparra."

"Nimah."

"Sparra sits prettier on the tongue." Zensha grinned, a slow smile revealing gold and diamond-capped teeth. "We pirates prefer monikers."

"Right." Correcting her had been foolish. This was her territory. Her say. "Thank you for taking the time to meet with me. Parlay. Sorry. Parlay." *Fuck. Me.* Why was she tripping all over herself like a greenie? "As second-in-command to Captain Indira Roscoe, on behalf of the *Stormchaser*, I'm here to seek permission for our crew to drift in your quads and hope we can come to terms."

Ro's voice crackled over comms. *"Slow it down, Sparrow. Let her come to you."*

That had been the plan. She knew that. With pirates, there was always ceremony and protocol. Parlays were known to stretch for hours, if not the better part of a day, but an infuriating itch forming under Nimah's skin made it hard to think. It crawled through her like ants scuttling between the layers of fat and flesh, the sensation as unsettling as stitches unraveling in the seam of her resolve.

And no matter how still she sat she couldn't stop the decay.

Reaching for her shot glass, Zensha downed the swirling liquor—luminescent purple—in one bracing swallow. Slapping the empty glass down to the linoleum tabletop, she blew out a breath that wafted against Nimah's face like a blast of voidburn on the RIM.

"What was that?" Nimah gestured to the shot glass.

"Call it the Black Hole." Zensha's eyes gleamed like black diamonds, bright with amusement. "'Cause you don't know where it leads, and no one can escape once it sucks you in." She wiggled the now-empty glass. "Want one?"

Nimah flinched. The smart thing to do would be to shut up and take the shot, but the last time she kicked back unknown alcohol, she'd nearly burned a hole through her intestinal tract. And at the resurfacing memory, her roiling stomach promised to unleash absolute hell if she dared to subject it to further trauma. "Is it stronger than seawater?"

"Does a mule kick?"

"Ah... then, no. Thanks."

"Your loss." Zensha signaled the robo-tender, an outdated model with a brass plate stamped with holes in lieu of a face and dressed in a century-old suit, ordering a second round.

A puff of blue smoke wafted across Nimah's face, and the snap of a Zippo sent her heartbeat to scatter like a flock of spooked birds. Instinctively, her head swiveled, eyes scanning the tavern, drawn to something she could only feel, when the crowd parted, and a breathless gasp escaped Nimah like air from a punctured lung. "Impossible..."

Reclined against the bar, lipstick smeared at the corner of her mouth, Dobs flashed a grin, bright as the end of her freshly lit cigarette that blazed like a dying sun as she sucked in more smoke.

"*What's the matter, kid?*" Although clear across the tavern, her voice carried as if she spoke directly into Nimah's ear. "*You look like you've seen a ghost.*"

Nimah pressed the edge of her thumbnail into the center of her palm to ground her attention on the parlay instead of a ghost who'd haunted her relentlessly in nightmares. But this wasn't a dream. She was awake. Eyes-wide-open awake.

"Alright, Sparra. Figure you got less than a quarter before I lose focus, so let's get to it." Zensha hunkered forward, elbows to table and eyes sharpened. But there was another sound cutting through the din of the tavern that made Nimah's blood run as cold as Zensha's breath.

Not the clink of glasses, or the barking of laughter. But the soft ping of teeth falling from the ruin of Dobs's bloody, smiling mouth. Little nuggets of bone that clattered to the floor like raindrops on a windowpane as she suddenly appeared at Nimah's side.

"She's looking at you like chum in the water," Dobs said with a soft, rasping chuckle, and more teeth dislodged.

Throat tight with terror, Nimah dropped her eyes like a child afraid of a monster lurking in the dark. *Not now.* Her heart gave a violent thud and squeeze. *Please, not now.* Eyes were on her. Too many eyes. Her grandmother, Chu, and Gertrude—and somewhere in here, Zensha's own crew, all carefully scattered at various tables—watching *her*.

"Walk away, kid. You ain't got the salt for this, heard?"

Delirium and panic surged, threatening to swallow everything except Dobs's grating voice and Nimah's own thundering heartbeat. If this wasn't a nightmare, it had to be a hallucination, probably a side effect triggered by her first dose of heliosmoke.

That's it. That's all. She's not real.

"Ain't I?" Dobs leered over Zensha's shoulder.

And Nimah froze in horror as her bloody grin split wide, like a belly opened by a blade, and fresh blood spilled forth. More than a single body could hold. It flowed like a surging river, red at first, then deepening to pitch black.

"If I ain't real . . ." Her skin bubbled, eyes near to bursting as flesh and gore melted away to reveal shocking white bones. "Then why you lookin' so pale, kid?"

Nimah recoiled so sharply she nearly flung out of her seat and onto the ground. "Sorry." A tremor racked her shoulders, rattling through every nerve and bone. Cold. She was suddenly so brutally cold.

Zensha frowned like Nimah had grown a second head. "Look at you. Trembling and soft as a chick fresh from the egg." She rolled her eyes. "Listen here, little bird. I ain't one to waste air. Shit's at a premium these days, even in this rusted heap. So here be my terms." She paused long enough to stub out her cigar and settled forward, her many rings catching the warm light. "If the *Stormchaser* wants to drift in my waters then the levy is thirty percent of whatever you haul in this quad. And that's only 'cause I'm playing nice."

Thirty percent was absolute thievery, nearly double what any other pirate ruling a quad would demand from her worst enemy. Calling Zensha out on that would blow the parlay, and without agreement, the *Stormchaser* was sunk. Nimah had to salvage this. Fast.

But before Nimah could speak, a shadow fell across her like a wall.

"See you're still busting balls like goose eggs." The jarring softness of her grandmother's voice was more terrifying than any apparition of Dobs could ever be.

Nimah closed her eyes. *Fuck.*

CHAPTER FOUR

"As I live and breathe." Zensha's brusque voice rang out. "La Voz." She tipped an imaginary brim.

Ro claimed a chair from a neighboring table and in the same instant, a slender Black woman rose from the table behind Zensha, her eyes gleaming bright as her red-dyed sister locs, and set down a clattering chair to the right of her captain. Had to be Zensha's second. Parlay was supposed to be a one-to-one endeavor, but as Nimah's grandmother joined the table, she'd come to even the odds.

Arms crossed, she pinned Nimah with a glare that wasn't all bluff. This girl had been born a pirate while Nimah was only pretending and, apparently, fooling no one.

Reaching for the green bottle on the table, Ro poured out amber liquid into a pair of empty shot glasses stacked on the tray next to it, and set one before Captain Blackfyre, arching a ruthless brow. "Thirty percent, Zen?"

"Ah, c'mon Ro, don't be iced." Gold and diamond-capped teeth flashed in a scoffing smile. "Was ruffling the hatchling's feathers, is all. Scrubbing off some of that down she's still covered in."

"That hatchling is *my* granddaughter." Ro's hand tightened around her shot. "And you were baiting her to get to me."

"So what if I was?" Zensha shrugged. "You're the one come nose to dirt to kiss my toes for scraps, otherwise you'd be loosening my teeth for the impudence."

Ah. And here it was. The squeeze. Zensha wanted something, and she'd twisted Nimah's arm near out of joint to lure Captain Ro to the table and get it.

"I have to know," Zensha settled closer, "did this little Sparra spring you from the noose?" She nodded to Nimah. "Void's been buzzing for weeks but hard to know truth from exaggeration when it comes to our ilk. Pirates love a good banty."

The muscle in Ro's jaw flexed before she nodded. "I wouldn't be here if it weren't for her. Nimah is new to the cloth, but she holds as much shine as my most seasoned of crew."

Warmth bloomed in Nimah's chest, but it was quickly dispelled at the derisive snort from Zensha's sullen second.

"Alright, Zen. You got what you wanted. So tell me what you're really after."

"Never could pull the mist over your eyes." Zensha raised her shot.

Ro brushed hers to Zen's in salute then both women kicked back the smoking liquor. Zensha hissed against the burn. Ro remained stoic as stone.

"Here be the problem—plain and true. Two days ago," Zensha began. "An entire commune of twenty thousand was smoked out. Don't know who or why, but it happens to be one of my best yielders for grain and produce. I be in need of a reliable crew to handle it quiet-like and return what was taken."

Drawn in by intrigue, eagerness latched onto Nimah's throat, refusing to let go. Now *this* was a job. Something she could sink her teeth into beyond the mundane tedium of drifting. The kind of job she'd expected the Valkyries to undertake when she'd surrendered her opportunity to claim her STARs badge. One with high stakes and higher impact.

"What did they take?" Nimah asked.

"Something . . . precious." Zensha poured a couple more shots, this time including Nimah and her own second. "As the presiding lord, part of my job is protection for these outposts that seed not only my coffers but Tortuga herself. For this to happen, under my nose, it's an offense not to be borne—but it should've been impossible. Whoever done it, they be . . . a problem perhaps more than Blackfyre can handle. But if all I hear be true, the banty about you and your little Sparra, well"—Zensha clicked her tongue—"that takes a lotta salt to pull off. So it seems to me like Source is smiling favor on both of us, eh, Ro?" Zensha held out her hand, and without hesitation, her second withdrew a folded sheet of paper, and slid it across the table for Ro.

"My terms, you'll find, are most generous. Since we be old *friends* and such."

Nimah's eyes fell to that little folded square, anticipation burning in her throat and eagerness flexing in her fingers, but this was no longer her parlay; it was between captains, now.

"No," Ro answered without even so much as glancing at the offer.

Zensha exhaled sharply. "*No?*"

"What?" Nimah turned to her grandmother, voice hushed. "What are you doing? We *need* work."

"She's not telling us everything," Ro answered, without pulling her eyes from Zensha or lowering her voice, rich with accusation. "Because it's a suicide mission. There's deeper roots to this and we can't afford to get tangled up in them. So, again, my answer is no. Clean up your own quad, Zen, and leave us out of it."

"But—" Nimah sputtered.

Zensha slammed her fist to the table, and it rattled like she was close to splitting it in half. The volatile outburst raising little more than a few stray eyebrows from the other patrons. "Who'd you think you are telling *me* no in my own fucking quad?"

Her grandmother rose from her seat, drawing all six foot and three inches into her spine like a cutlass drawn from its sheath. Then planted her palms to the table. "You know damn well who I am, and what I am capable of."

"Do I?" Zensha rose as well. Both women stood poised on either side of the table—twin waves ready to collide. Zensha barely clearing five-seven on her feet, but what she lacked in height made up for in the menacing set of her wide shoulders attached to strong arms and scarred hands.

"You've been gone a long time. Too long. And this *child* you call your second isn't cut from the cloth of a pirate, let alone capable to one day wear the brim of *captain*," Zensha continued, a little louder and bolder, drawing on the rapt attention of the Beak's patrons. "Perhaps neither is the infamous La Voz. Not anymore."

Nimah released a soft gasp at the insult, and around them the tavern drew to a tense hush. There were not many Nimah could recall who dared meet her grandmother's gaze, let alone eagerly sought to goad her temper. Zensha, it appeared, was more than comfortable with doing both.

"Methinks your colors have changed from black to yellow." She dropped her hand to rest on the golden pommel of her cutlass, shaped like a woman arched in the throes of ecstasy at her hip. "Shall we find out?"

Ro's eyes tracked the movement and the implied threat that followed. The whip she carried, while intimidating, was no match for cold steel.

"Wait!" Nimah leapt up, flagging her hands. "Please, can't we just—?"

But Ro swept Nimah to the side with the flat of her arm, her chin high and gaze clear. "You dare threaten me with steel during a parlay?"

Zensha prowled toward Ro—there was no other way to describe the feline way she moved—and rolled up her sleeves. Her left arm glowed with a subtle metallic sheen beneath a thin layer of protoskyn encasing a bionic arm. Cheaply made, protoskyn needed frequent patching, so whatever the cause of her injury, given the webbed seams visible between the pattern of her metallic tattoo, it hadn't been recent.

Stopping before Ro, Zensha drove a closed fist into Ro's abdomen and she folded like a new hinge, vein bulging in her brow and eyes wide as she fought to draw in air.

"Be grateful I only used my left." Zensha flexed her bionic right hand for good measure, a whirl of lights streaking up the length of her forearm and down into her knuckles, cinched tight with warning.

The protoskyn covering may have been cheap as shit, but the mechanisms encased within were not and had she in fact used it, Zensha would've punched a hole through her spine.

Ro straightened, hand pressed to her belly, breathing hard. "You really wanna do this, Blackfyre?" she rasped.

Zensha drew her cutlass and tapped steel against her thigh. "I've *dreamed* of this."

Ro nodded once—just a sharp drop of her chin—before the tavern erupted with cheers and shouts. She unfurled her whip, releasing it from the harness as Zensha flipped the table behind, knocking over steins full of beer, forming a cleared space in the center. Pirates and grifters clamored into a tight ring—forcing Nimah to the back corner, where she could barely make out the movement between the gaps of swaying heads and fists punching the air.

It took her a few tense seconds before she spotted Chu and Gertrude, hunched over the banister of the stairs by the entryway, and Nimah battled through the crowd until she reached the bottom step.

"We need to stop this!"

"You fucking fried—stop *this*?" Chu blinked at Nimah, eyes magnified three times their normal size behind her extended bifocals. Her small, bent body tucked into her usual oversized grease-splattered jumpsuit. "Told you we'd get a show." She ribbed Gertrude with a pointy elbow, already ensconced back in the fight. "Y'owe me fifteen credits."

"Only if Ro wins, darling, and last I checked a whip is no match for a blade." Gertrude waved a quieting hand at Chu. "Now shush and let me enjoy the spectacle."

"How can you be betting right now?" Nimah winced at the clang of steel to wood and the answering crack of a whip that followed, inciting the fervor to a frenzy, and the shouts of encouragement rose even brighter.

"You would too if you had any sense. Come." Hands knotted from decades of scrapping, Chu yanked Nimah up a couple more steps by the collar of her coat and tucked Nimah in between her and Gertrude. "Watch and learn, kiddo. Watch and *learn*."

Aghast, but unsure what to do to stop it, Nimah turned to the two women in the center of the circle. Ro gripped the length of her whip stretched taut in both hands, her braid swaying like a tiger's tail down the toned line of her back, while Zensha prowled, her blade held inverted at her side. The dull edge of her cutlass ran along the strong line of her forearm, sleeves pushed up to reveal arms corded with muscle beneath heavily scarred skin.

They came to a clash, all muscle and matched skill. Using the whip like a rope, Ro latched around Blackfyre's wrist and twisted hard, sending the cutlass skittering out of reach. But the move cost her, as Zensha yanked the whip free from Ro's grasp, forcing the women to fists.

Though it had been several weeks since Nimah and the Valkyries had rescued Ro from aboard the *Challenger*, the litany of injuries her grandmother had sustained from interrogation—including the gunshot to the thigh from Dobs's mutiny—hadn't quite healed.

It showed in the rough way Ro moved, and Zensha sought to leverage the weakness, driving her left fist into Ro's kidney. And the way Ro recoiled with a hard twist in her torso, another blow like that was going to topple her grandmother to her knees.

Using her elbow, Ro smashed the hard cap of bone into Zensha's jaw, creating space between them for her to recover—to breathe—before Zensha caught her with another left-handed punch, this one angled high up under her ribs. Even above the din of chaos, Nimah caught the sickening crunch of yielding bone, but instead of pulling away, Ro charged into it, absorbing the full force of the shock while taking Zensha off her feet into a body roll.

Chu punched both hands into the air, screaming like a kid howling at an arcade game.

"Don't let go—hold her arm." Nimah sank her teeth into the knuckle of her clenched fist.

"That's the spirit." Chu barked an approving laugh. "What's your rate?" She wiggled thin, brows at Nimah. "Twenty on Ro? Or you takin' them long odds and betting on the Blackfyre?"

"Get her, Ro!" Gertrude shouted before Nimah could respond.

Zensha and her grandmother tumbled around the sticky floor, a tangled, rolling ball of muscle and fury. But it was clear Ro held the advantage when she flipped onto her back, arms anchored around Zensha's throat in a triangle, cutting off circulation.

"No quarter! *NO QUARTER!*" Gertrude roared, hands cupped over her mouth, like an announcer at a prize fight.

That's it. Nimah watched with strained breath as Ro's arms cinched tighter, a noose drawing taut, and Zensha's eyes bulged against the pressure.

A few more seconds and she'd black out.

But then Ro twisted a little more to the left, instead of the right. The barest shift, subtly done, but it opened the hold instead of closing it, and that little gap was all Zensha needed to wriggle free, slick as a greased pipe.

"What?!" Gertrude and Chu roared in tandem before spouting various curses and shouts of encouragement for Ro to regain her advantage.

But Ro was now moving slower than she should have—even after those crushing blows to her torso that undoubtedly took a toll on her still-healing internal organs. Cutlass back in hand, Zensha loomed over her, a victorious grin on her face. Sweat gleaming on brown skin, she thrust a fist high over her head, rallying the crowd to celebrate her moment of triumph—when a sharp, high-pitched whine immediately brought the fervor to a silence so swift Nimah almost thought she'd suddenly gone deaf.

"What is going on?" Nimah asked, but both Gertrude and Chu appeared equally distracted as they rummaged in pockets and purses. And that ringing met with harmonizing notes that circled the room.

"The gold sings." Sheathing her cutlass, Zensha raised her amulet for all to see. The ankh vibrated like a struck bell and its keening whine echoed in signets adorning hands, hoops decorating ears or noses, and bracelets banding arms.

"The call has been made," someone uttered within the crowd.

"*To Tortuga!*" another bellowed. "*We hoist the mast for a new reign!*"

Fresh cheers roared, resounding against rafters of steel, and Nimah rushed through the dispersing crowd.

"Good to see you haven't lost your salt." Zensha hoisted Ro to her feet.

"Nor you." The women tapped fists in respect for a fight well fought. "My spleen'll carry the imprint of your knuckles for the next week, at least."

Zensha's laugh shot high. "Yeah, well, you've got ribs of carbide. Nearly broke my damn wrist. But next time, should we come to cross swords again," she added, a little lower, "I expect you not to fold your hand."

Ro pursed her lips with a smile. "Don't know what you're talking about."

"Bet you don't." Zensha shook her head, sighed. "Drift, if it please you. My levy be eight percent of whatever you haul from my quad. For an old friend."

"Five," Ro countered, drawing her braid across her shoulder.

"Six and a half."

Ro nodded in agreement; they shook on it.

"What was that? The ringing sound?" Nimah asked as Zensha sauntered away, still grinning as she rejoined her second and a trio of other captains offering their praise for a thrilling win.

"Council summoning all pirates for a gathering. The time of mourning for Siggy has passed and a new monarch will ascend." Ro grimaced, buckling an inch to her left. "So we must make our way to Tortuga."

Nimah's stomach twisted at the mention of Sigourney's name. "Are you okay?"

"Not here." Ro rolled away from Nimah's concerned touch, eyes scanning the tavern.

"Well fought," Chu sang as she and Gertrude approached. "Knew you could've cinched it but probably wise you dropped your guard for the sake of parlay."

"Blackfyre's given us a levy of six and a half." As Ro retrieved her whip with a wince, the room thinned out to a third of the crowd and rapidly declining as pirates and grifters rushed for the doors. "We'll need terms sealed in ink before we jump from this quad."

"I'll do it," Gertrude offered. "You should take care of those ribs."

"Chu, go with her." Unable to mask her discomfort much longer, Ro hugged her side and hissed a breath through clenched teeth. "I'll want us to burn from here in thirty."

"Aye." Chu tapped the side of her brow in salute.

Once alone, Ro swung her eyes to Nimah and her insides went icy beneath the shock of her grandmother's disappointment. "What happened to you?"

"I . . ." Nimah lowered her gaze, taking a keen interest in the toes of her scuffed, twice-recycled re-soled leather boots. "I don't know."

Her gaze sharpened. "Do you have any idea how it looks to have a second challenge her captain during a parlay?"

"I just . . . I thought the job could be good for us to do something bigger. Important."

"Good for us?" Ro winced, hand rubbing along her tender side. "Blackfyre has been a captain almost as long as I, and as a presiding lord, protection for outposts within her quads falls on *her* shoulders. There's only one reason a pirate as seasoned as her would push this onto another crew. Whatever happened—whatever she saw—it scared the salt out of her." Her golden-brown eyes flickered with heat. "And does Blackfyre look like the type to scare easy?"

No, she didn't.

Irritated, Ro pinched the bridge of her nose and sighed deeply. "I knew there was going to be a period of adjusting, Nimah, but you're not a cadet anymore, so stop dreaming like one. You're a pirate. My second-in-command, at that. My *second*. That means you have my back no matter what, and if at any point you disagree with me then you address it in private. *Never* go against me in front of anyone ever again. Am I clear?"

"You're right," Nimah muttered, trying her hardest not to cry. "I'm sorry."

"Sorry?" Ro scoffed, and closed in on Nimah like a storm. "*Sorry* is nothing but empty syllables to pirates. A weak word letting you pat yourself on the back, but it teaches you nothing. And when the next mistake happens, instead of credits, maybe it costs us someone's life. Apologies are a pointless waste of breath, and I don't want air, I want action—show me, Sparrow. *Do better.*"

Nimah obediently followed in silence as they exited the Beak. The lash of her grandmother's temper had stung more than any blow she'd received in all her training at the Academy, but Ro wasn't wrong for shooting her between the eyes with hard truth. Nimah wasn't on Lysandis anymore. She was sailing with hardened warriors who'd carved out their livelihood with steel and blood in a part of the void where life should not have been at all sustainable.

Where mistakes, even small ones, were detrimental, and any traces of weakness had to be ground to dust and replaced with unwavering grit. Ro was right—Nimah had fucked up. Now it was on her to learn from it.

CHAPTER FIVE

Back in her cabin, Nimah took a weary breath before dunking her face into the basin she'd filled with the coldest water their tanks could manage. She held for a count of sixty before rising to take a fresh breath and then dunked herself again.

Submerged, everything inside her went blissfully quiet. No ghosts. No noise. And she clung to those precious seconds of peace as if they were gold. One minute passed, and as the seconds stretched toward another, her lungs rebelled, and she burst from the water with a sputter, gripping the basin as she mopped water from her face.

"Careful, kid. Thought you were gonna drown on that last one."

Nimah clenched her eyes, smothering the urge to cry. "Go away."

Dobs's laugh crackled like electricity through the air, followed by steady puffs of cigarette smoke that floated through the cabin like ghosts with nowhere else to haunt except the fringes of Nimah's unraveling sanity.

"Over my dead body, heard?"

"You *are* dead." Nimah twisted to follow the shifting direction of her voice, but the lights were fully dimmed, so all she could make out was the rough outline of her bunk and nightstand. "Tormenting me won't change things, Dobs."

"No." Subtle movement streaked by the foot of her bunk. "But makes it more fun."

Smoke thickened. Then came the gleam—those glittering black eyes that shone with a pinpoint of waking hellfire red at the center. Nimah's heart kicked into a terrified gallop as those pinpricks moved closer, but she didn't clap her hands to signal the lights to activate. The only thing worse than being trapped with Dobs in the terror of darkness would be to see her in full light.

Her face a ruin of melting, bubbling skin. Her mouth grinning wide with teeth slipping free from her gums. Or the way her eyes exploded like sonic grenades as she screamed, locked in the throes of perpetual agony in those final moments of life.

"You're in my head," Nimah whispered. "A figment of my imagination."

Silence answered. Then broken by the dragging scuff of footfalls, unhurried in their approach. "Imagination is perception. And perception's as real as reality, kid."

Pale blue smoke rolled toward Nimah's face. So thick she could actually smell it—burnt paper and ash, and those bright red pinpricks now hovered only inches away. Haloed by the faintest ghostly outline of Dobs. Almost crisp enough to make out her smirking features and dense cloud of white curls dented by her brass aviator goggles nestled atop her brow.

I don't understand how this is happening. How is this happening?

"The mind is a fragile thing, heard?" Dob's answered like she'd heard her thoughts as clear as her own voice. "Reckon I'll enjoy seeing how long it takes to break yours."

A sudden burn seared Nimah's right bicep. She yelped, stumbling back, and caught the gleam of Dobs's sickening smile before she melted into the shadows like smoke vanishing into a vent shaft. But the sting remained. And so did her words.

Nimah gasped, her breathing shallow and frantic and heart thudding in a rhythm that felt too fast, too loud, like it was trying to outrun her own body. She clapped her hands, and the lights rose slowly, soft and warm, like the first blush of a sunrise. Her cabin was empty, but the cold inside her didn't budge. It had settled deep—like the void itself had crawled into her chest.

Trembling, she reached into the back pocket of her cargos and withdrew the vial of heliosmoke. She held it like an anchor. No. It was too soon. She'd already dosed for the day, but maybe if she took a little bit. A precaution. Just enough to keep her focus from fracturing again. Because after what happened at the Beak, and now here in her cabin, she couldn't afford another slip once they reached Tortuga.

A knock startled her, and the vial slipped from her hands and clinked into the basin as the door whispered open and Maverick entered.

"Hey." Nimah planted her back to the sink and crossed her arms to mask their trembling. "What's up?"

"Wanted to check in. Heard about the brawl with Blackfyre." He stopped his chair at the foot of her bunk. "Almost sorry I had to miss it."

"Yeah, it was . . . something." Nimah cleared her throat. "But we got our terms in the end." *No thanks to me*, her thoughts finished dryly.

"Guess Captain Ro wasn't the only one getting her licks in." His finger brushed along a tender spot on her arm. "Someone use you for an ashtray, Cadet?"

"What?" Nimah's gaze dropped to her right arm and there, on her bicep—where she'd felt the pinching sting—was a small round burn. The perfect size for a cigarette. Her stomach turned. "It's nothing." She tugged her sleeve down and kicked away from the sink. "Look, I don't mean to be rude, but if you're not here for anything particular . . . I'll see you at the bridge for my lessons when we have to dock."

As they'd burned from the Beak, Ro had decided docking at Tortuga was a perfect opportunity for her granddaughter to gain some valuable flight time in first chair. But Nimah saw it for what it really was. Punishment. While she'd come a long way with managing a shuttle, despite three months of flying under Maverick's tutelage, Nimah still struggled at the helm of the *Stormchaser*. And right now, the last thing she wanted to do was get behind the yoke, but she'd been kicked hard enough in the ass for one day; she could practically taste the leather of her grandmother's boot.

Any pirate worth her salt should know how to fly with authority and skill, but for a captain—it was mandatory. Otherwise, she had no hope of one day commanding a ship, or a crew.

"Nimah. You can't keep avoiding me." He said as she crossed to the other side of her tight cabin, doing whatever she could to do exactly what he'd accused her of—put yet more distance between them.

"I'm not."

"Aren't you?" Maverick arched a brow when she finally met his gaze. "Because you sure as shit couldn't wait to fly off to Kesh3 maybe an hour after saying you needed space to *think*."

Nimah pressed her lips into a flat grimace. "I was just doing my job as second."

His scrutinizing brow softened with a measure of sympathy. "I'm not trying to pick a fight. I'm worried about you."

I'm fine. The lie sat poised on the edge of her tongue, but she snapped her mouth shut and swallowed it back. "I don't know," she whispered instead. The closest she could bring herself to being honest. Vulnerable.

"I'm sorry if I sounded harsh," he continued. "The last few months, I know haven't been easy, and you should be proud of yourself. *I am proud of you.*"

Tears pressed against the back of her eyes, crushed glass that nicked and tore, but she held them in with a sniffle and something in his gaze broke, seeing her at the verge of falling apart.

"Nimah, please. Talk to me. Let me in." Reaching for her hand, Maverick tugged gently, trying to draw her into his lap, into his arms, into safety.

And she wanted to. By source and stars, she wanted to feel his chin against her shoulder, the assured rhythm of his breath steadying hers. But instead she dug in her heels and pulled away. "Don't do that."

He dropped his hand like she'd scalded him. "Do what?"

"I told you I need space."

Tenderness lifted from his gaze and was replaced with searing hurt. "Yes, you did, but not *why.* It's been two days; I think I deserve an explanation. Did I do something wrong?"

"There's no time for this, Maverick." But when his brows flattened, it was clear he wasn't going to relent. "It's complicated."

"Everything is complicated. We're pirates."

"I don't think you understand how much I have riding on me right now. I gave it all up to be here and—everything I know. Everything I believed in. My home. My friends. My dreams—gone."

"And?"

And I feel like I've made a huge mistake. All my instincts are wrong. I can't focus. I can't sleep. I can't get anything right. I'm holding on by a thread but barely. It's like I'm drowning in failure, and I don't know how to fix it. To make it all stop.

The walls of the *Stormchaser* closed in tighter, narrow as a coffin. Closing in on her, like the walls, like her skull, like the muscles in her chest—constricting to the point of pain. Her pulse roared in her ears, a whooshing pound drumming like fists, and Nimah wanted nothing more than to turn on her heels and run away. From him. From all of it.

But most importantly, herself.

"Be serious with me, Nimah. I know you won't admit it but you've been pulling away for weeks. My mistake was I let you because I knew fighting to hold on would only push you away faster. You want to end things between us, fine." He dashed a hand. "But I deserve to know *why*."

Nimah scanned his face, she saw the worry—but more importantly, the hurt that while choking on the venom of her own trauma, she'd inadvertently stepped on his. Triggering his fear of rejection. Abandonment. A wound they both shared.

And there . . . right there, cruel as it was, she saw her way out.

"You want to know?" Nimah crossed her arms. "I'm second-in-command. One day I will be captain, and the truth is, Maverick, this dalliance or flirtation or whatever you want to call it—isn't appropriate."

Shock flashed across his face. Darkened into anger. "Dalliance," he echoed.

If she'd drawn her blaser and shot him point-blank in the chest it would have hurt less, but there was no taking back the wound now, so she took aim and fired again. "I can't run a ship and cross lines with you. It was a mistake that never should've happened in the first place. I'm sorry, but it's over, and you need to accept it."

"Mistake." Maverick scored his teeth across his bottom lip, his words raw. "Well, if that's how you feel, then I'll tender my resignation to Captain Ro after we deboard at Tortuga and find work elsewhere."

Shock nearly took Nimah off her feet. "You'd leave the *Stormchaser* without a pilot?"

He shrugged. "Find another."

Fuck. Now her grandmother was really going to keelhaul her ass. "Maverick, don't be like this. You can stay. We can be civil."

"Civil?" His grin cut sharp as the hurt in his eyes. "How's this for civil." Anchoring his forearms to his thighs, he leaned in, teeth bared like a wolf warning her not to come any closer. "I chose to be here because I believed in you. I loved you."

"Mav—"

"But I'm done," he plowed on, silencing her cold. "I'm not stupid. You're hurting me because I keep demanding honesty and truth, because I know something is wrong and you don't want me finding out what it is. Because I refuse to be kept in the dark and you're more stubborn than sense. Whatever's got you so freaked out, Nimah, if you won't let me help you through it then I'm done fighting you for a foothold in that icebox you call a heart." He gripped his wheels, guiding his chair for the cabin door. "Since you're so determined to handle everything alone. Okay. Do it alone."

He exited without another backward look, and Nimah waited until the door sealed shut before she drew her first, shaken breath. That had been harder than she'd expected, and the raw ache of regret was a knife twisting in the chambers of her *icebox* heart.

<*Nimah, Second-in-Command.*> Mother's voice rattled through the overhead comms in her cabin, the light tracks ribboning in tandem with the smooth, robotic voice. <*We're approaching Tortuga; Captain Ro has requested your presence on the bridge.*>

"Yes, Ma. I am on my way."

<*Heard, Nimah, Second-in-Command.*>

Nimah jolted to a stop. ". . . What did you say?"

<*I said, Affirmative, Nimah, Second-in-Command.*>

No, she was almost certain it wasn't. Only Dobs had ever used *heard*, but doubt settled in. Quiet and heavy. "Thank you, Ma."

Stepping off the gangway, Nimah scanned across the imitation wood dock to the humming heart of Tortuga. Vibrant with life and energy, the floating spacity was shaped like a crescent island covered with lopsided buildings made of brick and stone, and in the distance—the spires of the conclave.

Overhead, holos of gulls wheeled through a simulation blue sky, their lilting calls floating on a warm, salty breeze and twisting her already bleeding heart in her chest. She'd only been here once before, with Dobs when they came seeking aid from Sigourney, the Queen of Bones, but that moment brought forward so many memories. And all of them cut like a knife.

"You going to stand there all day looking pretty, or are you going to clear the way so the rest of us can pass?"

Jolted by Gertrude's terse tone, Nimah shuffled down to the dock. "Looks like Blackfyre beat us here." She gestured to the tethered ship, large and gleaming with a carbide exterior lacquered in black paint that shifted to show flecks of red and yellow, depending on how the light struck her hull.

"Yes, well, she is a swift vessel, but there's more important things than speed."

Although Gertrude was tactful with her choice of words, Nimah knew what she really meant to say was that they'd have been here ages ago if it was Maverick in first chair.

"How does it work? The call?" Nimah asked, as Gertrude toyed with a pendant around her neck made from a simple gold coin with the face nearly worn away from years of passing hands.

Gertrude tucked it away with a sage grin and sparkle to her eyes, tinted icy blue to match her curls, picked out into a soft halo framing her high cheekbones. "Some things are best left with a bit of mystery, Sparrow, and not spoiled with explanation."

Striding onto the dock, Boomer planted his hands to his hips, arched his back, and breathed deep. "Fuck, it's good to be off that boat and getting some proper air."

"Well, breathe deep. We got us a solid twelve at least. Maybe more." Ro hooked a thumb through her belt loop and swung her head in the general direction of the three towering spires. "Go on, take your leave. Enjoy yourselves while Nimah and I make our way to the conclave. The gathering will be for first and seconds in attendance only, so no sense staying cooped on the boat."

"Razor." Boomer clapped his hands together and rubbed hard like he was trying to start a fire with his callouses. "I'm gonna find me a table and some dice."

Chu bounced on her toes. "Got a hundred and eighty-three credits to play with, thanks to the little breakout between Ro and Blackfyre at the Beak. And I like to keep my streak primed."

"Yes, well, consider it charity." Gertrude rolled an unbothered shoulder, though it was clear she was absolutely bothered by losing to Chu. "I'll wander to the shops and see what sort of wares may catch my eye. Maybe treat this one to some blackberry ice." She winked at Mumbles, who gasped at the mention of the sweet treat.

She'd have a purple tongue for three days and would be jittery as a sparkplug from all the chemicals, but the sight of her mile-wide gummy grin made it hard to imagine denying her now.

"Be nice to have a breather." Chu's features melted from her usual sulk to a sunny grin. The rim of her glasses perched on the round tip of her nose. Her cap of rough-chopped black hair shot with more and more gray as the weeks passed. "Ain't seen this many pirates gathered since a'fore Sigourney's reign."

"Everyone sync up before we go, and comms stay on at all times." Ro scanned her crew. Scowled. "Anyone seen Maverick?"

"He took off soon as the hatch opened." Chu hooked her thumb toward the central hub of the spacity. "Said something about errands."

"Well, someone make sure he's looped in. Set for six hours," Ro ordered. "We'll wave if the ceremony takes longer than that."

Six hours? The itching under Nimah's skin intensified. "You really think this will take that long?" Nimah asked as she and her grandmother made their way down the dock—a long, riveted walkway of rusted steel that staggered across three levels with multiple ports branching out like boughs on a tree.

"Generally, yes. All depends on how the council's chosen ascender is received by the conclave of captains." False sunlight washed across them from between a break in the buildings and turned her deep amber eyes molten with hints of gold and red at the core. "But if no one draws swords, we may get lucky."

Nimah could only hope but if her brief experience was any indication, *luck* and *pirate* rarely went hand in hand.

CHAPTER SIX

The streets of Tortuga drowned in bodies as every pirate in the void spilled their way onto the cobblestones—bringing Nimah shoulder to shoulder with some of the roughest rogues she'd ever seen.

All mottled skin and hard-lined faces with blackening teeth and yellowed eyes, a clear sign of malnutrition and failing livers. Pirates spent more time in space than they did on land. Most flew on ships that had patchwork sanitation systems and recyclers, forcing them to live in abhorrent conditions the longer they kept to the void with shields not strong enough to protect them from chronic exposure. As a result, most didn't die from blaserfire or cutlass—they died from radiation sickness.

Those with access to larger quads earned more income to provide for their crew and maintain the integrity of their ships. Those who hadn't managed to ingratiate themselves with a presider were pushed out to shallow waters where credits were thin.

What should've taken them no more than twenty minutes from the docks stretched into well over an hour before they reached the lifts, and from there another hour of waiting to ascend to the conclave.

"How did the Council of Black come to be?" Nimah asked, needing something to distract her mind from the tedium.

Ro balked at her question. "You don't already know our histories?"

"Academy texts were sparse on how piracy even began, let alone its continued evolution."

"Why am I not surprised." Ro shook a derisive head. "It began during the height of the Zone Wars, as reserves broke away from

SIGA control in revolt against the slaughter and ceaseless bloodshed. Those wartimes were catastrophic, and many abandoned their regiments to become outlaws. The brothers in black were the first twelve to call themselves pirates, inspired by the histories of Earth-Prior, and as tales of their exploits grew, more were drawn to the allure of freedom in the stars. As numbers escalated, the need for order became paramount.

"The conclave was established soon after, and this stronghold was built with all the spoils the brothers in black had amassed. Danbi was our first king, and the eleven brothers formed his council. They drafted our code, carved out territories, and established hierarchal order to ensure all had their fair share."

Finally it was their turn to board the lift—a flat, open shelf, with a single barrier shield that slotted into place before the lift whisked up at an ear-popping speed. The ground fell away to a broad landscape of haphazard structures and ramshackle towers, but it was the glimmering dots of ships tethered to the docks, with more flowing in on the horizon, that snatched the breath from her lungs. Almost enough to rival the stars in the sky.

"I had no idea there were so many," Nimah whispered, awed.

"So many what?"

"Pirates." During her studies at the Academy, it was estimated the total pirate population ran in the vicinity of one to every million in SIGA's militia. It appeared that estimate was off by quite a substantial sum.

At the summit, the lift brought them into the second spire, which was the largest of the three. As she and her grandmother deboarded, merging with the forming crowd, a particle doorway pixelated open into a shimmering energy curtain that sent pinpricks racing across Nimah's skin as they passed through the barrier between the inner and outer walls.

Thicker than most vaults, should the barrier ever be sealed, it could easily entomb thirty men deep and perhaps twice that across, leaving them to suffocate in solidified nanites. This was high-grade SIGA tech that pirates were not supposed to have in their possession.

The bodies before her peeled away and as Nimah entered the conclave, she nearly lost her breath. This wasn't the throne room where they'd first bent the knee to Sigourney, but a grand, tiered atrium framed by soaring vine-wrapped columns made of red marble veined with cobalt and gold. They supported the weight of wraparound balconies stacked so high Nimah could barely make out the faces of those already seated and awaiting the rest of the assembly to gather.

Overhead, a round viewport cast a spotlight upon the Council of Black. Unlike what their namesake would suggest, they wore draping coats in vibrant jewel-tone hues, some trimmed in gold filigree, and others cut with a more modern tailored edge. But all had metallic tattoos etched into their faces that shone against their skin like light tracks aboard the *Stormchaser*. By her count there were forty-three, with the split swinging a head or two in favor of women-presenting members.

"This way, Sparrow." Ro caught Nimah by the elbow before she'd turned for the twin stairways that led up to the gallery. "Marks must be made."

Confused, Nimah shuffled after her grandmother across the atrium where a mast lay on the floor. A stoic line of pirates passed on either side, heads bowed and hats removed like mourners paying their final respects.

This line moved even slower than the walk from the docks to the spires. Sighing, Nimah's gaze dropped to her feet as a glistening white fish, large as a lap dog, swam by beneath a sheet of diamond glass protecting a stream of water inlaid into the intricate mosaic-tiled flooring. Only when she caught the soft ripple across their scales did she realize they were a simulation.

To capture such richness of color, texture, and density of matter—the only other time she'd been so expertly deceived had been the day she'd met and collared Maverick.

Finally, the mast came into view. At least a hundred feet long, arched like the curve of a cutlass, with the base wider than the tip for support. The dark stained wood marred with millions of notches and grooves.

Nimah traced the overlapping markings. Some faded as scar tissue, blackened with dirt and age, and others vivid as a fresh wound. This was *real* wood. After spending most of her life on Lysandis, she had an eye for quality and could spot the real thing. Oak, if she had to guess, grown from seed to sapling and nurtured to maturity for at least a hundred years before it was cut for a mast of this size. Maybe even two. A process that would've cost a small fortune few could afford.

Ro made her mark, tears glimmering in her eyes. The first Nimah had seen from her in a very long time. She rubbed away the curled shaving with her thumb before she passed the hooked knife to Nimah. Little more than a finger in length, it was one she used almost daily, whether to slice apples off the core or to open ration cans.

Accepting the blade, Nimah pressed the pad of her thumb against the tip and a small bead of blood welled to the surface, glistening against the steel.

I'm sorry. She dug into the mast, leaving behind a red crescent to join the litany of others, like a thumbnail cutting into a tender palm out of anger or grief. *I'm sorry you died because of me. I'm sorry I couldn't save you.*

But the words didn't make her feel any better or at peace. They were too small and insubstantial to encompass everything Nimah had carried inside of her for weeks. Her grandmother was right.

Sorry was weak and empty as air. Utterly ineffectual on its own. Pathetic.

If she wanted to atone for Sigourney's death, then she would have to earn it through effort and change. She'd have to bleed for it.

"Captain Indira Roscoe."

Both women turned to face the man that had spoken. Short, with wide shoulders and a flat face pinched behind metallic tattoos that swirled like a current.

"Councillor Rennick." Ro inclined her head in greeting. "Been quite a long time."

"An age and a day." Rennick grinned, his teeth all replaced with emeralds. "Council asks that you remain on the floor while we hoist the banner of our fallen queen. Respect for the years she sailed with your crew as a Valkyrie."

"I . . ." Ro took a moment to shake off her surprise. "I'd be honored."

Her grandmother didn't look honored; she looked wary as a rattlesnake. And when Rennick's chin lifted with pleasure at her humble response, something in his eyes made Nimah's insides tense in warning that he wasn't someone to trust, but in a den of pirates—was anyone?

Across the chamber, a hulking guard strode inside. His skin white as bleached bone and covered with red tattoos in whorl-like patterns and a mallet slung across his shoulders, almost as long as he was tall.

Stopping beneath a rectangular gong that stretched almost from floor to ceiling, he hammered it with a fierce swing and the entire chamber vibrated from the singular, booming note.

The weathered gold cuff on Ro's wrist hummed in the same high-keening note Nimah had heard at the Beak, joined by a chorus of a hundred thousand, blending like voices harmonizing in a choir. As soon as the gong fell silent, so too did that song of gold.

"It's time." Rennick turned to rejoin the line of council members spanning the length of the mast.

And Ro steered Nimah over to the sidelines, away from the center floor where many others were gathered around the circumference of the chamber. A few of the faces Nimah recognized almost immediately from her years of study of pirate lords and their seconds. Including Pommen Grayscale—the lower half of his jaw, ripped off in a brawl, was replaced with one made of gold, giving him the look of a skull come alive.

It was then Nimah realized how underdressed she and her grandmother were compared to all the other captains and seconds in the chamber. They'd come adorned in their finest, like birds preening for attention, feathers bright and fluffed. Many dripped in gold and jewels, while others were trimmed in fine cloth and buttery leather.

This was a pageant. An intricate display of authority and prestige.

Choose me, they all seemed to say.

Captain Ro, on the other hand, in faded gray cargos and a simple black tank, said: *Leave me the hell alone.*

"Who are the prospects for ascension?" Nimah leaned into her grandmother. "Do we know yet?"

"Prospects?" Ro arched an amused brow. "It's already been decided by the council. All of this is merely a formality, Sparrow." She gestured around them before recrossing her arms, bare and corded with muscle.

"Wait . . . so we don't get any input?" Nimah frowned. "I thought pirates were democratic. This feels wrong."

"We're too ornery a bunch to agree on the color of the sky, let alone our leadership. There was a time when ascension was determined by combat. Three names were put forward and a fight to the death would ensue until there was a clear winner, but grudges often formed between crews after that sometimes went on for decades. It took a few changeovers of monarchs before it was determined the best approach was to have the council decide. And we've been far better off for it."

Two councillors raised their hands toward the gallery, and at the clap of their hands, sheer cables drew taut, pulling a flag to hang in the center of the chamber. Sigourney's former banner was white with blood-red fangs attached to sword hilts instead of blades, framed by the infamous wings of the Valkyrie crew in glow-thread. As the banner rippled with movement, the wings appeared to spread in flight.

To the void or Valhalla. Tears seared the corners of Nimah's eyes.

The banner was raised high and more of the alabaster guards flowed in, all bearing the same face, and the same tattoos. Clones, she realized in disbelief—yet more advanced tech she'd thought only available to SIGA—and between them they hauled a massive bronze brazier.

Sigourney's body lay within, dressed exactly as she had been in her final moments aboard the *Challenger*, in black leather armor and crackled war paint that clung to her graying skin like broken pottery. They'd claimed and returned her body to Tortuga by way of cryo-shipment, and Nimah would've thought by now she'd have been laid to rest.

The chamber fell into a sudden hush. Heads hung, shoulders sagged, and caps were removed. Even Ro's proud chin dropped a mournful inch as the flag lowered to drape over Sigourney's corpse. Then, softly, the pirates began to sing.

A song rich in tenor and deep with mourning. As the chamber swelled with the funeral ballad, a councillor activated an icon on his wristdeck and, descending from overhead, the colossal disc Nimah had admired earlier slanted open.

To the naked eye, the air only seemed to ripple, lapping forward like wind skimming the surface of the clearest water, but the second those ripples reached the brazier, the contents within erupted in a singular blast of light. A violent snap—so sudden that if she'd blinked, she'd have missed it entirely.

Smoke cleared, and all that once remained of Sigourney and her banner was a searing cube of compact ash.

The councillors closed in, and Nimah watched, confused at the spectacle, as the ashes were gathered and brought to the summit of the conclave's chamber, and they were then fed into the basin of a towering hourglass.

"Now our queen will preside over us always, along with the remnants of those who ruled before," Rennick called out loudly. "A reminder for all who will one day ascend to our throne: *memento mori*. Live long and live well, but eventually we all must die and to ashes we all must return."

Nimah's mouth tumbled open. Horrified. "No!"

"Quiet, Sparrow," Ro cautioned, jabbing her with a stern elbow.

"They're *entombing* her! She wouldn't want that," Nimah hissed. Sigourney, vibrant and fierce, shouldn't be trapped in a coffin of glass and bronze when she deserved to be scattered to the wind. Her spirit soaring, wild and unfettered. A Valkyrie on wing.

And whose fault is that, Dobs snickered inside of her.

Nimah cleared her tight throat, unable to prevent the tense spasm jerking her head on her shoulders. Her eyes dropped to the floor where a small chunk of compact ashes caught her attention. A coin-sized clump that must've broken away while being collected by the council. Under the guise of fixing the ankle strap on her boot, Nimah bent to her knee and gathered it with careful fingers. It held its shape like a nugget of firm soil, desiccated under unforgiving heat, and she slipped it into the pocket of her trench.

"As we send one queen to join the bones of her brethren, the time has come to welcome the rise of another. Captain Indira Roscoe."

Every bone in her grandmother's body jolted.

The chamber rumbled in surprise, the sound gathering in strength as it reached where Nimah and her grandmother stood on the flagstones beneath the stunned glare of five hundred thousand of the saltiest pirates in all the void.

"Oh shit," Nimah gasped. "Did you know?"

"No fucking idea," Ro barely breathed.

"You all know her name," Rennick continued, "but let us remind you what it means. La Voz didn't just sail the void—she carved it. Forging trade routes that became our main throughlines and the grid many of us still hold today; the very reason Tortuga still flies free. She's bled for this conclave more times than most of you have docked, and when the storms batter our shores, it is she who raises her sword first to stand in defense of all we hold dear. And so, by honor of this council, we have determined it is she who's to be our queen. Step forward, take a knee. And claim your throne."

Steeling herself, Ro joined the line of councillors, her face once more unreadable in the swath of sunlight, and for a heartbeat, all fell quiet. But before she could sink to her knees, a harsh voice cut through the silence.

"Queen? She barely has enough salt to call herself Captain." Zensha prowled from the base of the stairs into the center of the conclave. Platinum goddess braids loose beneath the slanted brim of a crimson tricorne hat, an array of gold hoops stacked along the shell of her ears, small at the top and growing larger as they reached her lobes.

"What is the meaning of your impudence?" A female councillor bristled.

Zensha raised her hands in truce, the tails of her alligator coat whisking the ground behind her like a train, dyed crimson to match her hat. "I'm merely exercising my right as a member of this conclave to question the merit of the council's decision."

"You dare—?"

"Yes!" Zensha shouted. "*I dare.* As should all of you!" she bellowed, swinging her arms wide to the hushed members of the gallery. "Aye, we have all heard the great stories of Ro and her Valkyries," she continued. "There was a time when I, too, would have said she was the fiercest of us. Born to bear the weight of a crown. To stand for us all." She stopped by Ro and raised her imperious chin, onyx eyes gleaming in challenge. "But that was twenty years ago. And the woman before us today is not the captain we all once so fiercely admired. Or loved."

Nimah watched, breath held, as history and heartbreak collided in that single glare.

"For nigh on fifteen years, she vanished—leaving her routes vulnerable and outposts unprotected. I ask you—is that the steel of a queen? And now our council would raise her to a throne that would otherwise still be occupied had it not been for the desperate song of a little *sparra*."

Nimah flinched as Zensha's words speared through her chest, heavy with accusation.

"Sigourney was steel and salt and blood—under her reign, Tortuga thrived like never before. Our coffers grew fat, our caches plentiful. We were at the pinnacle of our greatest glory. Our Queen of Bones . . . warrior was she! Drawn into the void on a fool's errand, and in defiance of our very code. And they returned her to us—as ashes."

Nimah looked to her grandmother, who glowered in quiet rage. Why was she saying nothing? Why was the council doing *nothing*? Nimah's heart pounded in her ears. She wanted to leap forward, to challenge Zensha, but then she caught Ro's raised brow—an unspoken command for restraint that Nimah reluctantly obeyed.

And Zensha was only too eager to fill the silence.

"The loss of Sigourney is more than a blow to our hearts, it's a blow to our survival. Sailing was challenging enough, beforehand." She spun back to face the gallery, her voice ringing out, pure with contempt, for all to hear. "Now we all bleed for *their recklessness*."

Roars hammered down from the gallery in agreement and Zensha raised her bionic fist, inciting them into a frothing frenzy until all within the conclave bayed for blood. Then she stilled them to silence with a single finger and the roar dropped into sudden calm. Even the light seemed to lean in with breathless wonder. And Nimah found it hard not to be both infuriated and impressed by how effortlessly she tamed a hurricane into a still breeze.

"If Ro thinks she has the salt to call herself our queen . . ." She set her chin, eyes dark as honed steel. "If we who have sailed and served are expected to bend our knees to the council's whim—I say let her prove herself. Let there be a Reckoning!" She threw her arms wide and spun again, for all in the gallery to see. "What say you?" she roared. "*What say you!*"

Once more, shouts of agreement crashed down from overhead, joined by the steady beat of fists to pillar, post, or chest, a dizzying thunder that pounded like a war drum calling for justice.

No, not justice, Nimah thought dully.

A Reckoning.

CHAPTER SEVEN

"Just so I got this clear . . ." Hands cupping knobby elbows, Chu crossed her feet at the ankles. "Ro's been named successor, but not until she completes a Reckoning, some such test in penance for Siggy eating lead during her rescue op. Now we got a handful a'days to save five hundred youngins before Siggy's ashes run out like sand in an hourglass? That the gist?"

An hour after the conclave concluded, Nimah and Ro returned to the ship to gather the crew on the communal deck of the *Stormchaser*. Including Zensha, assigned by the council to join them in the Reckoning as the slighted presider who had all the information and access to whatever resources they required to complete the mission. And, even more surprisingly, Maverick.

"Five hundred and seven children," Nimah corrected, drawing away from where she leaned against the arched industrial column that supported the girth of the *Stormchaser*'s belly like a belt. "And the hourglass—it wasn't just Siggy's ashes but all the kings' and queens'. Some kind of perverse reminder of mortality for the next presiding monarch."

Nimah stopped at the foot of the long trestle table, opting to stand while most of the others sat in the mismatched chairs. Ro remained off to the side, reclined against the ledge of the oval viewport that peered out at the glistening bioluminescent waves lapping at Tortuga's simulated shoreline. She'd barely said more than a grunt since leaving the conclave. A dangerous sign that when she did, hell was going to break loose.

"Bloody morbid, innit?" Gertrude commented, her gaze fixed to the worn pattern of the woven rug spread beneath their feet over the paneled wood flooring.

Mumbles, lost in her own little world, lay stretched out on her stomach with a pair of action figurines she'd cobbled together from spare toy parts fished out of an old bin in storage. A small seed of envy sprouted in Nimah's belly, tender roots twisting through the cavern of her guts at the sight of Mumbles, her feet kicked up, red boots clicking listlessly at the heels. Free to disappear from all burden of responsibility.

"And what exactly is the mission we're expected to do?" Maverick asked, drumming the edges of his wheels.

"Well." Boomer kicked out of his chair with a grunt, one hand pressed to the muscular plane of his belly. "If I gotta focus, I'ma need t'fill the hole in my gullet."

"Seriously, Boomer?" Nimah sighed. "This is kind of important."

"Shoulda had us convene on the bridge then," Boomer called from the adjacent kitchen, and yanked open an upper cabinet—the mossy green paint chipping around tarnished brass hardware.

"Since you's in there—pop a few cans for the rest of us, why dontcha," Chu called out, hands cupped around her mouth. "Boy's right." She shrugged at Nimah. "Might as well have a proper sit-down."

Fifteen minutes and half a dozen warmed ration cans later, Zensha picked one up then pulled a horrified face.

"This the best you have to offer?" She spooned out a sampling mouthful. "Tastes like . . . fermented beans stewed in shit and left to dry-rot."

Ration cans, packed with a full day's worth of calories, tasted like sweat and regret. They were laced with a layer of synapse-altering chemicals that convinced you to eat with the urgency of needing water after a month in the desert—but did absolutely nothing to mask the flavor. They weren't meant to enjoy, only sustain.

"You're lucky we ain't feedin' you the bottom of Gertrude's boot." Chu jabbed the mealy contents of her can with her spork, working in the seventeen dashes of her homemade hot sauce, because burnt tastebuds made choking down the slop easier.

Gertrude chuckled darkly, her blue afro traded in for a neon green buzz cut faded low at the nape. "One would be so lucky, darling."

Zensha, however, remained unfazed by either Chu's veiled threat or Gertrude's scathing insult. "Did you buy these during the Jafferesh administration?"

"More like Gandry."

At Chu's disgruntled response, Zensha dropped the can to the table like it had bitten her and wiped her hands against her ivory britches to rid herself of any offensive remnants. "I brought in nearly twelve tons of food for Tortuga's stronghold last week. I'll see that the cache admins provide us with a few crates to sustain us. Can't run a mission if we're not properly provisioned."

At that, Boomer's head shot up, an eager puppy scenting crisp bacon. "We talkin' food? Like *real* food?"

"Beans, barley, potatoes, and oats. Dried apricots, plums, and cherries. Plenty of smoked meats—from river fish to forest game. And," Zensha added with a proud nod, "if you can believe it, whole duck eggs."

Boomer slammed his palms to the table. "*With* the yolks?"

Zensha winked.

Eyes moon-wide and shimmering with hopeful tears, Boomer sucked in his bottom lip with a watery sniffle. "I love you."

"Food isn't enough. We'll also need a retainer," Maverick pointed out. "Our dummy sleeves are drained, and while I don't expect we plan to sail deep into the main grid where levies are steepest, until we know what we're up against, couldn't hurt to be properly seeded."

Nimah's heart twisted in her chest with hopeful optimism. Now that they were tasked with the Reckoning, if the *Stormchaser* lost their pilot, they'd have no chance of finding another one as skilled as him before the ashes run out. But if Maverick was asking questions, and engaging in the discussion, then maybe—just maybe—he wasn't planning to leave them in a bind after all.

"I'll wave my second," Zensha agreed. "We can float a couple thousand credits for the cause."

Gertrude raised her cup in salute. "Well, that's a start."

"It's a handout. And a meager one at that," Ro barked, and all heads swiveled to her as the captain broke her silence. She rose from the ledge of the viewport and strode ominously to join everyone gathered at the table. "If this is your way of apologizing for feeding our necks into a noose of your own making—we're far from square."

Zensha met Ro's heated glare with a haughty lift of her chin that was equal parts defiance and challenge. "I won't apologize for doing what needed be done."

"You had your *own* ship and crew!" Ro lunged, her thighs slamming against the table, and even though it weighed about as much as Boomer, it shifted a solid inch. "You could've left us out of it, Zen." She punched a finger against the tabletop, drilling into her the severity of her statement. "Instead, you made a spectacle at the conclave, forcing my hand after I'd already turned you down at the Beak!"

Gertrude and Chu exchanged arched-browed, wide-eyed, puckerlipped glances, Maverick released a tense sigh, and Boomer was too busy scraping the inside of his ration can clean with a spork like he hadn't eaten in a month instead of just that morning.

"Bet your ass." Zensha shot to her feet, every inch of her drawn taut with purpose. The light from the pendant lamp caught her stern face, highlighting cheekbones and brows as severe as her shoulders. "My crew may be fierce and willing to follow me straight to hell," she continued before Ro could gather the ire Nimah saw rising in her chest to cut Zensha down. "But this is beyond their scope of capabilities."

And that harshly admitted truth brought everyone around the table to breathless silence.

"You are *the* Valkyries!" Zensha gestured around, her eyes landing on each of their faces in turn. "You were military once, Ro. Decorated! And this here little Sparra? Academy trained! Toss in a couple of Hatchett's best skinbags, and you might be enough to pull this off."

Nimah shifted her attention to her grandmother, trying to decipher every subtle twitch and fleeting expression to flash across the rippling landscape of her tense face. And of all the emotions she expected to find there, regret was not one of them.

"Five hundred and seven." Attention swiveled to Maverick. "I'm sorry, but, that number." He drummed a restless thumb against his wheels. "Does it not strike anyone as odd? It's really fucking high."

Looking down at him, Zensha tossed her shoulders. "Your point being?"

"Kids make for difficult cargo. They kick. Scream. All the things that draw heat." Maverick scraped a hand behind his neck, scattering waves of his thick dark hair. "That's why only a few are ever taken at a time, maybe twenty at most—and *only* if you're feeling particularly brazen. But *hundreds* shouldn't be possible."

"I'm inclined to agree with our dashing pilot," Gertrude chimed in. "I've never heard of a cull this large. Ladies? Gents?"

"No," Nimah agreed, horrified to realize Maverick had struck a compelling and concerning point.

As part of her training, cadets examined cases from previous Academy investigations—building out their own analyses and criminal profiles. She'd worked through hundreds of trafficking reports, and of those that had pertained to children, the highest tally she'd ever seen was thirty-two. A figure so staggering it had been blasted across media waves for months. She remembered professors being bereft at the heartbreaking call for the return of the children, off for a school excursion to one of the most prolific museum sites in the void.

First reports were that they'd been caught in a massive accident that swept their cruiser off course near the coast of Soewel, only to be later recovered one hundred and eighty miles short of their destination site.

No bodies were found, only school bags still tucked under seats, and only because of a child's abandoned holopad playing a song on repeat that led authorities to the cruiser's recovery. Reporters had called the story *Soewel's Last Song*, and those children had never been found.

"Who would do this?" Nimah asked. "And what could they want with so many?"

Hunched against the table, Zensha hung her head. "All I know for certain is two days prior to the assault, my crew received a rogue wave from an encrypted channel stating they required clear passage through my quad. In exchange I'd receive a sizable payout so long as I ensured security measures were reduced in three specific grids and asked no questions."

"You complied with a request from a *rogue*?" Ro demanded, the whites of her eyes flashing bright as her teeth set in a grimace.

"It be more common these days then you think. My navigator determined the coords showed no threat. We did our due!" Zensha jerked a weary shoulder. "Judge me if you want, but the seas are rough, Ro. We saw an easy payout and thought little more." She dropped back into her seat, drawing Boomer's eyes to the unclaimed can left waiting on the table.

"You done with that?" He gestured with his spork.

"Be my guest."

Boomer plucked up Zensha's barely touched ration can and tucked in, shoveling what was supposed to be, far as Nimah could tell, beef stew into his mouth. Inhaling the contents like the void did oxygen from a breached hull.

"You remember the coords?" Gertrude asked, drawing Nimah's attention back to the discussion.

"Don't think I'll ever forget them."

"Read them out to me, darling. Let's see if we can make sense of the puzzle together. Ma, drop the projection map if you would, please?"

At Gertrude's request, the ship's navsystem rumbled like an old dog letting out a slow burp, causing the latticed pendant light to sway while Nimah and Chu cleared away the empty ration cans and water cups.

By the time Nimah returned from disposing of the empties in the kitchen, the map had descended across the length of the table, fed by two projectors from either side of the room, and a compartment in the tabletop had swiveled open, revealing a flat box of black pixels. A hybrid blend of tech and kinetic sand, programmed by the projection lasers and guided by the sound of Gertrude's voice, it took shape in a three-dimensional model replicating the intricate network of the Inner Circle and the Fringe void.

Following Zensha's instructions, Gertrude input the sequence of coordinates into her wristdeck and the map followed the keys, drawing a light trail in the rippling black canvas to outline their respective paths. Three points, but the paths between them were incoherent fragments.

"There's no sense to it." Maverick hunched closer, his eyes tracing every detail. "Even if they were intending to burn between them, they don't align. It'd be like jumping an air cruiser across multiple lanes in a freeway but stacked on completely different levels and headed into oncoming traffic."

Across from him, Gertrude rose to take it in from the top-view, her eyes shifting almost as quickly as the gears in her mind, running the math. A vivid green fingernail tapped urgently against her bottom lip. "The chaos is in fact the method, darling. See here." She swiveled the map around. "At first glance, I agree, it's purposeless—but that's because the coords weren't how they planned to enter your zone, Zen, nor was it about where they were going."

"Burn trails," Zensha finished, earning an approving smile from Gertrude.

"Correct, darling. By the time you were waved, they were already *in*. This was about presetting a way *out*. One of these three was the intended escape path. The other two were meant to be a diversion. Unfortunately, that gives us a hundred different flight paths, and none of which will have any existing ion trails to track without the original flight tag, which I guess your anonymous benefactor did not provide?"

"Could this be the work of ticks running a roundup for skinners?" Maverick asked. "The Boonhounds, maybe? Or the Zone-Pekks?"

"No, no this wasn't ticks." Zensha grimaced, her expression haunted. "It was too . . . clean."

"What do you mean *clean*?" Ro demanded.

"A single distress call broke through from the commune as the assault was underway. We burned straight for them. As presider, their lives are my responsibility. So I went to ground and saw what'd been done with mine own eyes." Zensha's mouth hardened with emotion. "Twenty-seven minutes. That's all it took. Twenty. Seven. Minutes. Almost every child between two and twelve, gone. Every adult, along with any children that weren't taken—even infants—slain."

"Blimey," Gertrude whispered.

"Ticks aren't particular about killing—they're sloppy and often ungraceful," Zensha continued, words brittle. "But each body on Solvanis was executed. Three clean strikes. Two in the chest—left of center and an inch apart—with a third in the head, between the eyes." She pressed the point on her brow for emphasis. "It was methodical. Precise to the exact degree."

"That . . . that can't be." Nimah shook a disbelieving head. "What you're describing—that's tactical. It's how all cadets and SIGA militia are taught to . . . you expect me to believe our government sanctioned the theft of children?"

"No." Zensha raised her chin. "I'm suggesting they did it."

Nimah recoiled at her declaration, and everything inside her ran cold with dread. "No, I refused to believe that." She planted her feet, standing on the matter as firmly as she did the *Stormchaser*.

Abandoning her earlier aspirations of serving as a STARs agent because she'd come to believe she'd be of greater service to the people through piracy was one thing, but to accept that SIGA mass-murdered an entire community and stole innocent children was not a reality she was prepared to embrace. Their government had many faults, sure, but this? This was unfathomable.

Soulless.

"I know you've spent most your life amongst Innies, but have you not opened your eyes yet, Sparra?" Zensha challenged. "SIGA is capable of far worse atrocities than any pirate or skinner has ever been accused of. Ask your grandma, here."

"Alright everyone, enough." Ro intervened and stood before them now with the firm authority of a captain. "Zen, hail your second—we'll see you back to your crew. After that, I want the *Stormchaser* to burn for the Faldor system."

"Why are we going to Faldor?" Nimah frowned, shifting her eyes from the map to her grandmother and back again. "There's nothing out there but a couple of outposts about as dead as the Boneyard Dobs tried to maroon us in."

"I know. It's where we're going to lay low and let this all blow over."

Nimah's eyes popped wide in shock. "We can't run! If we don't complete the Reckoning, you won't be queen."

"Good." Ro spread her arms, brows raised so that they vanished in the silver wing of her curtain bangs. "I don't want to rule. I never have. We'll hole up for two weeks and the council will appoint someone else."

"You yellow-bellied—"

"One more word from you," Ro roared, punching her finger toward Zensha like a fist, "and I'll vent you myself. Fuck the years we had and the love I once bore you."

Zensha sat down and held her tongue but not the venom in her dark brown eyes. She let that do all the cursing for her.

"Fine, you don't want to be queen. But what about the kids?" Nimah pressed, not willing to back down even though her grandmother was on the precipice of murder. "These are *innocents*—taken, like I was. Alone. Afraid. If we don't find them, they'll disappear, and no one is going to care about what happened to them. You really want us to abandon them?"

"Sparrow, I know this is horrible, but horrible things happen all the time in the void. It's the cost of living out here. This mission is too great, and quite frankly, I'm too old for it. I won't risk you or my crew or my ship for something that is going to get us all killed. Not against these odds. So we lay low."

"No." Nimah shook her head. Two weeks trapped in Faldor with nothing to occupy her mind but Dobs and the walls of the *Stormchaser*? She wouldn't make it six days. Nimah would rather be buried alive. "I'm not running. That's all you do. Life gets hard—run. Someone dies—run. Almost two decades! Haven't you had enough?"

Her grandmother's expression hardened even further, dropping to bone-chilling levels of cold. "Careful, Sparrow."

But Nimah wasn't prepared to surrender. Not when the alternative was a return to extreme isolation, rotting the fraying threads of her mental health. "I know this job comes with difficult odds, but as Zensha pointed out—we're Valkyries. We do the impossible. We saved you, didn't we? When everyone else would've said it we couldn't." Nimah felt a desperate smile form on her face. "But we did it!"

"And Siggy died," Ro countered. "Who else are you prepared to lose, Nimah? Chu this time? Gertrude? Or how about me?"

That stopped Nimah dead in her tracks. "That wasn't my fault," she whispered, but her voice lacked conviction. There wasn't a single day where she didn't blame herself or relive that terrible moment when Sigourney leapt before Nimah to take the bullet meant for her.

"What happened to doing the right thing? To standing for a cause, even if it comes at great risk?" Nimah clamped down on desperate tears that if released would drown her where she stood. "Ever since we left the Inner Circle, you've kept the crew on idle. No jobs. No missions. Just weeks of *nothing*! Every suggestion I made—you turned it down." *Don't you see? I'm going crazy out here.* The trapped words clawed at the inside of her throat, so intensely she almost tasted blood.

"I don't have to explain my—"

"*I gave up my badge!*" Nimah shouted, her voice threatening to shatter the last threads of her composure. "All my life, all I've ever wanted was to make a difference. And I became a pirate because I thought that was the best way I could achieve that dream. I wanted to help. *I wanted to be like you*," she continued, even though instinct warned her that she was pushing the matter too far "Why won't you let me?"

The vein in Ro's neck ticked ominously, every inch of her as rigid as if hewn from stone. She didn't blink. Didn't move. Barely even seemed to breathe. Only that continuous pulse beating against the strained line of her throat gave any indication of life, counting down like a timer on a bomb about to blow.

Nimah didn't dare pull her gaze away, but she felt the utter shock and disbelief of the crew in the heart-pounding silence at her back. No one spoke to Captain Ro this way. Even Zensha had the sense to shut her mouth when Ro had warned her not to speak another word. And while Nimah might be her granddaughter, she was pushing a very dangerous line. One that might see her cast from the ship altogether for sedition.

"You seem to forget yourself; I am captain of this ship and crew," Ro said at last, her voice a low, snarling hum. "I've made my decision, and I'm done discussing it."

"Then as second, I exact my right to call a vote," Nimah shouted to the wall of her grandmother's retreating back. "Ma, mark my words for the log that I, Nimah Dabo-124, SIC, am putting forward a call to vote to challenge the captain's orders re the mission entrusted to us by the Council of Black on the third sol cycle for the eighth month in the year 364 A.E.P."

<Your words have been marked, Nimah, Second-in-Command.>

Ro turned from the threshold and a shadow fell across her face. A slanted blade of darkness that made the molten shade of her amber eyes burn even brighter. "You'll need a senior officer to support you, and it'll only pass if unanimous, otherwise I pull rank. So . . ." She sliced her scathing glare across the table, ready to cut down anyone who dared step forward. "Anyone care to challenge me?"

The silence was profound, but after several tense moments, Gertrude rose with a slow, whooshing exhale. "Captain, I'm sorry, but . . . I'm with Sparrow on this. We've been cooped up long enough, innit, and I cannot abide harm befalling innocents. This mission is what we do, as Valkyries. So as Chief Navigator, I support Nimah's call to vote."

<Thank you, Gertrude, Chief Navigator. Your support for the SIC's call has been marked. The crew may now cast their vote in favor or against.>

Ro's bitter laugh was ice cold. "Unbelievable."

"She's a senior officer and has every right to exert her authority," Nimah reminded her grandmother before facing the table of silent, shocked faces with her own hand raised high. "The vote has been sanctioned—all in favor of accepting the reckoning mission say *aye*."

Chu was the first to break.

Boomer quickly followed.

Maverick remained pensive.

A knot of tension locked in Nimah's throat, tight as her clenched fists. He was still upset with her, and while that anger made him unpredictable, would it really be enough to push him to vote against her for no purpose other than scored pride? If it wasn't unanimous—then her grandmother could pull rank and bury them all.

Please . . . She let the urgency soften her eyes and pushed everything she had into the burning wish. Then, like a sudden gasp of starved lungs breaking above the surface, that fierce knot of tension inside her released when he finally raised his hand.

"It's decided." Relief flooded Nimah, so fast she was almost dizzy with it. "The *Stormchaser* has accepted the reckoning."

Ro grazed her teeth across her bottom lip, then sucked hard with a terse nod. "Be it on your heads, then," she growled, then disappeared through the doorway, all fire and steam.

Chu's thin, veiny hand slapped against Nimah's chest, halting her before she could signal her legs to follow. "Best to let her cool her pistons, Sparrow. Ro angry is a tempest you don't wanna cross. Trust me."

Chu was right. Soothing her grandmother's anger and hurt was a problem for later. They'd accepted the mission, and if Ro wasn't going to lead them forward, then it was on Nimah, as second, to do so.

"S'what now?" Boomer crossed his arms. "We ain't got little to nothing to go on and no leads. What's our next move?"

Hands on her hips, Nimah paced the length of the table in thought. *Never set foot in the unknown without one rooted in the familiar.*

"We can't make a move without intel, and time's against us," she said at last. Her emotions settled into the calm focus, now that she had a puzzle to chew on. "So if we want answers fast, then we need to tap in with someone with the capacity to get them."

Unsurprisingly, Maverick was the first to connect the dots. "You're looking to call in favors with old friends, Cadet?"

Following his path of realization, a collective rumble of groans moved through the crew.

"I appreciate the urgency, Sparrow, but the Inner Circle isn't exactly the kind of place we can jet about unnoticed." Gertrude joined Nimah beneath the arch of the viewport. "Forget the insane levies for a ship our size to enter their voidspace . . . we're talking defense patrols, security scanners." She listed off the risks on her fingers for emphasis. "Maybe if it was one or two of us, we'd slip through the cracks, but not even Mumbles could rig a Blind-Eye big enough to bypass *all* of them."

"Mav and I ain't exactly in the clear, ourselves." Boomer wiggled a thumb between him and a sullen Maverick. "Hatchett thinks we're dead, but we get spotted by just one tongue-waggler? We go right back to the top of his shit list."

"Or get brought in for flaying." Maverick rolled his right shoulder, as if imagining the blade Hatchett was rumored to use peeling him from scapula to hip.

"I know, I know." Nimah flagged her palms, calming the rise of voices, her temples beginning to throb from all the surrounding anxiety and tension. "I am not suggesting we dock the *Stormchaser*, only that we get as close as possible. After that, I'll take the shuttle down and make contact. Alone."

"Maybe we should tap in with our own networks here," Maverick suggested. "Neon is a whisper. She's got to know something that can guide us to—"

"If SIGA really is involved, this will be out of reach for the whispers, otherwise the council would already have answers," Nimah cut him off. "Through Liselle not only can we gain direct access to SIGA's network, her father, who happens to be chief legal counsel to the board, will have the highest possible clearance to anything confidential and redacted. No one—not even the whisper network—are more *in* than he is." She angled her wrist, checking her wristdeck for the timestamp she marked as soon as the council had set the hourglass to run. "We're already down one hour and forty-six minutes. What say you?" When no one seemed eager to budge in their stance, Nimah spread her hands. "Honestly, if anyone has a better idea—you have the floor."

"Very well, Sparrow, we'll do it your way . . . but send me." Gertrude set a hand on her shoulder. "You're too valuable, innit?"

"Thank you, but Liselle isn't going to like the idea of being asked to hack her father's private network." Nimah offered Gertrude a grateful smile. "I'm the only one who'll be able to convince her. It's got to be me."

"I think you underestimate my powers of persuasion." Gertrude wiggled her sculpted shoulders. Still every bit the performer who had captivated half the Fringe with her dazzling productions as the Minx of Sparta3, and there wasn't a man or woman or anyone in between who hadn't been enthralled by her commanding presence onstage.

Or in the bedroom.

"If you're set, then you're not going alone," she added. "Ro would never stand for it, nor will I." Chu hugged her arms to her chest and rocked onto the back of her heels. "Take the big lug with you." She wiggled bony, gloved fingers toward Boomer. "He ain't exactly subtle, but should things go sideways, 'least you know he'll be an asset at your six."

"Not bad, darling." Gertrude approvingly tapped Chu's shoulder with the tips of her bright green nails.

"I'm known to sprout a good idea or two."

"And here I thought all you sprouted were chin and chest hairs."

"Don't mind goin'." Boomer wiggled his jaw in thought. "But I'm taking my guns. *And* grenades."

"Yeah. Alright," Nimah agreed. "Boomer and I will drop in on the shuttle and contact Liselle. Once I have what I need, I'll return to the ship, and we can strategize on next steps." Bracing the console, she scanned the surrounding faces. "Are we all in agreement?"

"Aye." Chu was the first to raise her hand, and the rest quickly followed suit.

"Good. Zensha, did you take recordings while you were surface-level on Solvanis?"

"Of course."

"I want to see everything you have."

Zensha arched a brow. "My account not good enough for you, Sparra?"

"No," Nimah answered plainly. "Not if I'm going to ask my best friend to break several laws based on the insinuation that the government we'd both dreamt of serving is somehow behind this atrocity. I need to see for myself. I need to be sure."

Zensha released a tense breath before shrugging. "My second will transfer all you need."

"Perfect. Include all archival data you have on the commune—registry, citizen records, all of it." Crossing to Mumbles, Nimah dropped next to her on the rug and waved a hand, breaking her focus on the figurines she had at play. Then she waited for Mumbles's eyes to connect with hers and focus.

"Zensha is going to give you a disc soon. Upload it to the simulation chamber, and then run a trace for me on Liselle. Find out where she was stationed after grad. When you have our coords, give Gertrude the heading so she can set the flight path."

Mumbles nodded with a slanted grin, and pressed the flat of her hand against the side of her cheek, curling three fingers down, nails bitten low and ragged.

"She says, 'I'll handle it,'" Boomer translated.

"You've been teaching her RIM-SL?" Nimah asked, a little stunned.

"Sure." Boomer raised a bashful shoulder. "Figured might help her, y'know."

Touched at the thought of Mumbles and Boomer huddled together in secret, Nimah ruffled Mumbles's mess of coarse gray hair woven into fresh braids before rising to her feet again.

"You think maybe you should send Liselle a wave *first*," Maverick commented. "Let her know you're coming?"

"No. I have one chance to get through to her, and my best bet is face-to-face. Everyone else head to your cabins. I doubt most of us will have a chance to close our eyes for quite a while, so get some rest while you can."

"Hold a sec, little bird. Got somethin' for ya." As the bridge cleared, Chu rummaged through the deep pockets of her overalls before taking Nimah's hand and slapping something into her palm.

Confused, Nimah lifted a row of yellowed, chunky teeth. "Why are you giving me your dentures?"

"Fashioned me some new ones." Chu grinned, showing off an even clunkier pair in blinding white. "But these got plenty of kick left in 'em, if you catch my drift."

Oh, she did. Nimah remembered all too well what these teeth were capable of after Chu lobbed one like a mini sonic grenade on the

Challenger during their rescue mission. "And what am I supposed to do with them, exactly?"

"Bite someone in the ass." Chu winked. "Biggest bang is in the molars. "But the incisors and front chompers got some surprises. Details in the lid."

Nimah frowned, returning them into the container with a grimace. "These are clean, yes?"

Chu only cackled, scuttling down the corridor.

CHAPTER EIGHT

Down in the *Stormchaser*'s base level, Nimah entered the simulation deck and activated the lights with a swipe of her hand against the wall panel. The system awakened with a stutter, and a visor lowered from the ceiling as she approached one of three pods that sat idle.

The pod itself was a three-sixty swivel track connected to a body harness that would allow for mobility in all directions without the risk of slamming into walls. She could flip, roll, turn, and pivot with ease. Perfect for running drills, training exercises, or in this case, walking through miles of on-the-ground footage Zensha had recorded from the commune.

Stepping into the first booth, Nimah fastened herself in and removed the visor from its tether. "Ma, have we received the files from Blackfyre?"

<*Yes. We have a total of twenty-seven.*>

"Run an analysis on the files. Separate them into key categories, prioritizing recorded footage and commune records, then launch the simulation. When complete, link the recordings to my visor and loop them into one single stream, giving me full range and perspective, starting with the clearest POV."

<*Rendering complete. To engage simulation, say* ENGAGE.>

"Engage."

Falling into a simulation was like falling off a cliff. Sudden. Terrifying.

A breathless plummet into streaming light and code that had Nimah's heart shuddering violently in her chest as the *Stormchaser* evaporated into the shimmering planetary orb of Solvanis.

Nimah swiped *pause* and then pressed the pads of her thumbs and forefingers together before stretching them apart to expand and expand again. The focus magnified as crystalline atmosphere gave way to open sky then lush terrain with dense forest and wide farmlands until she was hovering over the entirety of the commune like an eagle perched on a towering bough.

Built in staggered rows connected by curved pathways, the commune sprawled in perfect, geometric proportions, maximizing efficiency without sacrificing square footage. To the left of her periphery, a readout pane from the *Stormchaser*'s systems fed her weather conditions, oxygenation, and contamination levels as documented by Zensha's recording. All of which indicated a planet in shockingly fantastic health. Nearly no pollution or toxicity readings. Oxygen was high, and gravity within a comfortable range.

A planet like this . . . in the Fringe?

"Ma, show me the crop yields for the last six quarters, include all financials in a chart below. Flag any discrepancies, such as sudden increases or withdrawals, or any recent loans leveraged against all accounts of the commune's registered inhabitants, personal and business."

Activating the simulation again, Nimah dropped firmly onto the ground, and the full weight of sensation flowed over her. Cool breeze, the pull of gravity in her joints. Fingers curling in the dirt beneath her, she smelled the musk of earth and sweetness of crops. Hay. Manure. Minerals and livestock.

Standing, she dusted her hands clean as her gaze skimmed the fields. They'd been recently harvested, maybe a day or so prior to Zensha's arrival after the assault. Next to prime, water, and air, food was the next most valuable natural resource. Could that have been a possible motive?

Tapping the left readout pane, rapidly filling with data, Nimah maximized it for easier reading and was met with her second pop of surprise in under ten minutes. The commune had been appropriately situated within the most fertile region and, according to specs, was the only settlement on the entire planet large enough to hold several billion.

"That can't be right," she murmured to herself, but kept scrolling over to the financials, combing through significant profits generated from high-output harvests. Quarter over quarter the commune was generating a significant amount of income. Most of it was being seeded back into the commune for upkeep, expenses, and levies, but the rest was siphoned into a corporate account. Not unusual. But Nimah flagged it anyway, as a point to come back and dig into more.

"Ma, are you seeing any sudden dips or increases?" Anything to suggest this assault was triggered through greed or extortion from a rival crew or rogue mercenaries who may have threatened the commune members with violence if they didn't meet the demand?"

<None.>

"How about recent expenditures? Outstanding loans or debts?"

<None.>

Taking a long, slow breath, Nimah tapped a restless finger against her thigh. "Ma, run a new analysis on all commune members. Pull up any persons of interest."

<Running.>

"Thank you." *Let's see who's living here.*

Two and a half minutes later, Ma had organized all members into a layered org chart, broken into a hierarchy based on position within the commune. Lines connected reporting ranks to direct managers as well as indicating their family members.

Only two were flagged as possible persons of interest. One, Pradnya Huin, cited for failing to show for her shift three times in one month, earning her a reprimand from her Scrum manager. The other, Kemset Sid, was fined five hundred credits for a noise complaint from his neighbor. His fourth infraction in two years.

"Are you kidding me?"

<No, Nimah, Second in—>

"It was rhetorical, Ma," Nimah snapped. "What I meant is, are you sure there's no one who's been collared at a lower-tier penitentiary? No one with a record of any kind whatsoever?"

The readout pane cleared and a series of dots flickered, indicating that Mother was running through the search before the blank screen filled with a single word.

<Negative.>

"Bullshit," Nimah grumbled, setting her hands on her hips after minimizing the readout pane. Someone here had to be hiding something. Something horrible enough that it warranted wiping out twenty thousand lives so they could abscond with hundreds of children. All harvest stores were untouched, so clearly this wasn't a raid for wealth or food. The only reasonable explanation left was personal vendetta.

<*Secondary user is seeking permission to join the simulation. Flight Officer Maverick Ethos-333. Access granted or denied?*>

Maverick? Nimah's heart shot high and gave a staggered thump in the tight walls of her throat. "Uh . . . granted."

He started as a spark in the simulated sky, streaking in fast as a comet that landed with a breathless whoosh six feet from her side. Dropped on one knee, hands braced to the ground for anchoring, he rose and wiped his palms clean on his thighs.

Nimah's mouth tumbled open and her eyes made the slow trip up to meet his. "You're *standing?*"

"Sims." Maverick shrugged as he stalked toward her, his boots leaving heavy prints in the soil with each steady stride. "They were all formatted for able-bodied rendering. It can't tell that my legs don't work. So. In here"—he threw his arms wide and gave a playful stamp and spin—"I can walk."

"Huh." Nimah cleared her throat and tried to shake off the unnerving sight of him peering down at her for a change. He stood at least half a foot over her. Boomer, who was eye-to-eye with her grandmother, beat him by maybe two inches. Three at most.

Her gaze was level with his jaw, shaded in dark stubble that parted on the left from his scar, which hooked down the line of his neck and cleaved through his metallic tattoo that caught the filmy sunlight and gleamed like molten gold against his tawny skin.

Nimah's throat tightened and she swallowed against the torturous rise of attraction pushing her to betray herself. She hadn't broken up with him because of his looks. He was chiseled perfection, with his broad shoulders, muscled arms, and strong hands. The wicked shape of his mouth a temptation she longed to surrender to even now.

"Why are you in here?" she asked, trying to shake off her nerves.

"Same as you." He tucked his hands into the pockets of his cargos. "Getting eyes on the ground to see what kind of information we can root up."

"Oh . . ."

"Oh?"

"Well . . . I'm sorry, it's just that . . ." Nimah scratched absently at her arm. "I didn't think you'd care to be around me right now, let alone see this mission through, after . . ."

Thick brows lowered over his dark green eyes and something like disappointment flashed through them. "I might be a lot of things, but a callous asshole isn't one. Whatever our differences, there are lives at stake, which makes our breakup pretty fucking insignificant by contrast, don't you think?"

Well, that hit like a roundhouse kick to her sternum, but Nimah absorbed the blow because, damn it, he was right. They were adults and perfectly capable of setting aside personal slights for the sake of a greater purpose. Thinking otherwise of him, even for a moment, made her stupid or arrogant, and Nimah wasn't comfortable with either of those labels.

"If you'd prefer to do this alone—"

"No!" Nimah interrupted. "You're right. And I'd be grateful to have a second set of keen eyes." Stepping back, she tapped her readout pane and expanded it to joint view. "I was just going through a process of elimination to suss out a possible motive. Something to give us clarity and push us toward a direction."

"What have you found out so far?" he asked, attention centered on the analysis summaries that Mother had cobbled together based on Nimah's requests.

"It doesn't appear that the assault was financially motivated. The financial accounts weren't hacked, and all harvest caches left untouched, so whoever came here wasn't interested in absconding with the wealth of produce and grain."

"And that's saying something." The soil yielded easily when he shoveled the toe of his boot into it. Stooping, he scooped up a small mound, and it rained in sodden clumps from the fold of his loosely closed fist. "Healthy soil. A commune like this must be banking tens of millions per quarter. If that wasn't a motive . . ." Dusting his palms, Maverick anchored his elbows on his knees and gave a low whistle. "Makes you wonder what could possibly be more important?"

What, indeed.

<*Attention, Nimah, my systems have flagged a note of possible interest.*>

"Go on," Nimah answered.

<Completed financial scans indicate that Solvanis, although established close to thirty-three years ago, is in fact unregistered.>

Nimah's scowl deepened. "Impossible."

<My information is accurate. There are no archival auditory records for Solvanis in SIGA's entire database.>

"Why is that impossible?" Maverick arched a brow.

"Unregistered means this planet and commune, according to SIGA, don't exist. But look at these logs." Nimah gestured back to the readout pane showing the quarterly yields spanning the last eighteen months. "You were right. Tens of millions a quarter in profits, and our government isn't seeing a single credit? The same government that holds our third-tier citizens to a levy of fifteen percent, *minimum*? This commune would net them close to five million per annum in taxes. Maybe more."

Maverick scanned the output data and shook his head. "And our government would never surrender claim to such a profit."

Not unless they were planning to gain something even greater in return, but Nimah held that to herself, not yet willing to allow herself to cross the line Zensha had so adamantly pointed out. If the planet was unregistered, then that meant it had to be off their radar, so how could they possibly know to send a retinue to wipe it out? Even then—destroying it versus allowing it to continue to grow and thrive made even less sense.

"Have you seen the dead yet?" he asked, angling his gaze up to hers.

And that immediate connection of their eyes almost struck the air from her lungs. Damn his stupidly beautiful face and the things it did to her every time she looked at him.

"Was just about to." Nimah nodded over her shoulder. "Terrain readings indicate the bodies are this way. Come on."

They fell into step together, and again Nimah had to shake off the strangeness of him walking next to her in a prowling stride that reminded her of Boomer. But where Boomer was heavy and almost blundering, boots bouncing off the corners of walls or furniture from the way he swung his large feet with carelessness, Maverick was light but lethal, almost graceful with intention.

They followed the winding pathway through the twin rows of commune homes, built in short blocks, all one story with the same dark-gray stucco walls, tinted windowpanes protecting the interiors from sunlight and elements, and black slate shingled rooftops. But no smoke billowed from the tin stacks and no voices floated from the empty courtyards or narrow lawns where flowers bloomed in bushes and ivy wrapped around trellises.

"Fuck," Maverick whispered.

Nimah whipped her gaze from the ghost town to what was labeled on the map stretched at the bottom of the readout pane as the central plaza. A place where the commune would've gathered for community meetings, celebrations, and morning markets, selling homemade goods, fresh eggs, and baked bread in woven baskets.

Now it was filled with bodies laid in neat, organized lines like dolls.

Maverick reached for Nimah, his hand taking hers in a firm grip she hadn't realized how much she needed until his fingers laced with hers. Grounding her with his warm, steadying presence. He was the first to move, and she shuffled with him, holding tight as they went from one end to the other, passing along each of the dead. Seeing every face.

Every. Single. One.

"They've been sorted," Maverick said when they'd gone more than two thirds of the way through, landing on the same thought she'd only just arrived at herself. "Why would they be sorted?"

Releasing his hand, Nimah stopped by the last body in the row. A young man with a twisted back. Lain to the right of him was another young man who at first glance seemed perfectly healthy until her gaze landed on his left wrist, which was stamped with a medical alert brand given to anyone with a life-threatening allergy or ailment. Tags and bracelets could be lost, but acid brands were impossible to remove.

"Ma . . ." Nimah pushed strength into her wavering voice. "Can you do an analysis of all the dead and run a comparison against the children who were taken. Compile your findings into a single outcome statement, giving your best guess as to why the missing children were chosen."

"What are you thinking?" Maverick's voice floated from behind her.

Nimah closed her eyes with a weary sigh. "That I hope I'm wrong."

<Analysis complete. Based on the data, compared to the deceased, all children missing from the commune are between the ages of two and twelve, with no documented defects, health impediments, or known mental

disorders. Of the five hundred and seven missing, there appears to have been no apparent preference toward gender. Additionally, when running a medical assessment on their parents, data also shows clear records of health, which signifies minimal chances for inherited predispositions toward illness or psychiatric disorders.>

Weaving to the last row, Nimah assessed a woman clutching a girl, her leg amputated below her right knee. While all the others lay apart, these two tried to run, and when felled—they'd refused to let one another go.

Stooping to her haunches, Nimah adjusted the hem of the woman's faded gray dress, not that it would make any difference. This was only a simulation, and the actual bodies would remain as they'd been recorded, rotting and forgotten beneath the soft sun of a distant world no one knew existed, but a part of her needed this connection. This small act of decency was her last defense against the surge of grief threatening to consume her.

"I've never seen anything like this, Mav."

"Me neither." Stopping at her side, Maverick held out his hand.

She took it, allowing him to help her to her feet and draw her into his embrace. His arms banded around her, strong and reassuring as a ship's anchor, and Nimah sank into them, savoring this moment of quiet comfort. A fragile lifeline amidst the surrounding pain. The grit of his stubble scraped across her brow and the warmth of his breath flashed against her neck. She'd missed this. She'd missed holding him. Escaping into him.

"I was nine when I was snatched by ticks." His chin bounced against her brow as he spoke, palms tracing the line of her waist. "They were vicious. Didn't care who they grabbed or why, just crammed us into shipping containers and stacked us on top of each other. Some were crushed under the weight. I don't think more than forty percent made it out of that container, and of those, even fewer survived Hatchett's onboarding."

It hadn't been vastly different for Nimah.

A contractor, hired by senior leadership for various prime mines that didn't want to get their hands dirty, had come to her boarding house on the RIM and rounded them up like chattel at auction. Pointing as they went down the line, deciding fates with a flick of their wrist. Afterward, those chosen were brought aboard a ship—the *Avenger*—already swelling with indentured men and women who'd sold themselves to bookies to pay off their impossible debts. The kind that crippled generations.

"Zensha was right," Nimah whispered, her voice as unsteady as a faulty comms signal. "This wasn't the work of mercenaries or thugs for hire." It was far too methodical and highly organized. Almost . . . clinical in its execution. It screamed of the kind of privilege and access that could come from only one source. A horrifying thought that tore through her like jagged shrapnel, cleaving through her chest wall to cut her where it hurt most.

She could no longer question the possibility that SIGA had some kind of involvement, if not sole responsibility. A realization almost as chilling as the stack of corpses laid out before her, and it lit an ember of righteous fury deep within Nimah's core. With the question no longer *who*, it then became an even more urgent *why*?

Why would they do this?

The ground beneath her feet slanted sharply, almost as if the simulation itself recoiled at her thoughts, and Nimah's brow knocked against Maverick's chin.

He steadied her with a "*Whoa*."

"What was that?" she asked once the ground leveled.

"Something from outside the sim," Maverick answered. And a warning screen flashed before them, connecting the sim to the comms of the *Stormchaser*.

"*Apologies, theydies and gentlethems—*" Gertrude's sunny voice sang. "*But we seem to have drawn a bit of company from a pod of negs who've taken a fancy to our ship. Expect a bit of rocking until thrusters hardburn in approximately thirty-five minutes. A burndown timer will be set on your wristdecks so you don't get plastered to walls.*"

"That's our cue, Cadet." Dropping his hands from her waist, Maverick put a foot of space between them. "Ma, we're done in here. End the simulation."

<*Yes, Flight Officer Maverick. Simulation terminating. To confirm, please say* DISENGAGE.>

"Disengage," they said in unison.

Nimah gasped to the surface of her consciousness and removed the visor from her face. Lights in the simulation pod gradually brightened, and by the time she'd extracted herself from the module, Maverick was seated in his chair, adjusting the straps on his waist. Those, and the support rings on his legs, kept them from atrophying, with constant electrical pulses that contracted and worked the muscle fibers.

"I should get back to the bridge," Maverick said and spun on his wheels.

She opened her mouth to stop him, to greedily hold on to the warmth and connection they'd found together in the sim, when nausea rose to slap Nimah off her feet. Stunned, she was saved only by the body harness that kept her fastened in place.

Ringing in her ears, a whining ache in her jaw, Nimah clamped her eyes tightly shut and panted against the growing pressure in her chest as another violent, queasy blow sent her spinning into a dizzying spiral.

Ship gave way to void. Steel to stars. And Sigourney hung suspended in the glittering darkness, her long silver locs twisting like live wires around her skull-painted face. No, not war paint, Nimah realized in horror as the searing gold and red from flames lit up her features. But her *actual* skull, gleaming through missing chunks of her decaying flesh.

Blackened eyes shone like liquid metal, gazing into Nimah. Through her. And she shot forward like a human ship set to hardburn, materializing in a breathtaking flash. Her hand latched around Nimah's throat. Fingers tipped like talons cut through her tender skin and closed around the pipe of her throat.

"Siggy . . ." Nimah panted, blood seeping into the neckline of her shirt as those talons clawed deeper. "Please."

"Little Sparrow," she rasped, her voice cracking like century-old bones. "Fly straight. Fly true!" The last word rang out of her in a never-ending scream. Her mouth yawning impossibly wide, a serpent unhinging her jaws, until it was big enough to drink in the void and swallow all life whole.

Nimah jolted in the dark, a violent snap back into her body, and it took several reorienting pants for her head to settle on her shoulders like a drunk coming out of a bender. Groaning, she straightened in the pod, fingers gripping her harness until her knuckles ached as a solid, heavy *thump-thump* faded along with the ringing between her ears.

Nimah dabbed at her throat, half expecting her hand to come away with blood, but in the pale blue glow of the pod lighting she saw the pads of her fingers were clean. Just a dream. Just a horrible, terrifyingly *realistic* dream. One that she was not at all ready to unpack. It had slammed into her like a fist to the gut, and she shuddered to think what might have happened if Maverick had lingered a minute longer.

"Ma," Nimah wiggled her jaw, temples throbbing. "Where is the captain?"

The ship's system hummed a moment before responding. <*Our sensors indicate that Captain Roscoe is currently in the gym.*>

"And how long until we reach our destination?"

<*According to navigation settings, just under four hours and fifty-three minutes.*>

Pushing aside her worries and doubts, Nimah grounded herself in the importance of the mission and could only hope that beating a bag had softened grandmother's temper enough to listen to what she'd discovered. Exiting the simulation deck, she heard the brutal slamming of a fist to leather long before she stepped inside the gym. To the far right was the squat rack stacked with weight plates and dumbbells that, with a press of a button, could be adjusted between ten to fifty-five pounds, and under one pound when set to rest, allowing for easier transportation and storage.

Gel mirrors ran along the side walls and rippled like the surface of water when touched. The center of the gym was a hard rubber mat, used for sparring and grappling on most days, but today a restored leather bag hung suspended from the rafter.

It swayed in a slow spin—like a body strung up—and Nimah had a moment where her mind flashed back to the shocking sight of her grandmother aboard the *Challenger*, unconscious and dangling from her wrists. The wings of her silver bangs obstructing her face, and her powerful body drenched in sweat and blood.

Finished with her water bottle, Ro returned to the bag and steadied it between her hands before launching into drills. Sweat soaked into the white of her shirt and ran in rivulets down her face as her wrapped fists flew with impressive speed and punishing precision, sending the body-sized bag to swing. She danced around it, feet light and shoulders slanted to absorb each blow. Her form near perfect until she switched to her left and she bowed in on herself from the recoil.

Nimah stopped at the edge of the mat. "You're still favoring your ribs after that fight with Blackfyre."

"That's 'cause I'm old," Ro snapped, left arm cradled to her side. "Too fucking old."

"Stop. Sit down and let me take a look before you injure yourself." Nimah gestured to the bench off to the side near the viewport. "Please."

Ro crossed over to it and plunked down with a reserved sigh. "You come to tell me where we're heading, Sparrow? Or should I call you *Captain?*"

Nimah hesitated a moment before raising Ro's left arm and bracing it across her own shoulder before gathering the hem of her shirt, exposing her left side. "This isn't a mutiny," she answered gently, eyes pinned to her grandmother's ribcage.

"Sure as shit feels like one." Ro grunted.

"I didn't want to go against you. I'm sorry."

"There's that word again," Ro cracked her neck before shaking off the foulness of her mood with a sigh. "Whatever. It's done now."

They fell into tense silence as Nimah pressed along the side of her ribs. Feeling for tenderness, bruising—anything that would indicate a cracked rib or worse. But relief replaced concern after ten minutes of investigation yielded nothing beyond a minor wince.

"You still have some internal bruising, but if you don't body-slam anyone anytime soon, I think you'll continue to knit well." Finished with her efforts, Nimah lowered her grandmother's shirt, then dropped her hands into her lap, unsure what to do with them. "How's your leg?"

Ro pressed a hand to her thigh—the one Dobs had shot before sending her and Nimah to the Boneyard to die. Jono had reported that removing the bullet had been difficult to do, given it had broken off shards of bone and lodged in a cluster of nerves surrounded by arteries. The surgery had required him to go in deep for several hours before he was able to extract the shell, and he had advised it would take weeks if not months to know the extent of possible damage.

When she was met with only silence, Nimah rose to leave.

"You grow more like her by the day, you know. Your mother."

Nimah settled back to the bench, surprised by the shift in conversation as well as the softness of her grandmother's tone. "What was she like? We never really . . . talked about her much."

"I know. I should have." Ro's throat tightened with emotion, teeth biting down so hard on her bottom lip the skin flashed white. "It was just so hard at first. You were so young it didn't seem to make much sense, and then as you got older I convinced myself perhaps it was kinder to let you forget. But that was . . . wrong. Zory may have been killed at the hands of cybers, but I'm the one who let her die by not keeping her memory alive in you." She touched her wristdeck, fixed with a sleek black band.

An old VCD file recording sprang up of her mother holding Nimah, rocking her gently to sleep and singing the lullaby of the little sparrow learning to fly. Her hair hung well past her waist in a single long braid—silver-blond to contrast her rich gold eyes and same warm-brown skin.

Ro stood in the distance, watching both mother and child, her hair shorn at the jawline with no real thought to style or aesthetics. And it was in that moment Nimah realized that only after Zoraida's death had she begun growing it out. And now wore it in the same long braid.

"Tech was trash back then, and most of what we have got corrupted from various system crashes. Everything I had of her is all just a pixelated mess now. Audio gone. Probably for the best in this case—she couldn't sing for dirt." Smiling tears brightened the whites of Ro's eyes so they shone against the blue glow from the grainy holo. "But she loved you. Her last words were for you, you know—right before it happened."

"What did she say?"

"She told me—over comms—tell Nimah to always fly straight. Fly true." Ro's smile wavered, like waves breaking along a shoreline.

And Nimah's heart gave a twisted leap as her ears rang with the echo of Sigourney's voice screaming the same words in her vivid dream.

"I close my eyes, and I try to hear her. Truly *hear* her and . . . it's not quite there anymore. Almost like trying to recall the exact colors of a specific sunrise." Ro sniffed back tears and double-tapped the screen on her wristdeck, retracting the recording. "I wanted so much more for Zory, and after she died, I tried to do it all for you—but I failed. I failed you both."

"No, you didn't." Nimah reached between them and grasped her hands, the knuckles red and inflamed where they'd broken through the wrap. "You saved me in the only way you knew how. Through sacrifice. It took me a long time to understand that, but knowing all that I do now, I wouldn't change any of it."

Ro exhaled deeply. Her gaze squinted as if struggling to see beyond something Nimah couldn't hope to understand. "The day Zoraida died, I knew something was wrong with her," she said so low it was almost a whisper. "I'd felt it gathering for weeks. Looming on the horizon like the threat of a rising storm. *Death.* Yet in my arrogance I sailed right into it and lost a daughter." Settling closer, she skimmed the calloused edge of her thumb against Nimah's cheek. "Now I feel it again, and all my instincts are screaming at me to stop before it's too late. Because whoever's behind this, we may not know what they're after or why, but one thing is clear: Death awaits us on the horizon." A tear rolled down Ro's cheek. "And I can't lose you, too."

Nimah took a moment, letting her gaze drift to the liquid stars raining against the diamond-lacquered viewport like molten drops of gold before. "I know you want me to run. But I can't," she whispered. "Not from this."

Ro swallowed a heavy exhale, and a curse. "You're not listening."

"I am." Nimah squeezed her hands urgently. "You think I'm sailing blind into the storm—that I'm too arrogant to see the risk and the real danger but I do. I reviewed the footage Zensha took from on the ground, and you're right. Whatever she saw scared the salt out of her. It scared me, too, but it doesn't change the fact those children are out there, lost and helpless . . . and while I don't expect you to understand why I must do this, I need you to trust me."

"Did it ever occur to you this mission could be a trap, Sparrow?" Ro arched a fierce black brow. "You've royally embarrassed a massive government organization and crippled the prime industry faster than I can snap, exposing not only corruption within the most affluent of households but also positioning SIGA as either complicit or incompetent. Neither of which is an insult to be borne. SIGA does not forgive easily, and they'll want to make an example of you."

Nimah worked her tongue along the edge of her teeth. "I can't believe they'd go to such lengths to capture me. This is *bigger* than me."

"Is it?" Ro brushed her finger to the silver and opal pendant she had gifted Nimah before her graduation ceremony to replace the one of elite which now powered the *Stormchaser*.

But unlike the stone sparrow, there were no echoes of voices or shocks of energy snapping through her when they were pinned by cybers aboard the *Challenger*. A wild, breathless power. Like harnessing lightning and something more primal—like the flow of life itself entering her body that she'd used to incinerate her enemies with a mere thought. Leaving behind charred husks of bone and ash.

The second time she'd channeled elite, it had drawn her deeper into herself, where she'd stepped into the very recesses of her mind to confront her deepest pains and traumas before emerging with astonishing clarity of self. She'd reached out into the Boneyard, and awoke dormant droids, commanded both krakens and negs to follow her into bringing down the *Challenger*'s defenses long enough to rescue her captured crew and stop Dobs from eradicating all life on the RIM.

Since then, her connection to elite had grown silent—overshadowed by something greater that festered in her heart and soul. Guilt. Depression. There were no voices or threads of energy tugging on her every nerve and instinct. Instead, there were only ghosts and shadows boring their way through her skull. No one knew how much she suffered, and on pain of death, she would never let them.

"They can't know about what I did on the *Challenger*." Nimah closed her fingers around the silver bird. "The Blind-Eye cloaked me from all cameras and sensors."

"You better fucking hope so," Ro challenged. Palms together and thumbs hooked under her chin, she took a deep breath to calm her frustration and worry. "If nothing I say can change your mind, all I ask is that we be careful. Vigilant. Because there's so much more at stake here than just your life. Or that of the crew."

"You're right. There are too many unknowns—but there's someone who can help us get the answers we need." Nimah rose to her feet. "So let's do this. Together."

"I'll follow you, Sparrow." Ro grimaced onto her feet as well. "To the void or Valhalla, I'll follow you."

CHAPTER NINE

When beginning a hunt, Vesper liked to find her starting line. The point where her prey was last sighted so she could get on the ground, shove her nose into the dirt, and sniff for clues. For Nimah, that starting line brought Vesper barreling to the foul-smelling cesspool of Kesh3.

It hadn't taken long. Nimah had made quite a spectacle in a clumsy snatch and grab. A few bribes, a few broken noses, and one very talkative dockhand later, Vesper found her scent and followed it all the way to a name: Groober. Freelance hawker.

Vesper found him in his bunk, perched overhead his shop—if you could call a rust-stained mattress wedged between coolant pipes and a half-dead fan a bunk. Her entry hadn't been crisp, either, so as soon as he heard her coming, he'd tried to run. She'd let him get as far as the grill-screen covering his narrow window before dropping him with a hook that loosened teeth, then pinning him to the ground with a knee to the gut and a blade to the throat.

Now, Groober was sat in a heap on the floor, bound and bruised, and Vesper stood over him, wiping blood from her hands with a microcloth. Crimson smeared into the fine lines of her palms and the pads of her fingers, darkening the whorls etched into her skin like paint strokes across a canvas.

It was almost beautiful.

Groober grunted and wheezed, blood and drool oozing from his swollen mouth, from which she'd extracted three teeth. Two molars and one incisor. They sat on the table in front of him, slightly yellowed and caked in plaque, along with two incised knuckles and half of his pinky. All from his nondominant hand, of course.

Vesper might be cruel, but she wasn't a sadist.

"You really ought to take better care of your oral hygiene." Vesper tsked. "Those came out far too easily."

Groober raised his chin, his lip curled with a sneer and his small dark eyes gleaming with equal parts contempt and spite. "Fek y'self."

So, even after all that he still wasn't going to talk. Admirable but also annoying when she didn't have time to waste. Vesper ran a blood-smeared hand through her short cap of hair and exhaled in frustration. In most cases, when her reputation failed to precede her, an extraction like this was more than enough to get even the most stubborn of tongues wagging. But Groober was either cut from tougher cloth or there was someone he feared far more than her.

Hard to blame him. Captain Indira Roscoe was a legend and a force in her day. Hard to imagine what she'd do to the man who turned on her granddaughter, or to the hunter seeking to bring her in. But Vesper almost relished finding out.

"Why was Nimah in your shop?" Picking up her hooked knife, Vesper reached for one of his knuckles on the table and began to carve into the puckered skin.

"Told ya already. She wanted t' trade parts. Told 'er they was junk. Sent 'er off."

"Yes, you did." Vesper nodded. "There's more that you're not telling me, and until you do, I'll be forced to continue."

"I ain't tellin' ya shite." Groober grunted, his arms straining against the magcuffs she'd used to lasso him to the steel water pipe running along the center of his bunk and on through the entirety of the spacity. Even though it was as thin as a sapling, it was made of carbide steel. He could struggle all he wanted, but not even a full-grown kraken could snap through it.

"Ye'r just a' Innie bitch think she's salt but really ye'r fluff." Groober flashed his teeth, what was left of them, like a cornered dog ready to snap at her throat if he had the chance. "It'll take more'n a pulled tooth t'rattle my tongue."

"Hmm." Vesper smiled with a soft laugh. "You're right, Groober. Being raised in the Inner Circle, I certainly never expected to fall into this line of work." She spread her hands, gesturing around her. "You know, when I was a girl, I actually wanted to be a carpenter. Can you believe that? Something about running a blade across wood and watching it gradually take shape—it's beautiful. Wood is strong, yes, but it's also supple. Almost . . . flesh-like, you could say. The way it *yields* and surrenders to the hard, ruthless edge of a blade." Emphasizing her point, Vesper stroked her knife down the center of the joint, carving a straight line through skin and tissue straight to the bone. "With enough pressure, and enough patience, you can transform it into anything you desire. A table. A chair. A statue."

The peeled curl of skin fell free, bouncing off her thigh before landing onto the table.

A perfect neat little spiral. Groober's eyes followed it and shone brighter with disgust. Pleased with his reaction, she reached for the second knuckle and carried on. Sometimes the fear of what was next was even more effective than inflicting pain itself, and she hoped he was imagining that blade whisking across one of his still intact fingers.

Skinning it like a crisp apple.

"People are not so dissimilar. All it takes is the right application of pressure and a sharp, unyielding edge to make them split open and pour themselves into your hands. I like watching them transform. I like seeing how far I need to go before they break and I find out what they're hiding." Vesper deposited the gleaming bits of bone in front of him.

The seam of Groober's throat bobbed and the sheen in his eyes transitioned from stubborn determination to the first true lick of fear.

Good. Now we're getting somewhere.

"I hope you understand this isn't personal. It's business." Vesper flipped her knife, catching it by the tang as she languidly moved around to the edge of the table. "But that doesn't mean I'm not enjoying it. So thank you, Groober, thank you for not making this easy. I don't mind a challenge. In fact—I welcome it." She sat down on the edge in front of him, her knife casually hooked in her fingers.

And his eyes bounced from his bone to her blade.

"Shall we begin?"

Ten minutes and one whole pinky later, Groober folded like an accordion hatch door.

Standing in his shop, Vesper ran a finger down the length of his ledger until she found what she was looking for. Though he'd told her all she wanted to know, she still broke into his shop just to be sure, and to her surprise, and pleasure, he'd been truthful.

Heliosmoke. It was the only sale made in the last six months, and the ones preceding it were all bulk orders—likely made to peddlers who would cut it with additives, degrading the quality but allowing them to stretch the product for more credits to desperate puffers too hooked on the drug to care. And according to his log, he sold the single dose at wholesale value, as well. A favorable decrease allowing for no profit on his end. Given his show of loyalty in refusing to talk about Nimah, it was only logical to deduce that he'd told Vesper the truth and the purchase did in fact belong to her.

Shutting the ledger, Vesper ran her tongue along the edge of her teeth in thought. Originally designed with the military in mind, heliosmoke was intended for soldiers in the field to rest. Thirty minutes of dreamless sleep under the substance would feel like eight hours, but it also came with a slew of side effects. Soldiers quickly grew dependent and unstable, thus it was deemed ineffective for military use. So naturally peddlers got a hold of it, and in less than three years heliosmoke became the most profitable drug trade in the void.

To imagine Nimah . . . a puffer? Very unexpected.

According to Groober, she came into his shop seeking to trade parts for credits, but only when he'd turned her away did she then ask about the drug. And when he'd tried to steer her away from the substance, her response to him had been a curious one: *I need something to stop me from dreaming.*

Vesper knew about wanting to escape the darkness of dreams.

She'd been haunted for almost a year after Ashleen's death—the sight of her flattened against marble. A pitiful splatter of flesh and blood and bone. Vesper would wake soaked in sweat from the shocking terror of free fall—as if she were Ashleen, tumbling from the balustrade of her balcony to embrace death. Only the fall never ended. The release of death never came. And the screams—of Yasmin and Chance . . . it was all she could hear above the rattle of her own galloping heart.

A never-ending wail.

Whatever Nimah's motivations for purchasing the drug, it was clearly tethered to a deep, internal torment. Something was haunting her, and Nimah was willing to dance with oblivion to make it stop. Yet based on the carefully curated folio SIGA had provided to Vesper to start her hunt, years of school charts and tests showed nothing about her having a problem with addictions, or even being the sort of person who'd succumb to them.

Very interesting.

Either the Academy didn't know their former student at all, or the intel SIGA had offered on her mark was useless. And somewhere deep inside, a little part of Vesper thrilled at the prospect of an unexpected twist or turn.

It made the hunt even more exciting.

While the Academy might not have known who Nimah was at the core, there was one person who did. Someone who'd shared a cabin with her every day from the moment she joined the STARs program. Someone who earned her trust and friendship, so much so that it was documented that the two girls were as close as true family.

The daughter of SIGA's chief legal counsel.

Liselle Namsara.

CHAPTER TEN

The drop into Corlys went about as smooth as a dry shave. Normally Nimah had a softer touch with a shuttle, but Corlys's atmo was thick as plasma gel from the electrical waves cast from the voidnetting, designed to capture harmful UV radiation. Passing through it made the shuttle's hull metal crackle and bounce like kernels of corn popping in a cast-iron skillet. To her surprise, Boomer, who never failed to take an opportunity to roast her awful flying, said absolutely nothing once they disembarked.

She chalked it up to him being in watch mode and embraced the tense silence between them as they made for the tram station.

Shaped like a sleek silver bullet, the tram hovered on the air track with nanite doors that pixelated open to allow the flow of passengers. Nimah kept her chin tucked while boarding to avoid retinal scanners and activated the Blind-Eye orb in the lining of her pocket. The scanners swept over her and Boomer twice before the partition hummed open, allowing them entry.

Boomer followed Nimah as she led him down the set of stairs to the base level of the tram where mostly delivery bots and working synths were clustered, their functions set to rest mode to preserve fuel cells while in transit.

Finding a couple of seats near the nose, Nimah slid into the empty booth and felt her second pop of surprise when Boomer took the booth on the opposite side of the aisle rather than seating himself across from her. Boosting his foot to the empty seat facing him, he sat with his brow to the nanite-glass and peered quietly out at the blurred cityscape.

Sighing to herself, Nimah did the same. The tram shot down the air track, streaming past massive towers—each building alone housing a city's worth of people. They were called megaholds. Positioned in the industry quads, Corlys was predominantly inhabited by second-tier citizens—the working class—and boasted an endless sea of towering buildings all wrapped with mirror façades that refracted light from the tens of thousands of shimmering neon holoverts that webbed across the airspace. The towers were so densely packed it was rare to see a scrap of daylight between them.

At night the entire city gleamed like a kaleidoscope, constantly shifting and swirling with so much light and shape and color it was almost hypnotizing. Often local citizens, those who couldn't afford a subscription to advert scrubbers, would be caught in what was known as a holohaze—a trancelike state induced by the holoverts embedding them with subliminal messaging urging them to buy overpriced shoes or the twice-repurposed leather handbag with hand-stitched detailing. Spending credits almost faster than they earned them, keeping the second tier in a perpetual state of living from hand to mouth.

As on most planets within the Inner Circle, the cities were built in tiers. The canopy, where only the wealthiest could afford to reside; the trunk for those working themselves to the bone with the hopes of clawing their way up; and then the roots for the poorest of the working class, who knew they'd never make it beyond their humble means and toiled hard in the dark and squalor, earning little more than enough to survive.

Where Nimah was heading was a little deeper.

The planet of Corlys had suffered a particularly horrible accident twenty-five years ago after the completion of what was to be the largest of the megaholds—a colossal fuel-cell explosion in its core generator that sent the massive building toppling to the ground. Its collapse claimed near fifty million lives and tore open a horrible wound that stretched for forty-six miles and took nearly seven years for city workers to mend.

What was left in its wake became known as the Scar. Few would wander down this deep, but Liselle was never one to shy away from the rush or the crowds. If anything, her best friend seemed to enjoy being in places stripped of polish and refinement.

Poor little rich girl, a dark voice inside of her sang. *How difficult a life of privilege must be that she'd need to escape to the realness of poverty just to feel alive. Some might call her pathetic. Or arrogant. Maybe even both.*

Nimah wrenched the foul thoughts aside with a hard shake of her head. That wasn't her. That could never come from her. Dobs's distant laughter slithered into the funnel of her ears. All smoke and shadows.

The tram shot into a tunnel and the inside of the cabin went almost completely dark. The Blind-Eye in Nimah's hand shimmered a soft, pale white, offering enough light for Nimah to see Boomer's fuming expression now pinned on her.

"What makes you so sure she's down all this way?"

"Corlys is one of the planets Liselle and I used to patrol as cadets." Part of their training was immersive on-the-ground experience. Not everything could be learned through books. Nimah rolled the orb in her palms, savoring the sparks of energy and heat emanating from its smooth surface. "Mumbles's trace showed that Liselle's been spending a lot of time down here when she's off shift."

And Liselle was nothing if not a creature of habit.

Boomer answered with a harsh grunt, his thick fingers tapping restlessly against his muscular thigh. Irritation. Defensiveness. Nimah nodded to herself as the dots connected.

"Listen . . . I'm not sure if I'm overthinking this, but if you're upset with me over what's happening between me and Maverick . . ."

Boomer cut his eye to her then shook his head with another grunt. "What goes on ain't none of my never-mind."

"No, it's not. But clearly, you're bothered." Tucking the orb into her pocket, Nimah adjusted herself so that her legs were positioned in the aisle and planted her elbows to her knees. "Let's talk about it."

Boomer worked his tongue against the pocket of his cheek and molars before also swinging his large legs out into the aisle to face her head on. Usually, when she was this close to Boomer, Nimah's first thought was surprise at how large he actually was. All wide shoulders and long arms corded with muscle. But right now, hunched in on himself, he appeared wilted.

Sighing, he scrubbed one of his large hands over the dome of his head—hair buzzed short so that his dark, tight curls rasped against his calloused palm and the lights from the tracks of his hearing implants shone vivid lavender against his dark brown skin.

"When Mav and I first met—didn't think much of him. He was just this skinny little shit kid. The kind you kick down and take what you can off 'em. But not Mav. There was no kicking him down. And even more surprisin', he somehow had a way 'bout him that got the big'uns to listen." Boomer paused with a laugh then held his hand up barely an inch taller than the line of his bent knee. "Can you imagine? Within a week of him showing up, the older kids were suddenly takin' orders from him. Stopped picking on the young'ns. Stopped nixing their food trays or swiping their sleepmats. He got 'em unified." Boomer laced his fingers together and locked his hands into a single, solid fist. "Working together. He made us a family."

"I didn't . . . We never really talked about his past."

"He doesn't like going back there. Not even in his head. But I know it chews on him." Boomer tapped his temple. "You ain't the only one living with ghosts, Nimah, but you sure as shit are the only one letting it twist your head off your shoulders."

"What did he tell you?"

"Only that you said some bullshit about needin' space to clear your head." Boomer chewed on something before he found the words to spit it out. "I ain't never seen him like this, Nimah. Not in all the years we known each other. He's always been the strong one. Never one to fold. Never one to break. Even after he lost his legs—he bounced back with so much humor and . . . I dunno . . . *spark*." He lifted his eyes so Nimah could see the sincerity and pleading in his gaze. "Ain't never seen nothing take the shine out of him 'til you."

Nimah swallowed the acrid rise of guilt burning the back of her esophagus. "Me?"

"He loves you. Not that puppy-dog shit, neither. Not the kind that flames you for a minute but tapers off after a good hard nu—uh," Boomer cleared his throat, catching himself before he finished the statement. "Respectfully. You know what I'm trying to say, right?"

"Yeah." Nimah nodded. "I think I do."

"So why'd you have to break him for?" His eyes narrowed to furious pinpricks. "It was plain you were mad for each other. I know it wasn't just him. I know he wasn't alone in it. But you left him in the dark anyway. And now he's stuck there, and I can't . . . I don't know what to do to get him out of it."

Nimah chewed her bottom lip, needing pain to stem the flood of tears wanting to burst from her. She had to keep them buried deep, where no one could know. No one could see. Not even Boomer. "These things are complicated. I'm complicated."

"No shit. But here's the ice, Nimah—he ain't just my friend, he's my brother. And you're *hurting him*. I can't allow that. So listen and listen good, I don't need to know the nitty grits. All I care about is keeping Mav from spiraling too deep over you that he can't ever find his way out." Boomer pointed a blunt finger at her, and despite the ferocity of his tone, the end of that finger trembled. "He said you needed a breather to sort your shit out. Razor. Take your time. Sort your shit out. But if you know, deep in your guts, he ain't it for you—then don't drag your damn heels like some puffed-up dancer with a broken ankle. Cut him loose. All the damn way loose. Got it?"

Shot between the eyes, Nimah felt her heart give a vicious lurch, but she urged the galloping beat to ease as she realized the "puffed" comment was a turn of phrase, not a call-out.

"You don't need to worry." She brushed down his pointed finger with a gentle swipe of her hand. "Maverick and I have already agreed to part ways soon as this job is done."

Taken aback by her response, his brows shot up and nearly kissed the edge of his meticulously trimmed hairline. "Well . . . no shit."

Nimah offered a soft smile. "Yeah."

After a moment of quiet reflection, his jaw tightened in scrutiny. "You really prepared to let him go?"

"I have to."

"Is that what you *want* to do?"

Somewhere deep in her chest, a fresh twist of guilt seized the tender muscles of her heart. Pinching them together like clamped eyelids not wanting to see the truth. "I don't know," Nimah answered honestly. "But it's the right thing to do."

Boomer grunted with a tense nod, somehow taking in what she couldn't find the heart to say. "Then . . . do it gentle. For me. For him."

They rode the rest of the way in silence, and in less than an hour the tram pulled to a stop at the final station deep within the belly of the Scar. They exited the tram onto a surface of rough concrete covered in the slop of grime and watery puddles that collected at the base of the buildings. Cast-off sludge slowly filtered its way through the slats of grating over the sewers. Steam wafted in alternating blasts from recyclers, and it took a few deep breaths before Nimah was able to adjust to the stench of chemicals and filth.

"Son of a—" Boomer pressed the back of his hand against his nose, eyes liquid with tears. "Who in their right senses would wanna be down here?"

"It's not as bad as it looks."

"Tell that to my nostrils." Boomer pressed a fist to his mouth, muffling a burp that promised vomit was not far behind. "I think the hairs been singed clean off."

Overhead, a glowering pink dragon, its slick body and powerful legs rippling as it prowled down the street, towed behind it a long sign with popping gold letters in Spantonese heralding the New Year.

A smile split across Nimah's face. "I know where she is. Come on."

Ten minutes later, Nimah and Boomer reached the main market, where vendor stalls were stacked atop one another like bricks and tables lined in neat rows. Patrons swelled through the streets with trays or bags laden with greasy food, while hundreds of service bots rushed back and forth, wiping down tabletops, carting empty trays, and dumping leftover scraps into metal incinerating bins that belched fire and smoke with each toss.

Sure enough, amid the chaos, there she was, tucked at a communal table shoveling heavily sauced noodles from a carton into her mouth like she hadn't seen food, let alone air, in a month. Still dressed in her agent suit, locs twisted away from her slender face, she stood out like a flying pig farting rainbows.

Elbowing Boomer, Nimah gestured toward Liselle and gave him the signal to hold back. He nodded in agreement, finding a position nearby to keep watch while Nimah approached an open seat at Liselle's table.

"I can't believe you're still eating that junk." Nimah chuckled.

At the sound of her voice, Liselle's eyes rolled up and her mouth widened with a silent gasp, chopsticks limp in her startled fingers.

"Stop." Nimah plunked down onto the bench across from her and reached for her frozen hand. "You're looking at me like I died."

"What are you doing here, Nims?"

"Can't I pay my best friend an unexpected visit?"

"Nimah, I'm serious." Liselle jammed her chopsticks into the carton, standing them upright like posts. "If you think you're welcome in the Inner Circle after the stunt you pulled at grad—snubbing SIGA to become a pirate—you're deluded. This is not the place where you want to be seen right now. Or ever." Liselle looked around uneasily, taking in how exposed they were.

"Well, someone once told me the best place to avoid being noticed is in the lion's den." Reaching for Liselle's beverage, Nimah took a casual sip of the carbonated drink. The flavor enhancers rippled across her tongue like voltage from a battery before mellowing to a subtle tangy sweetness. "I'll never understand why you enjoy eating this stuff."

"Don't do that."

"Do what?"

"Brush off what I said like it's a joke." Liselle slapped an aggrieved hand to the table in frustration.

"It's not that deep, Liselle. Sure, I bruised toes, but SIGA has bigger issues to worry about. They'll cool off eventually."

"No. I don't think they will. Do you have any idea the strings that were pulled to get us our badges after the mess that you made and the laws you broke? If you'd walked up to Chairwoman Aramir and spat in her face in front of the board, I think she'd have been less insulted. And my dad—he was locked in his office for *weeks* with all the meetings he got called into after you took off. I think he aged two years because of it."

"About your dad . . ."

Liselle's brows flattened. "What about him?"

Nimah folded her hands in her lap, fingers linked to stop herself from fidgeting. "I need a favor."

Understanding settled in the long beat of silence that followed. "Oh no. No, no, *no*! Are you out of your mind?"

"Liselle, it's serious."

"It's always something serious with you, Nimah. I can't. I'm an agent now." She touched her lapel, where a STARs badge was pinned, and something inside of Nimah rang hollow with the ache of regret.

"Whatever you want me to do, I can't. I won't risk this."

"Would ya look at that. Kicking you to the curb for a bit of brass."

Nimah clenched her eyes with a grimace as Dobs wriggled in the back of her skull like an eel. "Stop."

"Just saying, kid, that it didn't take long for her to turn her shoulder. So much for friendship. So much for family."

"Nims." Liselle waved a hand, flagging her attention. "Did you hear what I said?"

"Sorry . . ." Nimah shook off Dobs, recentering her focus on her best friend. "Five minutes, Liselle, give me that. And if you're not swayed by what I have to say, then I'll burn from Corlys and never bother you again."

Deep brown eyes scanned Nimah's face, hesitant. Wary. But also disappointed. "You even sound like a pirate now . . ." Rocking back with a deep sigh, Liselle nodded once. "Five minutes."

It took Nimah less than four to know she had her best friend hooked as she quickly outlined all that had happened across the last few days.

Disbelief and horror fell across Liselle's stunned face. "Nimah . . . what you're saying doesn't make sense. For an entire farming commune to have been wiped out—and five hundred children *taken* . . . there'd be ripples in the newscasts. Something! But no one, anywhere, is talking about this. As a strategic defense analyst, I would know. It's my *job* to know."

"This commune is part of an unregistered planet," Nimah answered. "I think this is being redacted *by* the board. To cover their hand in this."

"Unregistered planets?" Liselle gave a disbelieving laugh. "That's absurd. Impossible! Do you *really* expect me to believe our government would *steal* children?"

Nimah shifted uncomfortably. "I never told you why I chose to walk out of graduation. Why I gave up on my dream."

"No." Liselle folded her arms across her chest, arched one scrutinizing brow. "You didn't."

And it was time she amended that. So Nimah settled closer. "After my grandmother came to say goodbye, I was passing by your dad's office when I . . . I overheard something I shouldn't have." Nimah took a quick breath, then pushed herself to say it all. Relaying the wave she'd listened to where Annelise Aramir had told Lennox to not only stall the RIM Accord before it was executed, but to break it entirely.

"Nimah . . ." Liselle's eyes darted around them in alarm. "You can't be suggesting what I think you are."

"I am. Lis, I don't think Cormack was entirely responsible for the plan to wipe out RIMers. True, he set the plan in motion with Dobs, but if you think about it—really think about it—he must have had support from higher up. Much higher. And if SIGA can get their hands dirty with Cormack, is it really a stretch to imagine they'd do this—or worse?"

"Stop." Liselle flattened her palms to her ears, eyes squeezed shut in protest. "What proof do you even have?"

"That's where you come in."

"Un-fucking-believable. Are you listening to yourself?"

"I am. But I don't think *you* are."

"Oh, I'm listening. I'm listening to my best friend in the entire void imply that the government I serve is so morally bankrupt that it would kidnap children. And you want me to believe that my father is willingly complicit in this?" Hurt shone in her eyes, spilling forward in a single, glistening trail. "Thinking this is a crime. *Speaking* it—even here in the Scar, it's foolish to voice such accusations. You're asking to be put in a blackbag."

Nimah took a deep, sobering breath and nodded gently. She knew this wasn't going to be easy, but part of her was disappointed at Liselle's unwillingness to be swayed by the stakes.

"You know how much I love your family. How much I love you." Liselle shook her head with a harsh laugh, blinking away more tears as Nimah pressed on, "What I am saying is awful, and I swear on my soul I want to be wrong. I need to be wrong. And there's only one way to know for sure. Your dad's position with the board grants him the highest level of clearance. If you could just—"

"—commit a felony?" Liselle finished. "You realize this could not only strip me of my brass but also have me collared? I could lose everything. *Again.*"

"Lis . . . we're talking about kids. Some as young as two." But when Liselle only shrugged, something in Nimah hardened with absolution. Enough. If words weren't going to reach her, then she needed to see. Nimah removed a disc from her pocket, a copy of the footage she'd walked through with Maverick, and set it on the table next to the carton of rapidly congealing noodles. "This was recorded by someone who saw the aftermath firsthand. Take it. See with your own eyes, and if you can walk through those bodies and not feel as sick and twisted up as I do, okay. No harm done. Go back to your analyst job and forget I was ever here. But if you do, and even the smallest part of you agrees I'm right, then the only way I can possibly save those kids is through your dad."

Liselle sighed deeply, palms patting away the dampness on her cheeks. "There's an official dinner tonight. My dad is a keynote speaker. Super big deal. He's been sweating over his speech for weeks so . . . that solves the dilemma about how I'll get in. But the next issue is access to his console. He's not exactly going to be kind enough to leave it unlocked for me."

"Mumbles," Nimah offered. "She can crack anything."

"Great," Liselle said with a sardonic grin. "You have her tucked in your pocket?"

"Even better." Nimah withdrew the glowing silver orb, and Liselle's lips parted in a surprised O as, when her hand fell away, it continued to hover in the air. "This is what you'd call rogue tech. Mumbles named it Blind-Eye. With this device, you'll be able to shield yourself from all cameras and scanners on your family's property. When you're in his office, call Mumbles using my comms tag—I'll have Boomer flag her to be on standby for you. She'll help you navigate the rest."

A grim look of resignation settled across Liselle as she accepted the items and tucked the disc, comms tag, and Blind-Eye away into the satchel resting on the bench at her side, one strap looped around her thigh in case a grifter with quick hands got any ideas.

"I guess that's the plan," she muttered with a complete lack of enthusiasm. Apparently no longer interested in her food, Liselle tossed her carton into a passing incinerator. "Get a room in the Scar," she said as it disappeared with a puff of smoke and a belch of flames. "Detailing isn't sharp down here, so if you're lucky, you'll escape notice. How are you for credits? Chips?"

"Um . . ." Nimah winced.

Sighing, Liselle fished out a half-used roll of chips from her pocket and counted out a small stack before handing it over to Nimah. "One-fifty should be enough to cover a night's stay. The *Platinum Flamingo* has decent bunks and fewer critters. If this works—and I'm not saying it will—meet me back here in exactly twelve hours. If I fail to show after fifteen minutes, then it means I found nothing." She rose from the bench to leave, the strap of her satchel halfway to her shoulder before she paused with a thought. "I'm agreeing to this because I need to know for myself that my father isn't a monster. And once I've proven that . . . we're done, Nimah. Okay? Done." She dropped her chin and held Nimah's gaze with a firm arch of her brow. "No more surprise visits. No more favors."

"Lis—"

"No, Nimah. You've been gone for almost three months, and in all that time not once did you make any attempt to communicate or check-in, but soon as you need something, you're on my doorstep asking for favors that could get me fired. Or worse." Her lip curled. "It's infuriating and insulting."

The harshness of her words struck Nimah like a sonic blast that burned beyond layers of skin to bone, leaving behind an irreversible scar. She'd known asking this of Liselle would likely drive a wedge between them once and for all, but it had to be done, even if it meant sacrificing her friendship. Innocent lives were at stake—five hundred and seven of them. But understanding that didn't soften the sting of severing the last thread tethering her to Liselle.

She was right to draw a line. They couldn't be friends anymore, or family. Liselle was an agent. Nimah was a pirate. They'd each chosen their side, and now it was time to stand on it.

Nimah steadied herself, letting the weight settle as the wreckage of their friendship drifted into oblivion and the love they'd once shared collapsed into a black hole. Raising her chin, she met Liselle's stern gaze with a firm nod of acceptance.

"I understand."

CHAPTER ELEVEN

I *understand?*" Liselle slammed through the door of her loft apartment. "Of all the arrogant—" Tossing her uniform jacket to the floor, she scowled through furious tears. Fingers curled into fists at her sides, trembling with the force of rage crackling beneath her skin.

The surge of late-night air traffic streaked past the lone viewport, each glow of thrusters a reminder of a world that wasn't crumbling around her. But inside this room, inside her mind—it was collapsing, imploding under the weight of everything Nimah had insinuated.

To think her father, of all people— *No.* Nimah was wrong, and Liselle was prepared to burn through every firewall, decrypt every classified file, and break every law she could think of to prove it. Whatever it took.

Her home office hummed to life as she entered the main living space and activated a trio of curved holoscreens with a swipe of her finger to the console keyboard.

"Alright," she whispered, voice tight with determination, and slotted in the disc Nimah had provided. "System, run simulation."

Liselle threw up three times in the span of two hours.

Once after completing a thorough review of the footage on the disc, and twice more in the ride from her megahold and the lift to her parents' penthouse unit. Threading between planets with a stomach full of greasy, chemical-laced, synthetic noodles certainly hadn't helped matters, but it was the raw disbelief that left her stomach churning with ceaseless unease.

So many dead, and her mind raced over the many possible *whys*.

Standing outside the main entrance, Liselle raised her wristdeck and waved her personal key against the scanner. Within a moment the door opened and the butler rolled out, his smooth metal face shaped to emulate that of a refined older gentleman with a cap of combed and gelled pale white hair. His glass eyes shimmered with digital scans as he authenticated Liselle's biometrics before stooping into a stately bow.

"Mistress Liselle, we did not expect you to be in attendance this evening."

Liselle adjusted the weight of the fresh bouquet of peonies in her arms, swaddled in crisp paper dyed to match the powder-pink petals of her mother's favorite flowers. "I know, I opted to surprise my parents, but the air traffic was tremendous this evening. Have they left for the dinner already? I can leave these in her private sitting room."

Which was adjacent to her father's personal office and far removed from the household bots tasked with either cleaning or sweeping the home for security.

"Left?" The butler inclined his head slightly, in the manner of all bots when receiving information their processors didn't quite comprehend. "You mean, has the dinner commenced? Fear not, mistress, you are in time for the start of speeches, after which dinner will be served, promptly at seven forty-five."

"Served . . ." Her arms sagged beneath the weight of the flowers. "As in, my parents are hosting the state dinner?" *Shit*. Somehow she'd failed to recall that very important detail.

"Yes." The butler bobbed on his uniwheel, and even though his face was not designed to emote, he almost beamed with an aura of pride. "All guests are in attendance, including Chairwoman Annelise, newly appointed Admiral Kimora Wallace, and the key members of the UPN overseeing the RIM Accord."

UPN. RIM Accord . . .

Because she'd believed the dinner was happening offsite, she hadn't bothered to pay much attention to the details, but now her brain stumbled over various conversations she'd had with her mother in holo and tried to piece together what was going on.

It was no secret, given recent newscasts, that negotiations between SIGA and the RIMers were not landing well. It was reported that while

Cormack Shinoda was the mastermind behind the horrible atrocities that had nearly been inflicted on them, a high proportion of RIMers believed his actions had not only been supported but safeguarded by SIGA. While many wanted to sign, a greater number held little trust for a government that not only shunned them but failed them for the better part of a century.

The dinner tonight was an attempt to reach common ground with the ambassadors—elected by the RIMers to advocate on their behalf—through the age-old practice of bending over and kissing ass.

And here she was still dressed in her analyst uniform, fresh off the clock, hardly appropriate for a gathering of this magnitude. Slipping through a crowd this affluent unnoticed was going to be impossible, but there was no other way to reach her father's office.

Shit. Shit. Shit.

The butler rolled back on his uniwheel and Liselle stepped into the foyer, fingers locked around the stems of the peonies she now held tight to her chest like a shield. Thankfully she'd grabbed a large bouquet of fifty stems. Maybe if she held them high enough, she could pass for a member of the household staff carting a delivery of flowers.

Music, a collection of strings, rippled soft as the candlelight, joined by the robust sound of voices. If she had to guess, there must be at least a hundred to a hundred and fifty in the adjoining ballroom—reserved for gatherings and celebrations.

Overhead, soft airy fabric draped across the ceiling and was met with floating wisps of light that mimicked stars. Her mother had brought out the big guns, not surprising.

"Should I announce to your father that you've arrived to join us?"

"No!" Liselle blurted, then caught herself with an anxious smile. "No, I'm not fit for this level of company. I'll take this to my mother's sitting room and see about freshening up. Please, tend to the rest of your tasks for this evening. I'm sure you have an extensive list still to get through."

The butler straightened at the reminder of duty. "Yes. Quite a long list. If there is nothing else required of me, I shall leave you, mistress. You know the way."

He whisked off toward the crowd and Liselle released a steady breath.

The great thing about bots and synths was that, unlike people, they lacked the capacity for skepticism and weren't designed to question the motives behind Liselle's unexpected presence or gauge the integrity of her actions. As the daughter of Isabeau and Lennox Namsara, this was and would always be her home; therefore, Liselle showing up unannounced, amid a high-profile official dinner no less, gave the butler no choice but to adhere to his programming and the protocols of high society.

Bots were easy.

The household cameras and scanners, on the other hand, were another matter.

Raising the bouquet of flowers to obscure as much of her face as possible, Liselle wove down the foyer and veered left, away from the din of the party, toward the quiet private wing of her mom's personal suite. She deposited the bouquet on a center table already laden with a lush display of hydrangeas and roses topped with white peonies from her mother's own garden. Then she hurried back out into the hall and took a quick right, stopping outside her father's home office.

Here the camera activated with the doors, so the moment she entered her father's office there would be no way to shield her from the system. Not without cover. Reaching into her pocket, Liselle removed the smooth orb Nimah had given her earlier.

A Blind-Eye, she'd called it. Strange contraption. Liselle held up the orb, about the size of a peach and made of a smooth clear substance that felt denser than stone but lighter than glass. She swirled it in the palm of her hand as Nimah had shown her before parting ways, and as it had in the demonstration, the orb shimmered to life, emitting a soft, silver light that glistened like sunlight across still water.

Awakened, it hovered over the skin of her palm, barely touching, and somehow mirrored her movements precisely. Releasing an unsteady breath, Liselle lifted her eyes toward the camera and reached for the handle of the office door.

Palm sweating, she gave it a gentle turn. A soft nudge.

Overhead, the corridor camera remained stationary, no red dot indicating activation. Liselle sighed in relief then quickly stepped inside and shut the door behind her. The Blind-Eye tracked her movement, keeping in position by her left shoulder, and its soft silver glow created light for her to see by. Approaching the console, Liselle removed a disc from her back pocket with enough storage to download half of SIGA's archive.

The console hummed awake at the touch of her hand, and the clear holoscreen blinked with the request for login credentials.

She touched the back of her ear and the comms clicked on. "Hello?" Liselle whispered. "I'm in."

The comms hummed, a soft whisper of static before a rasping voice answered on the other end. "Goody-hi."

"You must be Mumbles." The Blind-Eye swiveled in front of Liselle and blinked twice as if in response. "Right. Well. Do what you do, I guess."

The holoscreen shuddered, and the password icon expanded as code scrolled in a blur. Three minutes. It only took this Mumbles three minutes to do what some of the most skilled hackers in the void would've struggled to do in under thirty.

"I'm in," Liselle breathed. A sour note of regret coated her senses as part of her hoped with secret longing that Mumbles would fail and she'd have a viable excuse to walk away. But there it was—wide open and waiting.

Mumbles giggled.

The remote connection ended, and the comms tag went silent. Leaving Liselle alone in the dark. Her gaze fell to a mug of stale coffee, left over from earlier in the day when her father had sat here, deep in work. Guilt lodged in her throat like a dry chicken bone and no amount of coughing was going to wrench it free.

Am I really doing this?

"You're not breaking into your dad's files," Liselle whispered to herself. "This is a rogue console, seized during an investigation, and you've been brought in to scour it for evidence. That's it. Just another day at the office."

As an analyst, she was taught where to dig for private accounts and locked folders with unusual file names or extensions. But the first place she preferred to look was in deleted files. Even if recently scrubbed, no matter how cleanly someone swept, crumbs were always left behind, and her father appeared to be a poor sweeper.

Given there was a party going on, she didn't have time to be especially particular or thorough. Every second she spent in here increased her chances of being caught. The most logical approach would be a bulk download of anything that seemed remotely suspect, then weed through it all once back in the safety of her own apartment. Using the drone of speeches as her countdown, Liselle set to work.

A lawyer's best defense, her father often said, was a strong archive of evidence.

Document everything, Liselle. You'll never know when something will prove useful. Cover your ass.

While the bulk download commenced, she scrolled back through his logs and found the recording made the day of their graduation ceremony. There were three audio files, but only one time-stamped for an hour before they'd left with Nimah to head to the Academy.

Swallowing hard, Liselle opened the file and a small projection of her father shimmered onto the screen in 3-D. The first thing she noticed, as an objective analyst, was the stress carved into the lines between his brows and in the way his hands braced the flat surface of his desk, as if he was struggling to find the strength to stand.

Muting the audio, her eyes tracked the subtitles transcribing the conversation between him and Chairwoman Aramir.

Namsara, Lennox: *The law may be malleable. But I can only stretch parameters so far.*

Aramir, Annelise: *Stretch them, break them, I don't really care what you do. But find a solution to this ordeal. The Circle is spiraling. If we lose our grip on this, we lose everything. And without us at the helm, we're facing anarchy. That cannot happen.*

Namara, Lennox: *I need time.*

Aramir, Annelise: *The RIM Accord goes to bed in eight weeks. You've got seven to find a way to break it.*

Liselle ended the recording, her heart barely beating out of cold fear. So Nimah hadn't lied about what she'd overheard. Not a complete surprise; Nimah had never lied to her, but Liselle had hoped—desperately hoped—this would be the first. While this didn't prove anything around Nimah's claims with the missing children, it painted her father in a light she'd never seen him in before.

The thundering roar of applause jolted Liselle back to present. That was it. Speeches were over and it was time to get moving. Typing furiously, Liselle ended the download sequence, having captured close to eighty-four percent of all documents and files, then closed out programs and was about to shut down when a notification caught her eye. The insignia identified it as directly from the Chairwoman's office.

Leave it, a dark part of her whispered. *Speeches are done. You have to go.* But the need to know was too great. She clicked the notification and a direct message opened on screen confirming that funds had been extracted from Shinoda's frozen assets and were ready for immediate disbursement once the private contract for Nimah Dabo-124 had been completed.

"Wait . . ." Liselle shook her head in disbelief. "Contract? On Nimah?"

The ring of cheers sent her heartbeat to scatter. *That's it.* She'd pushed it far enough. Removing the drive, Liselle closed out of the console and rushed out of the office with the Blind-Eye, all but sprinting for the foyer. Once she was far enough from the office, she swiveled the orb three times and it winked out, sinking into her palm like lead. She tucked it inside her work satchel, took the corner like a speed racer—tires screaming, engine revved—and nearly collided with her stunned father.

"Sweetheart, what are you doing here?"

"I'm sorry." Her window for escape gone, Liselle forced a bright smile and hoped it was enough to mask her alarm. "I dropped by to surprise you with a visit and brought some flowers for Mom. I completely forgot the dinner was tonight."

"Oh, don't worry about that, love." He drew away and his joy shifted to worry. "Are you alright? Why on earth were you running? You look flushed."

"Oh, well. I'm not fit for the party. Wanted to get clear before I . . . caused any embarrassment."

"Sweetheart."

He gathered her into another tight hug, and Liselle was almost overcome with the need to fold into him and weep in despair. *Daddy . . . Not my daddy. Not you.* Her father. Her hero. Did she even know him at all?

"I know what's really going on, Lissy." He sighed against her temple.

Everything inside of Liselle—heart, stomach, bowels—plummeted to her knees. "You do?"

"Of course I do. You're still grieving the loss of your best friend. It's why you hardly come home anymore. Too many memories." He cupped her cheek in his hand, his palm warm and soft and tender. So much so she felt herself shrink from a young woman into a little girl needing the comfort and assurance of her father. "I know it hasn't been easy. You and Nimah had all these plans—her running off left you confused and heartbroken. But she made her choice, sweetheart. It's time to move forward. To let her go."

A tear escaped, despite all efforts, but Liselle let it fall and didn't pull back as her father brushed it away from the point of her chin. The best lies were concealed in truth. "I know."

"Why don't you head to your room and freshen up and come join us? Maybe the dress you wore to the Winslow gala. There's a new Head of Strategic Affairs for the UPN that I'd like you to meet. She's a little older than you and I think she'd make an excellent mentor. Or friend."

Liselle opened her mouth to think of a way out, the stolen files beating like a heart against her hip, when across the line of his shoulders she saw a familiar face float through the crowd. White hair and searing golden HWKeyes—Admiral Kimora Wallace. She stood on her own, all stoic elegance, her athletic frame beautifully enhanced by an incredible dress that rippled with hues of a late sunset fading into dusk.

Liselle had never seen her outside the pristine white commander's uniform she wore at the Academy, and suddenly, hope sprung in her chest at a possible ally. "Yeah. Okay."

Twenty minutes later Liselle emerged from her room wearing a sheath dress cut to her ankles in shimmering silver scales. Her locs, twisted into a chignon, were studded with faceted crystal beads that caught the light like diamonds.

She joined the gathering, navigating the crowded room with ease born from years of experience bestowing graceful smiles and perfunctory *How are you*'s, pausing long enough to scoop a flute of champagne from a floating tray offered by a hired synth-server. Unlike the household bots, these moved like pieces of art with incredible shells of tinted steel and metallic whorls of enamel embedded with synthetic jewels that caught the light and dazzled with every movement.

Liselle nearly dropped her flute when a woman turned and she locked eyes with Chairwoman Annelise Aramir, surrounded by RIM ambassadors and SIGA brass. Her gown was obsidian silk, cut sharp at the shoulders and rolled like liquid shadows at her feet, giving her presence a magnetic and commanding aura.

"Chairwoman Aramir." Liselle held her smile with practiced poise while her heart thudded like a snared animal in her chest. "A pleasure to see you again."

Excusing herself from her circle of conversation, Annelise's answering smile was unreadable as she approached. "Liselle Namsara. I was wondering if you'd make an appearance tonight. This is quite an illustrious moment for your father."

"It is." Liselle fingers dug into her beaded clutch. "I hope the evening's been . . . productive."

"Productive?" Annelise's brows quirked in amusement. "Dear girl, we're redefining history. The RIM Accord is the most ambitious diplomatic effort of our generation. And tonight's offer—full citizenship in exchange for relinquishing ownership of elite—is a generous one. One I am proud to have presented to our esteemed delegates."

"Generous?" Liselle echoed. "Generous for whom?" Because nothing about that offer could be taken as anything other than blatant extortion. Not when analysts forecasted the value of elite would eclipse prime shares two thousand to one; a price tag that would cripple SIGA and the prestigious one percent of the Inner Circle who hoarded more wealth than could be spent in eight generations.

This offer was a ridiculous proposal that sought to strip RIMers of their rights through policy rather than force. Which made this entire spectacle little better than an attempt to seduce the ambassadors with a taste of wealth and privilege in return for their support with selling this offer to the masses.

Cut by Liselle's scathing retort, Annelise's gilded mask fractured, giving Liselle the barest glimmer of the monster hidden beneath porcelain skin and livid blue eyes.

Annelise sipped her wine, taking a moment to slip it firmly into place, cracks and all. "We can all agree that elite is the future and hoarding it out of spite is not serving anyone. We're simply aligning incentives to ensure a fair outcome for all."

A fair outcome would be to pay what was owed—as promised—but Liselle bit into those words rather than set them loose. She'd already lost control of her tongue once, and that was enough.

"I must say . . ." Annelise closed in and reached high to brush a mindful hand across Liselle's shoulde, clearing away filth that wasn't there. "I am so deeply relieved to hear reports from your father of your good work. He's so very proud of you, you know, and how far you've come—despite *questionable* persons you once held dear."

Liselle set her teeth, and did her level best not to crack. "You mean Nimah."

Annelise sipped again, this time not to regather herself but only to enhance the tension. "Such a passionate young woman, is Nimah. But passion without discipline is chaos. And chaos must always be dealt with. Let us count ourselves grateful you are not in her orbit anymore."

Liselle's throat tightened. "Excuse me," she said, bowing slightly. "I see Admiral Wallace, and I'd like to pay my respects."

Annelise stepped back with a wave of her flute. "Of course. Do enjoy the evening. And I look forward to us speaking again. Soon."

Liselle turned, heart hammering, and made her way toward Wallace—her heels clicking with each hurried step, the weight of her evening bag growing heavier by the second from the stolen secrets she carried within.

"I need to speak with you," she said, low and urgent, once at Wallace's side.

Wallace swept golden HWKeyes over Liselle and the subtle sheen that glimmered across the surface of her gaze signified she wasn't just seeing Liselle, she was reading her. "Not in here." She gestured with a slight incline of her head toward the terrace, and together they whisked out at the unhurried pace of two women seeking a quiet breath of fresh air amid the garden. Once they crossed the sound netting, the music and laughter immediately gave way to the soft silence of Lysandis at night.

"I haven't seen your stress signals this high since the day Nimah boosted Maverick from the Academy." Wallace braced the balustrade and overlooked the gardens to the glowing flow of a neon waterfall spilling a river of light to dance and coil above the carefully manicured flower bushes and live trees two stories below.

"Oh? And here I thought they'd be *worse*." Liselle laughed dryly, joining Wallace. "I have something I need to show you."

"It'll have to wait," Wallace whispered, her eyes continually scanning around them. "They know she's here."

Liselle snapped straight in alarm. "How?"

"She was flagged entering adjacent airspace earlier this evening. A warrant for Nimah's arrest was drafted a little over two and a half days ago, already stamped by SIGA, and has been sitting on my desk with orders not to execute until otherwise directed . . ."

"On what grounds?"

Wallace's jaw tightened. "I expect that is going to be filled in . . . *after*."

"That's not protocol." Liselle's brows furrowed.

"I don't think SIGA is particularly concerned with protocol right now. Not with the tension surrounding accord negotiations." Wallace sighed heavily, the edge of her restless thumb tapping against the balustrade. Three taps between the space of every heartbeat.

It was the closest to panicked Liselle had ever seen Wallace, and it was hard not to be unnerved. "Does this have anything to do with the private contract out for Nimah?" Liselle whispered, and Admiral Wallace tensed. The only confirmation Liselle needed. "So you already know about it."

"Yes. I know. I've been keeping an eye on her. Nothing invasive, I just wanted to make sure she was . . . After all that happened, I worried for her safety."

"Please tell me what is going on. Why are they hunting her?"

"You should be more concerned with who they're sending." Golden eyes flickered to Liselle. "Headless Crole."

The name sent a shock of recognition through Liselle that hit like a sonic grenade. Vesper Crole, former socialite turned sociopath. They called her the Headless because that was all she left behind of her mark, a headless corpse.

If Vesper had been hired to take Nimah down, then the draft warrant must be a manufactured ploy for SIGA to cover their asses later. Because whatever they had planned for Nimah wasn't about bringing her in. It was about taking her out. This was bad. This was very, very bad.

"Come back with me to Corlys. There's a disc I need to show you. This mess with Nimah and Vesper—it's all connected somehow and maybe together we can—"

"You're not listening," Wallace interrupted, the gold of her eyes heating with frustration and worry. "Forget whatever you saw or think you know—Nimah is being hunted, and so too will anyone associated with . . . with . . ." Wallace paused as her wristdeck hummed, indicating the receipt of correspondence. "Keep quiet," she cautioned, then activated the private receive function, jaw set.

Her pupils expanded with the inflow of information. She was taking the call internally, so Liselle couldn't hear anything beyond two words: Wallace's clipped *I understand* before she ended the transmission.

"What's going on?"

Wallace set her closed fist to her mouth. "Whatever you stepped in, you left footprints. And now the board wants you brought in for questioning, as well."

Liselle blanched, her mind firing like a primed thruster as she grappled for a hold on rationality and reason. "My dad . . . I can't—he would never let them . . ."

Wallace stepped in her path, stopping Liselle before she rushed back toward the glow of the party. "This is an order from the *chairwoman*, which means he won't be able to stop this even if he wanted to." Taking her by the arm, Wallace steered her off to the side of the terrace toward the drop of the marble staircase leading down into the shadowy gardens. "I can stall on executing the request, buy you a bit of time, but you need to move quickly." Her eyes dropped to Liselle's evening bag. "Do you have everything you need in there? Badge? Suit?"

"What?" Liselle struggled to move her leaden tongue. "Oh. Yes. Academy 101." She nodded. An agent in the field, even when off duty, must always have two things with them. Liselle had tucked both within a micro-capsule, minimizing to the size of a chicken egg, so it could be stored in her clutch.

"Good girl. Do you know where Nimah is?"

Dazed with disbelief, Liselle nodded like a heliohead puffed on too much smoke. How was this happening? She hadn't tripped any alarms in her father's office, of that she was almost certain . . . otherwise his household would've gone berserk, and house bots would've flooded in like precision-coded missiles. So where else had she mis-stepped? Unless the Blind-Eye had failed and there was a secondary layer of surveillance tethered directly to SIGA's base she didn't know about.

"You need to go to her," Wallace urged. "Stay low while I sort this out. I'll signal you when it's safe."

Nausea slid over Liselle and her knees nearly buckled from underneath her. "I can't run. Running makes me look guilty, right? Like I have something to hide." Teetering on the edge of panic, she flung her gaze back toward the party, to the soft glow of lights and even softer ring of music and laughter. "I should let them question me. I mean . . . what could they possibly know?" A deranged giggle slipped from her throat like the hiss of an over-pressurized valve.

Bright. Popping. Quickly chased by another—and another—until Liselle was doubled over and strangled by manic laughter. A reactor on the verge of meltdown.

Wallace cracked her palm hard against Liselle's cheek.

Liselle sobered immediately. "Yeah. You're right, I needed that." She pressed a hand to flaming skin. "Thank you."

"You're welcome. Now, keep to the gardens until you reach the landing pad. I suggest flagging an air-taxi instead of taking your own transpo. With a party of this magnitude, there's bound to be a hundred hovering nearby. Now go."

"But—"

"That's an order, Agent!" Wallace snapped, but her features quickly softened just enough for something close to grief to shine through. "For your own good, please do as I say."

CHAPTER TWELVE

Calling the *Platinum Flamingo* a motel was someone's idea of a bad joke.

Built from the abandoned skeleton of what Nimah guessed was supposed to be a megahold before it ran out of funding, it squatted between a strip plaza comprised of a burned-out repair shop and a defunct water purification station.

It was stacked three stories high with plastic sheeting for window screens. The motel's neon sign hung over the flat roofline, bearing a one-legged silver flamingo that spun in a glitching circle overtop half-dead lettering of INUM FLA—GO that pulsed in what once might've been hot pink but now was muddy yellow.

The front desk was manned by a bot built sometime in the early A.E.P. As for the room itself, a lopsided bunk covered in stained sheets sat atop mismatched linoleum, and a cracked holoscreen was fastened to a wall covered in bubbling blue paint. When the door shut behind them, the ventilation system rattled awake and gave a desperate cough as though it was trying—and failing—to breathe.

Boomer dropped his bag of gear with a beleaguered sigh that Nimah was hard-pressed not to match. Literally no one in their right mind would think to come here, which, she supposed, made it the perfect hole for them to hide in.

"Damn thing's fused shut," he grunted after trying without success to open the window, peering out over a parking-grid riddled with potholes and a few broken-down airbikes.

"This isn't exactly the kind of district you want to catch a breeze." Nimah flicked the knobs on three separate locks, none of which seemed particularly effective.

Irritated, he gave the frame a rattle. "Smells like someone lit a dried turd on fire in here."

"Take a deep breath. You won't notice it for long." Hauling his gear from the entryway, she dropped it at the foot of the collapsed bed. "Give me your comms. I'll update the crew while you grab us some food from the plaza downstairs. I'm starved."

Grudgingly, Boomer removed his tag and Nimah handed him the remaining chips from Liselle. The room had cost them close to eighty— a fucking crime, but at least they still had enough to get a decent slice of pizza, which was really the only thing Nimah would trust on this side of the Scar.

Soon as Boomer was gone, Nimah sent a recovered wave to the *Stormchaser*, updating them on her meet with Liselle. A few clipped responses came back from Zensha, who felt the twelve-hour wait was an egregious use of limited time, but Nimah wasn't in the mood to take her on or argue semantics. Whether Zensha liked it or not, they were all just going to have to suck it up and wait.

Reclining against the wall, Nimah propped her feet on the shelf of the windowsill and let her eyes roll shut. Only for a moment. Just to catch her breath. But the second her lids fell, she tumbled back into herself, a rock clattering down the chasm of a dark well.

At the firm touch of a hand, Nimah gasped awake with a panicked swing of her arms.

"Whoa." Boomer raised his hands, palms splayed wide. "Sorry, didn't mean to jolt you, but you were twitching like a neck in a noose."

"Sorry." Nimah knuckled her burning eyes with a groan. "How long was I out?"

Boomer jerked a shoulder. "Dunno. Was gone for thirty, so thereabouts, I guess?"

"Fuck me."

Boomer arched a stunned brow.

"What?"

"Nothing. Just ain't heard you curse so much before." Boomer backed up to the minuscule kitchenette where he'd deposited the takeout bags and busied himself with rummaging through them, plucking out cartons and a couple brown bottles of what Nimah suspected was home-brewed beer. "Couldn't find any pizza," he said over his shoulder. "Went for Spantonese—seeing as it's New Year's and all."

"Fine."

"You like whiskey?"

She heard the wet thwack of a cork being freed from the neck of a bottle, followed by the gurgling of liquid pouring into a glass.

"Prob'ly burn like a primefire-lit asshole, but I think we could both use the buzz." Boomer crossed the room with a couple glasses filled with two fingers of amber whiskey.

He handed one to Nimah just as her skull seemed to split down the center, and she caught the glass with trembling fingers.

"You look bleached." His scowling expression carried more concern than irritation—a rare softness in his otherwise hardened features. "What's got into you?"

She was really starting to grow tired of that question.

"Nothing." Nimah smiled, but the edges were brittle and uneven, as though her face might crack from the effort. Another jolt of agony ripped across the nerves at the base of her skull—an electric crackle across tender nerves—and she barely managed to hold her composure, let alone the glass, until he turned his back for food. Setting down the glass, Nimah pressed the heels of her palms to her eyes, the sockets screaming against the overload of pressure.

"No," she groaned. *Not now. Not here.*

Rising from the windowsill, Nimah shuffled to the basin of the sink. Its reservoir was shared with the toilet, collecting and storing wastewater for flushing. Turning on the faucet, Nimah let the water run, filling the basin before she submerged herself until her nose touched the bottom of the bowl. The shock of cold muffled the world, and Nimah held herself suspended in that blissful silence, counting each unsteady beat of her heart, a rhythm that felt as fragile as her state of mind. Stretching her lungs to their limit until the burn for release grew impossible to ignore.

She emerged gasping and grabbed the cloth hanging from the hook to wipe the beads of water from her face.

Behind her, Boomer perched on the windowsill she'd abandoned, peering out the hazy windowpane while running the blunt end of his finger—dampened with a bead of whiskey—around the edge of his glass until it sang. A high, keening note fractured in her ears, already throbbing and on the edge of pain.

Can't keep me out forever, Kid. Dobs crawled at the edges of Nimah's consciousness like a spider searching for a way in.

The heavy beat of a fist to the door had them both reaching for their weapons—Nimah the blaser strapped to her hip, and Boomer the sawed repeater looped across his back.

Signaling Boomer to cover her flank, Nimah scuttled to the door and primed her weapon. "Who is it?"

"Nims—open up!"

At the distressed sound of her best friend's voice, Nimah twisted open the locks.

Liselle shot inside and latched onto Nimah with hands that were far too cold given the warm night air. "You were right," she said before Nimah had a chance to open her mouth. "We have to leave. We have to leave *now*."

"What she—?"

"There's no time for that," Nimah interrupted Boomer. Whatever had Liselle so desperately spooked, it was clear questions had to wait. "Is anyone behind you?"

"No," Liselle answered, then squinted in uncertainty. "I mean . . . I don't think so."

"Okay. You, sit down." Nimah guided Liselle to the edge of the lopsided bunk. "We need quick transpo. Boomer, any ideas?"

Boomer scanned the decrepit lot below, his nose almost pressed to the filthy glass. "There's the shop across the street gotta couple jetbikes we can boost."

"Perfect. Go ahead and get them juiced and flag the *Stormchaser* while you're out there. Let them know we're making a burn for them, plus one. I'll gather our gear and be right behind you."

"Razor." Boomer bunted the windowpane with the end of his repeater. It took two hard knocks and a front kick to dislodge the sheet of the windowpane. Boomer tucked himself through the frame and disappeared out onto the fire escape.

"He wasn't supposed to be home." Liselle dragged her hands through her lengthy locs, studded with little crystal gems that complemented the silver scales of her sheath dress. "My father. But he was."

"The dinner?" Nimah asked, only now taking in Liselle from head to toe. She glowed like a movie star walking a red carpet. Even if no one was hot on her heels, she'd have drawn attention in a place like this.

Liselle nodded. "UPN delegation. RIM ambassadors. Fucking Chairwoman Aramir was there. Admiral Wallace, too."

"Wow. Must've been quite the event." Rucksack in hand, Nimah did her best to keep Liselle talking as she busied herself with stuffing their belongings into the gear-bag. But at the sound of Liselle's soft sob, Nimah's movements slid to a halt and she turned to her best friend hunched on the end of the bunk.

Disbelieving tears shone in Liselle's eyes, bright as the gems studding her locs. They glinted in her dark hair like stars in an evening sky.

"I did what you wanted. I was careful but . . . I don't know, I must've screwed up." Her thumbnail scraped against the side of her finger, picking at a bit of skin from a hangnail. An anxious quirk that Liselle had outgrown years ago. She'd worried that bit of skin to the point of irritation. Soon there would be blood.

Crossing to her, Nimah gripped Liselle's hands, trying to still their picking. "What about the files? Talk me through what you found. Did you see anything that could help us?" she asked, trying to guide Liselle away from the shock of whatever had happened and over to more stable ground. Get her focused on the task and away from the problem.

"I saw some emails. Messages and call recordings." Liselle answered. "Honestly, it was such a risk with everyone there for the dinner, so I sacrificed efficiency for speed. Just threw out a net and dragged it all back in—grabbing anything. Everything. Whatever. I don't know if what I copied is any good, or if it'll even help." Opening the bag, Liselle removed a micro-capsule before handing over her jeweled clutch.

Inside contained Nimah's comms tag, the Blind-Eye, the disc she'd copied for Liselle to review, and a coin-sized data drive that could hold every file on Liselle's father's personal network three times over.

"You did good." Nimah fastened her comms tag behind her left ear and added the evening bag inside her rucksack, minus the data drive. That she tucked into the inner pocket of her leather trench, feeling safer to have it as close to her as possible. "What's in the capsule?" Nimah asked as it vanished in the vee of Liselle's neckline.

"Suit and badge."

"Ah." Nimah nodded. "Smart."

"There's more, Nims. SIGA's hired a bounty hunter to find you. Vesper Crole." A tremble scored through Liselle. It wavered in her voice. "They call her the Headless Hunter. Because she always brings in the head. Not the body. The *head*, Nims."

"Catchy." Nimah clenched her jaw, the weight of guilt pressing in at every angle. That explained why Liselle hadn't used the comms tag to signal Nimah of any distress. Too easy to trace, and far easier to breach. If a bounty hunter was out for her, Liselle had been very wise to err on the side of caution. "Well, as it happens, I intend to keep mine."

Angling her wristdeck, Nimah tapped the screen, where her interface showed a search prompt for *Vesper Crole* and drew up a snapshot summary of the fierce hunter's identity profile from citizen registry archives. Former Academy trained, perfect. Socialite daughter of engineering executive Vector Crole and tri-city senator Dameris— "Stop!" Nimah scoffed. "She's a fucking Shinoda?"

"Sounds like a punchline to a bad joke." Liselle's brown eyes lifted, but instead of their usual sarcastic mirth, they were molten with shock and heartbreak. And the pain in them shattered Nimah right to the core. "Daddy was going to let them take me for questioning . . . can you believe that? But I ran . . ." Her voice went soft. A little distant, like fog burning off in sunlight. "Maybe now they'll send Vesper for my head, too."

"Hey." Nimah gripped her arms and gave her best friend a bit of a rough shake, forcing Liselle back from the precipice of tears. "I know you're freaking out, but I really need you to hold it together for me, okay? Boomer should have the bikes juiced. We'll get to the *Stormchaser*, review what you've found—and work out next steps from there." She swept her hands up Liselle's arms to her shoulders, anchoring her with a reassuring smile. "Everything is going to be okay. Promise."

Rising to her feet, Nimah reached down to loop an arm around Liselle's waist when every instinct went rigid in alarm. "Wait." She loosened her hold on Liselle, and turned toward the door—the door she'd failed to lock behind them—just as it swung open and a young woman sauntered in.

Barely a day over twenty-five, if Nimah had to guess, and built like a boxer, lithe and lean. She moved with the slow, cagey prowl of someone who knew how to fight and was quick on her feet. Nimah clocked the weapon in her hand, a custom blaser that had been modified for rapid fire and an extended cartridge for additional ammo, but it was the hybrid dog panting at her side that made Nimah ease back a step.

Tucked close to its owner's side, pointed ears flattened to its skull as it bared teeth in a low warning snarl, it was clearly well trained and waiting for a signal to attack. While Nimah was confident in her ability to take on a single adversary, the dog, an exotic breed with long legs—two of them bionic—a thin arched waist, and a whiplike tail, tipped the odds.

"Remove your weapon."

Nimah unholstered her blaser and tossed it to the ground between them. "You must be Vesper."

An eyebrow notched with a scar rose, and the corners of her mouth dipped down in a pleased smirk. "It's not often a mark gets wind of me before I've made my presence known." Her eyes jumped to Liselle, seated and shaking at the foot of the bunk. "Was it you who flagged her? If so—impressive. Even for an analyst."

"Maybe you're not as subtle as you think you are," Nimah challenged.

Vesper chuckled darkly and booted the door shut behind her. "Hold, Saint." She signaled her dog, and the animal planted its rump to the linoleum. Unblinking eyes fastened to Nimah as Vesper crossed to the kitchenette.

She'd never be able to make a move for her weapon before the dog lunged for her throat and tore it out.

"Thank you for making this easy. I wasn't expecting to find you here." Vesper helped herself to the whiskey and took a swig from the bottle with straight-faced ease. After a second pull, she capped the bottle then returned it to the counter at her side. Overhead, the shitty lights flickered like mosquitos popping in a UV lamp.

"My original plan was to facilitate a little sit-down with your bestie there." She gestured to Liselle with the muzzle of her blaser. "Instead, she led me straight to you."

Liselle's wet sniffle rasped in response.

"Okay. Well, you've got me. Let her go."

"And have her miss all the fun?" Vesper angled her head with a sunny smile, the dark shock of her bangs slanting across her slender face. "Shall we?" She gestured to the narrow side table fastened to the wall near the busted window.

The table was as small as a dinnerplate, with two weathered folding chairs made from white plastic yellowed from age and cigarette smoke. Nimah and Vesper claimed seats on opposing sides.

"You look different than your holos." Vesper swept her hair back, clearing her line of sight. "It's more than the haircut. Something in the eyes." Her grin sharpened. "Lack of sleep, maybe."

Cold punched through Nimah's chest as Vesper tossed something onto the tabletop. A tooth rattled to a stop in front of her. Haloed in gold with three holes drilled into it, and only one filled with a kernel of jade.

Groober's tooth, she realized in dull horror. There was no mistaking it.

"Is he dead?"

Vesper's smile stretched wider, cutting and cold. "No. Might wish he was. So." Hands clasped together, she leaned forward like a diplomat entering a negotiation over levies. "I'm going to offer you the chance to come along quietly. We walk out of here together. I turn you in and claim my bounty, and you'll have my word no one else gets hurt. But if you resist me, if you manage to run—" She pointed a blunt finger to the extracted tooth in warning. "I'll take apart anyone who helps or harbors you, starting with Miss Namsara. I'll tie you down and let you watch all the ways I'll make her scream."

Nimah's heart thundered in her ears and her mind spun out, a dizzying whirl of thoughts and panic. Vesper wasn't just a brawler with a blaser, she was Academy trained, which meant she knew all the tricks of the trade. Therefore, if she wanted to find a way out of this, Nimah would have to throw something at Vesper she'd never seen before.

Something unexpected. Nimah's gaze dipped to the table—to the plaque yellowed tooth. Like biting someone in the ass . . .

"I won't ask who sent you or why." Nimah had to move slow. So painfully slow. The barest increment of movements as the hand resting casually at her side slipped into her cargo pocket, fingers twisting and seeking until they looped around the horseshoe of Chu's dentures. "Just give me four days to settle some things, and on my word, I'll hand myself over to you. I won't resist."

"No."

"If this is about credits—"

"It is," Vesper interrupted Liselle's tearful plea. "Far more than even you or your father could hope to pay, Miss Namsara, even if you had three hundred lifetimes. And to save you the waste of effort, if you're thinking of appealing to my sympathies next—I don't have any." Vesper returned her attention to Nimah, and by the flattened gleam in her dark eyes, her capacity for games was nearing its end. "SIGA would like you brought in alive, but far as I'm concerned, dead is just as good, and personally, it's what I prefer. Question is"—she scored her tongue along the edge of her wicked smile—"how many do I have to hurt or bleed before I break you? What's it going to be, Nimah? We doing this easy or hard?"

Twisting off one of the molars, she extracted it from her pocket and squeezed it firmly in her closed fist until the porcelain shell cracked and the soft innards of the explosive gels began to fuse. "I guess we'll do hard." Leaping to her feet, Nimah threw the smoking tooth.

It struck Vesper's chest and exploded with a sharp *crack*—tossing Vesper clear across the room. Saint's howl of distress joined the fierce ringing in Nimah's ears as she spun for Liselle, who shielded herself with both arms from the blast.

"Come on!" Nimah shouted, the smoke and chaos a temporary delay. She reached for Liselle with one hand, her rucksack with the other, and turned for the window when a snarl and tug nearly yanked her clean off her feet.

Saint latched onto the rucksack, eyes wide and teeth relentless as the dog reared back and thrashed its neck.

"Leave it!" Liselle shouted, ducking onto the fire escape.

"Get down first," Nimah shouted back. Soon as she dropped the bag, the beast was going to come for her, and when it did, Nimah didn't want Liselle in the way.

Liselle disappeared from the open window and Nimah set her back to the frame. She had one chance and hoped she was quick enough on her feet to see it through. Holding the bag firmly, she gave it a tug and jerk.

Saint's teeth clenched, drool dripping from its jowls and fierce determination in its eyes. Releasing her grip, Nimah threw the rucksack at the dog and dove through the frame, hit the grating of the fire escape, and rolled just as Saint flung the bag aside—fifty pounds of gear as light as if it was a feather pillow.

Nimah slammed the security grate down and fastened it in place with half a second to spare as Saint collided with steel.

"Nimah! Hurry!" Liselle shouted from the ground.

Saint's muzzle wedged through the grating, tongue licking over teeth between snarls and snaps. Bracing the security ladder, Nimah slid down the side of the rungs like the brass pole aboard the *Stormchaser*, and at the bottom, her boots slammed to rain-soaked pavement.

"Is she dead?" Liselle demanded, feet bare as she stood in filthy puddle water that shimmering bright pink and blue from whirling holoverts.

"No. It would have just taken the wind out of her." And really, really pissed her off.

Boomer, already straddling one of the jetbikes, bounced his gaze from Liselle to Nimah in utter confusion. The second was propped and waiting a few feet away by a rusted waste bin. "What happened?"

"We're pinched. Take her." Nimah shoved Liselle against Boomer. "Get to the shuttle and burn out of here. That's an order."

"What about you?" Boomer pumped the throttle with his foot and the engine roared between his thighs as Liselle hopped on behind him, her dress splitting along the seam up to her hip.

"I have to lead her away." Drawn by the sound of breaking glass, Nimah's gaze shot up to see Vesper's elbow punching through the window of the adjacent room. "Go. I'll find a way to rejoin you when I can."

"No, Nims, don't!" Liselle reached for her, but Boomer punched the gas and took off on the jetbike, quickly disappearing in the surging lines of air traffic.

Vaulting onto the seat of the second, Nimah jumpstarted the jetbike with a crank of the pedal lever and the engine coughed like a smoker before catching its breath and roaring into motion. "Nimah to *Stormchaser*."

"*Cadet*." Maverick's voice flowed through her warm and steady. A balm to her frantic mind. "*What's wrong?*"

"Boomer and Liselle are en route to the shuttle. I'm holding back to shake off a tail." She kicked the throttle and bolted from the alley just as Vesper surged onto the fire escape and fired two sharp blasts, one striking the back of the jetbike, and the second the corner of a garbage bin, raining sparks that pressed like hot kisses against her cheek.

Nimah shot out the mouth of the alley into the Scar. Alive with neon and chaos, its roadways were a maze of tight corridors that funneled between crumbling concrete and flickering holoverts, advertising everything from counterfeit IDs to illegal bodymods.

She pushed the geriatric jetbike as hard as its rusted engine could handle, cutting through the flow of vehicles and pedestrians like a knife. The delivery trunk hitched on the back of her seat rattled against the frame, threatening to shake apart with every air bump or hard tilt as she did her best to weave around the worst of the craters in the poorly maintained road.

"You have an exit strategy?"

"Not exactly." The traffic lights changed to red, and not wanting to get caught in the congestion at a stoplight, giving Vesper an opportunity to close in, Nimah followed the green and veered hard right, turning into the next intersection. "Figure I'll run her in circles in the Scar then hitch a ride on a transport vessel from Suldamn. Will send a wave to you once clear." Preparing to change lanes, Nimah adjusted her side mirror then swore under her breath.

"What? What's wrong?"

"She's *still* on me." Nimah glanced over her shoulder as Vesper leapt from the side of a transport car and onto the flat back of an eighteen-hoverwheel rig. "She's fast, Maverick. She's making me look like an amateur."

Blaserfire lit up the path in front of Nimah like the pop of violent fireworks, shattering vendor crates stacked on the side-lanes and sending pedestrians to scatter. A couple of panicked vendor carts collided, and a crate careened into the road. It clipped Nimah on the backend, forcing her to swerve hard, and sent the jetbike into a dizzying fishtail.

Nimah threw her weight against the force of momentum, alternating between brake and gas until she regained control in time to swerve clear of another rain of blasts that would've taken out her front tire, sending her into a nosedive through a chain-link fence.

"Nimah—are you okay? Talk to me."

"I'm okay." Nimah swallowed the acrid taste of terror. Her arms rigid and palms damp as she raced around pedestrians and posts. "She almost got me there, Mav . . . I don't think I'm going to make it."

"Yes, you will. I've sent coords to your wristdeck—head for Marlo, in the loading quays. I'll take care of the rest."

"But . . ." Nimah frowned as the coords auto-synced with the map on the jetbike's nav screen, adjusting her path for a half a mile from her position. "How are you going to help me? The *Stormchaser*'s out of range."

"I took the secondary shuttle and have been on standby in Corlys since you left. I'll be to you in less than ten, Cadet."

Nimah struggled to find her voice around the sudden weight of emotion in her chest. "You came for me?"

"Always."

Nimah dove into a narrow split between megaholds as her side mirror exploded in a rain of sparks and glass, and she followed the lumpy path lit by the burnt orange yolk of a simulated sun perched on the horizon, leading her to Marlo.

Breaking through the gate, she glimpsed the loading quay through the haze of exhaust and neon lights.

"I see you, Cadet." Maverick flashed the lights on the prow of the shuttle, signaling her attention as she blazed down the lane. *"Swing left. Quay 2342."*

Nimah swung a glance over her shoulder and cursed as a land vehicle roared behind her. Vesper was hot on her in a stolen cab. If Maverick stopped to dock the shuttle, she'd close in on them in no time.

Nimah needed a plan. A *reckless* one.

"Mav, wait. You see that loading ramp? The unfinished one at the far end?"

"Nimah," Maverick's voice flattened with uncertainty. *"Are you thinking of doing what I think you're doing?"*

"Unfortunately." Teeth set in a hard grimace, Nimah cranked the throttle, revving the jetbike. "Get in close and drop the hatch."

The silence over the comms stretched, and she could almost imagine the look on his face when he grumbled, *". . . Shit."*

The thrusters on the shuttle sparked, and she watched as he sped ahead of her toward the end of the upcoming ramp. Good man. Nimah swerved on her jetbike, evading the front bumper of Vesper's cab as it swung for her back tire, then throttled hard and launched for the ramp. Workers flailed arms, hailing her to stop, then flung themselves cursing from her path as she tore through the safety lines.

And shot straight off the end—sending her and the jetbike flying into empty air. Nimah's heart seized, and the weight of the bike fell away from between her thighs. Kicking off the seat, she spun in the air, blaser hot, firing every shot she had—emptying her clip into Vesper's engine. Smoke burst from under the hood and Vesper yanked hard on the wheel, slamming the cab into the sidewall.

She had a moment, a single glorious second to think *fuck yes* before gravity snatched her waist and that moment of triumph was immediately replaced with *fuck no!*

Falling, Nimah kicked at open air.

Clawed a naked sky.

Then the hatch of the speeding shuttle yawned underneath her like an open mouth, scooping her into the belly of the airlock. She landed with a hard thud and the hatch snapped shut just in time as a barrage of blaserfire pelted along the hull.

"*Fuck, Cadet, please don't ever do that to me again.*"

"Don't worry." Nimah rolled flat onto her back as the shuttle tore off from the quay, thrusters screaming as they broke for atmo. "I won't."

CHAPTER THIRTEEN

It took a lot for Vesper to be impressed.

Somehow, not only had Nimah managed to evade her on a rusted jetbike—ribboning through the Scar with impressive skill for someone with an abysmal Academy flight score—she'd shot herself off the end of an unfinished loading ramp, into open voiddamn air, like she had wings.

The girl was fucking insane. And Vesper admired her for it.

Sure, it was annoying when a mark escaped, but the setback was minor. Nimah could run, but Vesper had nicked her quarry, and the scent of her blood was thick in the air. All she had to do was follow it.

Vesper returned to the *Platinum Flamingo*, and spent the next several hours combing the motel room Nimah had holed away in for clues, as well as tapping the surrounding security drones to download any archival footage. Some might call it a wasted effort, but often it was the smallest details that yielded the most promising fruit.

Tossing her ID tag to the dock worker seated in a control booth, Vesper waited for him to authenticate her clearance, and the gate swung open. Her baby sat anchored and waiting. A customized Interceptor-class single-chair fighter she'd named *Wraith Runner*.

She was thirty meters from prow to stern with a matte-black hull laced with camo-mesh panels to deflect light as well as radial scan signals. To the naked eye, when in flight, she appeared more like a shadow than a ship. Powered by twin ramjet plasma thrusters backed with a vector-thrust maneuver drive, she could handle short hyperjumps without sacrificing agility. Twisting through zero-G like a sharpened knife where most other vessels would fracture when trying to pivot against such force.

Vesper had poured all she had into its design and build, every inch optimized for stealth, speed, and efficiency. The *Wraith* was as cold, dark, and ruthless as her heart, and there was nowhere in the void she felt more at home then at its yoke.

Saint panted at her side as she entered the side airlock and took the meter-wide main corridor that ran along the spine of the ship, plated in carbide-graphene, recessed floor lighting cast pale blue shadows across its matte walls. She deposited her gear in one of the storage compartments adjacent the snare. A compact single-person lockup for the rare occasions she transported a live mark.

In four years, she'd only used it twice. Nimah would make for a third. Potentially.

Veering for the cockpit, bright track lights snapped on as the door folded into the seam of the wall. This was the largest room aboard the fighter and where she spent most of her time. Complete with an adjoined kitchenette, where Saint made a beeline to plant her rump alongside her gleaming, empty bowl.

Vesper smirked. "Got it. Chow time." Opening the cabinet-sized fridge, she drew out a pre-portioned pack of raw-feed. "What's on the menu today?" She smiled over at Saint. "Minced lamb, raw duck egg—powdered shell and membrane included—two rabbit ears with skin and fur, a goose neck, beef liver, pumpkin purée, and whole blueberries. Yum!" Vesper sliced open the vacuum-sealed pack with her personal knife, sheathed at her boot, and emptied the contents into the bowl.

Saint was a hybrid Lycaon descended from wild Earth-Prior hunting dogs. She'd found the pup about a month after she left home—a feral little thing hiding behind a factory dumpster, all skin and bones and missing her two front legs. A birth defect that likely led to her disposal, despite being a rare breed from what must've been a carefully arranged litter.

Vesper fed Saint only raw foods, when possible, balanced with supplements to meet all nutritional requirements to keep her healthy and strong. After her rough start in life, Saint deserved only the best. She was more than a dog—she was Vesper's. And Vesper took care of what was hers.

She deposited the bowl on Saint's feeding tray. Saint sat still, patiently awaiting her release command, as tendrils of drool slipped from her jowls, her eager coal-black eyes unblinking. She'd sit there for hours. Even days. And no matter how starved, she wouldn't dare lift a paw forward without permission.

"That's my girl." Vesper nodded to her bowl. "Feed."

Saint moved faster than a blink and stuffed her face into her bowl, devouring her meal with swift, impressive gulps. It was a wonder she didn't choke.

While Saint feasted, Vesper opened a top cabinet and fished out a sealed packet of freeze-dried steak and eggs leftover from her last supply run. Rehydrated with boiled water, she gave it a careful mix with a metal spoon to ensure it was evenly coated before she forked out a chunk of bland meat most would grapple with swallowing.

Food was fuel, and so long as she got in her protein and necessary fats, Vesper couldn't care less what went into her body. Scooping out a bite of rubbery eggs, she felt the comms on her wristdeck pulse and Vesper gave the dial a swipe with her thumb to read the scrolling notification.

Incoming: *Urgent wave from Chairwoman Aramir.*
Connect to holocomms for live projection.
Five minutes.

Vesper sighed deeply. She'd expected a wave from the chairwoman in perhaps a day or two, but for it to come through quite this soon meant only one thing. She knew Nimah had been on Corlys. And that she'd got away.

"Kennel up when you're done," Vesper ordered as Saint's large gray tongue licked her bowl clean.

Settling into the flight chair, Vesper put on a visor, and after tagging in the provided meeting ID codes, braced for the disorienting rush of connecting to the comms' bridge, where she would be projecting as a holo into a meeting room.

It started like a pinpoint of light on the horizon before that little dot split across and expanded until her world went from black to the bright warmth of a sunny day.

Huh. So not a meeting room, then.

Annelise sat inside what appeared to be a sitting room with fourteen-foot ceilings, walls laden with centuries-old artwork, some of which Vesper recognized from history books about the greats of Earth-Prior. Vintage pieces that had been meticulously preserved in the thousand years it took for humanity to resettle, and worth an incalculable fortune.

It was a collection to rival that of her uncle Cormack, and Vesper wondered if some of these pieces had not been acquired by the chairwoman following his fall from grace.

"Vesper." Annelise sat on a curved sectional of exquisite emerald velvet trimmed in gold, almost like a jewel wrapped in a bezel setting. "I'm so pleased you could make it."

In lieu of her formal SIGA suits, the chairwoman was dressed in loose-fitting slacks made of ivory cotton and a butter-yellow sleeveless blouse. Her precise chin-length bob had been swept up in a loose chignon so that wisps of blond framed her oval face and revealed the long smooth column of her throat.

"Don't think I've ever seen you without glasses. Or a suit."

Annelise smiled. "Between us, I don't need them. Part of being a public figure—optics. It was determined that my numbers fared better when I wore them. Instills the impression of intellect and authority, while also making me appear nonthreatening."

Her deep blue eyes twinkled with the mystery of a woman sharing intimate secrets that some might view as an effort to connect or establish trust, but Vesper saw through to the heart of her intentions.

It was a power move.

She was saying through actions instead of words that if everything was a carefully crafted illusion, Vesper couldn't trust her eyes to form any opinions. Only her instincts. She'd have to question everything. Even the softness of Annelise's outfit, which made her appear older than her fifty-five years, was a careful part of her mind game. A declaration that even in such relaxed conditions, Annelise was capable of extreme danger.

The knowing gleam in her eyes deepened, as if reading Vesper's very thoughts. Annelise raised a teacup to her lips and, taking a small sip, nodded approvingly. "My home is what I would call my sacred space.

Few have set eyes on it, let alone have received an invitation to stand where you are right now."

"Well, I'm not really here, am I." Vesper raised a hand, sheer and washed-out gray—holos were shit for rendering color or holding saturation. She swept it toward a lamp with a pearlstone base and passed right through, her entire figure stuttering as it struggled to hold together from the disruption of holo meeting solid matter.

Annelise's lips twisted with a hint of a rueful smile. "True enough. Come with me." She led Vesper out of the sitting room and across an outdoor terrace to a greenhouse.

Inside, a lush paradise of plants, from flowers to bushes and trees. An impossible landscape of greenery from hundreds of different worlds, seamlessly integrated into a thriving ecosystem.

"Aren't they beautiful?" Annelise asked as they walked down a stone-paved center walkway. The entire greenhouse must've been three miles long, at least, and required a full-scale team to manage its upkeep. "Everything you see in here I planted with my own hands and took twenty-six years to curate. This garden reflects a lifetime of acquisition. There are over fourteen thousand different species from nine hundred worlds. Most were sent to me as seedlings or saplings, but others I carefully grew myself. Like this one." She stopped before a collection of flowers Vesper recognized. A beautiful but shockingly dangerous bloom that, if handled incorrectly, would lead to a horrendously slow death.

"Pharaoh's Curse."

Annelise peered at her with a bemused grin. "My, my, my. You are well versed in botany, it seems. I am impressed." Opening a chest perched near the blooming flowers, Annelise settled to her knees and withdrew a pair of gloves that covered her from elbow to wrist, and a gardening hat complete with a protective veil.

"I thought all plants such as these were destroyed by SIGA mandate?"

"They were," Annelise agreed. "But a few seeds were stored in our repository. I now own what I am sure is the last of its kind." She adoringly stroked the vibrant green petals with a gloved hand, each leaf tipped with a claw-shaped thorn. "She will bloom only twice in her lifetime. Count yourself blessed, Vesper, few have ever seen her in her full glory."

Fine white hairs covered the stalk, appearing soft and fuzzy as down on a baby duck, but if touched by a bare hand, you'd find they were in fact barbed. Once they met skin, they immediately embedded into the dermis and burrowed in like worms seeking earth, rapidly dissolving once they entered the bloodstream, releasing a potent neurotoxic.

The pain, it was said, was immediate and profound. Every nerve in the body attacked by the toxin that could not be abated by any opiate or sedative. Unconscious or awake, the victim experienced a constant agony so absolute it drove them to the point of searing madness. Most took their own lives within a matter of hours. Those who didn't were overtaken by a fever that resulted in an internal hemorrhage, liquefying the organs and scrambling the brain. It ravaged the body slowly until internal fluid and organs oozed from every orifice, like the ritual of mummification worked on the ancients of Earth-Prior, leaving behind a dried husk preserved in perpetual agony.

Not even the leaves or the petals were safe. A sniff of the pollen would yield blindness. Dried and crushed petals could be brewed into a lethal tea that smelled of burnt oranges and almonds. In all cases, no matter the point of contact, death was guaranteed within forty-eight hours. Only someone truly confident in their knowledge of botany would dare house such a specimen, and Vesper doubted most would even want to, knowing of its risks.

Another declaration.

Chairwoman Annelise was either incredibly arrogant, or far more dangerous than most would perceive her to be. A silent threat to Vesper not to underestimate her as an adversary.

"If your summons is about Corlys—" Vesper began. "Marks can be slippery. The will to keep their heads tends to be a strong incentive for anyone to evade capture. But she won't evade me for long."

"Do not worry, I am not surprised she managed to get away. She is, after all, Academy trained, and despite her humble origins, Nimah's file indicates that she is nothing if not resourceful." Raising a pair of shears, Annelise snipped off a shriveled brown leaf from the stalk and crumbled it into a glass vial she removed from her pocket, sealing it with a press of a cap that welded shut on contact. "Have you any thoughts or insights as to where she's headed?"

"Yes."

Annelise held the vial to eye level and gave the contents a little shake. The brown flakes of the leaf swirling within tinted the clear liquid to a rich toffee hue. "Care to share them?"

"No."

The line of her jaw flickered with the barest indication of irritation. "While I appreciate you have your methods, I think it's time we implement some modifications."

"She won't get far." Vesper crossed her arms. "That's all you need to know or concern yourself with."

The whir of an approaching housebot grew louder as it swiveled down a side path, obscured by dense foliage, then stopped when its sensors detected Chairwoman Annelise, glowering like she wanted to strike Vesper, and probably would have if she were flesh instead of a holo.

"Pardon the intrusion," the bot's metallic voice intoned, a single blue light blinking in the orb of its central body. "Senator Dameris and her wards have arrived."

And just like that, the storm of Annelise's fury gave way to vivid sunshine. "Ah, right on time." Her knees popped as she stood, hands dusting dirt from the ivory cotton—impossibly stained now, not that Vesper expected she cared. The chairwoman would likely toss those in the bin and buy more without a single thought.

"What is she doing here?" Vesper demanded, her voice low and glacial.

"Your mother?" Annelise asked sweetly, weaving down the walkway to a side path that ended at a clear sheet of glass overlooking the meticulously groomed garden by the terrace.

Resplendent in a dress suit of soft gray, Senator Dameris stood watching with a tender expression as Chance and Yasmin raced through the bright green grass. Sorrow and love punched Vesper in the heart, and tears she couldn't quite hold in sprang to her eyes at the sight of them, so grown and so close after all these years.

"They can't see us." Annelise's cheerful voice broke the tender moment like a shoe stomping on a budding flower. "The windows are veiled from the outside. Stops the birds and other animals from seeking to enter."

"Why are they here?"

"Dameris and I have important matters of state."

"I meant the kids."

"Oh, come now, it's just a few cakes. And tea." Annelise twisted the vial of the decayed leaf she'd collected. Another not-so-veiled threat.

Vesper turned toward the chairwoman, incandescently aware that as a holo she was utterly helpless to do anything to protect Chance and Yasmin. Or her mother. Annelise could kill all three of them and there wouldn't be anything she could do to intervene.

She'd brought Vesper here to remind her that she was small. Helpless. And on the hook.

I see you, Vesper let her gaze say, *now see me*. She closed in until there was barely a breath between them. Until the blue of Annelise's eyes grew as large as a world. Until she was nearly swallowed whole in the spheres of her pupils that tensed like the muscles of Vesper's shoulders, arching down into her palms where her fingers curled into fists.

"There isn't a mark I haven't caught. I'll finish the job and get you Nimah Dabo-124. But if you harm either my niece or my nephew before I do—death by Pharaoh's Curse will be a blessing in comparison to what I'll do to you."

The world shuddered and the holo seized before fading into a pixelated blur, sealing Annelise behind a firewall as a warning blared loudly in three sharp blasts, followed by a clipped pre-recorded official voice that flashed before Vesper in subtitles:

<*Vesper Crole, you are hereby cited and fined one hundred and fifteen thousand credits for threatening harm to a representative of the SIGA body. Should you wish to challenge this citation, you are welcome to request a hearing, and court-appointed representation, if you are unable to afford such. How do you wish to plead?*>

"Strike that citation from record, on my authority," Annelise commanded, and the holo shuddered again as the system recalibrated to respond.

<*Please present official credentials to approve this request.*>

Removing a signet from around her neck, Annelise raised it to the flashing icon and stamped the air, and the icon changed from red to green.

<*Citation has been stricken. Your holo will now proceed without interruption. Thank you. By the hands of many we are united in trust!*>

The holo cleared, and Annelise returned her signet around her neck, tucking it beneath the neckline of her blouse. "Careful, Vesper. I can only strike one of those in a day."

Vesper raised her chin with a cutting smile. "Then don't make me repeat myself."

Annelise's expression was equal parts annoyed and impressed. "I'm glad we understand each other."

An alert notification from the *Wraith's* navsystem flickered into view, drawing footage from her ship of two figures waiting outside her airlock entry and requesting access to board. Their drawn hoods made identification impossible, but the alert flagged their weapons—primeswords. Weapons available only to cybers.

Annelise's knowing grin indicated she was aware of but also responsible for the unannounced visitors.

"Don't worry, they're not there to harm you." She clasped her gloved hands together. "Your recent encounter with Nimah made me realize you're woefully under-resourced, so I've enlisted two decommissioned cybers to serve under you for the completion of this contract."

"Decommissioned?"

"No longer fit for active duty. Once they're finished assisting you, they'll be terminated and harvested for any viable genetic material to be recycled for organ resynthesis for future cybers."

"You speak of them as if they're not human."

"They're not. And it's best you do the same," Annelise said with a coldness that even Vesper found biting, and tapped the display on her wristdeck.

The holo disconnected, slamming Vesper back into the flight chair of her ship. Removing her visor, she took a deep breath, allowing her senses to reacclimate before she crossed to the airlock and released the hatch.

Cybers. Fucking great. Clones derived from human genetic sequencing, they operated more like machines than people. At first glance, the added support made sense. Nimah was crewed up with seasoned pirates. Legends. Going after them solo was foolish now that she'd lost the element of surprise. But there was a reason why she preferred to work alone. You didn't have to guard your back or worry about loyalties being swayed. And while cybers weren't corruptible—they answered only to

SIGA—with Annelise in control of puppeteering their strings, she'd have to be especially cautious and assume that their presence was to serve a dual purpose.

Bring in Nimah . . . and tie up any loose ends once the job was complete.

Saint padded a few steps forward, ears pricked and on alert.

"Eyes on me, Saint," Vesper ordered as she disengaged the door locks. "Hold for three." Meaning if Vesper raised three fingers on her left hand, then Saint would go for the closest target with lethal force.

Steam billowed from the door pistons, and she cleared the way as the cybers entered, unmasked and unsuited. One male and one female, both had brown eyes and hair. White, if she had to guess ethnicity, and close enough in features to be related. Not an unlikely possibility, but she knew little to nothing about the cybers program. It was one of SIGA's most protected and safeguarded assets, and a frequent source of contention between religious purists and new-age reformers.

She'd never seen a cyber unmasked before. No one had. And children loved to whisper over ghost stories of the garish cybertronic warriors who were more metal than human, speculating all kinds of horrific modifications hidden behind their liquid-metal masks. But these were just a couple of kids. Eighteen, maybe twenty at most, and without a mark visible on either of them. Surely too young to be decommissioned like a pair of recycled trash cubes.

"Vesper Crole," they said in unison. "We are here to serve, as mandated by order—"

"Spare me the drill," Vesper interrupted. "I'm guessing you don't have transpo?"

Both cybers looked to each other, then shook their heads no. The way they moved in silent synchronization was fucking creepy. Almost like they shared a damn brain.

"Well, this is gonna be fun," Vesper grunted.

Her bunk was in the tail of the *Wraith*, a compressed sleeping unit with just enough space for a narrow closet set into the flooring, and a toilet that recessed into the wall when not in use. Aside from that, the only other space was the snare locker. It wouldn't be comfortable, but it would do as a makeshift cabin.

"Guess we'll have to rotate sleep schedules . . ." she said more to herself, then frowned. "Do cybers even sleep?"

"Four hours, when in the field," the girl answered.

"Or less," the boy continued. "Depending on circumstances."

"Hm." Vesper nodded. "Alright. What do I call you?"

"I am S4A5H0," she answered.

"8R3N0N."

"Fuck me, that's impossible. We're going to have to change that." Hands on her hips, Vesper dragged her teeth across her bottom lip. "Sasha." She pointed to the one she presumed was female. "And you"—she pointed to the boy—"Brenon."

They looked to each other then back to Vesper. "If you command, we obey."

Vesper sighed. "Fucking cybers."

CHAPTER FOURTEEN

Nimah barely had time to catch her breath before she strode onto the bridge of the *Stormchaser* behind Maverick, the air thick with a ring of tension as though they'd arrived mid-argument.

"How are we looking?" Ro demanded.

"Clear waters, from what I can see." Gertrude leaned over the nav console, the dim glow of holodisplays painting sharp angles across her face. "Bumped our radial scans to max, and all vessels in vicinity have clear tags with preset coords and permits. If anyone's after us, they've either got some razor tech or are holding back to avoid our sensors."

Ro settled into the captain's chair, arms crossed. "I think it's time we had a debrief. Who the hell was chasing you?"

"Bounty hunter. Vesper Crole." Nimah planted her hands on her hips. "I don't know much about her—yet—aside from she's Shinoda's niece."

Ro blinked, stunned. "Who hired her?"

"Who else?" Maverick rolled his chair to the base of the pilot's console. "Clearly it's about retribution for taking down Cormack."

"No, I don't think her motive is familial vendetta." Nimah peered out from the viewport as stars streaked in liquid drops of light, the shimmer of negs rippling in between them and the void like wind breaking across the surface of a still pond. "When she had us pinned, Vesper said something about credits. *More than Liselle's father could hope to ever earn in three hundred lifetimes* . . . but that can't be right, can it?" Nimah turned back to her crew. "SIGA could never set a bounty that high."

Ro dragged her thumb across her bottom lip. "The Shinoda estate. SIGA would've absorbed his assets, which means his family was stripped of inheriting considerable wealth."

"So they're leveraging that pot to hunt me down." Nimah cursed under her breath, frustration skipping across every notch of her spine. "It's always something."

"Puts a hell of a target on us." Chu rocked on her heels, her bifocals catching the blue glint of overhead status lights as she scanned the bridge, taking stock of the worry exchanged between the rest of the crew. "We prepared for this kind of heat?"

"Don't have much choice now, darling." Gertrude snorted. "Best we can do is keep running." She paused, rolling her shoulders. "Maybe we need to rethink this mission, Sparrow. Captain might've been right about breaking for Faldor and laying low."

Nimah had braced herself for this on the shuttle ride back to the *Stormchaser*, knowing someone—mainly her grandmother—would see the increased risk and convince the others to abandon the mission. But she hadn't expected for that voice of opposition to be Gertrude, the same person who'd stood in support of her a day ago. And something inside of her wilted in defeat.

"What about Zen?" Chu rasped. "Chuck her from the airlock and burn thrusters?"

Gertrude's eyes glimmered darkly. "I'm in favor of that plan."

"I'd like to see you try." Zensha sauntered onto the bridge, sweat beading her brown skin, with a towel draped around her powerful shoulders and her bionic fist flexing in challenge.

"Enough," Ro interrupted, rising from her seat. "Running is not an option anymore. We complete the job. After I take the throne, we have the protection of the council and every pirate at our back. SIGA will have no choice but to withdraw the contract on Nimah or risk igniting a civil war. And this time? It won't be a skirmish—it'll be the full force of every pirate crew in the Fringe." Her gaze flicked toward Nimah, softer now. "I didn't want to be queen, but if it means keeping you safe, so be it."

Emotion burned a little too bright, making it hard for Nimah to breathe. "Thank you."

Ro's expression once more took on the stoic conviction of a formidable captain leading her crew. "Where's Liselle? We need to go through those files. Find us a heading."

"Medbay." Boomer jerked a thumb over his shoulder.

"What?" Nimah stiffened in alarm. "Is she hurt? Why wasn't I told?"

"She's fine. Had to sedate her after all that excitement, s'all."

"Well, what of the files, then?" Ro sighed.

"I have them." Removing the chip from her trench, Nimah handed it to Mumbles. "Can you get started with the download?"

Humming gently to herself in a corner, Mumbles lifted her hands in a rapid flurry of half-sensible, half-chaotic gestures ending with what looked suspiciously like bunny ears.

"She's saying yes," Boomer translated, "but it's got 'ncryption. She'll need a place with better gear."

Nimah muttered another curse. Of course it was encrypted. Her father was SIGA's chief legal officer, no way would he leave his data wide open, even on his home network. And if they couldn't crack it, this entire effort had been nothing but a monumental waste of time.

"Makes sense that we'd need SIGA-level tech if we're going to break through SIGA-level encryption," Ro agreed. "The *Stormchaser* isn't provisioned for that."

Nimah tapped her fingers against the console, thinking fast on how to navigate the problem. Then it struck her like a zap from a live wire. "Jono's lab is." She'd only seen it briefly when they'd stopped by the RIM three months ago, but from what she recalled, even though he was housed in a rundown shack, Jono had installed some of the best tech money could buy. Nimah turned to Gertrude. "How long for us to get to Port Fibris from here?"

"If we want to shake Vesper?" Gertrude cracked her knuckles. "Six hours."

Nimah scrubbed a hand through her curls. "That's too long." Cracking the chip, making sense of the contents—all was going to require valuable time, and that was best-case scenario that Liselle had extracted something of value. They couldn't afford to piss away seconds, let alone minutes, and the wait in Corlys had cost them more than they had to bargain with. "What can we do to shave off time?"

Gertrude pulled up her navsystem's holodisplay, washing sharp blue light across her face. "We can run it in two if we jump from the nearest Socket, but that'll put us in heavily monitored thoroughfares. And I won't be able to scrub the trail." She exhaled, stretching the tension from her fingers before continuing. "Vesper'll know where we're headed, Sparrow."

"Can we divert her with decoys?" Nimah asked.

"We deployed all we had getting Ro," Chu grunted. "They ain't exactly easy to come by."

Nimah chewed the inside of her cheek, weighing a bad option against a worse one: They could either take the long way, shake Vesper but lose valuable time, or cut through regulated voidspace and risk another encounter with SIGA. Under ideal circumstances, Nimah would've preferred to err on the side of caution, but every minute spent stalling was another minute those children were lost in the void.

Priorities had to come first. Risks, second.

"I don't see any way around it," Nimah said, jaw tight with resolve. "Set the coords for the RIM—fastest route possible. If we're lucky, Vesper will assume we're stopping to resupply and hold off until we're somewhere more isolated to cross us. We can shake her off then."

Gertrude didn't look convinced, but she went to work, adjusting their trajectory with brisk efficiency. "And if we get flagged for onboarding? This vessel screams pirate, Sparrow. No way we're passing by without inspection."

"I know." The *Stormchaser* wasn't a gleaming warship or a sleek luxury cruiser—she was a battle-worn beast with atmo-scorched panels and welding-patch scars from old skirmishes. Trouble was written into every inch of her hull. Even if the dummy sleeve passed clearance, the second they pulled up into the queue, she'd be flagged by the Socket control team. "We're gonna need a scrubdown."

"I can do it in an hour." Chu raised her hand. "Twenty minutes, if I get an extra set of hands."

"Been a while, but I still know my way around a good scrub," Zensha offered, holding the ends of the towel looped around her neck. "Might as well start earning my keep."

"Get on it then." Nimah turned on her heel, determination settling into the stiff lines of her posture. "I'm going to check on Liselle. And learn about our enemy."

* * *

The *Stormchaser*'s medbay was built for necessity rather than comfort. Compact in size, the walls lined with mostly empty storage units, and dim overhead track lights that flickered in a weak sputtering were a reminder that the ship was as aged as its crew.

Liselle lay curled on the examining table, a foam mattress atop a rusted gurney welded to the metal grating of the floor. The rise and fall of her chest was steady, but every now and then her fingers twitched against the foil sheet, restless even in unconsciousness.

Nimah stared down at her best friend—a girl who'd once been closer to her than family and now felt as distant as a rogue planet in an uncharted zone. She swallowed that thought and crossed to the medbay console, fingers gliding across the worn keypad, drawing up the interface for the Interstellar Repository Network.

The one great thing about sailing within the Inner Circle grid meant access to the IRN.

Typing in *Vesper Crole*, Nimah quickly drew up everything she could on the former socialite turned bounty hunter. Given her illustrious familial ties, the search hits were plenty.

She began with Vesper's years of training at the Academy, five years ahead of Nimah—which explained how they'd never crossed paths, and dropped out eight months shy of graduation, despite holding rank in the top two percent of her year. Nimah's brows quirked in surprise and confirmed through the final term grading records on the public-facing site, where all cadets, past and present were listed, Vesper was well on track to earn her badge. So if she hadn't been failing, what would have pushed her to abandon her education?

Ten minutes and three search links later, Nimah got her answer.
ASHLEEN SHINODA, FIRST-BORN DAUGHTER OF SENATOR DAMERIS SHINODA, AND MOTHER OF TWO, COMMITS SUICIDE AT FAMILY ESTATE.

The date stamp on the newscast aligned with when Vesper withdrew from training and fled the Inner Circle, within what appeared to be hours after her sister's funeral.

A sharp inhale from the examining table broke her focus and Nimah turned just as Liselle stirred, blinking against the dim lighting, her breath hitching on the edge of panic.

"Hey." Nimah rushed to her side, holding her shoulders down until Liselle calmed enough to regain focus. "Easy."

"Where am I?"

"You're on the *Stormchaser*. We're heading out to the RIM. Jono's got better equipment for Mumbles to crack through the SIGA encryption and decode the files you copied from your father's mainframe."

The fight died in Liselle and her shoulders went limp as tears welled in her eyes. "So it's real. It all really happened." She pressed closed fists to her face and openly wept.

"Lis . . ." Nimah whispered, not knowing what to do or say. "It's going to be okay. You're safe now."

The sniffles stopped. Liselle's shoulders tensed, and when her fists fell away, her gaze was sharp and wet with fury. "Safe?" The whites of her eyes simmered red. "My life is ruined, thanks to you. Do you understand that?"

Nimah stiffened as Liselle slid off the table, her silver dress a ruined mess of split seams and missing scales.

"I was finally settling into a rhythm again. My life had *purpose*. Even if it ached with emptiness from missing you—that hole inside me was filling." Liselle set a trembling fist to her chest. "My father . . . I'll never get to explain . . . and my mom . . ." Her voice cracked under the weight of emotion, choking back the devastation threatening to drag her under. "Do you have any idea what you've done to them? What you've done to me?"

"I didn't mean to." Nimah barely managed above a tearful whisper.

"You selfish *bitch*." Tears streaked Liselle's flushed cheeks, her anguish heightened by the residual meds, which stripped away her calm control and left her bare as a raw nerve. "It's over. I've lost everything. I can't go home. I can *never* go home."

Nimah stood frozen her chest tightening with the surge of sorrow and shame as Liselle dissolved into hysterical sobs, clutching her stomach in despair. "Liselle, please—"

Liselle reared back and swung, but her movements were uncoordinated from the lingering effects of the sedatives, otherwise she would have caught Nimah by the jaw, and sent her spinning.

"Come on." She swayed like a drunk trying to hold her ground, fists raised.

"I don't want to fight you."

"I don't care what *you* want!" Liselle lunged for Nimah again with sloppy punches and stunted jabs. "It's always about you! *Fuck! You!*"

Pinned in the corner between storage shelves, Nimah braced against the barrage of wild haymakers then caught Liselle's roundhouse kick. Trapping her leg against her side, Nimah swept Liselle's stabilizing leg out from under her—sending them both toppling back. They locked into a chaotic tangle of limbs and curses, colliding with the edge of the examining table before spiraling around to ricochet off the medicine cabinet.

Supplies rattled, a box of gauze tumbling to the floor, scattering like snowflakes in the chaos. Now Nimah understood why Boomer had sedated Liselle earlier. Consumed by shock and hysteria, her emotions were a volatile mix of rage and despair. There was no reasoning with her like this. But as enraged as Liselle was, she was burning out fast.

Straddled atop her, Nimah caught Liselle's wrists and pinned them down as she scanned the medbay for a solution when her gaze landed on the upended tray and there, amidst the scattered supplies—within arm's reach—was a sedation syringe.

"No!" Liselle panted, her voice hoarse and desperate as she bucked her hips. "Don't you fucking dare!"

"I'm sorry," Nimah whispered, her voice breaking. She grabbed the syringe, yanked off the cap with her teeth, and plunged the needle into the furious veins bulging on Liselle's neck. It took barely a second, and the remaining fight drained from Liselle's body with a whimper.

"Why couldn't you just stay away?" Her eyelids fluttered shut. "Wish you . . . away."

Nimah removed the empty syringe and tossed it onto the tray, then hauled Liselle's dead weight back onto the examining table. Hands trembling, she checked the pulse points against the delicate skin of Liselle's wrist then drew back her eyelids. The pinpricks of her pupils responded limply to the stark light, confirming she was deep under sedation.

"I'll make it right," she vowed, and tucked the foil blanket once more around Liselle, smoothing it over her bare shoulders with trembling hands. "Somehow, I'll make it right. I promise."

Liselle's only response was a soft, unconscious sigh.

"*Sorry* be empty words, kid."

Nimah turned sharply, her breath catching as Dobs flicked open her Zippo, the flame sparking to life with a sharp crack of flint.

Leaning back, Dobs exhaled a thick cloud of pale blue smoke with a smirk on her face that cut deeper than any blade. "But that's about all you're good for. Hot air."

"Shut up!" Nimah snarled through clenched teeth and fresh tears. "Why can't you just leave me alone?"

"Over my dead body." Dobs smiled over the blazing end of the cigarette perched between the edges of her teeth, her expression maddeningly calm. "Heard?"

Nimah lunged, a roar tearing from her throat as she swung at the air with bruised fists. The blow snapped Dobs's head to the side, but there was no shock of color blooming in her cheeks, no blood dripping from what should've been a split lip.

"Try again," Dobs taunted, her grin widening. "I'll pretend it hurt something awful."

Defeated, Nimah's fists fell limp at her sides as a sob rattled free from her throat. It was no use. She'd have more luck fighting her own shadow. "Fuck you," she whispered, as weakly as she felt. Then bolted from the medbay on legs that struggled to hold her weight against the perpetual grief and shame that clung to her like heavy chains made of lead.

The track lights embedded in the grated flooring ribboned with every heavy footfall, but no matter how fast Nimah ran, there was no escaping Dobs. She appeared at every corner, hovered at every turn, waiting with that same horrible smirk as she puffed on her cigarette like she had all the time in the world.

Because she did.

Dobs wasn't just haunting her. She was *inside* her—a ghostly echo dragging Nimah's worst thoughts and fears to the surface. Her failures. Her regrets. Adding kerosene to the fire burning within, pushing her closer to the edge.

Then came the sound. The strange, rhythmic thumping, loud as a heartbeat between her ears. Nimah swiveled on her heel, blinking a cold sweat from her eyes as it rattled through the cavern of the corridors, and the walls of the *Stormchaser* seemed to expand and retract like a ribcage in a breathing chest.

Thump-thump.

Thump-thump.

"Ma, what is that?"

<*Can you be more specific, Nimah, Second-in-Command?*>

"That sound." It echoed through her, and her own heart stumbled in the same rhythm. Mirroring it beat for beat. "Run diagnostics on the ship. Is there a problem with the gravity boosters? The recyclers? Is there a breach in the hull?"

Older ships like the *Stormchaser* were prone to sleepers—fine-line fractures too small to detect at first but that grew over time like cavities in a cracked tooth. Degrading slowly. Stealthily. Until one day, under the right pressure or strain, they snapped—gutting the ship without warning.

<*All systems are functioning at normal operational capacity. I detect no anomalies or concerns with our systems or structural integrity.*>

"But that sound." Nimah pressed her fists to her ears as it grew louder, more urgent, her own heart suddenly feeling too large for her body to hold. "What is that sound? Make it stop!" A wave of dizziness struck her, expanding to her chest, where her heart seized and shuddered. She gasped, pressing a hand above that frantic beat, panic clawing at her throat. "Come on, Nimah, you've got to calm down."

"You're looking pretty gray, kid." Hovering over her, Dobs tilted her head as she popped and snapped the cap repeatedly until it almost drowned out the ghostly thump flooding through the hull.

"Shut up." Nimah's heart gave another painful lurch, and she couldn't hold back the whimper that escaped her lips. Arms hugged to her chest, she struggled to slow the frantic rhythm of her heart, throbbing like a fresh wound. An erratic and impossible to follow beat that threatened to come to a violent stop without warning.

"I think you're about one foot in the grave."

"It's just an anxiety attack," Nimah whispered as the tips of her trembling fingers went numb, and tingling arced across her palms.

"Is it?" Dobs sank to Nimah's side, tapping the butt of her cigarette against her bottom lip as she drank in Nimah's panic. "Let's find out." She drew hard on the end of her cigarette, and it blazed a violent red before she punched a fist to Nimah's chest and—like a pencil through paper—muscle and bone went through muscle and bone.

Pressure. So much pressure. Nimah couldn't breathe against the sudden density and watched in horror as Dobs's arm sank *into* her down to the elbow.

"It's not real."

"Feels pretty real, don't it?"

It did. Dobs's hand writhed between the wings of her lungs to coil viciously around her heart, threatening to squeeze the organ. Crushing it completely.

"How are you doing this?" Nimah panted, all sweat and cold terror.

Dobs's grin widened, and the blue of her eyes switched to laser red in a blink, glowing as hot as a dying star as those fingers inside of Nimah tightened and her heart gave another wicked squeeze, wrenching a panicked cry from her.

In that moment, the metal grating rattled and the walls of the *Stormchaser* suddenly splintered apart, like panes of shattered glass in a collision. The shards spiraled into the glittering dark of the void, leaving her surrounded by nothing but stars and blackness. Her mind fragmented like the walls of the ship and she spun helpless in the endless chasm of a rapid barrage of too many images and sounds and textures and scents.

Voices clamored in the dark. Similar to the ones that first began calling to her the moment she touched elite. But rising above it all, the beating of a frantic heart that wasn't her own but felt connected to her all the same. With no time to make sense of the chaos, the arcing blast of electricity seared across nerves and bones and everything, then flashed away.

White walls. The sterile smell of surgical steel. Her wrists and ankles restrained. The gleaming smile of a woman she couldn't quite see—the rest of her swallowed up in the searing glow of a white-hot light.

"Brace yourself, my dear," that grinning, faceless voice said. *"Because you're going to scream. Very, very loudly."*

The light swiveled away, and the weight of death settled on Nimah's chest. It poured itself down her gasping throat—thick and hot and black as ink. Suffocating.

Nimah's eyes rolled back into her skull as she fought to focus. To breathe.

"Nimsy?"

Nimah recoiled, fists raised, ready to strike—but it was Mumbles's startled face that froze her seconds before her knuckles would've made impact. Panting, she scuttled away. Head swiveling as she took in her surroundings. Steel and wires and Mumbles. She was safe. She was alive.

"I'm sorry." Nimah trembled so fiercely it was difficult to stand. "I'm fine."

But she wasn't fine. She felt like she'd been sucked into the void and spat back into her bones all at once. Whatever had just happened to her wasn't like anything she'd ever experienced with elite. This had been so much sharper, and terrifying. Almost like experiencing two realities at once.

What is happening to me?

"Are we ready to jump through the Socket?" she asked, fighting to ground herself back in sanity. "Is that why you've come looking for me?" She met Mumbles's silent gaze and was shocked to see the tense scrutiny in her eyes. Staring at Nimah almost like she was a stranger. Or an enemy.

"Ship goody hop skip. Purple toes and wind bubbles, yes?" Mumbles said, her brows tightening another notch before she shuffled away.

Alone, Nimah slumped against the wall and breathed slow and deep, listening to the heavy clomp of Mumbles's retreating steps until the corridor fell silent. Empty. But in her chest, Nimah's heart still throbbed like a tender bruise, her lungs sore from the compression of anxiety that had taken such violent hold of her breath along with the fading pressure of Dobs's all-too-real fist.

Limping to her cabin, Nimah poured herself inside and sealed the door, locking it behind her.

The mind is a fragile thing, heard? The echo of Dobs's threat rang sharp as the point of a knife slicing tender skin. *Reckon it won't take long for yours to break.*

Whether real or a figment of her imagination, Nimah couldn't deny that her sanity was unraveling as fast as a popped seam. What if the next episode sent her walking out the hatch and into the snatching vacuum of the void, or if she made a lethal mistake that put everyone she loved and cared about in harm's way?

Slumped on her floor, Nimah pulled the vial of heliosmoke from her pocket and her fingers brushed across the peeling label. If she took the rest all at once it would keep her mind clear for a week, but the consequences... the risk...

"You really think that'll keep me out?" Dobs appeared in the corner of her bunk, grin wide.

"It was working pretty well so far."

She answered with a soft, smoky laugh. "How much longer you wanna go on like this, kid?"

"As long as it takes." Gripping the vial tightly, Nimah popped the top. Fuck the consequences. Five hundred and seven children were counting on her to get them home, and she'd be of no use if her mind was splintering apart like brittle bones beneath Dobs's bootheel.

No more questions. No more hesitations.

Nimah brought the vial to her lips and swallowed it all.

CHAPTER FIFTEEN

"Approaching the queue." Maverick guided the prow of the *Stormchaser* into the line of void traffic. A glittering trail of ship-lights that snaked in a slow-moving line toward the horizon, where a ring of carbide steel hung suspended in the glittering vastness of the void, large enough to encircle a whole planet. Tens of thousands of plasma portals—Eyes—studded the center and pulsed in concentric circles of radiant blue energy, each a calibrated gateway that regulated heavy void traffic across the Inner Circle like blood through arteries.

A single Socket managed the flow of a hundred million vessels an hour and required a diligent control team of one hundred thousand to manage it. Flight paths, destination sectors, and vessel IDs were submitted to the SCT and injected into their sequencing system so that, once verified, each ship would then receive its grid point—an exact spatial coordinate to align with their designated assigned Eye, along with a timestamp and queue code for entry.

"Socket control team scanning dummy sleeve for verification on fabricated crew identity tags," Gertrude confirmed, her neon green stiletto nails tapping a restless melody against her armrest. "Cross fingers and clench cheeks, theydies."

A tense hush fell across the bridge. Dummies had a thirty percent chance of failing inspection scans, which was why pirates avoided traveling through heavily regulated Inner Circle voidspace. Should theirs fail to clear, the SCT would lock the *Stormchaser* in an immobilization frequency, and tow them aside for onboarding by an inspection crew. Then they'd really be fucked. But the risk was worth the reward of covering significant ground and saving invaluable time.

Nimah's wristdeck pulsed, indicating her tag had been accessed for review. The face blinked red, and, scanning across the bridge, she saw it was the same for the rest of the crew.

"Clear!" Maverick called out, and a whoosh of relief circled the bridge. "Pulling up to our entry-grid. Stand by for threading in three minutes, forty-three seconds."

The *Stormchaser* shuddered as it eased into the canal, lights flickering in the tracks and the consoles rattling in their rivets.

"Here we go!" Gertrude braced one hand to the nav console.

Chu cackled.

Boomer whooped.

And Nimah sucked in a rallying breath before she was slammed back against her flight chair. You didn't fly through a Socket so much as you were yanked into it, and the *Stormchaser* quivered against the relentless force catapulting them through the stars. The bones of her skull compressed, the wall of her chest strained, and when the ship snapped to a sudden stop, Nimah wheezed against her harness.

Holy fuck.

Threading through an Eye might be rough on the body, but leaping through a Socket with an entire ship? That was exhilarating as hell.

"Yeah!" Boomer clapped his hands like a kid at the end of an amusement park ride.

His excitement was echoed in Nimah's laugh, and over the rise of his shoulder, Maverick cast her a knowing grin before he throttled the *Stormchaser* toward the RIM. Formed from a dense cluster of asteroids cinched together by gravity dampeners and magni-cables into a solid plateau, it hooked like a grin into the void.

Encased in an atmo-netting and ozone shield, pulsing waves of purple, blue, pink, and green shimmered in an aurora formed by flickering energy currents instead of natural light. The sky never darkened here, and those shifting hues drew Nimah back to her distant childhood with a fond smile.

What was meant to be a wasteland was later forged into a sanctuary by the people who'd been torn from their homes during the integration following the Zone Wars and forced to live where life should not have been at all possible.

RIMers were the discarded. The underestimated and forgotten. But those who'd never known the soft comforts of luxury were also spared its weakness, and where SIGA had expected RIMers to wither in the asteroid dust, suffocated by desolation and neglect, instead they had taken scraps of nothing and honed them into an impressive feat of survival.

Jono was already waiting for them at the end of the quay and waved like a giddy school kid greeting his parents after being dropped off by his chauffeur as Nimah stepped off the gangway, crew in tow.

"Welcome." He grinned, shielding his eyes from asteroid dust kicked by the final gust from the shutdown of the *Stormchaser*'s thrusters. "How was the flight?"

"Jono, although it's great to see you, this isn't a social call," Nimah said after she clasped him in a firm hug.

"Right. Your wave did say it was urgent. I have a rover parked nearby. I can take three of you. The rest of the crew will have to wait aboard the ship or nearby."

"Not a problem. It'll be just us." Nimah gestured to Mumbles and Boomer, standing idly at her side.

Jono swung his gaze over Boomer, all bulk and quiet menace, and then Mumbles, huddled close to the comfort of Boomer's shadow as she twisted a ratty pigtail around her finger. The three of them fell into step with Jono as he led the way down the quay, packed with dock workers and tradesmen pulling in with fresh cargo.

"Things are busy," Nimah commented as a cart rattled by laden with crates, nearly rolling over her foot in its haste.

"Like you wouldn't believe! Just wait until we reach my lab. I have so much to show you!" Jono activated the rover, and the track lights on the doors winked pale green before the doors whisked up like the spread of wings, allowing them all to crawl into the body of the vehicle.

Nimah and Jono claimed the front, leaving Boomer and Mumbles to wedge into the back.

Knees hugged to his chest, Boomer scowled at Nimah in the rearview mirror. "Really?"

"Sorry." Nimah gave him an impish wink as Jono steered them out of the lot.

Ghost-grass swayed as they rolled past, thick moon-white stalks that moved like foam-capped waves. One of the many genetic innovations created by the early fore-settlers, who'd cultivated a minor ecosystem of asteroid trees and resilient critters that had adapted to the harsh terrain. A testament to the kind of ingenuity bred from necessity rather than abundance, and perseverance rather than privilege.

Without its own source of fresh water or air, the RIM sustained itself with ruthlessly maintained recyclers and strict guidelines on consumption such that anyone who failed to honor them was vented for their hubris. But those who lived here knew the only thing to kill you quicker than hunger or thirst on the RIM was a seasonal frost so sharp it could flay flesh from bone if one made the mistake of failing to gear up properly.

And the RIM held no mercy for carelessness.

"Them sticks on the yonder," Boomer commented, punching his thick finger against the window. "Looks like the makings of a megahold."

"You've a keen eye," Jono answered, veering the rover onto the grid of a main roadway, which wasn't built so much as was carved like a river through the ramshackle landscape.

Gasping, Nimah swiveled around in the passenger seat to the half-formed skeleton etched across the horizon. "The RIM is building a *city?*"

"Crazy, right?" Bodies parted grudgingly with the firm blast of Jono's horn. "It'll take a year, maybe more, to complete. But despite delays with executing the RIM Accord, we've managed to open pathways for commerce and trade. The ambassadors committee has worked tirelessly alongside the UPN, who have brought in shipments of medicine and materials to enhance security and sanitation."

The rover plowed over rubbled wasteland with smooth ease thanks to its thick wheels and sturdy engine, and light fell away as a towering wall of trash rose above them like the sheer face of a mountain, swallowing that glowing promise of a better future from view.

"The hospital is also undergoing extensive renovation," Jono continued as they maneuvered through a reinforced tunnel carved through the wall, the interior studded with holospheres which, although expensive, were the only way to provide light in the tunnel without risk of setting the wall of trash ablaze.

"We're nearly finished with an expansion of a secondary wing which will increase inpatient capacity by one hundred and twenty-seven percent. New operating rooms, all equipped with state-of-the-art medical imaging equipment and integrated-synth diagnostics support. We even have recovery pods!" Shooting out the end of the tunnel, he beamed at Nimah, bright as an amplifier. "In less than three months, we'll go from being a threadbare medical facility to almost close enough to rival some of the more prominent planets of the Inner Circle!"

"I'm glad to see things are going so well."

"We've a long way to go, but it's a start, Nimah. A real start. For the first time in our history, we can bring positive change to lives of those who've been wronged for so long."

Nimah assessed him with a bemused shake of her head. It was shocking to believe that this bright-eyed youth was the son of Cormack Shinoda. Once the prodigal heir to an incredible fortune, yet he had thrown it all away—not only helping Nimah to expose his father as a genocidal maniac but also exonerate her grandmother after she'd been framed for his crimes.

"What's going on there?" Nimah asked, drawing her attention to a gathering of people chanting loudly and holding plyboard signs etched with heated slogans, their cries lost in the roar of the rover's engine.

"Protests opposing the accord led by folks who call themselves *Descendants of the Source*." Jono's lips pressed into a tense line. "After centuries of mistreatment, many believe SIGA can't be trusted, and question why they should integrate with the Inner Circle or share resources with a government that nearly eradicated them."

"They ain't wrong," Boomer grunted, earning a nod from Jono.

"On top of that, we've had a surge of grifters flocking to the RIM, trying to extract elite themselves and make off with a fortune." Jono twisted the wheel, guiding them off the main roadway and onto a jaunty narrow path she recognized as the one that led toward the remote flat-lands where his lab was situated. "Thankfully, most can't tell elite from fossilized waste," he added with a dark chuckle.

"Hence the need for increased security," Nimah commented.

"Decidedly so. I've done what I can to help support efforts here, using what's left of the personal assets I'd safeguarded outside of my father's control. The UPN offered me the role of chief ambassador because of it, but I turned them down."

"Why didn't you take it?" Nimah asked, genuinely confused at the thought of him refusing not only a high honor but a chance to be a part of making integral decisions to the betterment of the RIM, of which he appeared so deeply invested.

"Because I'm just the privileged son of some asshole," he said with a bitter smile. "Decision-making authority is a power that deserves to reside in the hands of those who were forced to live out here, discarded and neglected, for three generations. Instead, I offer counsel and expert opinion when requested, otherwise, I keep to myself and to my research which, for now, the ambassadors have graciously allowed me to continue. Provided I honor the conditions of *data sovereignty*. My findings go to the ambassadors first and are to be treated as the RIM's intellectual property."

"Speaking of findings—were you able to review the materials I sent along with the wave?"

"I have." Jono nodded.

"Do you think there's a connection between these missing children and SIGA? Particularly as it pertains to the RIM Accord?"

"I don't see how." Jono brought the rover to a stop and threw the brake lever. "But life out here has taught me to never underestimate what SIGA can or will do for progress."

Slipping from the rover door, Nimah landed on her feet outside Jono's lab. "Wow. You *have* been busy."

What had once been little more than a shack with a slanted tin rooftop was now a two-story structure built from slabs of concrete made from the dark-gray sediment of the asteroids, and tinted panes of pressurized glass strong enough to withstand the volatile solar winds that often plagued the RIM during energy re-allocation.

"Helps that I'm not hiding anymore." Jono set his hands on his hips, chest puffed proudly. "Also, the RIM ambassadors are eager to support my studies into elite," he said with a sheepish grin and a gleam of excitement he could barely contain. "We're on the precipice of history. Can't say I blame them for wanting to be at the forefront of it."

Offering his hand, Jono helped Mumbles as she struggled on short legs and locked hips, followed by Boomer, who couldn't wait to crack his back and stretch his long limbs.

Inside, his lab was even more impressive than its exterior. Almost as much a home as it was a workspace, the rooms flowed through a moderately furnished living room, complete with a full kitchen and floating two-person bunk. The second half was dedicated to the lab and adjoining medbay, fused with what appeared to be a sealed greenhouse.

"Samples I've collected across this ridge," Jono explained, joining Nimah by the wall of plastic, misted by the spouts feeding the plants housed inside.

"These were *growing* in the flatlands?"

Jono's grin shot wide. "If that popped the top of your skull, I have something even more exciting to show you." Drawing back across to his workstation, Jono activated the semi-circular console. The worn surface blinked to life under his touch. "Alright," he said as Mumbles shuffled to his side, her lopsided pigtails swaying as she clutched her satchel stuffed with snacks and her favorite puzzle toys. "So, to access the mainframe, you have to go—"

Brushing him aside, Mumbles flopped into the ergonomic console chair. Dragging her headphones over her ears, large soft cups and a cushioned headband, her fingers danced over the interface with the remarkable grace and skill of a concert pianist. Code snapped onto large curved holoscreens, whizzing through system protocols faster than Nimah's eyes could follow.

"Well, you really weren't kidding." Jono looked to Nimah with a bemused smirk and cocked his head. "Shall we?"

"Yes." Nimah halted by the console. "How much time do you need?"

Mumbles barely spared her a glance, her expression sharp with something that wasn't quite contempt, but close enough to sting. Nimah tried not to let the hurt sour in her stomach at the way Mumbles, who had never been anything but warm and affectionate, seemed to shy away from her with a wariness that was almost painful to watch unfold.

"She says give her an hour and a half," Boomer translated, without breaking stride, as Mumbles forked her fingers beneath her chin then brushed them in three strokes under her left ear. His voice carried the quiet fondness of a proud teacher watching a student find their footing after weeks of stumbles and falls.

"Alright then." She hesitated on the threshold. "You coming, Booms?"

"To what, look at rocks?" Settled into a corner of the deep and plush sectional, Boomer tore open a bag of ham and cheese flavored chips in his lap, eyes glued to Mumbles and the blur of the holoscreens. "Watching her work is fucking art. Go have fun playing in dirt."

Leaving them to it, Nimah followed Jono out of the lab. Their boots crunched over brittle terrain as they crossed through the field of rubble and over the ridge where the wind howled between the jagged boughs of an asteroid tree, ruffling Nimah's loose curls and twists like unseen fingers.

The crude X, once a solemn grave marker, now lay several feet away from a gaping wound in the ground that was covered with a weighted tarp. Alongside it sat a couple of generators, a stand with floodlights, and a digger.

"You exhumed them?"

"With the utmost respect, I assure you," Jono replied, his posture rigid, as if bracing for judgment. "Would you like to see them?"

Nimah swallowed hard. "Please."

Stepping down a worn path into the ten-foot-wide crater, Jono peeled away the tarp, and the pressure in Nimah's chest expanded like the moment before a supernova.

What was left of her mother and grandfather lay within a few feet of each other, their remains almost entirely calcified in stone—like the sparrow her grandmother had carved for her that now powered the ship. Shimmering tendrils webbed from the petrified remains like roots at the base of a tree, fine as spider silk. Soft wisps of gleaming silver that fed into the ground, a mixture of regolith—asteroid dust—and imported soil harvested from planets during construction and hauled to the RIM in massive tankers to dump.

Jono knelt at the head of the bodies and assessed Nimah carefully. "The last time you were here, you felt it—the heartbeat of elite in the ground." His voice went hushed, reverent. "Do you still feel it? How does it sound to you now?"

Lowering to her knees, Nimah pressed her palm to the earth and closed her eyes. The sensation rose, featherlight and soft as the whisper of a breeze before dawn. The ringing hum sang through her, warm and achingly familiar, and Nimah released a tender gasp. It was like being enfolded in an embrace that brought with it true peace, and oh how she wanted to sink into that sensation and never let go.

"I feel it." She curled her fingers into the ground, allowing the energy to seep into her veins; it climbed up her arm and threaded through her bones.

Home. Something inside of her thrummed. *Lead us home.*

"I've missed you," Nimah whispered, and brushed a single tear from her cheek.

Excited by whatever he saw on her face, Jono beamed. "Does it feel the same or different?" he asked.

"Different." Nimah lifted her gaze, scanning the landscape with fresh clarity. The orbital breeze tickled the back of her neck, sharp and clean where the air had once been thick with dust. "It's much clearer. And the ground." She scooped up a handful of the soil, rolling it between her fingers. "It looks rich. Like farming soil."

"That's because it is." Jono grinned, his excitement radiating like solar flares. "Nutrient-dense, brimming with minerals. Readings from core samples have gone off the charts in the last six weeks. It's like . . . whatever was planted here is finally waking up."

"How?"

Jono pressed a finger to his lips before speaking. "I think it's connected to you."

"Me?"

"These are your relatives." He gestured to the two bodies. "Grandfather and mother, respectively. My research confirmed my theories that he seeded the earth, and she fertilized it. But nothing happened—nothing truly took root—until you encountered elite. You were the life spark. I believe the three of you, together, have forged a sort of symbiotic ecosystem. Interconnected, despite death and distance, and that spark you have given it is developing like a zygote in the womb. It's *growing.*"

Nimah's heartbeat stuttered. "Into what?"

"I think . . ." Jono exhaled, searching her face. *"A planet."*

Nimah blinked, her breath catching. "But asteroids are too small to become planets."

"On their own, yes," Jono agreed. "But the RIM isn't just a single asteroid, it's *millions* of them fused together, giving it the required mass. Elite, it seems, is doing the rest and, even more impressively, accelerating the process. What should take tens or hundreds of millions of years is happening in a fraction of that time." He shook his head, his voice bright with fascination at being able to share his findings. "At this rate, the RIM could be a fully-fledged planet in a century. Maybe less."

"Growing planets." The silver web of elite glimmered beneath her fingers. "Sounds more like magic than science."

Jono's eyes flared with a laugh. "I told you my research would be galaxy-changing."

"I don't understand how such a thing could be possible."

"Neither do I, which is why while you're here, I'd love to run some tests."

Hesitation gripped Nimah by the throat, her pulse quickening against her temples. Instinct told her to leave whatever was happening inside her body a mystery, but the rational part of her knew better than to succumb to anxiety. But what if what was happening to her couldn't be stopped? What if it only got worse? Nimah swallowed down the bitter surge of fear. Willful ignorance wouldn't save her. Better to know the truth now than hide behind illusions and denial. "Okay."

Jono's brows popped up in surprise. "Really?"

"Yeah. Let's do it."

"Wow." He ran a hand through his hair with a laugh. "Honestly, I didn't think you'd agree so quickly. I had a whole pitch prepared."

"Glad I could make your day easier," Nimah replied dryly.

Using a side entrance, so as not to disturb Mumbles hard at work, Jono brought Nimah into his medbay, a hermetically sealed and fully pressurized habitat module. Its design was sleek and efficient, with walls that expanded and contracted like the lungs of a living organism, a testament to the cutting-edge technology meant to protect from the vacuum and radiation of space.

Nimah hesitated at the threshold. The smooth, insulated walls gleamed under the hot white lights and the air inside somehow felt heavier. Charged. As though vials containing various samples of elite had seeped into the dome.

"I wish we had more time together so I could take you to the hospital for a proper screening." Jono sighed as he put on a white medical coat. "The tests won't be as thorough as I'd like, but I should be able to cover most of the bases. Take a seat here." He tapped a padded exam chair that was raised to chest level.

"Before we start . . . I have one condition." Nimah stopped at the side of the chair and brought her gaze to his. "Any tests you run or samples you take from me remain separate from your research. Do not share the results with anyone. And if you find anything strange, I want to know immediately."

Jono's expression tightened with concern. "What do you mean by 'strange'?"

She hesitated, the words catching in her throat. "I need to tell you about some things that have been happening to me."

"Okay," he said gently, his usual easygoing demeanor shifting to the professional grace of a trained doctor. "Why don't you fill me in while I get organized?"

Nimah heaved herself into the exam chair, settling into the padded foam. "I'm having trouble sleeping," she began.

"What kind of trouble?"

"Insomnia. Night terrors." Clenching her teeth, Nimah withdrew the vial of stained heliosmoke and held it out for Jono. "I've been treating it with this."

Sighing, he took it from her. "How long have you been puffing?"

"Not long," Nimah admitted. "It's helped me get some rest and blocked out the dreams but . . . there are other issues and they're getting worse."

"Like?" Jono arched a brow.

"Hallucinations. Vivid ones."

"How often are they occurring?" he asked, swapping his regular glasses for a pair of medi-focals, their lenses glinting with embedded nanotech designed to scan into the body, gauging blood pressure and oxygen levels, and even mapping the body's nervous system. "And when was the last one?"

"Daily. And my last occurrence was a few hours ago." Nimah winced as a needle plunged into the tender skin in the crook of her elbow and blood shot into a glass cylinder, rapidly filling the vial.

"Any ideas what could've triggered it?" Jono swapped in a second, then a third, depositing each into a clear holder at his side.

The memory of her fight with Liselle surfaced like an unexpected slap, and the fresh sting of regret bloomed in a physical weight in her chest. Almost as dense and unyielding as the sensation of Dobs's fist reaching inside of her to seize her heart.

"Stress."

Jono clicked his tongue. "No shortage of that in your life right now, I'm guessing." Finished with drawing blood, he extracted the needle and pressed a rolled wad of gauze against the wound before covering that with a bit of medtape. Jono rolled his hands at the wrists, his focus shifting to the holoscreens that haloed Nimah, each displaying a different layer of her anatomy—bones, muscles, organs—in intricate detail. "When did they start?"

Head angled in thought, Nimah worked back through her memories, trying to pinpoint when exactly the scales had tipped from sanity into madness. "In Commander Wallace's office almost three months ago." When she'd first touched the stone sparrow. "But those visions were different—more like someone else's memories funneling into me only when I was connecting to elite. Now it's like I'm being haunted by a ghost that can actually touch me."

"A ghost?" Jono's tone was curious, not dismissive. "Of whom?"

Nimah fell silent, her clasped hands pressed against her lips as she took a moment to reflect on how best to answer his question. How much was too much? If she told him the truth—would he think her insane? Because she certainly felt insane.

"Nimah." Jono's gloved hand settled on her shoulder, his touch grounding. "Whatever it is, you can tell me. I promise I'll listen. There's nothing to be afraid of and I want to help you, but I can't if you won't trust me." He settled closer, the tender gleam in his gaze offering both confidence and comfort.

Nimah lowered her hands. "It's Dobs."

Jono's brows quirked but to his credit he didn't interrupt her once as Nimah told him about her dark encounters, and the awful gnawing fear she hadn't been able to shake from her bones since Sigourney's death. Finally saying it aloud was like lancing pus from a wound—painful, but necessary, and while part of her shuddered in apprehension of what he was going to think, a greater part of her warmed with relief.

When she was done, Jono sat back, his expression thoughtful.

"Interesting." He dragged his palms across his thighs in slow, concentric circles, latex catching against the fabric of his pants. "If I had to hypothesize, considering all that's happened, I think it's highly probable these hallucinations are a result of post-traumatic stress. You're carrying tremendous guilt about Sigourney, arguably even Dobs, and that guilt is manifesting, so to speak. Exacerbated and induced by your connection to elite."

Nimah set her teeth on edge. "Meaning what, exactly?"

"The mind is a tricky thing." His lips pursed and he gave a soft shrug. "We often create all kinds of delusions as a means of coping with trauma. Therefore, to cope with yours, you created a villain to punish you, so you wouldn't have to face yourself."

"Fuck you." White-hot anger shot through Nimah like a solar flare. "This isn't just in my head."

"I'm not trying to offend or attack you, Nimah."

"If Dobs isn't real—" She raised her sleeve, exposing the circular burn on her bicep from the first time Dobs appeared in her bunk after the Beak. "Then explain this."

Jono rolled her bicep gently in the light as his medi-focals scanned the freshly scabbed wound, processing the results only he could see. "Definitely a third-degree burn, but there's no surface damage to the tissue or any trace chemicals that would indicate it's the result of a lit cigarette." Releasing her, Jono chewed the corner of his lip. "Is it possible that, while in a state of psychosis, you did this to yourself?"

"With what?" Nimah arched a brow. "I don't smoke. What else could I use to do this?"

Jono's breath hissed between his teeth before he finally shook his head in defeat. "I don't know but . . . let's run some tests and see what we can find out." Taking her hand in his, he gripped it tight, his smile steady and sure. "We'll get answers, Nimah. I promise you."

For the next hour, Jono put Nimah through the gamut.

Hair, saliva, blood, urine, and more. She felt like a specimen under a microscope by the time he was done, arms tender and muscles stiff. But instead of fear tightening in her chest, it eased—an impossible knot finally coming undone. Not knowing had made her feel helpless and small, like a child lost in the abyss of the void. This . . . this was a step forward. And hope bloomed in the reassurance of getting answers that would carve out a clear path, freeing her from the chasm of madness she'd spiraled into.

"When will you have results?"

"Six . . . maybe seven hours at most." Jono said without lifting his head as he scribbled into his notepad. "I'll send you a wave soon as they're ready."

Nimah buttoned her shirt, rolling her shoulders as she stood. "Don't . . . tell anyone about this, okay? Not even my grandmother."

Jono paused mid-note and looked at her. "As your physician, I am bound to discretion. No one will know anything that you don't personally disclose."

With that reassurance, the last remnants of tension peeled away, and Nimah drew in the first easy breath she'd taken in months. "Thank you." A crackle splitting through her comms, and Jono's response was lost as Boomer's excited voice burst between her ears. "Whoa, slow down." Nimah stretched and wiggled her jaw, lowering the volume. "Everything okay?"

"*Sharp as a freshly minted razor!*" he sang back. "*Mumbles finished her decrypt, and you ain't gonna believe what she's found.*"

CHAPTER SIXTEEN

The most important part of any hunt was knowing when to exercise patience.

Vesper dragged out a chair and sat down at an empty table, one of the four legs uneven and the top coated in a sticky layer of grime and old booze. Perched to the far left of the bar, she had open sight lines clear across the bustling establishment, including the main doorway—the only entry point in or out.

The derelict cantina overflowed with grifters, and other void-weary souls hunkered on the RIM who sought to lose themselves to hops, cards, and live music. Burning tobacco and stale liquor hung thick like a sticky perfume that clung to every breath, and weak solar lamps shed pale golden light across hard-weathered faces crammed at tables or against walls lined with booth seating designed to be just comfortable enough until the booze numbed your ass.

"Pitcher of brew. Kalstack, if you got it. Otherwise whatever's on house tap." She ordered from the bot—a welded ball of reclaimed tech that swiveled and spun with a single blue lightbulb that flickered like a blinking eye. "And bring three glasses. Clean ones," she grunted, before it spun away with the order to the half-dozen tenders working furiously behind the bar to meet the demand.

"Something wrong?" Vesper asked when neither of the cybers moved to sit.

Sasha and Brenon stood in military formation alongside her table, and though she'd dressed them in plain attire from her own cache of belongings to blend in on the RIM, she had yet to scrub all traces of SIGA from their poise or demeanor.

"I don't understand your directives." Brenon's stern face tightened with what she interpreted as confused frustration. "Felon Nimah Dabo-124 must be apprehended. We know she is near our location, so why are we ordering alcoholic libations instead of closing in on our mark?"

Vesper sat forward, elbows propped on the table. "Do you know how big the RIM is?"

"Precisely one—"

"That was rhetorical, Sasha."

Sasha clamped her mouth shut with an indignant grimace as the bot returned with a tray hovering over the sphere of its body, secured by magnetic and anti-grav sensors. Vesper removed the pitcher of amber beer and the trio of stacked glasses. Moderately clean, aside from a couple smears on the exterior.

"We're here because the RIM is a labyrinth of tunnels, above and below ground, which are impossible for any navsystem to map." Vesper poured beer with expert precision, until a fine layer of foam settled a finger below the rim of each pint glass. "I already lost Nimah on Corlys because I chose to advance too quickly, and I'm not about to repeat that mistake. The RIM is not the right strike point, but it is the perfect opportunity to get close enough to loop a tether around the hind leg of our prey."

"So . . . you have a clear objective," Brenon said cautiously, frowning down at the three full glasses. "Other than public intoxication."

"Sometimes the most efficient way to catch a mark is to find out what they're after—and get to it first. You don't trail behind, you leap ahead and set your trap." Vesper raised her pint and took a long, bracing swallow of ice-cold brew that was heavy on the hops but finished with a pleasant hint of bitter citrus. "Now sit before you begin to draw eyes."

The cybers exchanged a look that stretched between them in a way that seemed to articulate more than words ever could. Then, in precise tandem, they drew out the adjacent chairs and sat.

Vesper shook a bemused head. Sighed. "Drink." She scooted the glasses closer to them. "Loosen up, for fuck's sake." Without complaint, they picked up their pints and drained them dry in four chugging gulps.

Her brows winged as high as her surprised laugh. "Well, damn." She poured fresh pints. "Didn't think you had it in you."

Brenon examined his refilled glass, brows lowering over clear brown eyes that almost shimmered with the first sparks of life and curiosity. "It tastes . . . like liquefied electricity. Everything inside me hums. And I feel warmth settling here." He pressed at hand to his flat stomach. "Despite the fact the beverage is cold."

"It's called getting a buzz." Vesper smirked, then kicked back the rest of her glass, right down to the suds.

"It's agreeable," Sasha added, this time sipping from her beer instead of gulping it down like air. "Surprisingly refined in composition. I detect . . . persimmon?"

"Jade fruit, too," Brenon agreed, and both vanished into their beer, tasting and puzzling their way through the newfound experience. Halfway through their third, Vesper caught the bloom of a rosy haze in their cheeks and the hint of actual smiles. One even teased its way onto her own usually stern face.

It had been a long time since she'd had what she'd call crew. Or even friends. Since she put thrusters to Illysium, Vesper had shed all forms of connection for solitude. Convincing herself it was a strength as well as a necessity, as letting people in led to disappointment and heartbreak, either through death or betrayal. And emotions were vicious little beasts, all sharp teeth and claws that multiplied until you were infested by feeling.

After the loss of Ashleen, suffering the relentless ache of despair following her death, isolating herself seemed like the smartest move. Can't get hurt if you didn't let anyone in. But across the last couple of days, as puzzling as the cybers were with their stiff spines and almost robotic personalities, having them around hadn't been all that bad. Deep within her chest, a crack formed along the hardened walls of her defenses, and a small part of her began to wonder if maybe . . . maybe it was time for a change.

At the clap of the opening door, Vesper scanned across the cantina as members of the Valkyrie crew swaggered inside. Magaly Estevez, also known as Chu; Gertrude, the renowned Minx of Sparta3; and a platinum-haired third Vesper didn't recognize. Not a Valkyrie, but her metallic tattoos and the strong line of her shoulders held the command of a pirate. Possible friend, she mused. Comrades reconnecting over a drink. The RIM, after all, was a place of gathering as much as it was business.

They stopped by a round table near the center of the establishment, pulling over a couple of empty seats as a dealer set up for a fresh game of glo-cards and dice. Chu was the first to sit and from the way she handled her cards as the game played through its first round, steady and sharp-eyed, Vesper was willing to wager all three of them were veterans in more ways than one. They weren't careless players, which meant they weren't careless people, and that would make planting the sniffer difficult.

She'd have to get in real close, and she'd have to do it alone.

While the beer had scuffed away some of their military polish, Brenon and Sasha still screamed of brass. The Valkyries had once sailed under SIGA and would not be fooled, even with them out of uniform and glowing in the cheeks. Vesper, on the other hand, was adept at camouflage. She knew how to stalk close to her prey without spooking a single hair on their head. It was the part of the hunt she loved most.

Rolling a mouthful of beer across her tongue, Vesper studied her marks. Going for the unknown platinum-haired goddess would've been the easy approach, but when she raised a fan of glo-cards, wires shone beneath a thin layer of protoskyn and Vesper immediately crossed that off the list. A bionic hand could crush her windpipe or snap her femur. Chu's *fuck-you-and-fuck-off* scowl also made her a no-go. But Gertrude, the consummate performer, was all sunshine and smiles as she brought the other players at the table to stitches of laughter over whatever joke she'd shared—apparently at Chu's expense.

"Stay here and don't move until you've finished that pitcher," Vesper ordered.

The two of them nodded with boozy grins as she stepped away, and Vesper wove around crowded tables, rolling the tension out of her shoulders as she shed her usual air of command for something casual and unassuming as she approached her target.

"Mind if I join?"

Chu shrugged without looking up, sweeping plastic chips, iron nuts, and glo-cards toward her, claiming the pot. "Long as you got something to bet."

Vesper tossed an unopened roll of chips worth three hundred onto the table.

"Take a seat, dove." Gertrude jabbed her elbow into the side of a man glowering over losing what was left of his stack to Chu, clearing a stool. "I do hope you're ready to be plucked."

Vesper sat with a cagey grin as a fresh hand was dealt. "If it's by anyone but the Minx herself, I might take umbrage."

Gertrude's eyes sparkled, irises enhanced to a vivid green that matched the short haze of hair faded against her dark brown skin. "A fan, are we?"

"An ardent worshipper," Vesper corrected, and set a hand over her heart. "Your portrayal of Lola was my awakening. *Time and Tide Waits for No Man, Love, So Why Should I?* Genius. Wore my album to a nub for that track alone."

"Yup. That's gone and done it," Chu grunted, chin lowered so her bifocals perched on the tip of her discerning nose. "Her already massive head inflated another three inches. She'll never fit through them doors now."

"Play your hand and let me enjoy a bit of cooing from this dove." Gertrude winked, her knee sliding companionably against Vesper's thigh. "You have an intriguing look about you." Her gaze traced Vesper's jawline, which she'd been told more than once was her best feature, then flicked back to meet her eyes boldly in appraisal. "I'm not one to be presumptive—are we a madam or a monsieur?"

"Mainly keep to she/her, but I don't mind they/them. Prefer to follow the wind, as they say."

Gertrude's answering smile shone so bright it was, admittedly, hard not to be dazzled. "As do I, darling. As do I."

It wasn't until the game picked up, drinks flowing and laughter curling into the smoky air like vapor trails from a spent engine, that Vesper went to work. Rogue tech, while often temperamental, meant there was an array of gadgets far beyond anything the RIM's backwater bar patrons would recognize.

Much like Vesper's insignia ring worn on her left pinkie. To the untrained eye, it was a simple circlet of gold stamped with a single initial: A, for Ashleen. But inside was a microchip coded with a sniffer program capable of burrowing into Gertrude's wristdeck without detection. Once complete, she'd be able to track Gertrude within a mile of her location, as well as skim her text threads and personal files to hopefully ascertain the Valkyrie's next steps and spring a trap. All she had to do was remain in close contact with her quarry for at least ten uninterrupted minutes.

Easier said than done. Ten minutes was a lifetime under such strenuous conditions, so Vesper masked her concentration through the easy guise of flirtatious conversation that let her linger close. The thrill of deception hummed through her—being *right* here, with her prey unaware of who she was or the threat she posed.

Undetected, like poison in a glass.

"Maverick!" the blond shouted, waving her arm to flag someone in the distance before setting her bionic fingers between her lips and teeth.

Vesper tensed at the rip of her sharp whistle before she turned her head. Maverick Ethos-333. Even though he'd already been identified by the blond, she'd have recognized him straight away by both the hooked scar cleaving down the side of his neck as well as the hoverchair. Judging by his assessing gaze, he wasn't here to waste time with drink or cards, and although the tightly packed crowd slowed him down some, it wouldn't take long for him to battle his way through.

Vesper wasn't about to be sitting at this table when he arrived. Maverick was a skinner trained by Hatchett. One of his best. His kind could smell deception like a starhound tracking krakens across the void, and while Vesper prided herself on her skills, she wasn't foolish enough to test them against *his*.

Resting her cards against the table, Vesper's mind worked on a quick excuse to leave. Based on the spread in play and her lackluster hand, the best she could determine would be to bet reckless and lose big. "All in." She pushed her stack of chips into the pot that she'd doubled in the last round.

A collection of whistles and groans circled as the tumble of dice and pair of drawn cards turned the pot in favor of the third unknown pirate who'd stalked in with Chu and Gertrude.

Gertrude's brows winged high over the fanned edge of her cards as Vesper tossed down her losing hand. "All in for a pair of swords on the back of a courtly spread favoring crowns?" She tsked sadly. "Call me green, but one might think you'd intended to lose."

"A game without risk is hardly one worth playing." Vesper slid back on the legs of her stool. "I came for banter and booze; I've had my fill."

"That so?" Gertrude chuckled. "And here I thought it was so you could soften me with those delicious dark eyes of yours. *Vesper*."

Vesper stiffened as three sets of eyes pinned her where she stood, the air thick enough to choke. They'd *known*. They'd known the whole damn time. Of fucking course. They weren't just pirates. They were *Valkyries*. Women who had more than earned their fierce reputations across thirty years of hard sailing, and despite now being very senior in age, Vesper had made the mistake of underestimating them.

"Now, now." The muzzle of Gertrude's weapon settled against the table's edge in a casual, almost polite manner, but the glimmer in her eyes was charged with the kind of warning that could snap at any second. "Let's not make this situation hot."

Vesper exhaled, slow and measured, raising empty hands to reveal she had nothing holstered, and nothing hidden. Coming to their table alone and unarmed had been a gamble but one worth the risk, as her insignia ring pulsed, indicating the download was successful. She was in. Now she just had to find a way to extract herself with her head still on her shoulders.

"How long have you known?"

"'Bout three minutes before your skinny ass touched that stool." Chu spat a wad at her feet, elbows planted to the table, her blaser held primed and steady.

"We thought it was best to keep you tucked right here where we could keep eyes on you," the blond chimed in. "Rather than roaming and making trouble."

Vesper tilted her head, amusement ghosting across her lips. It wasn't often she found herself skillfully outmaneuvered; it was hard not to be impressed. "Well played."

Gertrude tipped an imaginary brim. "You as well, dove." And then she inclined her head slightly, likely receiving incoming comms from Maverick, who was apparently unable to cut through the belly of the cantina. "Copy." She nodded to her colleagues. "Time to burn, theydies."

"What'll we do 'bout this one?" Chu grunted, her eyes narrowed behind her bifocals.

The blond flexed her bionic fist with a menacing grin.

"Violence is not necessary. She's going to stay put, like a good little dove." Gertrude leaned over Vesper as Chu and their colleague rose from the table. "I'm a sucker for a pretty face, dove, and I'd hate to put holes in yours." She whisked a finger beneath the point of Vesper's chin. "Don't follow."

And she didn't.

Vesper remained seated as the Valkyries vanished from the cantina into the chaos of the RIM with Maverick in tow. Tapping her wristdeck, she watched the blinking connection to Gertrude pulse, steady and strong. A perfect signal. They may have spotted the wolf in sheep's clothing, but she'd still accomplished what she'd set out to achieve. She gave it a full five minutes before rallying Brenon and Sasha, then the three of them returned to her ship.

"We should go after them!" Brenon urged, following Vesper into the cockpit.

"I already told you." Vesper stopped by the kitchenette and pulled out a packet of raw-feed for Saint, who sat by her bowl with drooling patience. "We can't strike on the RIM." At the snap of her fingers, Saint lunged for her bowl.

"You have a wave notification." Sasha gestured to the main console, where an icon blinked with the seal of Annelise Aramir.

"Fuck." Dropping into her flight chair, Vesper brushed dust from her sleeve and activated the wave recall. Three quiet chimes, and the screen flickered to life and Chairwoman Annelise's sharp, cutting presence floated onto glass.

"I waved three hours ago."

"I'm aware." Vesper crossed her arms. "I don't have much to report other than I've made contact. Not with the mark directly, but with the Valkyrie crew. I was able to plant a sniffer that gave me access to the Chief Navigator's wristdeck. It's not strong enough to crack the *Stormchaser*'s firewall, but I'll be able to keep a tight leash on them now until I can set a proper trap."

"Why are you waiting? If Nimah is within reach—take her now!"

Brenon's *I-told-you-so* grunt had Vesper struggling not to roll her eyes into the back of her skull. "It's not that simple. Four days ago, the Valkyries were tasked by the Council of Black to complete a Reckoning.

Pirates everywhere are flapping their lips about it, but no one has any idea what the mission is, only that the stakes are high."

Reckonings were a trial of atonement. The greater the insult, the greater the odds, and whatever Nimah and the Valkyries had been slapped with, it was huge.

"Problem is this Reckoning has the Valkyries primed for assault," she continued. "Can't get close, even with the cybers you sent me; it would be hubris to take Nimah head-on. Therefore, my best advantage is *after* they've succeeded." Once the crew was glutting themselves on victory, guards would drop, making it easy for Vesper to swoop in.

"Is that really the best you can do?" Annelise skimmed her gaze over Vesper's shoulder line, and something passed over her face that Vesper couldn't quite comprehend. "I must admit, I'm disappointed. Your reputation held such . . . promise, and I thought we were quite clear about the urgency behind this matter."

Vesper set her teeth, the muscle in her jaw clenching from the effort to keep her aggravation leashed. "It is if you want Nimah alive," she scoffed. "Otherwise a full-on assault with cybers and crew only guarantees she dies in the skirmish. My gut tells me the Valkyries are close to concluding their Reckoning; I should have Nimah in a couple of days. Three at most."

"I'll hold you to that, Vesper."

The wave ended and Vesper finally let loose the fist-clenching snarl she'd strangled in her chest before turning to Brenon and Sasha, neither of whom appeared particularly fazed by the flames she felt burning in her eyes.

"Clear the pit. Go . . . scrape soot off the thrusters or something."

They left without argument, and that was perhaps the one good attribute of cybers—they didn't argue or bemoan, they obeyed.

Once she was alone, Vesper pulled off her insignia ring and set it onto the download tray of the console. It took a few moments for the files to sync, and she paced the narrow cockpit, the grated flooring singing with every heavy step, until the console chimed—signaling the sync was complete. Gripping the edge of the console, Vesper leveled her gaze as she whisked through Gertrude's cloned message threads, scrolling through them across the screen when the words *encrypted files* and *Solvanis* caught her particular attention.

"Interesting," she murmured, voice edged with something dangerous. "Let's see what you're after."

CHAPTER SEVENTEEN

Liselle was awake by the time Nimah rushed into the cargo hold of the *Stormchaser* with Mumbles and Boomer in tow. And it was clear from the way her smile dissolved that sedation hadn't softened her mood. But while her eyes still carried the virulent embers of her anger, they were clearer at least.

"So." Ro crossed her arms, one boot braced against the grated stairway that led up to the bridge. "How'd it go?"

"Razor!" Boomer's grin shot wide enough to light the room. "Mumbles is a damn *decryption savant*."

Mumbles, standing just behind him, vibrated with barely contained pride.

"We still need to organize the data," Nimah scanned the hold, shying away from Liselle's scathing gaze.

"Great, why don't you and Liselle get to work on making sense of the files." Ro's gaze flicked from Nimah to Liselle, reading the tension with ease. "I've already sent Maverick to wrangle the strays. I'll prep thrusters so we can burn out of here."

Reclined against the sealed doorway, Liselle let out an indignant huff of breath before gathering her locs and twisting them behind her head to secure in place with a hair tie from around her wrist. Clearly less than pleased with Ro's suggestion of being paired with Nimah.

"There's more space on the communal deck than on the bridge," Nimah offered, trying to switch her focus from raw hurt to the work ahead. "Mumbles, feed everything to Ma's system, and show us what you've found."

Once settled on the communal deck, Nimah set up three holoscreens as Mumbles siphoned batches of documents into their network—emails, reports, call logs, minutes from classified meetings. And even some of Liselle's father's personal notes. Boomer translated for Mumbles, his voice layering over her excited gestures, and between the four of them, they pieced together the entire sordid puzzle in less than an hour.

"Holy shit." Liselle stepped back, hands braced behind her head—the shock of their discovery temporarily pushing aside her anger. "Are you seeing what I'm seeing?"

Nimah's eyes watered in shock. "I think so."

Voices rose from beyond the corridor and onto the communal deck, Gertrude and Chu bickering like a couple of malfunctioning droids in a scrapyard with Maverick and Zensha close behind.

"How do you survive these two?" Zensha demanded. "Been like this for thirty minutes!"

"Easy." Ro set herself between the squabbling pair, one hand on Gertrude's shoulder and the other flat to Chu's narrow chest. "What's got you so amped? Start at the beginning."

"We was at the Rusty Screw." Chu grumbled, skinny arms crossed over her flat chest, white tank stained yellow around her pits. "Got set up over dice and glow-cards when Zen happened to take note of a pair of eyes beading us."

"Vesper?" Nimah gasped.

Chu pointed at Nimah with a confirming nod. "So, we think—bet, Nimah needs time to handle particulars, so let's keep the hunter tight, thinking she's got a couple goats in the grass to chew on." Scuttling to the kitchen, Chu yanked open the fridge to wrestle out a bottle of homemade brew. "Next thing you know, Vesper comes over, all suave." Chu cracked the cap off with furious teeth and sauntered back from the kitchen.

And oh, how it took everything in Nimah not to laugh as Chu rose on tiptoe with a performative strut, hips wiggling and lashes fluttering.

"Gets all slanty and such with Gertrude, burying herself to the bridge of her nose in her crack—" She wiggled a damning finger at

Gertrude. "And you let it swell your head, getting fat as a kitten lapping milk from a teat."

"Guilty as charged, darling." Gertrude drew out an empty seat from the table and sat with a smirk. "What can I say? Vesper may be the reddest flag I've seen standing on two legs, but I'm a bull. Flash a bit of crimson—and I charge right for it."

"Fuck." Nimah's shoulders slumped in defeat. "I thought we'd have at least another day before we needed to worry about her again."

"She's on us like shit on an asshole." Bubbles frothed at the corner of her lips as Chu took a swig of beer then frowned down the neck of her brew before squinting at Maverick with a slow swallow. "Not to insult your ace flying, but how sure are we that we've shaken her off our rump?"

"I paid a couple of the dockers to scrub our departure trail," Maverick answered, drawing his chair to the foot of the trestle table. "Vesper'll find remnants eventually, but she's working off a threadbare scent. Should give us the time we need to drop anchor and form a plan."

"Then let's not waste a second of it," Nimah suggested, drawing the attention of the crew to the three boards she and Liselle had worked hard on putting together, covered in clipped images, videos, and highlighted sections of texts. "We started with what we knew. The attack on Solvanis. Yes, the planet is unregistered, but the voidspace surrounding it? That's heavily regulated. So while Mumbles extracted stills from the Inner Circle's surveillance networks during the estimate assault window, Liselle and I went through her father's files and found this." Nimah pulled the finalized rendering onto an expanded screen for everyone to read the harrowing words.

/ *Solvanis is ripe.*
Send Cobalt to ground for harvest.
No witnesses. /

"Three hours after the assault on Solvanis, the board had a cloaked meeting, which Lennox Namsara captured minutes and stored on his personal console. Those notes also indicate details about a shipment which matched a bovine shipment Mumbles traced leaving that quad." Nimah tapped on the board and a manifest from one of the many SIGA redacted emails expanded next.

Asset Classification: Type 4, 507 Units
Destination: Sector 9 Transit Hub, Zone R676
Timestamp: 03:42 ICT

"*Ensure units are sedated prior to transfer,*" Nimah read aloud from the highlighted subsection of notes they'd connected with a dotted line to keep all the pieces organized. "*Biometrics must remain below threshold. Socket control team has cleared Eye-3G662 for silent dispatch for the following vessels.* It goes on to list flight tags for six ships."

Gertrude raised a hand. "I hate to be skeptical, darling, especially since Chu lives and breathes for the chance, but how are we so certain this ship is in fact children and not cows?"

Nimah ran a line beneath the expanded heading. "Take a look at the units."

"Five hundred and seven." Zensha swayed on her feet. "It's them."

"We strongly believe so," Liselle agreed. "Based on the log description, and the subsequent vessels listed, we can determine the stolen children were split into smaller groups and boarded onto six separate vessels which were then launched in a relay sequence through a Socket, with a thirteen-hour window between them to minimize the risk of suspicion and seizure."

"But that's not the worst part." Whisking the second board forward, Nimah pulled up the next batch of documents and files revealing countless reports and spreadsheets—years of evidence stacked on top of each other. "Solvanis wasn't the first."

"How many zones have been struck?" Zensha asked, words hushed in horror.

"Hundreds. And tens of thousands taken, that we know of, from registered systems." Nimah's pulse spiked. "With clear plans to take *hundreds of thousands* more across the next five years."

All hidden behind cover stories of natural disasters—ruptured atmosphere nets, floods, chemical leaks. Falsified tragedies meant to mask something designed. *Deliberate.* Small in scale, so they wouldn't set off any alarms. Trafficking was not new. Ticks kidnapped men, women, and children for anything from illegal prime mining to sex trade, or worse, but the volume implied in what they'd uncovered today was not only unprecedented, SIGA's part went back decades.

"Mother of pearl . . ." Chu gasped. "We ain't got the jaws to chew on somethin' this big." Her words punctured like lead to the heart of the crew.

Ro stopped by the first board. "What do they want with these kids?" she said under her breath, more to herself than to the crew as she tried to guide her thoughts toward making sense of the bigger picture. "And why take so many *now*?"

"That's the only thing we don't know. It's clearly an act of urgency." Liselle scowled at the holoscreen.

"And that means something important has changed." What that could be, Nimah didn't have an answer for, but cold dread unfurled inside of her like frost seeping into damp earth.

"How about a heading?" Gertrude asked. "Do we know where they're taking them?"

"Glad you asked." Boomer took the floor next and brought up the third and final screen, scattered with code.

"Well, that's about as helpful as trying to get honey from a hornet," Chu grumbled. "Thought you said she'd got it all decrypted?"

Boomer threw an arm around Mumbles's shoulder in an affectionate squeeze. "Work your magic, sis."

A gummy grin stretched across her wrinkled face and Mumbles raised her wristdeck, humming as she transformed deconstructed data into a coherent string of coords.

Without wasting time Gertrude input them into her wristdeck, connecting to the ship's navsystem, and the holoprojection map spread across the center of the table. "This is us." She gestured to a point where the start of a trail glimmered like a minuscule star. "If decoding is accurate, these keys bring us well within the San Rose Belt."

"Ain't that a dead zone?" Chu adjusted her bifocals, and her magnified eyes squinted in uncertainty.

"Yes, darling, it's *supposed* to be."

"Well then how we supposed to go floatin' all the way out yonder?"

Belts were unsailable zones that trapped cosmic radiation particles charged with extremely toxic levels of energy not even SIGA-grade tech could withstand. Once entered, contamination levels resulted in extreme danger to both ship and crew, which was why they were roped off with barrier buoys to stop ships from flying too deep into a poisoned quad. Nothing should be out there besides negs and krakens that flocked for feeding and breeding."

"What if it's just a ruse to keep people *out?*" Maverick suggested.

"You can't just fake a dead zone," Liselle argued. "That would break at least a hundred different codes."

"If I were doing something illegal and wanted to hide in plain sight"—he shrugged—"sealing myself inside a fake belt seems pretty fucking smart."

"I've sailed past the Rose, many a time," Ro interjected. "And I've known pirates who disregarded the buoys. Anyone who enters is never heard from again."

"Well, *something* is in there our government doesn't want us to see," Zensha planted a determined fist on the table, the gears in her knuckles whirring. "If the Rose be where the children are heading, then into the Rose we go!"

"How long can our shields hold in a belt?"

Gertrude took a moment to weigh Nimah's question and run the numbers. "My guess is four hours. We could push close to twelve *if* we all suit up."

"Ma, do you support Gertrude's estimation?" Nimah asked.

<*Yes, based on my analysis, Chief Navigator Gertrude is correct, with a probability of ninety-four percent in favor.*>

"We got enough suits on this boat?" Chu scratched her chin.

"There's the six we stole from the lunar outpost during Ro's rescue mission, which are all SIGA-grade nanite tech." Nimah counted off on her fingers. "We also have four suits that belonged to the *Stormchaser*, which aren't as efficient but should absolutely hold up for the duration required. So overall, yes, but to avoid any unnecessary risks I propose I go ahead in a shuttle to do a recon and report back with a clear picture of what we're up against."

"We should use both shuttles," Ro suggested. "Cover more ground."

"That just increases our chances of being spotted or accidentally triggering any security measures," Nimah argued.

Maverick straightened in his chair. "I'll pilot the shuttle."

"No, I'll take Zensha. You should stay with the *Stormchaser* in case of any trouble."

Hard green eyes met Nimah, uncompromising. "Depending on what's out there—I'm the best pilot to face extreme conditions whether that's evading territorial krakens amped for breeding, or SIGA security."

"He's right, Sparrow," Ro added before Nimah could think of a counterargument. "His skills make him indispensable, and if you insist on going in there then as captain, I'm sending you with the best we have."

Backed into a corner with no way out, Nimah's jaw slanted with a sigh. "Okay. Fine."

<Pardon the interruption, but there is an urgent wave from Tortuga.>

"Thank you, Ma. Feed us the wave. We'll take it in here."

The gravitational sand on the table bubbled, taking shape of a woman. Her face was little more than a featureless mask, but the rest of her was otherwise perfectly rendered with shoulders set and hands clasped at her waist.

"Hail, Captain Indira, and Second-in-Command Nimah. I am Eshe, Hand of the Council. We trust that you are faring well in your Reckoning?"

"I'm happy to report we've had some progress," Ro answered. "Along with some possible setbacks."

The sand bristled around the edges of Eshe's figure, as if registering her concern. "Such as?"

Ro looked to Nimah and inclined her head, suggesting Nimah be the one to share the unfortunate news.

"SIGA has issued a bounty for me." Nimah stepped forward, being sure to speak clearly so that the transmission would flow seamlessly on Eshe's end. Gravitational sand was not the best medium to capture audio, but the *Stormchaser* was not yet equipped with more modernized tech beyond the bridge. "So far it hasn't hindered us, but it's bound to complicate things as we approach our target."

After a brief pause—likely caused by transmission lag—Eshe's voice emerged, steady and resolute. "We anticipated there would be challenges," she said. "But that is the point. Restitution can only be achieved through risk equal to that of our loss."

"I understand." Nimah ground her molars. "But if we could just get an extension—"

"There are no extensions in a Reckoning." Eshe's tone cut like the hard edge of a hand striking against a tender throat. "The conditions were clear: You were given five days—until the last of the ashes are spent—to rescue the stolen children. By our measure you have fifty-two hours left. Fail to meet the requirements in time, and not only will Indira lose her standing as captain of the *Stormchaser*, but every Valkyrie under her banner will be stricken from Tortuga's shores."

Chu slammed her bottle to the table, suds and brew firing up the neck like a geyser. "Since *fucking* when?"

"Since Zensha, captain of the Blackfyre, whom I will remind you all is there acting in the official capacity of observer, brought to our attention the discourse between Captain Ro and her crew as to whether or not the terms of the Reckoning would even be honored. For all we know, this alleged bounty hunter and request for *more time* are merely ploys for you to evade our justice." Eshe swiveled her cool gaze to Ro, and even through pixel sand, Nimah felt the heat of her blistering gaze. "As you appear to hold so little regard for your future, as a pirate or even our queen, to ensure your unwavering commitment to the Reckoning and the will of this council—now it's not only your neck in the noose, but your crew. And your granddaughter."

Well . . . fuck.

Ro raised an imperious chin. "As you wish."

The transmission ended and a quiet tension settled as the dire reality pressed in from all sides, unforgiving as a vise clamped around their skulls.

Met with vicious glares, Zensha raised her unapologetic chin. "I did what needed doing."

Gertude's laughing snort was nearly lost in the clap of Chu's chair knocking to the floor as she bounced onto her feet. "You fucking bilge rat. I oughta—!"

"That's enough."

Chu halted at Ro's firm command; one knee hitched onto the table like she was about to crawl across it to ram her bony fist straight into Zensha's tense mouth. "But Cap—!"

"We don't have the time or luxury for anger." Ro turned to the ashen faces of Nimah and her crew, and instead of the blistering rage one would've expected there was only the stoic calm of a seasoned captain prepared to lead her crew into the fray. Or hell.

No, Ro was not the sort to lose dignity or control when the circumstances demanded clearheaded focus and decisive leadership, but when this was over? A cool shudder rippled across Nimah's shoulders. She almost pitied Zensha what was coming for her after treacherously throwing her grandmother to the wolves.

"The council has spoken." Ro set determined hands on her hips. "Fifty-two hours on the clock, and not a second more. Let's get to work."

CHAPTER EIGHTEEN

Nimah fastened the anchors of the suit around her wrist and neck, and the nanites rippled as the suit awakened against her skin. Glossy black, almost metallic, with a subtle sheen of blue. She'd dreamt of wearing one ever since she first saw agents walking into the medical center after her near-death experience of being stranded in deep void.

They'd moved like superheroes. All gleaming and powerful. And regret coiled in Nimah's belly with a sour twist knowing this suit wasn't one she'd earned—she'd stolen it to rescue her grandmother, and standing in the mirror all she saw was a pale shadow of what she'd never become.

"Now that's a sight to tickle my dead heart." Dobs chuckled, emerging from shadows as if conjured by Nimah's black mood. "Bet you wishing you never traded brass for salt, thinking you had what it took to call yourself pirate." The phantom weight of her arm settled around Nimah's shoulder. Heavy as her thoughts. And vivid blue eyes met Nimah's in the reflection of the mirror, brimming with cruel amusement. "Truth is you never had it in you to call yourself neither. Stars or sea, you were always gonna fail no matter which way you went."

"Shut up." Nimah batted away a plume of smoke Dobs blew at her face, her phantom fading with ripples of her laughter. But her words found their mark, twisting like a knife between Nimah's ribs as she steered out of her cabin and reached the open hatch of the shuttle where Maverick was already suited and behind the yoke.

He glanced her way as she wordlessly strapped into the co-seat, working through the flight check with an ease Nimah could never hope to acquire even after a decade of experience. Ships spoke to Maverick the way code spoke to Mumbles—like old friends sharing secrets and with a trust they reserved for no one else.

"You ready?" He drew on the yoke with a gentle tug, and the shuttle detached from the *Stormchaser* with a slight tremor of anticipation.

Nimah's nails gripped the armrest of her co-seat. "As I'll ever be." Her heart punched into her throat the same moment he punched the throttle, without warning or hesitation—because he knew that's what she preferred. And in a matter of moments, it all fell away.

The *Stormchaser*. Her fears and burdens. All of it, suddenly so finite in the expanding scatter of a million stars.

She let those distant pinpricks of light cradle her like a lullaby as the shuttle sliced into the swirling expanse of cosmic dust and gas, and through tendrils of luminescent vapor of a nebula cloud that moved in slow, graceful currents. Fiery red and orange diffused by soulful wisps of sapphire and violet, and at the center, deepest gold pulsing like the heart of a sleeping dragon.

"Approaching the buoy line," Maverick cautioned, flicking a few more switches on the console. "Activate helms."

They tapped the visor buttons at their napes and helms materialized into place. Liquid and snug. Her sight line was tinged blue from the flickering glow of her vis-feed, running with stats as she scanned the buoys. Each as large as the shuttle, they studded the horizon as far as she could see and within a few seconds of crossing, an immediate surge of radiation warnings flashed on her vis.

"Guess Liselle was right, and I was wrong." Maverick clicked his tongue. "Check out the scans."

"Definitely not fake," Nimah agreed, chewing on the inner corner of her bottom lip. But not nearly as high as she would have expected, given the Rose's fearsome reputation. "How far are we from the coords?"

"About halfway." Maverick swerved the nose of the shuttle and a surging ripple of light lit up the horizon.

"What's that? The intense glowing in the distance?" Nimah narrowed her eyes as something squirmed low in her belly. An awareness. A knowing. "Rad clouds?"

"That's a halo." When Nimah only blinked at him dryly, Maverick continued with a laugh, "Krakens require a ton of energy for sustaining their clutches, so belts make perfect nurseries. The eggs are loaded with prime, which then generates a halo." He swiveled to her with a bemused scowl. "*How* do you not know this?"

Nimah shrugged. "Guess the Academy curriculum isn't interested in the mating habits of void creatures unless it pertains to a threat to public safety."

"Oh, it's a threat alright. Ever seen a male kraken inflated on hormones *and* prime guarding his clutch? Not something you want to get close to." He punched a couple buttons on the console, then toggled a few switches. "Not picking up any movement, but we'll need to be careful. A halo that big means the clutch is *massive*."

"Correct me if I'm wrong, but it looks like the coords are heading *in* there?" Nimah gestured toward the halo.

Maverick inhaled deeply, nostrils flaring, and his brows lowered into a flat line over his flinty, blue-lit gaze. "You're not wrong."

Nimah snorted. "Fantastic." Something struck them off the port side, and panic winged high in her throat as the shuttle rolled hard to the left and the rippling iridescent body of a neg, almost twice the size of the shuttle, swam out from underneath them. And it wasn't alone.

"Looks like we've lured in another pod." Maverick slanted a smirk to Nimah. "They caught your scent."

"It's got to be the suit." Last time she wore it, she'd taken in a significant charge from elite during the assault from the cybers aboard the *Challenger*.

Right before she'd charred them to ash.

As nanites absorbed the genetic material of their wearer, this suit adapted to both her biochemistry *and* elite, fusing with the substance as intimately as it had to her and would remain part of it.

"Are we safe?"

"It's alright. Unlike krakens, negs get more docile in belts. They're like puppies drunk on milk." Driving the yoke, Maverick spun into a dive then swiveled up, giving Nimah a staggering view of the pod circling over and around them. A cyclone of shimmering bodies that rippled almost like sunlight through water and, for a moment, rendered her speechless.

The shuttle thrummed from the waves of the negs singing, generated through controlled pulses of light mixed with photonic vibrations that manipulated electromagnetic fields in melodic patterns. They reverberated through the hull, a bioluminescent radio wave. Haunting and achingly beautiful.

Shadows rippled across the viewport as one of the negs—smaller, faster—circled the shuttle with eerie grace.

Nimah settled closer to the glass, smiled. "I think he's looking at me."

"She," Maverick corrected, gesturing toward the streaks along her belly. "See the teal and jade markings forming a crosshatch across her flank? Bit of a runt from the looks of it—and fewer fins than the matured ones. But she's *fast*. I'll give her that."

More than fast, she was agile, rippling through the abyss like a dancer. Playful, untamed. As she looped around the nose, eyes like liquid opals connected with Nimah. Eighteen of them. And for a second, Nimah swore she saw something *familiar* in their glittering depths. A sensation that reached deep inside. A ceaseless, pulsing vibration that resonated through her bones. Not a sound. Not a feeling. Something *in between*.

It coated her senses and ran down her spine like the sticky slowness of honey, gentle as blades of grass threading between fingertips, crackling like the static of an empty comms channel. The longer they held one another's gaze, it built. Stretched. Then—a sudden blink—it was gone.

Nimah settled back with a breathless, "Whoa . . ."

"Hey, take a look at this." Maverick turned the nose of the shuttle away from the negs and Nimah squinted as the main viewport flashed with markers indicating obstructions ahead. Thousands of them, scattered like a field of matte-black stars the size of bowling balls, and impossible to see with the naked eye unless you were holding one.

"Are those . . . ?"

"Mines," Maverick finished, jaw grim.

"Strap in, Cadet. These are novas."

Nimah cursed. Ship sinkers. Used during the Integration Zone Wars to cut through whole swaths of enemy brigades, novas were gravitational bombs designed to simulate the collapse of a dying star. One wrong move, one stray drift into their grav-field, and the nova sucked you in with a force no ship's thruster was strong enough to break. Once the hull made contact with the mine . . . the ship wouldn't explode.

It collapsed into nothing.

Between the mines were the torn wreckages of vessels, gutted by the fury of territorial krakens seeking to prevent anything from passing near birthing females. It was a miracle anyone passed through at all, and then it struck her not only was that the point but clearly also how the Rose must've earned its lethal reputation.

"There's at least eight ships floating out there." Maverick cursed, eyes sweeping the scanner. "We've got to steer wide if we don't want to risk getting caught in the undertow of a nova." He swooped out, arching toward the halo. A glowing orb formed from clutches of kraken eggs—tens of *thousands* of them—floating in sticky clusters woven almost like a spherical net.

"That's not normal." Maverick frowned as they glided around the perimeter, taking in the size and scale of what was clearly manmade. "The young come out ready to scrap. Packing clusters this close almost guarantees most won't survive beyond hatching. What's the angle?"

"To absorb the radiation," Nimah answered. "The kraken eggs absorb the majority of the toxic particles and radiation, which then, in theory, would significantly reduce shield degradation from prolonged exposure. Whoever designed this place is leveraging the needs of clusters to their advantage. It's . . . genius. Mad, but genius."

"And the mines?"

It took her a second, but the answer clicked. "Kraken control." Given the number of clusters, and the intensely territorial nature of males during and after mating, the belt should have been swarming with them, but they'd yet to sight even one.

So, if a kraken got rowdy, the ruptured mine sucked them into a collapsing explosion that would prevent any possible damage to the cluster netting built to protect whatever was tucked behind it.

"It's a good thing we took the shuttle in," Nimah mused. The smaller vessel allowed for greater maneuverability through the death trap with ease. Not that she doubted Maverick's prowess. "Someone has definitely gone to great trouble to keep people away."

"Let's find out what they're hiding." Maverick throttled the shuttle through the web of clusters, and once they passed the glowing barrier, a floating station came into view.

Bubbled spheres of glass stacked atop each other, with tubular walkways of carbide steel that stretched like arteries to smaller domes, each pulsing with life. Too large to be a ship, too small to be a spacity. The kind of facility that couldn't exist without deep pockets and deeper secrets.

"This place must've cost *hundreds of billions* to build," she gasped. "Plus tens of millions more to maintain."

"Guess we now know where the undisclosed earnings from Solvanis were going."

"Before they came back to raze it to the ground," Nimah finished dryly. "It looks . . . clinical," she commented. "Everyone's in lab coats and tech uniforms."

"Hospital?"

"I don't think so." Uncoupling her harness, Nimah rose from her seat and moved to the side viewport and switched her visor settings to X-ray and thermal. "You take security and systems. I'll concentrate on mapping the interior."

Maverick tapped his brow with a salute, and the two of them set to work, flowing in smooth, efficient silence.

"What the fuck," Nimah grumbled, frowning at error notifications on her holoscreen. "This fucking shuttle!" She bounced her fist to the console, and more error notifications erupted in flashing yellow. "Every time I try to initiate a recording, it gets fucking corrupted."

Maverick leaned over to her screen, brows drawn and nostrils flaring with a deep sigh. "It's not the shuttle." He tapped the error code. "This place is cloaked."

"Which part?"

"All of it."

Nimah's mouth tumbled open. "That's not possible!" Cloaks were severely limited in range and couldn't cover more than an eight-foot radius for a handful of hours at most. When activated, sensors emitted a particle-bearing frequency that created a cloud of static-like fog so dense it was solid to the touch. Gazing out from the viewport, there was no such haze to indicate a cloak was in place; to imagine one large enough to shield an entire spacity? That kind of tech was unimaginable.

"That's why they don't have cameras positioned anywhere." Maverick nodded to himself as if he'd finally solved a riddle. "Cloaking would cancel out all video feeds for them as well. The novas, the krakens, the buoys—all of that is meant to compensate for the fact they're sitting out here blind."

"Well, that's just great," Nimah grumbled, crossing her arms in protest. "How are we supposed to map this place if we can't record anything?"

Amused by her sulking expression, Maverick chuckled and bounced a fist to a compartment on the console. A tray popped down, and inside was a worn manual, a half-eaten breakfast bar that was probably as old as the shuttle, and a flimsy paper notepad with a chewed-up pencil. "We go analog."

Nimah scowled at the notepad and removed it from the tray. The few remaining pages were scuffed from old notes someone had carelessly erased, leaving behind streaks of rubber and lead.

"Cheer up, Cadet, I have some good news that should put a smile back on your adorable face." He winked when she slanted an unamused scowl his way. "I found them."

And, damn him. That did coax out a smile. "Where?"

"Second level, third dome to the right. It's solid hull metal, but thankfully their cloak doesn't stop us from penetrating with thermals." Maverick adjusted his visor settings, and the heat signatures of bodies and the crude outlines of stacked bunks swam onto the console screen direct from his vis-feed. "Looks like some kind of dorm."

"That door is measuring eighteen inches thick." Nimah sketched roughly into the pad, outlining the shape of the room, number of bunks, and loose measurements. "Any thoughts on a way in?"

"There's some possible entry points through a few engineering hatches here and here." He gestured to the large central dome and a couple smaller ones at the bottom, third tier. "Far as I can tell, their sensors are not equipped for movement. Probably due to extensive neg and kraken activity—motion alarms would fire every ten minutes. My guess is they banked on no one getting past the mines or the nest." He eased the throttle, shifting the shuttle's trajectory to circle around for a third pass.

"Then let's be thankful for their arrogance." Nimah braced the back of his flight chair. "Do you think you can fly the *Stormchaser* through here?"

"It's not impossible," Maverick answered. "But it's absolutely going to require a slow and cautious hand. Steady in. Steady out."

"Okay. Let's double back and get the crew ready. We can form a plan once we're all together." Nimah fastened herself into the co-seat as Maverick shot free of the cluster web, and as they approached the sea of novas, movement from a passing neg drew her eyes to the metallic body of a sunken ship floating among the sea of novas.

Splashes of red that pulsed on her visor—still set to thermal—and Nimah slapped a hand to Maverick's forearm. "I'm getting biometrics. There's someone alive in that ship!"

"Which one?"

Nimah zoomed in amidst the graveyard of dead ships to the wreckage. And on her vis-feed, more red spots bloomed, sending her chest to tighten in alarm. "*Stormchaser*, this is Nimah. Liselle, come in."

Her comms crackled for a long pause before a dry voice answered. "*What?*"

"Lis, I need you to confirm a vessel tag from the six we flagged in the manifest."

"*One sec. Alright—what's the tag?*"

Nimah squinted hard. "Y-D-6-V-3-7-R-1."

"*37R1?*" Liselle echoed back. "*It's a match. You have eyes on it?*"

Nimah met Maverick's gaze. "Yes. It sunk. Looks like a kraken split it open, killing almost everyone on board. But thermals show maybe twenty survivors in what I'm guessing are cryopods, since their core temps are stable but low." So low, the shuttle's nav scan had missed them on the flight in. And would've missed them on the flight out, if Maverick had adjusted the shuttle's nose another degree starboard.

"*Copy, Sparrow.*" Ro joined the comms line. "*We're passing the buoys to lend recovery support.*"

"Great, but drop speed and pull in soft," Nimah cautioned. "This place is studded with novas, and it looks like this sinker is caught on the edge of a grav-field."

"*Ain't that razor,*" Chu grunted.

"*How long do we have?*" Ro interjected.

Maverick swung the shuttle for the sinker, while Nimah ran a scan on the ship's integrity. "An hour, perhaps, before it crosses the detonation barrier." And the nova obliterated everyone onboard.

"*We'll be on you in ten,*" Ro answered.

"Copy." Killing comms, Nimah unfastened her harness as the sinker filled the viewport. A ruined shell, one thruster torn off from the left flank exposing a pitch-black interior. Blacker than the void.

Maverick removed the straps of his harness and toggled the gravity stabilizers off. His body floated from his seat. "What's the plan?"

Nimah brought her hands to the doorway, steadying herself in the sudden weightlessness. "First, I'll need to go aboard to confirm proof of life. From there we can see what our options are." She exhaled in a hard blast, fogging her visor. "Drop anchor and wait for the crew. I'll go ahead so we don't lose valuable time."

Dragging herself to the hatch, Nimah took a moment to gather her nerve before she punched the release button. The hatch split open, and with a firm pull against the frame, Nimah shot out into the void. A solitary speck, surrounded by unrelenting darkness and stars. The sheer vastness sent a wave of terror and awe to wash through her, twisting her stomach and setting her heart to pounding in her ears with the ominous tick of a metronome.

Steady. Punctuated. Beats.

Nimah blinked sweat from her eyes, using her palm thrusters to steer to the torn side of the sunken ship where blackness waited to swallow her whole. She approached slowly and slipped inside that dark crevice, careful to avoid the sharp edges of torn hull metal. Nimah tapped her helm and her visor's search lights snapped on; she swept the strong beam from left to right, flooding the dark cavity.

"I'm inside." She wove toward the prow of the ship, swatting her way through fragments of debris, weaving around pipes and wires, then gasped in sudden alarm as she almost collided with a body. It spun upside down, back arched and arms bent, like a dancer caught in a wild pirouette. His swollen and frosted face locked in a mask of screaming terror.

"*Are you okay?*" Maverick called out.

"Just bumped into a floater." Nimah breathed slow and deep. "I wasn't expecting it. Sorry."

"*I see the headlights of the* Stormchaser *in approach. I'll deboard to you in two minutes.*"

"Okay. I'm going to grab the flight recorder, then meet you at the hold." Scooting into the nose of the ship where a pair of dead pilots bobbed in the flight chairs, Nimah reached for the console. Activated by motion, the whole of the ship sputtered to life. Track lights shot in flickering pulses down the length of the entire vessel like a half-gutted fish—an inch away from death and still struggling to breathe.

"Flight recorder," she whispered aloud, to keep her thoughts focused on the task instead of the grisly sight of the dead, and braced the headrest of the two flight chairs. "This is a transport vessel. Flight recorders should be docked beneath the console of the first chair." Reaching across the dead pilot's lap, she slapped her hand underneath the metal plating and grimaced as her fingers dug around, seeking the latch that would eject the recorder. When her fingers finally hooked around a small lever, Nimah snapped it like a tab on a soda can, and the flight recorder popped out.

A semicircle of clear hologlass, the surface covered in finely etched lines from the stored recordings. Based on the coverage of markings, this was little over halfway full. Opening a pocket on her suit, Nimah was tucking the disc inside when a timestamp on the console caught her attention. Frowning, she kicked off the chairs and shot like a bullet toward the hold, using the bent end of a snapped pipe to slow her to a stop before Maverick, waiting for her by the entry to the hold.

"All good?" he asked.

"Great." She pressed a hand to the sealed doorway, floating at his side. "The flight recorder wasn't damaged, but while extracting the disc, I noticed a transmission error message on the main console. There were two wave attempts made in the past hour, both failed."

"Meaning?"

"I don't think the station we passed has any idea this ship crossed the buoy line, let alone sunk."

Maverick pursed his lips. "Well, let's hope they stay in the dark while we get these kids out of here." He turned to face the hold. "Locks are disengaged, but the door held up." Reaching for the round handle, he gripped the wheel and twisted three times to the left.

The doors split open to the hold. Most of the cryopods had toppled from their anchors and lay in a tangled pile of bent metal at the back end of the ship. Coldness reached out for Nimah like an errant hand yearning for her throat, fingers squeezing tight until the edges of her vision bloomed with darkness.

Death.

The impossible weight of it settled against tender nerves, until all Nimah could take in was the harrowing, absolute silence, so thick she feared she would drown. "So many." She blinked through the burn of tears. "We were too late."

Maverick's hand reached for hers, anchoring Nimah to him rather than letting her spiral in grief alone.

"I'm okay." She squeezed back. "I'll be okay." And the two of them flowed forward.

Maverick stopped by the log screen and it limped on after a few urgent taps. "Less than twenty pods appear to be still operational."

"*Sparrow. Do you copy?*" her grandmother's voice crackled through static.

"We're inside," Nimah answered, then spun around to Maverick. "What do you think? Can we use a mooring line and tow the sinker out?"

"The ship has already breached the nova's grav-field. We can't tug it free without blasting thrusters, and that would make flight control over the *Stormchaser* unwieldy. If we strike another mine in the process, we're all sunk."

The bones of the ship rattled, much like Nimah's aching teeth clenched far too tight, confirming Maverick's dire prognosis. Nimah set an anxious hand against steel and reminded herself to breathe.

"Okay. Well, if towing isn't going to work, then we'll need to eject the cryopods and feed them into the belly of the *Stormchaser*." It was going to be an impossibly snug fit, but the alternative was leaving more children behind to die, and that was simply not an option. Nimah swiped her wristdeck for her comms link to broadcast across the entire crew. "Chu, how much time would you need to detach the active pods?"

"*Gotta go one by one. Best I figure is . . . two minutes per?*"

"Seventeen pods, that puts us at little over thirty-four minutes." Nimah braced the snapped beam for grounding as well as support. The ship rattled again, sending the warning vibrations through the flat of her palm, where they ricocheted along the bones of her arm and straight to her galloping heart. "We don't have that kind of time."

"Give me an extra set of hands." Maverick offered. "I can help."

"Oh?" Nimah arched a brow.

"Part of my glorious skinner days." He smiled tightly.

"Great. Okay, Chu. I'll give you two sets of hands, me and Mav. The rest of the crew forms a line. Chu will detach the pods, Mav and I will guide them out." Like ants working together in a colony.

Less than a handful of minutes later, Chu arrived in the hold carting her box of tools, and they went to work. Sparks rained from carbide shears, a cascading shower of bright pops of red and gold. Chu dismantled the anchored pods—closing the loop on their circuitry so that the systems fed off an auxiliary power supply, activated in times of duress.

Nimah and Maverick took turns collecting and guiding them from the hold to where Gertrude and Ro waited near the torn side carving along the ship's belly, and they launched pod after pod, floating across the void to the *Stormchaser* like an assembly line.

"How did so many of the pods fail?" Nimah asked while Chu finished welding the circuitry on the next pod.

Chu gestured to the gaping hole torn clean through the side of the ship from nose to tail. "Kraken must've come through—all primed—ripping through guts and sending the system into a catastrophic power surge. Pods popped like a man's nuts in a closed fist. In all that bustle, Kraken drifts too close to a nova, gets sucked in, leaving the ship to float."

The walls of the belly pinched as something bounced hard off the side.

"I don't think it's going to hold for much longer," Nimah broadcast to the entire crew. "We need to pick up the pace."

"We're burning prime, but we got negs out here," Zensha answered. *"And they're loopy."*

Nimah closed her eyes with a soft sigh. Negs were nimble, at least, and she trusted they'd steer clear of the mines with ease, but their presence added another frustrating layer for them to worry about. "We're down to our last five pods. Let's do our best not to rile them," Nimah cautioned. Another bump to the hull could drive them deeper into the grav-field, and once they ruptured the detonation barrier, they'd vanish into the mine like a foot in quicksand in under a minute-eighty.

"Hey, Cadet, give me a hand with this one." Maverick waved her over and Nimah floated to his side. "See that wire? Strip it to the copper then twist it with this exposed gray."

Nimah followed his instructions, hand shaking with tense concentration. "What now?"

"Pop the anchor on your side. It's a wide, flat handle. About three inches."

"I see it." Safety latch removed, the cryopod released from the wall with a rush of steam. "I'll take this one. Get the next." Gathering the pod by the carriage, Nimah pushed it toward the doorway of the hold, narrowly missing Zensha as she swam inside, nearly colliding into the pod.

"Whoa! What are you doing? You're supposed to be out there helping the others load!"

"What do you mean, we're 'down to our last five'?" she snapped. "By my count, we barely offloaded fifteen from a ship that has over one hundred and fifty. *Where are the rest!*"

"They're nonviable. Wait—what are you doing?" Nimah called out as Zensha shot for the hold's log screen. "Zensha—we don't have time for this. We need you loading the survivors!"

"Back off," Zensha snarled. Taking the partially cracked glass in hand, she drew up the manifest and whisked through the individual pods, registered both with the unit number and photo of the child within. "Please," she whispered, eyes combing over the screen as furiously as the whisk of her finger. "He's not here." Relief quickly morphed into rage, and Zensha tossed the screen. It spiraled in a slow roll down the length of the shattered ship to collide with the mess of ruined pods heaped in the stern. "He's not *here!*"

"Who is not—?" The rest of her words slammed into the back of her throat as the ship violently pitched and sent Nimah reeling. She spun like a throwing star, head over heels, then slammed into the shifting stack of broken cryopods. Her body punched through a narrow crevice, steel and glass clawing across her flight suit, leaving microtears in the nanites.

"Nimah!" Maverick roared. "Are you alright?"

"Fine." Nimah grunted, then groaned around a breathless wiggle, unable to move the lower half of her body wedged between two pods while a third settled across her back, pressing her into a stiff bow. "Actually... I'm stuck."

"Hold on, I'm coming to you. No, *fuck off*, Zensha. You and Chu get the rest of these pods out while I fix your fucking mess!"

Flailing in the dark, Nimah pressed her hands against the flat surface of a pod and grunted around another tense wiggle. The unstable pods shifted more tightly around her, a cruel fist closing around her aching thighs. Tapping her visor, Nimah activated her search lights—and death punched her between the eyes.

Her gaze ricocheted from one child to the next. Some had tumbled free of their harnesses and pressed against frosted glass. Others had broken clean through and hung against the shattered edges, sawing into them like teeth. And one—directly facing her—was hollowed out completely, the face smashed open like a ruined porcelain doll, leaving behind little more than the crater of an empty skull. So much death. It crawled over her, sickly and wrong. The ring of their laughter. Their tears. Their screams. A brutal echo of all the lives that would never be.

"I'm almost there." The twisted wall rattled and Maverick's voice tore through the cracks. "Hold on, Cadet. Just hold on!"

But Nimah barely heard him. He was little more than a whisper above the surge of so much anguish. Then a corpse moved. Small. Maybe three. His face blue and swollen from the sudden loss of pressure, causing bodily fluids to boil and expand. Ebullism. The Academy had drilled into all cadets what happened if someone was ejected into the vacuum of space.

He blinked at her with milky eyes and battled his way to her between jaws made of glass. Flesh ripped away from the apples of his cheeks and peeled from his forearm, and he clamped a broken hand around her wrist. Laughing as he hummed her mother's lullaby. A song meant to soothe and comfort now rang through her with terror.

"No." Nimah struggled against the prison of twisted metal trapping her on all sides. And a raw sob clawed at her throat as he pressed in closer, his empty gaze almost burning in the flood of her search lights. "*No! No! No!*"

The grip on her wrist tightened, tugged. And the jagged edge of terror sawed her open from her belly to the hollow of her throat, exposing her vulnerable heart as the child's grinning mouth expanded wide—impossibly wide—and when he laughed, it was Sigourney's voice that rang within the depths of her soul.

A third tug, and Nimah tumbled screaming into Maverick's arms.

Maverick drew back so he could see her tear-streaked face. The light of his helm made his eyes shine neon blue. "Are you okay?" he panted. "Are you hurt?"

"They're dead!" Nimah battled against him and her head spun in wild search of ghosts. "They're all dead. Screaming. Laughing. I can *hear them*!"

"I've got you, Cadet." Maverick held her against him. His chest, a wall. His arms, a shield. The steady drum of his heart, an anchor. "You're okay. Breathe. There, that's it." He stroked her back in calming circles, coaxing a muffled sob from her throat.

"That could have been me." Nimah hiccupped and struggled to rein in her breathing and rapidly beating heart. "All those years ago. It could have been me."

"But it wasn't," he crooned. "You're safe. Nothing like that will ever happen to you. I promise."

The hold pinched and the beams bracing the walls snapped, one after the other, like toothpicks between Chu's fingers, shocking them back to reality.

"Come on." Maverick took her hand and pushed for the door.

"Wait!" Nimah yanked hard as a sense of urgency anchored at the base of her skull and pulled her toward a broken pod, wedged beneath one of the collapsed beams. Life . . . the barest spark, but it was there. The elite churning inside of her sniffed it out and fused her in place. "This one is alive. He's *alive*!"

Maverick swiveled around, aghast. "Nimah, leave it. We're out of time!"

Walls crunched and split, the floor shook, and cables trembled as the nova chewed on the ship like a hungry animal breaking down a hunk of flesh torn from a carcass.

"He's alive!" Nimah shouted again, her eyes pleading. "Seventeen out of one hundred and fifty, Mav."

Maverick set his jaw, realizing there was no way to convince her to move even if the ship was moments away from flattening around them. "Alright. With me." Grabbing the pod by the carriage, Maverick planted his back between the pod and the shuddering hull metal. Hands braced to polished steel, he bench-pressed into a roar, while on the other side, Nimah looped her arms around the riveted beam and pulled.

The pod rattled, the weight giving inch by inch as the back end of the hold vanished into the twisted, angry mouth of the nova devouring steel in fast gulps.

"One more," Maverick wheezed, arms trembling. "Give it everything you got! *Now!*"

Together they slammed into the pod, straining with determination as death clawed for them—when the pod finally popped free.

"Go!" Maverick shouted.

Taking hold of either side of the carriage, Nimah and Maverick sparked their palm thrusters. The snap of the nova clawed for their heels like a violent riptide that threatened to drag them into oblivion.

And they burst from the belly of the ship with seconds to spare.

CHAPTER NINETEEN

Nimah sat at the communal table, still numb with cold shock. A feeling that also etched itself into the faces of the crew, their expressions a bleak mixture of fatigue and heartbreak after they'd finished stacking the last of the cryopods, crammed into every available square inch the hold could yield.

A pitiful handful from one hundred and sixty-nine.

The crew assembled around the table, the silence tense until Maverick threw his chair into Zensha's path. "What the actual fuck happened back there?" he roared, and the harshness of his tone spooled Nimah out of her bleak thoughts and back into her body.

"You trying to crack my toes there, skinbag?"

Hands gripping the edges of his wheels with white-knuckled fury, Maverick wrenched his chair forward an inch, forcing Zensha to jump back before he did just that. "You nearly got us both killed!"

Zensha clenched fingers tight into a fist, the gears in her arm whining. "Maybe I ought to finish the job then, eh?"

"That's enough, both of you." Ro pried Zensha back but beneath the calm, her own barely leashed rage shimmered in the tense draw of her breaths. "Now's not the time for quarreling among crew."

"Cargo full of ghosts, that one." Nimah turned at the unexpected rasp of Dobs's voice. She leaned against the riveted post, lurking from the shadows and crowned by a cloud of pale blue smoke rising from the end of a lit cigarette she was never without. "Find out what she's hiding, kid, before it all goes breach."

"What makes you so sure she's hiding something?" Her hesitant question was easily masked by the clamor of voices.

"Ain't you learn nothing from me, kid?" Dobs tapped the point of her pinky beneath her left eye. *Keep a weather eye open.* Dobs stubbed the butt against steel and flicked the bent nub toward the tense tableau of captain and crew.

He's not here. Zensha's frenzied words returned to Nimah, along with the twin emotions of relief and rage that overtook her features after she'd said it. Dobs was right—there was more at play here, and it was past time she got to the bottom of it.

Rising from her seat, Nimah picked up her chair with both hands, then slammed it down hard enough to shock everyone into silence.

"Now that I have your attention." Nimah smiled sweetly, passing over each of them before pinning Zensha with her unrelenting gaze last. "Something just occurred to me. Back when I sat down with you to parlay at the Beak, you told me you needed a reliable crew to find out what happened on Solvanis and, most importantly, return what was taken." Nimah tucked her hands into the pockets of her cargos and eased into a casual stroll. "When I asked you what that was—you answer was . . . interesting." She stopped before Zensha. "Do you recall what you said?"

Zensha held steady, but a waver of tension formed across her shoulders. "I don't—"

"Something *precious.*" Nimah rolled her teeth across her bottom lip in a scathing smile. "I believe those were your exact words."

"Sparrow, what are you—?"

"I'm getting to it," she promised, interrupting her grandmother's question while never once breaking her gaze from Zensha. "One could argue that the lives of children are inherently precious. Of course they are, none of us would contest that, or question that as a presiding lord, naturally you have a vested interest in restoring what was meant to be under your protection. But it goes deeper than that for you, doesn't it?"

"Don't go mistaking spit for rain." Zensha set her chin, but the shift of her weight caused a telltale creak of the steel plating under her boots, as though the ship itself longed to whisper her dark secrets.

"*He's not here.*" Nimah tightened the space between them. "That's what you said to me, aboard the sinker, after you came blazing in and refused to return to the recovery line until you searched the logs like a woman possessed by fear. *He's. Not. Here.*" She molded those three words to the edge of her teeth so that they cut almost as sharply as her bite. "You didn't join the Reckoning for duty, or honor, or even loyalty to the council. This is about love. Not some*thing* precious . . . some*one*."

Zensha's lips parted with a disbelieving gasp, whisper soft, but damning as a gunshot.

"No more lies, Zensha. It's time you explain yourself, or so help me, this mission is dead in the black." A bluff. But one Nimah deployed with every ounce of her training to uphold. She let the intention overflow like water, spilling from her with unwavering sincerity until the first sparks of doubt took root in the seasoned captain. Her resolve rapidly fading from a righteous blaze to a waning ember.

Exhausted and defeated, Zensha tossed her hands. "Six and twenty years ago, I met with a woman who offered a proposal only a fool would turn down. She told me about Solvanis and hired me to safeguard it. My job requirements were simple. Keep void traffic clear of the commune and ensure the income generated from the harvest was allocated into the designated accounts. Other than that, ask no questions—get paid handsomely."

Nimah nodded in consideration. "Paid by who?"

"I don't know."

"I said no more lies, Zensha."

"On my salt, I never knew with whom I was dealing. Aside from the initial meet, which was facilitated by a third-party mediator, all other communication was funneled through encrypted channels. Payment came same as clockwork and always from a different dummy. We're talking four payments per annum across two and a half decades—that's a hundred different identity tags and accounts."

"Only SIGA has that kind of sway," Chu grunted, earning a reciprocal nod from Gertrude.

"Aye." Zensha threaded her hands through her flowing braids. "That's why I knew better than to ask questions, true? Why would I? I had an uncontested pipeline to a lucrative commune seeding not only the other divisions within my quad, but Tortuga. The profit from this alone is why I took over that entire zone and never deviated from it. It's mostly Fringe settlements, so it was easy to muscle out the competition and keep 'em out. It was—"

"Too fucking good to be true and you should've known it." Ro's tone snapped like the sharp crack of her coiled whip. "Mother of pearl, Zen, how could you be so naïve?"

"Figured whoever was involved was shady, true—but I never would've sent her there if I thought them dangerous." Zensha rolled her shoulders, but it wasn't enough to shake off twenty-six years of secrets and shame. "I had a second named Kimbset. The sharpest to ever stand at my side," she continued, her voice flat beneath the weight of profound guilt. "Eight years, thereabouts, she comes up pregnant and something in her changed, true? She went from salt and sea to wanting to taste simple. To be a mother. So I pulled what strings I could and got her integrated on Solvanis."

All hostility melted from Ro with a soft curse. "Oh, Zen."

"The woman in the recording." Nimah's head tilted with a startling thought. "The one clutching the little girl."

Zensha's eyes flashed to Nimah, searing bright with tears and virtuous rage. "Aye. She died clutching the girl, Ingrid. But she'd had twins, and it was the boy they took." Her voice hoarsened with the grit of sorrow. "And Kimbset would've burned down her world before she'd allow them to take either."

At the time, Nimah had ascribed the intense detail rendered around those two slain figures in the recording to the particularly gripping display of a mother and child. Zensha had lingered there the longest not out of shock at the horrific tableau, but out of mourning. And guilt. Something Nimah understood all too well.

"Had I known . . ." Ro set a comforting hand on Zensha's shoulder. "You could've told us."

"I didn't trust you to listen." Her bruised laugh rang hollow. "But now you know it all. I can't bring back the dead, true, and nothing done will ever set right those scales, but I can save her son. That I can do."

"Hey," Boomer called from the doorway. "If you're done throwing piss and fists—we gots them logs from the sinker's flight-box ready. So, haul ass." He scooped a summoning hand and disappeared, the stomp of his boots fading as he dashed back to the bridge.

"You heard the man." Nimah gestured.

Mumbles sat on the edge of the console, snapping her gum, her boots swinging with impatience as they entered the bridge.

"Prime my thrusters and burn me to stardust . . ." Zensha's stunned face was lit from the glow of the rough image Nimah had sketched on her flyby with Maverick of the floating station. "The Eyes of Doom."

Boomer snorted. "The eyes of who?"

"Doom," Ro repeated, tenuous fear molding the hard lines of her stern features.

"I feel like we're missing something." Nimah whisked her gaze between the two women. "Who the hell is that?"

"They be a foul whisper," Zensha replied. "But all who have sailed long as we have heard the stories. The dark kind that turns yer stomach and sets the wee hairs on edge." She released a steady sigh. "But in every story, there is a thread of truth."

"What?" Nimah demanded.

"The Doom is a place where the poorest of unfortunates are taken, where a madman dabbles in the foulest of studies. And in all the stories and songs, they warn of three glass orbs that shine like eyes in the darkest of seas. You look into them, you are ne'er heard from ever again."

Zensha punched her finger to the screen where Nimah's sketch shimmered, which, come to think of it, did in fact kind of look like three, unblinking eyes.

The silence held for one tense beat before Boomer razzed his lips. "That's the lamest shit I ever heard. A kid-snatching lunatic named Doom?"

"It *is* absurd," Ro agreed before Nimah could speak. "Hiding behind such a moniker paints them more as a bedtime monster than man, but I think that's the point. To leverage incredulity of ghost stories as a shield, rather than expose a much more digestible and terrifying reality." Her gaze dropped to the flooring as if she could see past the grating and through steel, down into the hold where the cryopods were stacked, filled with sleeping children. "I had my suspicions at the Beak, but I didn't dare speak on them lest it somehow made it real . . . if Doom is behind this," Ro continued, this time directly to Nimah, "whatever awaits the children is worse than death."

Sorrow glistened on the fringe of grandmother's dark lashes. And the only thing more horrifying then being surrounded by the innocent dead lost to the sinker was beholding the fiercely commanding Indira Roscoe a breath away from hopeless tears.

"'Splain's why they cleared all them people on the ground." Chu cursed darkly, arms crossed and eyes blown wide behind her bifocals. "Dead don't speak."

"According to the records from my father"—Liselle stepped forward—"the sunken ship was the last on their manifest. We lost the majority before we got to them, and the rest have already reached the Doom facility. We're too late." She released a steady breath, worrying her fingers in her lap. "Do we circle back to Tortuga with the few we saved? Cut our losses?"

"No." Nimah inhaled deep, steadying herself. "The council won't accept a meager seventeen out of five hundred and seven." She swept her gaze around the console, meeting everyone's gaze. "And neither will I."

Ro crossed her arms. "What's your play, Sparrow?"

"The sinker was scrubbed, likely to slip through the Sockets undetected—same as we did—but their comms were shot in the jump. When I boarded the ship, I noticed the last two transmissions never got out, which is probably why they were caught in the minefield. The station didn't know they were en route to clear their path, and as of now likely still have no idea the ship even sunk."

A slow smile of understanding crept across Ro's face. "So they might still think their prize is incoming."

"Exactly. I figure we probably have at least another hour before they grow suspicious, and I say we use this to our advantage." Nimah's fingers skimmed over the cracked disc she'd pulled from the wreckage before escaping the collapse. "This holds not only all logs and transmission recordings, but the ship's registration tags as well. Mumbles can swap it with ours, disguising us as the vessel they're expecting."

"It's a way in," Ro agreed with a nod. "But this little ruse of yours won't hold for long, Sparrow."

"It doesn't have to." Nimah's voice hardened to steel. "Because once we're inside, we switch tactics and go in loud. Vicious."

Boomer whooped, cracking his knuckles. "You had me at loud!"

"Far as we could tell, the bulk of station security is external," Nimah continued. "Minefields, cloaking shields, and krakens. But inside, there can't be more than a small security team comprised of maybe ten to twelve, max. Probably armed with only close-range blasers, batons, but not much else in the way of weaponry."

"Enough to put up a bit of scuffle." Gertrude grinned. "But not near enough to stop us."

"When we dock, we'll be greeted by lab workers who won't be expecting an assault, or equipped to handle one," Nimah pressed on. "So we use that moment of surprise to our advantage to seize the hanger before we move on to recovery. Maverick and I confirmed with thermal scans that the children are being housed two levels down, in a sealed chamber behind an eighteen-inch carbide steel door."

"Light work," Chu grunted. "My shears'll chew through it like butter."

"The biggest problem we have to solve for is transportation. Four hundred is far more than the *Stormchaser* can handle. We'll need another ship. Maybe two." Ro braced the captain's console, her mind working the problem.

"A station of this size will have at least half a dozen emergency evac ships," Maverick commented. "If we commandeer a couple of theirs, three, including the *Stormchaser*, should be plenty."

"Three ships. Three pilots to fly them." Nimah nodded. "Maverick, Captain Ro, and Liselle—you're the strongest fliers, so each of you will pilot a craft. The rest of us will split between you as gunners, forming teams. First and second teams will focus on rescue while the third holds the hanger and scoops the ships, and Mumbles will stay aboard the *Stormchaser* to crack their network remotely through the Blind-Eye. We hit our targets in tandem—forcing them to diverge their already threadbare security—and reconvene at the hanger to break for the RIM. Once we're in the clear, we send a wave to the council for immediate collection of the children, and that's it." Nimah dusted her hands. "Mission complete."

A couple of chuckles circled the bridge.

"Oh, that all?" Gertrude sighed and elbowed Nimah with a smirk.

"After the children are collected," Nimah continued, smothering her answering grin. "Liselle will return to the Inner Circle. I'll flag ahead to Admiral Wallace so she can meet with Liselle and take her into SIGA so she can barter for reinstatement."

"Stay the mast." Zensha's frown was slow-forming as frost over a still pond. "What about the Doom? Surely we're blowing that place to all hell before we go blazing for the horizon."

"Well . . ." Nimah clicked her tongue. "Actually, no. We can't."

"What do you mean *can't*?" Zensha roared. "This one stole one of them novas along with them crates she hauled on board from the sinker!" She shot a finger to Chu, who rocked back like she'd swung a pistol at her nose. "I say we use it to send them screaming to hell!"

"If we destroy the facility, Liselle will lose her leverage." Nimah set her shoulders, bracing for a whole lot of rage about to come her way. "When this is over, Liselle will stand before the board and swear under oath that after I contacted her on Corlys, she only agreed to join my mission so she could infiltrate my crew and outmaneuver our efforts, and that she had every intention of arresting me herself once she'd succeeded. But I escaped, so she returned to the Inner Circle to share her report and plead forgiveness for acting without official capacity. She will produce a key piece of evidence to support her statement—a copy of the research that we allegedly attempted to steal, which Mumbles will download while we clear out the children, proving her fidelity to SIGA and to her badge."

Yes, SIGA would be wary, but they would want to save face even more, and would take Liselle back into the fold immediately, if only to ensure they had her in close contact.

"Are you fucking stupid?" Zensha erupted, fists clenched. "Your plan not only ensures SIGA gets away with this, but that they'll *keep going*."

"Probably," Nimah agreed. "But that's a problem for tomorrow. Today—this is how Liselle gets her life back." Her expression hardened. "And whatever your feelings, Zensha, I owe her that much." She looked to Liselle, her best friend, and at one time, her only source of family. "I owe her everything."

"Why are you worrying about stroking the belly of SIGA's ego, instead of aiming to take them down with a harpoon to the throat?"

Nimah crossed her arms. "And how do you suggest we do that?"

"The same as you did with Shinoda." Zensha tossed her hands with an aggrieved huff. "Use what we have—the files, the reports, everything you've pieced together. Melt it down into a single, smoldering bullet and blast it across the newscasts! Show the entire Inner Circle how deep SIGA's corruption runs!"

"Sounds poetic, innit?" Gertrude sighed. "Much as I want to side with you, soon as we pull the trigger, SIGA snaps their fingers and the bullet vanishes into naught but static—then it's us they come blazing for, and I don't know about you, darling, but I happen to find my neck too pretty for a noose."

"You yellow-bellied gobshites!" Zensha's rage boiled over, bubbling and thick as tar. "They have to pay for this. *They have to!*"

"And they will." Nimah squared her shoulders, her presence commanding. "But dismantling an organization as powerful and vast as SIGA will take a lot of time, and careful planning. What we do here today can't accomplish that, but it can save these children and restore one broken life. For me, that's enough. If you can't set aside your hard feelings, you're free to walk away—we'll see it done without you, and your conscience can remain clear." She stepped closer, voice lethal with warning. "But if make any attempt to circumvent our efforts—destroying any chance of restoring Liselle's future—I promise you . . . *I promise you* . . . I will snatch the life from your body with my bare hands."

"See the Sparra didn't fly far from the tree." Zensha's lips pressed into a thin line, her gaze flicking from Nimah to Ro and then back. "You're making a mistake. A big one. But this isn't my ship, so what choice do I have?"

"None," Nimah agreed. Then she turned her attention from Zensha to the rest of her family and crew. "I know you're all probably exhausted. It's been hard sailing over the last few days, and the hardest part is yet to come, but we're so close. We can do this. Together we can do anything. And the children we save will be another mark in the already unshakable legacy of the Valkyrie crew. I'm honored to sail with you."

Gertrude beat a celebratory fist to the wall, ringing the hull. "To the void!"

"Or Valhalla!" everyone but Zensha and Liselle echoed.

And beneath Nimah's boots, the *Stormchaser* shuddered, as if bracing for what would come next.

CHAPTER TWENTY

Contact: Jono Shinoda
Msg marked urgent: *I have your results.*

Jono's notification flashed on Nimah's wristdeck and everything slowed to a stop, her chest tightening in a terrified squeeze. Urgent? *Fuck.* She planted her hands to the table as a sudden wave of nausea brought with it a ringing echo in her ears. Sharp as a scream.

"Let's get our bearings before we go gallivanting off into the void." Ro took command of the table. "How are we for supplies?"

Chu raised her hand. "Them crates I hauled off the sinker. One was full to the brim with premium meds, enough to seed our account for a year if we hawk to the blackbooks. But the other two." A proud smile hooked across her sagging face. "Brand new med gear. Uniforms and shit. Got me thinking maybe Gertrude can put that needle of hers to use and fix us some disguises to pass as the delivery team."

"Excellent idea," Ro agreed. "The longer we can hold the pretense, the better our odds."

Another wave, this one strong enough to make Nimah's eyes wheel in her sockets, and a spear of cold raced down her spine. *Oh no.* She was about to have another hallucinatory episode. And if she didn't get away from the table, fast, it was going to slam into her like a transport vessel blowing through a traffic light.

"How are we for artillery?" Ro went on, thankfully too caught up in leadership to notice Nimah as she pushed out her chair.

The tension in her chest seizing tighter. Slow. She had to move slow. Not too rushed. Not too bothered. But every step was a struggle when her knees wanted to buckle and collapse.

"Blasers need to be cleaned and charged, but we got us plenty of mags for twenty clicks a piece," Boomer answered, drawing up a log from his wristdeck. As lead gunner, he was responsible for keeping an account of the *Stormchaser*'s weapons cache and overall supplies. "Wish we had a few more extended clips, but as we ain't anticipating heavy heat—we're razor."

"Sparrow?"

Nimah only just reached the doorway when her grandmother's seeking voice stopped her cold.

"Where are you going?"

"To call Jono." Black spots danced around the corner of vision, and she masked her nauseated sway by leaning into the jamb, thinking fast. "The hospital is empty, and huge. We can use it to hold the children while we contact the council."

"It's a great idea." Ro stopped before Nimah, arms crossed. "But we can call him en route, Sparrow. Right now we need everyone together to—"

Sweat, cold and thick shook through her with a tremble that Nimah couldn't fully suppress. "I won't be long. Twenty minutes, tops."

Her grandmother settled closer, her penetrating gaze heavy with concern. "Tell me I don't have a reason to be worried about you, and I won't."

Nimah pushed a smile onto her face. Not too bright to appear insincere, just enough to hopefully dispel the weight of worry carving hard lines around her grandmother's mouth. "Void sickness. Still happens sometimes."

Ro nodded, and when she drew back to the table to rejoin her crew, Nimah catapulted down the corridor, sprinting for her cabin.

Once inside, she set the door locks and reclined against it. Her heart rattled against her ribs, struggling for rhythm, for breath against the storm swelling in her chest. Pain grabbed hold of her lungs, sudden and cruel, and her vision tunneled as the hull of the ship splintered away, reality breaking apart like fragmented recordings on a fried disc. Sound warped as jagged bolts of electricity chewed along her bones and seared behind her eyes, driving deep into the tender orbs.

Then—*white walls. Hot lights. Currents slammed through her until Nimah's teeth wanted to pop like sonic grenades, and the taste of blood filled her mouth. Until it swam in her eyes, turning everything to vivid red.*

"*More!*" *A woman's shrill voice, sharp as the point of a scalpel.* "*I said more!*"

Another wicked explosion of pain and light, and suddenly Nimah wasn't in her body anymore—she was yanked free and floated untethered, weightless as a kite cut from its string. A soul without the anchor of flesh. Drifting. No more pain. The taste of blood gone from her mouth. No, not her mouth.

Something had called her here. Something she'd had felt many times before. And she looked around her, trying to find out what it was.

Shadow figures moved in the light, faceless things against the searing glare. Brighter than any sun. But between them, another shape—this one shimmering and faded around the edges like dying stardust. And that awareness, that knowing, tightened inside of her.

"*What are you?*" *Its voice, deep and ancient, expanded around Nimah, vast as the void itself as it reached for her—hesitant and uncertain, seeking not with fingers but with its mind. A cautious unspooling of energy that crept toward her with uncertainty until she came into focus.* "*What,*" *it repeated,* "*are you?*"

Then—fear. That prodding tendril of curiosity snapped back, severing whatever cord had bound her in place.

Nimah spun out of the light, a whizzing tornado, then slammed back into her body like a boot to the jaw. She hit the floor, cheek burning, and gasped against the sudden return to consciousness. Everything was too much—too real, too solid, too loud all at once, and a single screaming word rang sharply in her ears.

Just one.

Abomination.

Crawling onto her knees, Nimah vomited until her stomach was empty then spat her mouth clear. While the episodes were getting more frequent, whatever had seized her just now had been so much stronger. Almost desperate. This was nothing like being terrorized by Dobs or haunted by Sigourney. Rather, it had felt more like being sucked into a vortex that ripped her very consciousness out of her body and thrust her into someone else.

Into a memory.

Nimah flexed cold fingers and shook out numb hands. No time. She spat again and adjusted her jaw with a grunting wiggle. Jono was waiting, and that episode had her cost precious time she didn't have to spare. Drawing up her comms channel from her cabin's console, the holo flickered as Jono's face filled the screen.

"We have to be quick, Jono. What do you have for me?"

"First, I want to emphasize that my tests aren't entirely complete, so this is only a high-level analysis." His stern features tightened as Jono pushed his glasses up the bridge of his nose. "Second, I would ask that you sit down."

"I'm fine with standing."

"I really must insist."

"For fuck's sake Jono, lighten up. You look like you're about to tell me I'm dying." Her snorting laughter quickly faded when his tense expression not only didn't improve, it darkened. Nimah lowered to the foot of her bunk and the holoscreen lowered with her. "Am I dying?"

Jono spun away, and images swirled into view, showing the scans of her pulsing heart, magnified in eerie detail. "This is your heart. It's thirty percent larger than normal," Jono began. "Elite is putting tremendous strain on your system, which has led to acute failure of the ventricular muscle. Basically, it's pumping so hard the anterior walls are almost as thin as recycled paper."

Air sat thick as cement in her lungs. "How much time do I have?"

"This kind of damage is irreversible, Nimah." Jono's face switched back onto the screen. "It can be stabilized, but eventually you'll need a replacement."

Replacement. That word struck like a hammer against her skull. There was a reason retrofitting happened during childhood—synth organs, while readily available, had to be implanted before the age of five to prevent rejection. After that, failure was almost a guarantee at sixty percent after the first decade, increasing ten percent every year thereafter.

As for cloned organs, those could be grown, sure, but the process took years and as a RIM-rat, now pirate, she wasn't the kind of candidate who could push to the front of the line for a procedure she could never hope to afford, anyway. At least not until the RIM Accord settled, but even if that somehow happened within the next few weeks, the government would likely find a way to deny her out of spite.

Nimah sighed. "How did this happen to me? Why?"

"That . . . It's a little harder to explain. As you are part Valhallan, elite is an organic part of your genetic ancestry. Now that you've bonded to it, you've awoken dormant strands in your DNA which have triggered a kind of biological transformation. Think of it like a second puberty. Hormones are elevated and rapid changes are taking place on a cellular level—it's aggressive, and it's not going to stop until it's completed maturation."

"But if this is supposed to happen, why is it killing me?"

"That brings me to my next point." Jono released a heavy sigh. "I want to apologize for not believing you about Dobs."

"You believe me now?"

"I do." His eyes shone bright with remorse. "Your neural scans were . . . impossible, and the only sense I can make from them is that your mind is fighting to support dual consciousness and it's frying your brain. I also believe this is exacerbating your heart. Somehow, a fragment of Dobs's consciousness latched onto you like a parasite. Small at first, barely noticeable. But she's growing stronger every single day, feeding from your energy to keep herself alive. The stress of supporting you both is more than your body can handle."

Nimah's shoulders hunched with a grimace. "First my heart. Now my brain." And there was no synth or clone option to replace that. "Jono, what do I do? How do I get her out of me?"

Jono swiped a hand through his hair, disheveling black locks into a chaotic tumble around his gaunt face. "I don't know yet. But for now, you have to cut yourself off from elite."

"What? I'm not using it."

"Nimah." His voice darkened with concern. "Your blood levels indicate you have a high concentration in your system. You'd have to be using it daily for weeks to account for these results."

"I told you I'm not using it," Nimah snapped. "I haven't touched it since we saved my grandmother. After that, I gave it to Chu to redesign the *Stormchaser*'s core generator and power the ship."

Jono studied her. Silent. Calculating. His expression shifted into surprise, erasing the tense lines between his brows. "Of course! You're bonded now, and the ship is saturated in elite. It's all around you. In the floors. In the walls. In the air, reaching for you. And you must be reaching back, unconsciously, every time you have these episodes, like an automatic survival instinct."

"So what do I do?"

His gaze flickered to something off-screen and his mouth pressed into a grim line. "You need to get back to me as soon as possible. We can run dialysis to siphon elite out of your bloodstream, and maybe in a month or two, I don't know . . ." He thrust a hand through his hair, scattering the already wild black strands. "It's a long shot, and I only have theory to go on, but it might be enough to—"

"—cure me?" Nimah finished, but she knew the answer even before his features fell with regret.

"Buy you time. Your other organs can be salvaged with careful attention, but your heart . . ." He hesitated. "There's no saving your heart. And if we can't stop you from drawing on elite, you're a ticking bomb—eventually you will go off, and when you do . . ."

He didn't need to finish. It had happened before to her mother, all those years ago. This was what her grandmother had been afraid of— Nimah succumbing to the same explosive end—and was the reason behind why she'd dropped Nimah off on the RIM, never looking back.

Deep within her chest, something dark and bitter bubbled from her belly and into her throat. The hollow ring of laughter. Soft and deranged. Was it Dobs, she wondered, or was it her? Did it even matter anymore? Between sanity or madness—it was hard to tell which side of the line she stood on these days.

"Worst case scenario, how long do I have?"

He clicked his tongue, arms crossed in measured thought. "If all goes well, we could probably squeeze out a year or two. Otherwise, if not . . ." Jono stared off-screen, his gaze likely boring into the scanned images of Nimah's cardiovascular system, where she imagined a network of nerves and blood vessels blinking in alternating bursts of red and blue—like distant stars winking out, one by one. "A few months? Six, maybe. Certainly far less if you *activate* yourself again. The greater the surge—the greater the damage . . . the less time you'll have."

The truth sat between them. Heavy. Unavoidable.

"So no matter what we do"—the weight in her chest pressed harder—"I'm going to die."

"That's not going to happen." Jono settled closer, his face filling the frame of the holoscreen. "I may not have a solution right now, Nimah, but I will find one. I need you to trust me."

A tight smile wove across her lips. "You're one of the few people I do trust, Jono."

"How soon can you get out to me?"

"Not for at least another forty-eight hours." Nimah scrubbed a hand across her face as if trying to erase all traces of fear and uncertainty from her thoughts so she could focus on more important matters, and she brought him up to speed with the events aboard the sinker, as well as their rough plan for recovery. "We'll need help with finding somewhere safe to hold them until we can contact Tortuga."

"The hospital is still a bit of a construction zone, but it's large enough and currently empty of patients. I can call in the medical staff to ensure the children receive all the care and attention they'll need."

"I owe you."

"No. This is what the RIM does: it provides for and protects those who need it most. Keep me in the loop once you're en route back to us, and Nimah—after we get them situated, let's continue this conversation to work out our own next steps."

"I'll be in touch."

"And remember what I said, Nimah. Keep away from elite. The more you take, the stronger Dobs appears to get. If we want to stand a chance of extracting her from your mind, we'll need to weaken her source of energy."

"Got it." Shucking her arms into the sleeves of her leather jacket, Nimah ended the wave and the holoscreen collapsed into itself—a green line that cut like a fading miniature horizon.

She'd known the results wouldn't be great, but this had gone far darker than she'd expected or mentally prepared for. Nimah pressed the heel of her palm against her breastbone and kneaded away the tender ache. But to her surprise, while there was a spark of fear, it was small as a waning candle instead of a growing bonfire.

She'd spent her whole life afraid, but it wasn't fear that gripped her now. It was acceptance. Death was a biological certainty. It could be delayed and cheated, for a time, but in the end everything died. At least now Nimah had an idea of when it would come for her, and that knowledge was oddly . . . freeing.

The crack of a Zippo had Nimah turning to find Dobs standing in the far corner with a fresh cigarette blazing between hooked fingers.

"Guessing you heard all that, huh?"

Dobs didn't answer. Only gazed from the shadowy corner in expressionless silence as a thin curl of smoke plumed from the end of her cigarette.

"I'm done cowering from you." Nimah boosted from the foot of her bunk and closed the gap between them. Drawing every inch she could into her spine but still arching her head back to meet Dobs's stony yet slightly amused gaze. "I may be stuck with you in my head, but know this—you're tied to me. Whatever happens out there, if you jeopardize this mission and put those children's lives at risk, you're in my head so you know I'm not bullshitting when I say I will lobotomize myself, and trap us both in hell until my body fails and you fade into nothing."

Lifting her cigarette with the barest hook of a grin, Dobs sucked long and deep. Then exhaled. "Heard."

Dobs vanished in that puff of smoke and, for first time since she'd appeared, a sense of victory and control flooded Nimah. So bright she was dizzy with it. She'd challenged her demons head-on and won a battle. A small win, one she sorely needed, but now was not the time to get big in the head when there was a greater battle still to face. So Nimah donned her cutlass and set her sights to the storm brewing on the horizon.

CHAPTER TWENTY-ONE

"There. Now you're perfect." Gertrude beamed like a proud auntie before turning Liselle around by her shoulders. "See for yourself."

Liselle did a half turn in the mirror, then a quarter in the other direction, and adjusted the lapels of the lab coat. The bright white cotton, though plain, was expertly made and expensive. Gertrude had to sharpen the lines of Liselle's cheekbones with makeup, adding shadows for depth beneath her eyes that morphed Liselle from a baby-faced twenty-two to a very hardworking thirty-plus after ten years of med school and a handful more in the punishing beat of residency.

"You're good." Liselle tucked a freshly retwisted loc behind her left ear. "Honestly, I don't know who is more of a genius. You or Mumbles." She gestured vaguely to Mumbles, hunched over a portable holoscreen, code whizzing with blurring speed as she forged documents and identity tags so they could bypass any security checks at the Doom station. It was a job that would've required a small team at least a solid twelve hours to accomplish, yet she was doing it alone and with only an hour on the clock.

"Oh, that's an easy one, innit. Mumbles, by a thousand." Gertrude winked as she cracked open another micro-capsule, pouring out a pair of black combat boots that expanded from a grain of rice to full-size before they struck the floor.

Between the gear they'd extracted from the crates, and a few pieces collected from Gertrude's own stage wardrobe, the crew had been transformed from a ragtag bunch of pirates into uniformed technicians.

"Don't let the way she trips over her tongue fool you. Or the state of her cabin," Gertude added with a visible shudder that had Liselle laughing.

"I think them crossed wires be a blessing," Zensha said from the kitchen, her usual white blouse and khaki britches replaced with a slate-gray uniform, stamped with the emblem from the sunken ship. Her platinum hair was knotted into a low bun, hiding her face and highlighting cheekbones. "On the other side of madness there be genius. Isn't that what them powdery philosophers say?"

"Touché," Liselle conceded.

And as the flurry of conversation continued, Liselle stooped to gather her discarded clothes and tuck them into her rucksack. Inside was one of two possessions she had left—her badge. The other, she wore underneath the lab coat. Her STARs suit. Familiar to her as her own skin . . . yet wearing it now served only as a terrifying reminder of all that she'd lost and might not ever get back.

It made her angry. It made her scared. It made her want to fall to her knees and scream until her lungs throbbed like a fresh wound. Was this how Nimah had felt? Driving her to break into the Academy and free Maverick and Boomer from the cells—setting the events that followed into precipitous motion? Nothing had been the same since, and sometimes Liselle wondered what might have been had she chosen not to help Nimah that day.

Then Nimah's grandmother would be dead, she tried to remind herself. Surely helping her best friend save the last surviving member of her family was worth it, on top of preventing what would've been the most horrific act of mass genocide in their known history. She knew that. Understood it. But she still begrudged all that it had cost them. Their shared aspirations of being agents together, climbing their way to the echelons of SIGA. A lifetime of dreaming gone in an instant and the sour taste of loss curdled in the back of her throat.

Was it selfish? Sure. She could admit that. Was her anger at Nimah both misguided and misplaced? Perhaps. But it didn't make it any easier to swallow, nor was it a truth she was ready to admit or accept.

<*Attention*, Stormchaser *crew. Captain has requested all personnel make their way to the cargo hold and prepare for deboarding. T-minus ten minutes to dock.*>

Gertrude held out a hand for Liselle. "You ready, darling?"

Liselle set her rucksack aside and took a slow, deep breath. "Ready as I'll ever be."

"Don't worry. A heist is a lot like performing in a play. And acting is easy." Gertrude leaned in close, and looping her arm through Liselle's, she led her out into the corridor behind Zensha, who was practically jogging. "The key lies in purpose. For every character you play, you allow that truth to anchor you to your goal. Every thought, every action, every emotion will be connected to that truth like an artist using a vanishing point on the horizon."

"And what is my purpose?"

Gertrude raised her chin in thought. "You are a young physician eager to make a change in impoverished communities, but overwhelming loans and piling student debts have pushed you into darker pursuits. You know this job is questionable, but you aren't going to ask unnecessary questions, because if you default on your debt you'll be stripped of your hard-earned degree, and the siblings who rely on you for survival will be tossed onto the RIM."

"Wow." Liselle blinked. "That's quite the backstory."

"Ta, darling."

The rest of the crew was already gathered below in the cargo hold as the *Stormchaser* groaned into position. Liselle braced the banister at the top of the stairway. The steel pipe vibrated against her palm from the docking sequence, slowing the ship's speed so it could flow steadily into anchor.

At the center of the hold, Nimah was also dressed in a crisp lab coat, her hair tucked under a straight black wig cut into a bob that reminded Liselle of the fierce and commanding Admiral Wallace. It brought authority to Nimah's features and intensity to her posture, or maybe it was just her, finally coming into her confidence behind the security of a disguise.

Liselle reached the bottom of the step, their eyes met, and for a moment Nimah faltered, breaking the illusion. Suddenly they were just a couple of cadets in the halls of the Academy instead of rogue fugitives in the belly of the *Stormchaser*.

"Hey." Nimah was the first to speak.

"Hey." Liselle was the first to look away.

* * *

Hurt curled low in Nimah's belly like a fist, but she crushed it with focused determination. Now was not the time for her to give sway to her emotions. The hold shuddered as the anchoring locks engaged, and the hatch doors pushed open like the yawn of a great metal beast.

The loading dock was narrow but organized, and teeming with a small contingent of ten personnel who smiled as if they were about to give a tour to a group of Academy cadets rather than receive a shipment of stolen children.

"Captain Phaedra." A woman approached the hatch, approximately thirty, with a short cap of wavy teal hair tied away in a clip. Sleek black mono-frames sat on her pointed nose, kept in place by facial anchoring technology instead of earpieces. "Wonderful, we were starting to grow concerned when the other shipments arrived and we hadn't heard from you."

"Comms trouble. Caught some friction jumping through the Socket," Nimah answered, and held out her hand with a warm smile. "Pleasure to finally make your acquaintance, Ms. . . . ?"

"Pleasure is all ours." She accepted Nimah's hand and shook briskly. "And I am Deidre, site manager for *BPRO*. Or the Hill, as we like to call it. I'm impressed you cleared our external security measures."

"We have a very skilled pilot." Nimah's gaze dipped to Deidre's lapel, stamped with a logo and the words *Biogenic Programs and Research Organization*, before she scanned across the hangar. She counted only three support workers wearing one-piece uniforms, and seven additional personnel, aside from Deidre, in white coats. But, as Maverick had suspected, no internal cameras or sensors, and not a single guard on post.

"I don't see any sentries," Nimah commented, returning her attention to Deidre.

"Not at our hangar, no." Deidre hugged her tablet to her chest. "We have a large facility to manage and prefer to keep security to the more *official* areas."

"And no hangar team? Who is going to handle the offboarding?"

"Myself, and my colleagues here, will receive and catalog your shipment."

Nimah whisked a smirking gaze over her shoulder. "Boomer, wipe the clock, except six and two." He fired four sharp blasts, dropping bodies faster than Deidre could form the breath to scream. "*Shhh.*" Nimah clapped a hand over Deidre's open mouth. "Make a sound and Boomer will punch a hole in your throat. Now, step back, if you please. Slow and steady. That's it."

"Well, that was easy." Boomer swaggered down the steps into the hangar.

"Now comes the fun part." Chu rubbed her hands together.

"Bind these two," Nimah ordered, shoving Deidre against her subordinate, who huddled on the spot, arms tucked to chest and lip quivering like she was seconds from falling into a blubbering mess. "And muzzle the younger one."

"Well done, Sparrow." Ro stopped at her side while Boomer and Gertrude tended to the task. "You were right. No cameras. Minimal security. Begs the question, is it arrogance or stupidity?"

"I'll take either. Their lack of security gives us an edge but only a marginal one." Once both women were bound, Nimah stared them down until they squirmed in the uncomfortable silence. "How many children have been delivered?"

Deidre breathed hard like a spooked doe. Eyes wide and nostrils flaring, her gaze flickered from Nimah to her grandmother and back. "Three hundred and eighty-eight. I coded the last of them maybe six hours before you issued your docking request."

"Are they conscious?" Ro demanded.

Deidre nodded stiffly.

"Good," Nimah answered. That meant all were accounted for, minus those that died aboard the sinker. She lowered to her haunches and set her elbows to her knees. "What is the nature of the work you do here?"

"You . . . you don't know?" Deidre whispered apprehensively. "This is a research facility. We're scientists."

"What *kind* of research requires *children?*" Zensha demanded, a growl edging her words.

"We . . . we, um . . ." Deidre closed her eyes and swallowed hard, finding the voice to continue. "The cybers. Cloning and genetics. Advanced genetics."

Zensha rocked forward, fists clenched, but Nimah stopped her with the flat of her hand, then settled in a little closer and let the menace in her glare pierce Deidre to the core.

"Here's what you're going to do. Call whoever is required to arrange for the children to be brought to the hangar. I don't care what authority you have to pull, or what bullshit you need to spin from thin fucking air—do it. Or I'll kill you both, but I'll make you watch her go first." Nimah pointed to the young assistant, who whimpered and pressed her tear-dampened face into Deidre's shoulder.

"I can't—"

"No, no." The muscle at Nimah's temple ticked. "This isn't a negotiation."

"No shit," Deidre snapped. "But that doesn't change facts. I am a site manager. I oversee administration—maintenance bots, supply shipments, kitchen detail—fucking *grunt work*. I don't have the codes or the credibility to make that kind of a request, and the second I do, I promise you this entire facility will lock down. You want the children? Fine. I won't stop you. But you'll have to go in and get them yourself."

Nimah set her teeth then pushed to stand and faced her crew. "Alright, everyone. New plan. Lose the lab coats." She turned to Liselle. "Please tell me you still have your badge."

Liselle's brows pinched into a frown. "Of course."

"Good. Go and get it. We're going to bluff our way in as SIGA delegates."

Liselle laughed. Then quickly sobered. "Please tell me you're kidding?"

"Look at this place." Nimah swung out her arms. "SIGA is bankrolling whatever is going on beyond those doors. You and I"—she gestured between them—"we're Academy trained. We know how to move and speak like agents. We can sell the lie, and if we're stopped by security or anyone official, your badge is our key. It's one thing that can't be forged. It'll work."

"That gets us in," Ro agreed. "But what about getting out? Four hundred terrified kids—that's a lot to move without raising alarms."

"One problem at a time." Nimah pinched her nose. "Maverick and Chu, you two will stay back and hold the hangar. The rest will follow as part of our retinue." They'd need as many hands and blasers for recovery as possible. "No one speaks to anyone for any reasons. Leave that to Liselle and I." Because the second anyone caught a hint of the rough brogue common among pirates, the entire charade went straight to hell. "Once we have the children, getting them loaded will take the most time, so let's move quick and make every second count." She swung her attention to Chu. "I'd leave Boomer with you, but if things go sideways out there, we'll need his muscle to safeguard the children."

As a veritable one-man militia, only Boomer could hold back a garrison of sentries, buying them critical moments should the alarms be triggered.

"I'm counting on you to hold the hangar." Nimah set her hand on Chu's shoulder. "If we lose it, we're sunk."

Unholstering the repeater strapped across her hunched back, Chu spun it by the barrel around the flat of her hand, like a whirling baton, and caught it with practiced ease. "We ain't losing shit on my watch. Go on and get them kids."

Now that they had an in, and a holding strategy, all that was left was a guide.

"Untie her." Nimah pointed to Deidre. "And get her on her feet."

"What?" Deidre sputtered as Boomer plucked her up by her bound wrist then sawed his combat knife through the knotted rope. "No, I won't leave Cassandra."

"You're going to be our guide." Nimah stopped before Deidre and let her eyes darken with the severity of her words. "Once the children are all safely onboard, we will leave without incident, but if you try to raise the alarms, should you resist or do anything other than what you are expressly told to do—" Nimah grinned, the curve of her smile cold as the embrace of the void itself. "My colleague will vent your subordinate, and then I'll send you to float after her."

For good measure, Chu cocked the hammer on the repeater and Cassandra flinched at her feet, weeping around her gag.

"Please." A hot tear rolled down Deidre's freckled cheek, quickly followed by several more, and splattered against the white lapel of her coat. "I'm not a bad person. I . . . I just work here."

"I don't care." Nimah shrugged.

Gertrude worked swift magic, cleaning the blotchy redness from Deidre's face, restoring her to a polished and poised version of a site manager. "Chin up, put on a good show now." She tapped Deidre's shoulder and winked at Nimah.

Then together, they exited the hangar and stepped out into a corridor that opened to the heart of a sprawling atrium. White columns supported the hundred-foot-high domed glass ceiling and gleamed under the glow of artificial daylight. Sleek metallic architecture was seamlessly interwoven with lush greenery of cloned trees to soften the harsh clinical design. The slender boughs grazed high enough to draw the eye to towering walkways that crisscrossed in all directions, connecting a massive observation deck to two other spherical chambers beyond the vast central sphere.

The atrium buzzed with conversations twined with the faint electrical pulse of hovering service drones and automated cleaning bots that glided between levels, scrubbing already pristine floors and glass to a mirror finish. And transparent pixel walls revealed bustling work-rooms filled with personnel hard at work in coats and uniforms, too deep in focus to pay any mind to the small retinue weaving by.

"This might be easier than we thought," Nimah whispered to Liselle. "How much further?" she asked once they reached the bank of lifts opposite a twenty-foot-wide spiraling staircase that corkscrewed on the opposite side.

"Down two levels, and three doors to the left of the corridor," Deidre said beneath her breath. "Please, just take my credentials. You'll have clear access to anywhere you need to go. I won't stop you."

"Shut up." Nimah bunted the muzzle of her blaser into the young woman's ribs. "Any sentries in position?"

"No." The sheen of tears was thick in her voice. "The entire lower level is cleared."

Nimah bunted her again. "Don't lie to me."

"I'm not."

The doors to one of the five lifts opened and Deidre halted as a stream of bodies stepped off. One, an older man, hesitated when he saw her and broke into a sunny smile, paying neither Nimah nor anyone else from her crew any real attention. "Ah, Deidre. How goes it?"

"Hello, Todd, busy day in the Hill, as you know," Deidre answered a little too shrilly, her smile on the verge of forced.

"Busy, indeed. All senior staff have been summoned to the amphitheater and I was asked *personally* to sub in on the Exo. Can you believe it?" He wiggled brassy brows. "The doctor thinks maybe an increase in voltage might actually crack—"

"Hate to interrupt." Nimah offered an apologetic grimace. "But we have a schedule to adhere to."

Todd blinked at Nimah as if she'd suddenly manifested out of thin air, then dragged his confused gaze across the line of her crew, his frown deepening when he ended on Boomer.

"Oh, sorry, yes, Todd. These are delegates from SIGA, here to run an inspection of the Eidolon Project."

"SIGA?" He bristled, struggling to pull his attention from Boomer back to Deidre. "I wasn't aware we were expecting any involvement at this stage."

"This was a major acquisition." Liselle squared her shoulders, matching Nimah for presence and posture. "Did you really think it wouldn't come with provisos? After all that we've invested in this initiative?"

"No. I apologize, of course. It's just . . . a heads-up would've—?"

"—allowed you opportunity to present a front rather than fact. Enough. Step aside."

"Sorry, Todd." Deidre flattened her arm against the doors, gesturing for Nimah and the others to get on. "Good luck with the, *um*, Exo. Pretty exciting. Wish I was invited into the room for, um . . . that."

"Oh—wait, before you go, any updates you'd like me to bring to the Eidolon—?"

"No!" Deidre's already stark features went pale as the station's white walls. "No, no updates on . . . *that*. Um. I doubt there will be much progress for hours, yet. You know how . . . delicate these things are."

"Indeed." He nodded, uncertainty falling across his face. "Well. Can't keep the boss waiting." Todd stepped back, and the lift doors snapped shut.

"Sorry." Deidre's eyes shot to her toes. "I'm known for being chatty. Ignoring him would've been glitch."

Ro frowned. "Glitch?"

"Suspicious," Gertrude clarified, tapping Ro's shoulder in consolation.

"How long do you think until he opens his mouth to someone?" Nimah asked aloud.

"If he hasn't already?" Liselle focused on the descending numbers on the screen. "Twenty minutes, tops. Another twenty for senior leadership to make internal inquiries for confirmation. Maybe ten more before they send security to intercept and lock down the hangar."

That left them less than one hour—after that, the entire house of cards was going to collapse. When the doors opened, Nimah stepped out first with her grandmother—blasers drawn in a quick sweep. Nimah swung left and Ro covered right.

"Clear." Ro eased her finger off the trigger.

"Same." Nimah holstered her weapon.

"I told you." Deidre removed her clearance badge from her breast pocket. "Here." She thrust it at Nimah. "Entry code 3057."

Nimah arched a warning brow. "Are there sentries *inside*?"

"No. Only a couple of bots on standby in case . . . well, in case."

Ro bunted the end of her blaser beneath Deidre's chin. "Are they programmed for assault?"

"We've never . . . never had to worry about . . . that."

Gertrude chuckled dryly. "Well then, darlings, let's not tarry."

Nimah handed Zensha the clearance badge. "Go on. You first."

Zensha's eyes softened before her jaw firmed with resolve. She swiped the pad with the badge, keyed in the entry code, and the carbide steel door hissed open.

Nimah nudged Deidre ahead, her movements stiff with fear but resigned as they entered the bunker behind Zensha. Bright lights reflected off glossy white walls lined with staggered rows of three-level bunks, each capped with a paper-thin foam mattress and no bedding.

The children—so many of them!—were huddled in the center of the octagonal room or tucked into the safety of the bunks. Their faces mottled and eyes glassy from cryo-sedation that hadn't quite vacated their systems.

Zensha wove through the little bodies, pausing to search, until she landed on one that made her stop, and her breath quickened. Lowering to her knees, she took the boy's chin in her hand and scanned his eyes in the light.

"Devere," she whispered, and something flickered beneath the surface of his empty expression—a brief flash of awareness that had Zensha gasp in relief. Wrapping her arms around him, she hugged the boy close, her strong shoulders folding inward as she shuddered with the rise of tears. "I've got you, lad. I've got you."

"A wafer of soy-bread, couple slices of cloned apples, and a nugget of hard cheese." Gertrude, stopping by a cart laden with untouched food trays, picked one up and tossed the tray in disgust. It clattered at her feet, scattering the meager meal like paint across a canvas. "I've seen better food served in a prison cell."

Jostled into service mode by the sudden influx of noise, the stationary bots whirred into motion, but Deidre disabled them, punching in her management codes to take them offline. "I don't think the handlers were alerted," she said as the last one powered off.

Nimah swept her gaze back to the children. So many. In theory, she'd known, but seeing the reality made her stomach twist with doubt. A few of the children started mewling in panic, but Zensha was quick to soothe them with soft hushes.

Nimah stepped back, thoughts racing. "We can't march hundreds of kids through the atrium. Not without taking it first. Ro, Boomer, Liselle, and I will clear the floor, then together we hold the corners while Zensha takes the children through. It'll be tight. It'll be messy. And loud." And the last thing they needed was to get locked in a blaser fight with sentries when they had half-sedated children caught in the middle, but it was the best play they had.

"Wait!" Deidre waved her hands like flags calling a truce before a war. "You do realize we're standing *beneath* the hangar, yes? It's like fifteen . . . twenty feet above us."

"And?" Boomer snorted. "You suggesting we punch a hole through solid carbide?"

"Yes." Deidre adjusted her mono-frames on her nose. "That's exactly what I'm suggesting."

Nimah swiped the comms tag behind her ear. "Chu? You there?"

"Perched on a branch like a canary."

"Take ten long strides from the hatch, switch on your bifocals, and scan the flooring beneath your feet."

"What am I looking for?"

Nimah flashed her middle finger and smirked at Chu's barking laugh. "Think your welding shears can carve through to where we are?"

The comms hummed for a moment as Chu muttered too low under her breath for Nimah to make out. *"Lotta piping and prime cables, so it'll slant by a few degrees, but sure. Give me thirty, thereabouts."*

"Make it wide. Ten feet at least."

"Copy."

Swiping off comms, Nimah turned her attention back to her team. "There's our exit. It won't be quick, but it'll be easier to hold off assault from here versus the atrium."

"Once we disable that door," Ro agreed. "And if we blast the bolts on the feet of those bunks, we can stack them in the center. Use them as ladders to climb out."

Nimah's smile widened. "Great idea."

Zensha closed in on Deidre, Devere in her arms and tucked close to her chest. "Why would you help us?"

Deidre flinched at the sharpness in her tone. "I don't want to see anyone I care about die."

"But you're fine so long as it's these children." Zensha's lip curled with a sneer, and if her arms weren't already full with Devere, and no intention of putting him down, she'd likely have punched Deidre with her right instead of her left.

It wasn't long before the rattle of the carbide sheers hummed above them, and in less than thirty minutes, Chu punched a large hole through the ceiling, her head popping through the nearly perfect circle while suspended like a bat from a pulley, her bifocals expanded into telescopes and gloved hands holding the flaming end of her welding shears.

"Sonofa . . . I knew we were talking in the hundreds but, fuck me with a cactus, would ya look at 'em all."

"Okay, let's get them into rows of three feeding up each of these bunks," Nimah ordered, keeping an eye on time.

"Sparrow." Gertrude closed in at Nimah's side. "We have a small problem. I've run a head count and we're short thirty-one. I counted twice," she added before Nimah could suggest it. "Thirty-one."

Ice curled around Nimah's heart. Of course. This had been too easy. And as she turned to Deidre, her face, already ashen with fear, went a paler shade of white. "Where are they?"

Deidre breathed sharply, her chest fluttering like a terrified bird. "Under observation. Eidolon Project."

Eidolon. Nimah's thoughts shot back to the brief exchange between Deidre and Todd at the lift. And the way she'd blanched when Todd had said the name and how she'd brushed him aside in panic. Nimah hadn't thought much of it given they were on a time crunch, but now it was coming together. Her willingness to let them inside the chamber, offering a convenient exit under the guise of protecting colleagues and staff, when really she'd wanted them gone before they noticed the deficit and uncovered whatever dark secrets they were hiding.

Nimah set her teeth. "Finish getting the children out of here. I'll secure those that are missing and meet you at the hangar," she said to her grandmother. "You"—she lanced Deidre with a glare—"take me to them."

"I . . . No, we can't . . . You don't want to see—"

Seizing Deidre by the throat, Nimah slammed her against the wall. Hard enough to make her skull ring. "I said *take me to them*."

"Okay." Deidre wheezed. "I'll take you."

"Sparrow." Ro touched Nimah's arm, and she released the terrified site manager. "It should be me. Let me go."

"You're still nursing those ribs." Nimah gestured with a thrust of her chin. "I've trained for this, and I know what I'm doing."

"You can't go alone."

"I'm not." Unholstering a blaser, Nimah tossed it to Liselle with a fresh mag. "What d'you say? Have my back on this?"

Liselle caught both with ease. Checking the mag, she tucked the weapon into the belt of her agent suit. "Just like old times."

CHAPTER TWENTY-TWO

To a child, death was a faceless beast.

And the first time Nimah had confronted it, she'd been ten. Stolen from the RIM and taken aboard a transport vessel where a hundred and eighty-seven poor souls, illegally sourced, were indentured to extract highly radioactive prime mineral from asteroids until their flesh melted from their bones.

Only they'd never made it to their destination. Instead, the ship had stalled deep in the void, and it wasn't long before terror gave way to brutality. Adults turned on each other in a massacre driven by utter panic. Huddled in the dark vents, hands clamped over her ears, Nimah was drenched in the endless screams of slaughter and the tang of fresh blood that quickly moldered into the sweet stench of decay in the overwhelming silence that followed.

The stench haunted her in nightmares, as did the echoing cries of ghosts that rang in her ears. A frequency only she could hear. Exiting the lift, the dead sang to her again. A low, vibrating hum in her marrow that grew louder by the second as they approached a round nanite door. So many had come through here, and Nimah was almost convinced if she reached out, she could touch the dead buried within BPRO's glossy walls like bones in earth. The remnants of the dead.

"Are you okay?" Liselle's brows tightened with tension as well as concern.

Nimah swiped sweat from her forehead and the nerves in her teeth sent screaming bolts of pain to push behind the socket of her left eye. The promise of a blooming migraine. "Fine."

Liselle kissed her teeth. "Forget I even asked."

Deidre approached the doorway and, in immediate response to her biometric signature, the nanite door pixelated from solid to plasma.

Nimah and Liselle pushed through, blasers primed, but whatever nightmare she'd braced for—the reality they walked into was so much worse.

Glass partitions ran from floor to ceiling with the sedated children slung in between, suspended by anti-gravity and dressed in pale green patient gowns. Their heads were cleanshaven and tubes protruded from their arms and behind skulls, pumping something into their bloodstreams that had their veins shining black beneath sallow skin.

A team of technicians, all dressed in white coats and black gloves, huddled together to review holocharts with broadcasting data streamed from their sedated subjects. Their murmuring voices punctuated by the steady, mechanical beep of monitors and the whisper of sterilized air through grated vents.

Startled by the reflection of their movement, one of the male lab technicians dropped his tablet, and it shattered at his feet. "Breach!" he shouted. "Hit the alarms!"

A woman bolted for the console. Nimah set her blaser to stun and fired, striking her in the back, and she dropped to the floor, flopping on her belly like a fish as tendrils of electricity webbed across her spine.

Chaos erupted and Nimah and Liselle moved in tandem, fast and with practiced ease, and in under ten minutes eight techs lay unconscious and crumpled on the cold floor.

Nimah holstered her blaser, the whimpering from the tech at her feet fading into silence. "You good?"

"Yeah." Liselle turned full circle, taking in the full extent of the awful display. "What were they doing to them?" Her blaser trembled in her grip. "Are they making them into cybers? Is that even possible?"

"No. This is something else." A wave of gut-coiling sickness washed across Nimah, and movement shimmered in the air like sound waves reverberating off walls. They sank into her, layered echoes of the past overlapped with the present. Instinct gave way to sudden clarity and recognition. Almost like déjà vu.

I know this place. She'd been here before—not physically, but somewhere in the fractures between time during the volatile surges, when elite forced her to spiral across the edges of reality and memory.

Nimah turned full circle where she stood. "I've been here before."

"What?"

Cold sweat. Prickling nerves. And that voice. *Free me.*

Queasy, Nimah pressed her palm to her cheek. "I don't know. I don't..."

And when she pulled her hand away, a soft gasp tore from her. Auras shimmered around the children where there hadn't been any before. Vivid, searing blue, and they thrummed with energy, strong and familiar, that drew to Nimah's heart like a magnet.

"It's not possible." Needing to be wrong, Nimah rushed to the console connected to the diagnostic screens and raced through the touchscreen interface, throat burning as she scanned the recent files for something to explain what deep down she already knew but didn't want to believe.

But there it was. A single grainy image, drawn from the camera feeds on the *Challenger* during the rescue mission for her grandmother. It was badly corrupted by the Blind-Eye, but this one frame had been enhanced just enough to reveal Nimah, facing off with three cybers, engulfed in elite in that split second before she'd cast surging energy through them like a vengeful deity sending the cybers straight to Hell.

"Nims?" Liselle closed in at her side. "What's going on?"

"This place... these children..." She turned to her best friend. "It's elite. They're weaponizing elite." Her breath came shallow, ragged, and Nimah shot toward Deidre, who hadn't moved an inch from a few feet of the doorway. "How did you get elite?"

Deidre recoiled, her chest rising with sharp, panicked breaths. "I can't tell you that."

"Did you steal it from the RIM?" Nimah demanded. "*Where!*"

"It was delivered to *us.* Thirty-six years ago." Deidre shrank from her, hands raised as if to shield herself from the fire Nimah felt burning in her eyes. "This lab was built in dedication to studying and understanding it."

"Thirty-six years . . . ?" Elite would've only existed in one place. For them to have had it this long meant only one thing. Someone smuggled it off Valhalla. "Dobs," Nimah said, voice little more than a weary whisper.

A realization that brought with it another blow, one that nearly took Nimah's legs out from under her. *Why so many children? What changed?* The answer to the questions that had gnawed at her relentlessly for days finally punched through Nimah like thrusters set to full burn. ". . . Me." The blood drained from her head, and she staggered back a step.

She was the catalyst. The reason for all the recent death and sorrow.

"I know it looks . . . unpalatable." Deidre cleared her throat. "Even for those of us who work here—we struggle with it, too, at times. But we also understand we're part of something important. Revolutionary."

"Revolutionary?" Rage. White and searing hot as the surgical lights glaring off the walls, it filled Nimah like a sudden, violent storm. Seizing Deidre by the back of her neck, Nimah forced her to the splayed body of a little girl suspended in anti-grav. Still as a floating corpse. "Look at her and tell me again how noble your work is! How *fucking* revolutionary!"

Tears swam in Deidre's eyes but it wasn't grief or sympathy for the child, only fear for herself.

Disgusted, Nimah released her. No, she was devoid of empathy. Unholstering her blaser, Nimah aimed for Deidre's black heart. "You don't see a child, only a subject to be used for study. A means to an end."

"Please," Deidre whispered, hands raised and trembling. "I . . . I've spent my whole life on the Hill. This place, the work . . . it's all I know. It's my home."

"They had a home, too." Nimah adjusted the setting on her blaser. "And you fucking assholes razed it to the ground." She pulled the trigger.

Deidre collapsed, dead before she hit the floor, a grapefruit-sized wound sizzled in her chest like burning charcoal around the edges. And Nimah didn't intend to stop there. She swung her searing muzzle toward the next prone body, ready to fire kill shot after kill shot when Liselle caught her by the arm.

"What are you doing, Nims?" Liselle forced Nimah's blaser-muzzle toward the ceiling and away from her next target. "We don't *kill* innocent, unarmed people."

"These people"—Nimah set her teeth—"are *not* innocent."

"Maybe not, but they are unconscious." Her grip tightened on Nimah's wrist when she tried to pull away, gaze pleading. "I know you're angry, and hurt, but coldblooded murder isn't the answer. It's not who you are."

It should be. But before Nimah could say the words aloud, Boomer's voice crackled through her comms.

"We nearly done loading down here. You guys taking a vacation or what?"

"We found the missing children and are working on an exit," Nimah answered, turning away from Liselle and Deidre's smoking corpse. "How close are you to finished?"

"Down to the last fifty heads."

"Any ripples from security?"

"Nah, quiet as a fart in the void down 'ere."

It's too easy, a dark voice echoed inside her, but Nimah shrugged it off. "Get thrusters primed. We'll be on our way to you soon."

"Soon?" Liselle swept out her hand with a sigh. "Nims, these kids are in rough shape. I don't know what we're going to do. We need help getting them out, but we can't call in the crew. It's too risky." She whisked to Nimah, her features stricken. "Maybe . . . maybe we need to consider an alternative option."

"I know," Nimah whispered hoarsely, and turned to the suspended bodies of the children, hands shaking as she scanned their streaming vitals. The youngest was maybe four, and she swallowed tears that fought to break free. Liselle wasn't wrong. These children were likely to die in a matter of days or weeks. Ending their suffering now would be a kindness.

Just a stroke of a few keys on the holoscreen.

PURGE.

Nimah's fingertip hovered over the command, trembling, before pulling away. "We take them." Her voice was hard. Final. "Whatever their odds for survival, they deserve a chance—even if it's only to die free and not trapped in this hell." And a distant part of her dared hope that maybe, just maybe, once they were at the RIM, Jono could somehow undo whatever had been done to their poor little bodies.

Liselle hesitated, then nodded. "We can't wake them. The shock might put too much stress on their systems. And there's no way we can carry thirty-one, so we need to find a method of transport."

Nimah chuckled darkly. "Guess I should have waited a little longer before killing our guide."

Despite herself, Liselle smirked. "Yeah, might've been helpful," she agreed then frowned as Nimah swung her gaze to Deidre's sprawled body. "I know that look. What are you thinking?"

Nimah tapped a restless finger against her thigh as her mind rewound the last few moments, right before she'd pulled the trigger. "She said something earlier about the work being unpalatable, even to the staff."

"Yeah, okay." Liselle planted her hands on her hips, trying to keep up.

"If I was a deranged sociopath carving open children, I'd want to keep my subjects out of sight and out of mind. So how do you move hundreds of kids from one end of this facility to the other without being seen?"

Stunned brows popped up over Liselle's eager eyes. "There's a private pathway."

"Scan the walls. Look for a handle or a lever. Something discreet." Moving to opposite sides of the lab, they ran their hands along smooth panels and narrows seams until Nimah's fingers slipped against something that moved. A flat, barely visible handle that, when met with pressure, ended with a soft snick. Nimah twisted the handle and a door mounted flush into the seams of the wall swung open, leading into a narrow service corridor.

Liselle rushed to her side. "Bots and drones must use this to navigate between floors, as well. How much you want to bet this'll take us anywhere we want to go, including straight to the docks?"

"I'm willing to play those odds." Nimah grinned. "They had floating gurneys at the hangar. Maybe we can ping our location to Boomer's wristdeck so he can bring them to us?"

"We don't need gurneys. Service bots!" Liselle clapped her hands together. "They're designed for all kinds of tasks, included relocating supplies and heavy furniture. Deidre's credentials will have full administrative control—we call as many in as we need and program them to carry the children and head straight to the hangar for unloading."

"And no one will suspect a thing." Nimah perked up. "Please tell me you remember her code?"

"Of course I do." Liselle dusted her knuckles on her lapel.

"I could kiss you." Nimah punched a victorious fist in the air. "You reprogram the bots, I'll disconnect the children from suspension. Together we load. Good?"

"Razor."

In the time it took Nimah to call ahead to Boomer, services bots flowed in, summoned by Liselle, and together they worked in smooth, efficient silence. Detaching the children from the tubes and monitors, and tucking sedated bodies within the inner compartments of the bots, each able to carry three, before whisking out into the private corridor in a flowing assembly line to the hangar.

"Almost finished with this last one," Liselle called out.

"Great, after this, we can—" Movement over Liselle's shoulder drew Nimah's gaze, and her breath fell away.

A shimmering entity of light stood at the far end of the lab. Same as the one that had come to her on the lunar outpost the day she'd fought Senior Agent Gallani.

Her feet stumbled to a stop. And as it reached for her, frantic fingers connecting with skin—sliding into her, through her—the world beneath Nimah tilted. She was yanked from her body and shot into the white glare, her mind shattering under the force driving through the bones of her skull and into the softest parts of her brain.

Free me! Its voice rattled against her teeth, and pain sluiced over every nerve. So much pain. It gathered into a bloodcurdling scream, before the hallucination shattered in a million shards of light.

Nimah shot back into the walls of her own skin, and Liselle caught her before she struck the ground.

"Hey!" She slapped Nimah's cheek, clearing her vision. "What happened? Are you okay?"

"Something else is here." Nimah panted, gripping Liselle's arm with an urgency she couldn't explain. Gone. It was gone. The connection between them violently severed, but she still felt it, and that awareness came with layers of information, crumpled into a tight wad her mind struggled to unfold. "It's trapped. Fighting for a way out."

"Nimah, you're not making sense."

No, she wasn't, and there were no words she could find to explain what she'd felt or seen. Only an awareness she hadn't been able to grasp before, that suddenly drew a line across her memories, tethering every strange hallucination across the last few days to the starting point, when it had first reached out to her. Begging. Pleading.

Free me.

"Come on." Liselle scooped an arm around Nimah's waist, helping her back onto her feet. "The last bot is gone, and we've got to get going. Can you run?"

"Yeah." Nimah steadied herself, her grip so tight on her blaser that her fingers screamed, when suddenly the wail of alarms flowed through speakers.

Liselle cursed as, when they turned in tandem, the door to the passageway sealed with an emergency door of solid carbide.

<Attention all personnel, we have a security breach.
Sentries and drones have been dispatched to Observation Lab 6A.
For their safety, staff are to lock down where they are,
and remain thus until further notice.>

"Drones?" Liselle whispered. "Fucking fantastic."

"That's a dead end." Nimah nodded to the passageway. "They're coming right for us, we have to move fast."

"Agreed."

"Boomer." Nimah swiped her comms as they loped for the doorway. "Do you have all the children yet?"

"Last bot just cleared the hangar. But I don't see you?"

"We're pinched." Nimah swallowed. "The passage was sealed in the lockdown. Liselle and I have to punch our way out from the atrium." The comms crackled with tense static, confirming how dire their predicament truly was. "Boomer." Nimah closed her eyes. "Keep to code, okay? You load and you burn."

"But—"

"Liselle and I will manage." She looked to her best friend, Liselle's back braced to the door frame as she scanned out into the corridor before she signaled her agreement with a tight nod. "Tell Maverick and my grandmother whatever it takes to get voidborne. Promise me?"

Another tense beat. "*Yeah. Razor.*"

"Corridor is clear," Liselle said once Nimah closed her comms link. "But it won't be for long."

"Then let's get moving." Nimah flowed tight behind Liselle and both girls shot into a dead run, arms pumping and feet pounding, when they were stopped by a sudden barrage of blaserfire ripping around the bend. Dropping to the ground, they tucked against the wall, arms braced around their heads for cover.

The fire came from the lift bank—which was the only way back to the atrium. And the buzz of approaching drones, loud as a swarm of angry bees, indicated the sentries were closing in, protected behind the drone's shields. Chu's dentures weren't going to be enough to punch a way through.

If only they had Boomer and his grenades... Nimah rolled her eyes with a sigh, then frowned down the other end of the corridor to the diamond glass wall, illuminated by the glow of kraken eggs, but it was the flash of vivid yellow headlights followed by the glint of steel that made her heart swell in her chest. *Maverick.*

As if he heard her, he flashed the shuttle beams twice.

Nimah tapped her knuckles against Liselle's bent knee. "Remember when we debated the reclamation of Paxroy, winter term last year?"

"Call me crazy." Liselle flinched as more blaserfire peppered down the corridor, striking inches above their heads. "But I'm not exactly in the mood to recall my stance on Newnheimer's military theory at this very moment."

"Look behind you."

Liselle swung her head around. "Oh fuck, Nimah. Seriously?"

"Divide and conquer?"

Liselle pumped her blaser, ejecting the cartridge and slapped in a fresh mag. "Go!"

Both girls broke from their cover at the wall, Liselle veering to the left and Nimah taking the rounded bend to the right. She activated her helm, liquid nanites sealing her inside her suit. Its scanners read the threat before her as ten sentries in tessellated armor, hunched behind six battlefield drones shaped like oval shields.

Nimah charged toward them and dodged as scattered fire followed her every step, so close that her suit registered the ripple of each blast slicing through the air. If one struck the suit, it wouldn't hurt, but the scorched hole would take the nanites at least five minutes to knit, and for her plan to work, she couldn't afford a single scratch.

Nimah fired back, weaving and spinning. Every hit she landed was absorbed into the bodies of the drones and cycled back through them for added power and ammo. It would take the heat from a thousand rounds, point-blank, to so much as make a scratch, and she didn't have a thousand rounds. But she wasn't aiming to inflict damage, only to draw attention and time.

"Hold!" a sentry shouted, and the firing ceased.

Braced on her knees, Nimah panted hard, her blaser raised as the sentry who'd given the command flicked his half-visor up and revealed his grimacing, heavily lined face.

"That's enough. You're alone and outgunned. Drop the weapon and come quietly or we'll cold-bag you, here and now."

Nimah didn't need the integrity scans on her vis-feed to know he wasn't bluffing. Extending her arm out to her side, she dropped the weapon and the drones parted at his command so that a column of sentries broke through the center.

They approached her with blasers searing hot and Nimah kept her hands raised as they closed around her in a tight circle.

"Remove your helm," the leader commanded, holding a pair of activated magnicuffs. When Nimah didn't move, his teeth flashed in a snarl. "I said *remove your helm!*"

"No." She raised her chin. "But you might want to put yours back on."

A loud snap and crunch. Gravity seized, and the vacuum of the void snatched bodies off their feet, dragging everything—drones and screaming sentries—from the corridor into a cyclone. Nimah spun in the chaos, her vis-feed firing from all the sensory activity as the corridor was swept away and replaced with the dizzying void.

"*To your left!*" Liselle called out.

Somersaulting in the dark, Nimah angled her head, activating her palm thrusters to stabilize her momentum moments before colliding with a clutch of kraken eggs. A shaken breath rattled through her chest as she pushed away from the webbed net, guiding herself to a safer distance. Spinning out into the void to die slow would've been a mercy compared to what would've happened if she hadn't stopped herself in time.

Liselle glided to her, and Nimah they braced a second before the hull of the *Stormchaser* slid up from underneath them, flattening them against the prow.

Maverick tipped a salute at them through the viewport. *"Get to secondary airlock, Cadet."*

"Copy."

The *Stormchaser* hovered, thrusters pulsing with restrained power as Liselle and Nimah cleared the airlock and barreled onto the bridge.

"Strap in, this is going to get bumpy," Maverick shouted as they fastened themselves into their chairs just as a sentry struck the viewport and rolled off, arms flailing into a spin.

"I told all the ships to clear as soon as they were loaded." Nimah tightened the harness around her chest. "Why did you stay?"

"Why do you think?" Maverick didn't look away from his controls. "Now shut up and let me *fly*." He shot through a gap in the mesh webbing, his focus on furiously charting a path through the novas when the void around them erupted into violent shockwaves that blasted the hull from either side, turning space into a maelstrom. And *Stormchaser* was caught in the middle of it.

"What's happening?" Liselle demanded through clenched teeth.

"They're triggering the novas."

Maverick's words sent ice down Nimah's spine. "How many?"

"All of them." The drag snatched and pulled, and Maverick groaned through hot curses, his neck and shoulders tense with urgency as he yanked and spiraled and dove. Maverick flew like a man possessed, weaving through the chaos as if anticipating the detonations before they struck.

But there were too many, and the overlapping grav-fields thickened the void into rapidly setting cement. The yoke strained beneath his grip as they sucked speed from the thrusters and pushed the engine to the verge of stalling from exertion.

If that happened—Nimah closed her eyes and willed her mind to calm. To empty and expand. To reach. The faintest tendrils tickled along the edges of her dulled senses, but she pushed herself to go further and take hold. *Please.* She let the urgency flow through her and cast it out as far as it could go. *Help.*

Those tendrils rippled with awareness. Reached back.

Nimah's eyes shot open, and there in the shimmering distance, a pod of negs arced for them like shooting stars. Closing in fast.

"What the hell did you do, Cadet?"

Nimah's breath trembled, her fingers tightening around her harness. "I called for reinforcements." It had been a long shot, but as Jono had discovered she was brimming with elite, Nimah figured it had to be enough to allow her to communicate to the negs in a frequency only they could hear. And they'd not only heard her, they'd chosen to act.

Their slick bodies tightened around the Stormchaser, the pod shielding the ship like they would when protecting their vulnerable young. Negs, able to withstand the nova's magnetic pull, created the buffer Maverick needed to regain speed, and as he shot forward, they flowed swiftly alongside, weaving in a concentric pattern of a spiraling vee. Clearing their flight path.

"Almost there!" Maverick grunted—when suddenly the ship rocked, thrown violently off course and into direct contact with a nova. "Fuck, we blew a thruster—hold on!" Maverick braced all his weight against the yoke, battling against the dizzying strain.

Liselle screamed.

Unconsciousness clawed at the edges of Nimah's vision. She was seconds from passing out, and perhaps it was for the best. Better to be unconscious before death.

A massive wall of light passed over them and a neg slammed into the nova that would've swallowed them whole. Its body burst and the *Stormchaser* bucked into a chaotic roll—then with a final wrench, Maverick caught the rotation and stabilized their momentum just as the buoy line flashed past their helm.

Nimah's heart released from the walls of her throat and fell solidly back into place within her chest.

"Fuck." Maverick panted. "We made it. We're clear." His laugh shot out, but it was lost in a sudden thrum vibrating in Nimah's skull.

Vivid white walls. Searing bursts of pain. The void pushed in through the viewport, and glimmering arms reached for her. Screaming. Screaming. Screaming.

Free me.
Free me!
FREE ME!

They caught Nimah by the throat and yanked her, clawing into the dark.

CHAPTER TWENTY-THREE

Cloth was yanked away from her eyes and Nimah blinked her vision clear with a hiss. Chu came into focus first, then the rest of the *Stormchaser*—the riveted posts and swaying anchor cables behind her.

"Where are we?" Nimah groaned, her voice rough as sandpaper.

"Back on the RIM." Chu set her elbows to her knees as she sank onto her haunches, bones in her hips creaking with the movement. "Been here 'bout an hour or such. Mav was brought to the field adjacent the hospital. Crew helped Jono and his team with deboarding them kids for revival and assessment."

"An hour?" Nimah tried to stand but was met with resistance, and when she dropped her gaze, she then realized it was because she'd been bound to the support beam in the hold with tension cables around her torso and legs. "What the fuck?" She struggled against her bonds. "Unstrap me!"

"Easy there, little bird," Chu tapped her shoulder. "Cap said you should stay put until . . . you've calmed down."

"Calm down? What are you talking about?"

Chu cocked her head, her magnified eyes narrowed to fine slits in scrutiny. "Ain't you remember? You lost your fucking gob." She tapped the side of her salt-and-pepper temple. "Started ranting and raving. But it was your eyes—glowing like fucking laser beams again. Had to tie you up and hood you before you hurt yourself. Or us."

Nimah swallowed hard. "I don't remember that." Or at least, not much beyond venting the sentries during her escape from the lab with Liselle.

"Once you were secured, you stopped struggling, at least," Chu shifted her weight from her right leg over onto her left. "Went still as a stone but kept muttering in tongues. Saying words I ain't heard since we'd been grounded on Valhalla. Repeating one phrase like it was the only words you knew."

Nimah didn't have to ask what it was.

Free me. That frantic wail tore through her like blaserfire and even now, she could still hear it. Ceaseless. Desperate. Each repetition carving into the bone wall of her skull.

"Where's my grandmother?"

"On the bridge." Chu jerked a thumb toward the corridor at her back. "About to debrief the council."

"Get these off me." Nimah struggled against her bonds. "I have to be there."

"I don't think—"

"Fucking unstrap me, Chu, now!"

Chu flagged her hands in surrender before uncoupling the tension cables. One by one they dropped away with a clank and thud, and when the last cable was released, Nimah sprinted for the bridge, her boots pounding heavy as her heart against the grating and as she drew closer the voices of the council drowned out the burst of her sudden entrance.

Juanchim, head of the council, flooded the screen. The massive hourglass was visible behind him, the ashes ominously close to spent. Ro stood in the glow, shoulders drawn and hands clasped. "—pleased to report we have found and recovered most of the stolen children."

"Most?" Eshe emerged to join Juanchim on screen.

"There were losses sustained before we reached them. My second would be able to provide a more detailed account, but unfortunately she is—"

"—right here," Nimah interrupted, and looked away from the ashen shock on her grandmother's face as she approached the holoscreen. "Apologies for my lateness. There's a lot of work to do and so few hands to tend to it all."

"Of course." Juanchim nodded. "Captain Ro was in the midst of providing a rundown, and it sounded like recovery was an arduous challenge."

"To say the least," Nimah agreed, tucking her hands behind her back like a cadet facing her general.

"How fair the survivors?" Eshe asked.

"Hale and hearty, Councillor." Ro cleared her throat, taking command of the floor. "But there are a few among them who were subjected to . . . a foulness I struggle to find words for. Given the complexity of this mission, I suggest we provide a detailed report for your review, which will be drafted by my second." Ro gestured to Nimah.

And Nimah didn't miss the way her tone darkened on the last part of her statement, nor the ripple of tension in her grandmother's shoulders.

Murmurs whisked through the attending council members offscreen, and Eshe drew a circle above her brow in prayer for the unfortunate dead.

"In the interim," Ro continued, "Jonothan Shinoda, Chief Physician for the RIM's hospital, has requested fifty or so affected children remain onsite with him for a period of quarantine. The rest can be transported immediately to Tortuga for reunification."

"Thank you, Captain. We look forward to reviewing your report thoroughly once received." Juanchim lowered back to his seat. "Allow us a moment to deliberate, if you will."

The wave went dim, all sound muted behind a cloak.

"What now?" Nimah asked, keeping her words hushed in case audio hadn't been cloaked both ways.

"The council will determine if we have passed or failed," Ro answered just as softly, confirming Nimah's suspicions. She cast wary eyes to her granddaughter, scanning her from head to toe. "Are you—?"

The cloak lifted and stern faces reemerged. "Congratulations, Captain." Juanchim clapped his hands together. "It is my honor to proclaim the terms of the Reckoning have been met to our satisfaction. We also approve Jonothan Shinoda's request for a period of quarantine for any affected survivors, and as for recovery—two wardogs will be dispatched to escort those fit for travel. The council will begin the process of reunification with any surviving family, and those without will find sanctuary at Tortuga."

"Council, if I may speak." Nimah stepped forward, and the two heads on screen swiveled to her. "Before we end the wave, it's my belief that BPRO was running experimentation on those children in an effort to bio-weaponize elite." Ro's stunned gasp was immediately lost as Nimah hammered on. "I'd like to formally petition assistance to send a small contingent to destroy not only the facility but all those responsible for its application."

Juanchim settled closer to the screen and something like rapt fascination shone across his face. "Do you have proof of this? Footage captured during your recovery efforts, perhaps? Data extracted from their network files or detailed copies of any experimentation records?"

Nimah set her teeth. "No. The facility was cloaked by advanced tech that disabled all attempts at recording or data extraction."

Ro flinched at her side, shocked by the lie. But Nimah wasn't about to hand over what they'd stolen to anyone, not even the council. Knowledge such as this couldn't be entrusted. Only destroyed.

"So what exactly are you able to provide to support this allegation?"

"My word. I can only confirm what I saw with my own eyes."

A tense moment of silence followed before Juanchim shook his head. "While I appreciate that you may be Indira's second, and granddaughter, I can't and won't enlist support for any endeavors that will put all pirates at risk of greater retaliation from SIGA based on your word alone."

Nimah ground her molars, her heart rate surging with panicked urgency. "Councillor, please—that place is evil. You're sending wardogs, all I'm asking for is *one*. Just one! Give me that, and not only will I destroy it, but I'll bring you the person responsible for the atrocities so that they can stand before the council and receive justice for their crimes."

Built by resistance fighters during the Zone Wars, wardogs were massive gunners fitted with dozens of blaser cannons to take down dreadnaughts. Afterward, the vessels were repurposed as high-priority transport to protect high-value shipments of goods or personnel. A lone wardog could blow BPRO to space dust without even breaching the buoy line, putting neither vessel nor the crew in any significant danger.

"Taking back what was stolen is one thing," Eshe interrupted, "but destroying SIGA property would be a declaration of war against an entity too great for us to challenge. We've kicked the hornet's nest enough, but our hope is that by allowing the facility to remain intact, SIGA will . . . be less inclined to retaliate."

Nimah blinked swiftly, her mind struggling to process what she'd just been told. "You realize if we do *nothing*—they'll continue harming innocent *children*." She enunciated her words carefully, in case the council was somehow too stupid to understand the implications that inaction would render.

"Possibly. But, provided they keep clear of the territories and outposts safeguarded under our protection"—Eshe shrugged—"that's not our problem."

Nimah's mouth fell open. "Are you fucking—?"

"Forgive my second." Ro interceded before Nimah could finish her searing words. "As you can expect, it's been a trying few days and we're all feeling the wear from it. Thank you for your time, councillors. We will await the retrieval team and any further instructions."

"Drink deep as the stars tonight, Captain Indira. You and your crew have earned the reprieve." Juanchim raised a fist in salute. "Three weeks hence we will hold your official coronation in Tortuga. Listen for the gold."

Ro pressed her palm over her heart. "May it ring true."

The wave ended with a snap and silence descended on the bridge, broken only by the violent rush of Nimah's heart hammering between her ears like a furious fist beating against a hull metal.

"Have you *lost* your mind?" Ro faced her with a seething whisper, eyes wide in accusation. "What possessed you to speak to the council in such a manner?"

"What possessed me?" Nimah's laugh tore from her, harsh and jagged. "I can't believe you're just going to abide by their bullshit decision. Aren't you the fucking queen? Why aren't you standing up to them?"

"What world do you live in?" Ro shook her head, hands on her hips. "I am not queen *yet*, and until then I have no choice but to comply with the council. We all do."

"Fuck the council." Nimah paced the bridge, restless and agitated—*free me, free me, free me* hammering like a fist behind her eyes. "The RIM has plenty of weapons and ships we can rally. We can do this without their support."

"No, Sparrow, we can't." Ro shook a despondent head. "Insurrection against the council is punishable by death. The last pirate who defied their order was keelhauled through a clutch of hatched krakens, his death live-streamed as a warning. They ate him slow."

Nimah kicked up her chin. "I am not afraid of them."

"You should be." Ro's brows shot high. "Because right now a lot of very powerful people want you dead, and I can't protect you from all of them by myself."

"I don't need protecting!" Nimah rounded on her grandmother, fists clenched. "I need answers. I needed you. But instead of either, you've just pushed me aside or tucked me away like a breakable object." Bracing the console, adrenaline scored through her as finally everything she'd been fighting to repress came seething to the surface. "My whole life you've told me nothing, and now I'm losing my fucking mind because I have no one to guide me through what's happening to me."

"What are you talking about?" Ro's voice hoarsened. "Sparrow, tell me what's going on?" The scuff of her boots fell heavy behind Nimah as she closed the distance between them.

"It doesn't matter." Nimah shoved away from the console and resumed her agitated pacing. Annoyed that she'd shared far more than she'd meant to. "You can't save me from what's happening to me. I don't think anyone can. But there's something out there, and it's begging for my help." She thrust a finger toward the horizon glimmering beyond the viewport where the distant tugs of that energy spooled like an outstretched hand beckoning for her to come back.

Free me.
Free me.
FREE. ME!

Ro shifted her gaze from the horizon back to Nimah. "Sparrow, you're not making any sense."

"And you're not listening!" Hands pressed to her face, she dragged them away as something inside of her core trembled like an animal caged, fighting to break out. Grief. Rage. Terror. Anguish.

All of it compressed and tangled into a knotted mess low in her belly. "I need you," Nimah whispered, allowing the hopeful surge of vulnerability to come to the surface. "Why aren't you backing me on this?"

"Because the council is right, and I am not about to start a war. I've seen war. I've seen what it does, and there are no winners, Sparrow—only billions of innocents caught in the crossfire. I'll be damned if I'm responsible for that." Ro closed the distance between them, the hard lines of her determined face softening in sympathy and regret. "We have done the impossible, Sparrow. We saved a lot of lives today. Why can't that be enough?"

"Because it's my fault. All of it!" She bounced her fist against her chest, hard enough for it to hurt, the dam inside of her finally breaking free. "That place—what they were doing to those children. SIGA knows about me. They have the footage from the *Challenger*. They *know*." Nimah waited for the words to settle. For the shock and terror to take root in her grandmother's soul. "Everything that has happened, all of it, is because I harnessed elite *to save you*, and now SIGA wants to bioengineer it into a weapon, and I can't—I can't." Tears shook through her chest, swelled in her eyes, made her words brittle and sharp as broken glass slicing her open to expose the raw and vulnerable truth eating at her soul. "I brought this hell upon them. So long as that place still exists . . . I'll never know peace."

Ro swallowed hard, her own eyes gleaming and throat tight with emotion. "We all have our ghosts, Sparrow. It's time you learn how to live with yours."

Her grandmother's hoarse words, heavy with the strain of responsibility, struck harder than a fist to the sternum, and Nimah staggered back with a limp exhale.

"No, I have to do something." Nimah set her chin. "And if you're not going to help me—then fuck you, too."

"Fine. Fuck me, then." Ro crossed her arms, unwavering in her stance. "Because I am *not* going back there, Sparrow, and as your captain, I fucking forbid you."

Nimah's brows winged high. "You *forbid me*?"

"Damn right." Ro tossed her braid over her shoulder, and it swung against her strong back. "You forced my hand once with the Reckoning, and I let it slide, but if you try to outmaneuver me again, I'll strip you as my second."

Cold disbelief pierced Nimah through her chest. "You wouldn't dare."

"I am the captain of this ship," Ro warned. "Try me and find out."

"Have it your way. *Captain.*" Furious, she stalked from the bridge in search of the crew gathered over steaming plates at the communal table. Fatigue was carved in deep grooves around eyes and mouths, but the walls of the ship rumbled from the chorus of their voices and laughter.

"Sparrow!" Gertrude raised her stein with a wide grin. "Come, join us. Noodles are hot and chicken wings are crisp."

"Honey ginger. Fried in peanut oil." Chu licked greasy sauced fingers like she was cleaning herself down to the bone. "Jono brought us some of his goods to celebrate."

"Good-good!" Mumbles repeated, thrusting her gnawed chicken bone like it was a sword, sauce and grease splattered on her faded gray t-shirt.

"I'm not hungry." Nimah stopped at the foot of the table. "Where's Maverick and Liselle?"

"Liselle stayed back to float at the hospital," Chu grunted.

"And Mav is putting in some work in the gym," Boomer answered, cracking open a chicken bone so he could suck out the marrow.

It would've been better to have the full crew, but Nimah wasn't about to waste more time tracking them down.

"Seriously, you gotta try these." Boomer wiggled a flat. "Get in now, 'cause I ain't leaving nothing for leftovers."

Plates were passed. Beer flowed from bottle to glass. And a tin mug was set to the table inches from where Nimah stood, foam settling beneath the rim. She slapped it off the edge of the table, spraying suds across the weathered hardwood floor.

All laughter and chattering voices ceased—plates and cups hovering in midair, the crew rendered into a stark and silent tableau of disbelief.

"What says the council?" Zensha arched a brow, rising from the edge of her seat. "Is there a problem?"

"Oh, there's a problem," Nimah seethed, hands on her hips. "Question is, what are you going to help me do about it?" They listened, features darkening as Nimah brought them up to speed. "Well?" She tossed aggrieved hands when silence lapsed, each of them deep in spiraling thought. "Someone, speak!"

"Captain is right, bird." Chu spoke first, perched against the edge of the floating island separating the kitchen from the dining table. "You know I love me a chance to bust SIGA's balls, sure. But defy the council?" She pursed wrinkled lips. "I'd rather dry-shag a cactus back on Sahara9."

"We're pirates, darling," Gertrude added after Nimah swung hopeful eyes to her. "All that separates us from hawkers and mercs is our code. It must be kept."

Unbelievable. "What about you?" She rounded on Zensha next, but even Zensha seemed to have lost the defiant spark for the justice she'd raged for only hours ago.

"The council has spoken."

Nimah curled her lip. "I see. So because you got what you wanted, you can so easily look away? That it?"

The bridge of Zensha's nose wrinkled with a snarl. "Had you listened to me *before*—we could've asked for forgiveness instead of permission. But yeah, now I've got Devere to do right by, and I won't risk the axe swinging for his neck, or mine."

"Boomer!" Nimah struck her knuckles to the flat of the table. "I'm giving you a chance to pull every weapon you have. *Come on!*"

Boomer's chin dipped against the hard wall of his chest. "I ain't never had much." He scraped blunt nails against the scruff of a growing beard. "But now I gots me a crew. A captain. A home." He lifted shining eyes to Nimah, bright with apology and regret. "If Cap Ro sides with the council, I ain't gonna be the one to fly past her."

Nimah scored her teeth across her bottom lip as she fought to hold in her violent and vicious words. Cowards. All of them. "Fine." She let her disgust show as bright as a noonday sun on her face. "Be it on your heads."

Nimah stalked to the medbay, not quite sure where she was going or why until she got there. The one place where no one would bother her. The only place where she could be alone to truly vent her rage. Nimah screamed and let the tears come. The full weight of all that she held in as the dead descended on her. So many cries and screams.

She'd never be free of them now.

<*Nimah, Second-in-Command,*> Ma's voice hummed.

"What?" Nimah straightened, swiping tears from her face.

<*During deboarding of the cryopods from the sunken vessel, my systems detected additional data stored within chips implanted in each pod. I was able to extract those files into a compressed folder which I then downloaded into my network. Those files are now accessible for review.*>

Nimah blinked her vision clear, her mind struggling to keep up. "What kind of files?"

In response, Ma activated the medbay's console and the holoscreens expanded into three arched panels that swelled with glowing thumbnails of the children's faces, each coded by logging numbers.

<*Based on my analysis, archival video footage of interviews run over several years that belong to, I presume, a case study.*>

"Who gave the instruction to do this?"

<*Based on your frustrated outburst both with the captain and crew, I determined this might be information you would like to have and self-initiated the task.*>

"You determined?" Systems weren't designed to determine, only execute orders. This was almost . . . human.

<*I've been listening,*> Ma answered. An even more puzzling response. <*Shall I sync to a solo-vis for you?*>

"Yes. Yes, please." Rummaging through the console drawers, Nimah dug around in search until she found the auxiliary visor. She blew dust off the lens before setting the mask across her eyes and fastening the anchoring strap behind her head. "Show me the footage of the ones who died."

<*How many of the 133 would you like to review?*>

"All of them."

Nimah lowered to the edge of the recovery cot.

The first video expanded. Stamped on the corner of the video file: **Subject ELIJAH POOLE – 4 years, 7 months.**

Elijah sat on a metal chair dressed in soft gray clothes—a tunic and wide-leg pants with flat-soled shoes. His feet swung against the chair legs, and sunlight shone through an open window by his left shoulder, casting warm light across his oval face. Elijah was all cheeks and dimples as he grinned at his interviewer, one of his front teeth slightly chipped.

The interviewer—a woman, mostly off-screen—asked him a series of questions, starting with the basics. His name and age, who were his parents, did he have any siblings, and if so, what were their names and ages. Who were his best friends, and their names and ages. His teachers at his communal school, and what were his favorite subjects.

"Are we done?" Elijah sighed. "I wanna snack. Cheese cubes and green jelly."

"Soon. Just one more. Who do you hope to be?" the interviewer asked. "When you grow up?"

Elijah's face pinched in thought, head tilted like a puppy hearing the squeak of a toy for the first time. "Um. I dunno."

"There must be something," the interviewer pressed, tapping her pen against the side of her knee, the only part of her Nimah could see clearly. "Anything in the void. There is no wrong answer, Elijah. Nothing too great or too small."

Elijah shifted on the chair, wiggling his thighs like he was tired of sitting. "Sometimes when I dream, I dream of being a kraken!" He splayed his arms, fingers writhing like tentacles as he mimicked a yawning roar. "The biggest kraken *ever*! I swallow ships *whole*!"

Soft chuckles rolled in from further in the room and the interviewer rapped her pen against her tablet, silencing them as well as startling little Elijah.

"That's a very creative dream," she spoke sweetly. Almost cloyingly so. Her pen tip resumed whisking over the smooth surface of her glass tablet. "Do you recall what your answer was last year?"

Elijah shook his head no.

"I do." She slotted her pen into the loop on the side of the tablet. "Thank you, Elijah. You may now go find your parents and have your snack. You must be very, very hungry."

Elijah shot from his chair with a squealing *yayyyyy* as the interviewer turned to whomever else was in the room and requested the next subject just as the video cut out.

The next file opened, and this time Elijah was little over five, his cheeks still full and eyes bright with the kind of innocence that could only be possible from a life where he knew only safety and love. All the things Nimah no longer had by the time she was his age. At the end of his interview, when prompted yet again, he wished to be a sky captain.

Someone who tracked the weather, predicting the rains and shifts in forecasts for harvest. Then year after it changed again to an explorer—going deep into space to find new planets and people.

There were seven more videos of him in the study, and in the last he was twelve. His boyish face was narrower in the cheeks and a little sullen in the mouth as youth yielded to adolescence.

"It's good to see you, Elijah."

Elijah merely sighed. Bored before they'd even begun. His wide, dark eyes rolled then landed on the interviewer. His arms crossed over his chest were lean and toned from the hours he must have toiled in the fields from sowing to harvest. "Can I ask you something?"

"Of course." The interviewer settled closer. "What's on your mind?"

"This." He swung a finger between and around them. "What's the point? We do this every single year, but like . . . not all of us?"

"Please elaborate."

"Paxton." His eyes narrowed a little more, almost accusatorily. "He's never tested."

"Well—"

"And Bethany." He began listing off on his fingers. "Kevin, Ruan, Norman, or even Priyanka—and she's the smartest in my class! None of them ain't ever been tested either!"

"Elijah." The interviewer raised the point of her finger. "You know how we feel about proper grammar. Please use your words appropriately."

"I'll speak how I want. I don't care if you're iced by it."

The interviewer breathed deep and slow, as if gathering her composure. "That's an interesting word. Iced." She set her closed fist against her knee, her thumb stroking over her knuckle. "Based on the context in which you used it, it's what we call slang. A vulgar subset of language derived mostly from poorer communities or mainstream media."

Elijah's eyes flashed wide for the barest moment, as if startled that he'd revealed something he hadn't quite intended.

"It happens to be quite a popular term right now," the interviewer continued. "Though I don't believe I've heard it used by anyone raised this far from the Inner Circle. Where did you happen to hear it?"

Elijah's breathing went shallow as he made every effort to appear nonchalant. "Uh-nuh." He shrugged. "Somewhere, I guess."

"You are aware that leaving Solvanis is illegal," the interviewer pressed. "And that those enlisted in Eidolon are forbidden from receiving access to anyone or anything beyond what has been sanctioned by the Hill."

Elijah bit his lip hard, a sheen of sweat forming on his brow.

"Kill the video," the interviewer commanded softly.

The screen went black. Nimah yanked the vis-feed off, eyes burning and the heat of frustration trapped in her throat. Elijah was only one of dozens more. All those children taken and tortured and gone—because of her. It was her fault. And if no one was willing to back her, then she'd tear it down with her bare fucking hands if necessary.

"Let it go, kid. You played your hand and lost."

"Come to rub salt in the wound?" Nimah furiously wrenched open a drawer from the cabinet, clattering through supplies. For fuck's sake, they were running low on just about everything. Furious, she slammed another drawer shut then yanked open a third, and at the sight of the sedation packet her heartbeat slowed to a less thunderous degree.

"What's your plan?"

Nimah shrugged. "Zensha said it best." *Ask for forgiveness instead of permission.* Sounded good enough for her, and if her grandmother stripped her as second, well, whoop-de-fucking-do. According to Jono, she was one foot in the grave anyway. What did she really have to lose at this point?

Dobs snorted at her side as Nimah tucked the sedation syringe into her back pocket. "Ro is gonna string you up by your toenails." Grinning wide, she folded her arms across her chest. "Fuck, I'll love watching that."

Nimah jolted at the sound of knuckles rapping against the entryway of the medbay, and turned to find Dobs gone and Maverick whisking across the threshold.

"Heard you lost it on the crew." He stopped his chair by her at the foot of the cot where her vis rested. "Figured I'd let you cool down before I came to check in on you." Leaning forward, he set his elbows on his knees, dark green eyes sweeping over her in concern. "You good, Cadet?"

"No." Nimah swiped a hand across her face, clearing it of tears and fatigue as she returned to the cot and slunk down. "Ma extracted videos of the children from the sinker. I'm getting to know the dead." Because if she didn't remember the ones they couldn't save, it would be like they never existed, and somehow that was worse than failing them.

"Nimah." Maverick sighed. "You have to stop punishing yourself."

"I'm not punishing myself *enough*. I fucked up, Maverick. Zensha was right. I tried to be pragmatic and think like . . . I don't know . . . like a pirate. Focus on the means and forget the rest, but I *can't forget*."

"No one is asking you to." He fixed his gaze to a point over her shoulder, and something in him hardened with the bitter grief of his own memories. And while he hadn't seen the children strung up with tubes and wires firsthand, the crew had witnessed the aftermath as they'd rushed the children into beds at the hospital.

It had marked him, too.

"Well then." He clapped his hands together. "What's your plan?"

Nimah frowned. "What are you talking about?"

"Don't play me for an idiot, Cadet." Maverick arched a bemused brow. "I know you're planning something stupid and there's no talking you to out of it. So what's your plan?"

Nimah hooked her tongue along the edge of her teeth, hesitating for a moment before giving in with a sigh. Maverick was sharp. If anyone could help her find the holes in her strategy, it would be him. "When we were first forming a plan to breach BPRO—Zensha suggested blowing it to hell using the nova Chu took after we unloaded the sinker. So that's what I'm going to do."

"Novas are extremely dangerous, Nimah. Isn't there a less drastic way?"

"Sure. But destroying that place with their own tech gives me deniability. I'll plant it inside, set it off and to anyone investigating it'll seem like a freak accident."

Seeing her point, Maverick's smile sparked like primed thrusters for a full second before his expression rapidly dimmed. "Detonating inside a gravity-stabilized environment will both increase a nova's range and speed up the collapse time. You're talking seconds instead of minutes for you to clear the blast radius."

A fact she'd hoped he wouldn't quite catch on to. Damn him and his fucking sharp mind. "I don't have a choice. BPRO is huge." Therefore, if she wanted to destroy it all, detonation had to happen *inside* at the core.

"Alright then." Sighing heavily, Maverick angled his wristdeck, assessing the time. "In about another hour, most of the crew will have turned into their cabins. Everyone's exhausted, and they'll either want to seek out rest or distraction. Once they do, that's our window to sneak away and gather a few essentials from the RIM's armory before taking the shuttle I left recharging at the quay. There and back, I figure we're looking at six hours. Maybe seven."

"We?" Nimah's voice wavered.

"Yes. We."

Tears came again and she furiously blinked her eyes clear. "It's going to be dangerous, Mav. Are you sure you want to do this?"

"Am I sure?" Maverick gathered her face in his hands, his thumbs sweeping away tears from her cheeks—his gaze steady even as the seam of his throat bobbed. "Don't you know by now?" he whispered, every word molten with yearning. "I'm with you, Cadet. I'm always with you."

Something in her chest seized. Softened. Allowing everything she'd been so carefully holding back to come forward in a dizzying rush of emotion that would've taken her legs out from under her if she wasn't already seated. Only a breath separated them, and even though it was clear Maverick longed to close the distance, he wouldn't. She'd set this boundary, and it was hers to scrub away. So she did.

Yielding to impulse, to need, Nimah crawled onto his lap and sank into him, their lips meeting in a starved and furious kiss that held everything she couldn't find the words to say and instead poured into him. Through him.

I'm sorry. I'm here. I love you.

He deserved this from her. This singular tender moment centered in vulnerability and truth. A moment without hesitation or doubt or worry. Because what came next could very well be the end for them both, but right now, Nimah clung to hope as she clung to him. Hands dragging through his hair, she angled his head back and took him deeper, until his panting breaths gave way to soft moans, each carrying the whisper of her name.

Reverent as a prayer.

Together they tumbled from the chair onto the cot, his body all slick heat and molten desire. Skin met skin, mouths and hands fused,

Nimah surrendered and took, rose and fell, guided by frantic desire as Maverick pushed her to the blinding edge of wicked release.

"With me," he whispered against the skin of her throat, followed by the graze of teeth in a demanding bite. "With me."

Nimah brought his mouth back to hers for another drugging kiss as that pressure spiraled. Expanded. Soared. "Always."

And together—*together*—they fell.

Nimah woke in Maverick's arms, chased into waking by another nightmare and the heat of a scream trapped in her throat. Careful not to stir him, she lifted Maverick's arm from her side and swung her legs over the edge of the cot. She stroked her palms over her sweating thighs, shaken to the core with the chill of anguish.

In her dreams, Maverick died in her arms as the blast of primefire roared in a cyclone around them. She watched his eyes burst and melt from their sockets, heard his cries ringing through her so loudly her ears bled. Then as his skin and bones flaked away, Nimah rose in the cosmos of void and stars, her skin glowing from the surging force of elite. She faced the spread of planets—all one thousand five hundred and eighty-four—and, with a lift of her palms, she set them ablaze.

While she understood it was just a dream, part of her knew it held a darker truth.

Who else are you prepared to lose, Nimah? Chu this time? Gertrude? Or how about me? Her grandmother's words struck Nimah hard, piercing her already tender heart with certainty.

Death was a storm, and Nimah was heading straight for the epicenter—alone.

She dressed quickly, drawing on her discarded cargos and t-shirt, then laced up her boots before returning to the cot. Maverick lay stretched on his side, lashes fluttering against the curve of his high cheekbones. So peaceful. She almost wanted to curl up with him again and forget. Just for a little longer. But if she gave in to the impulse, she'd never want to leave his side and this had to be done. For all of them.

Lowering next to him, she stroked an arm across his back while she withdrew the syringe she'd hidden in her back pocket as he stirred against her touch.

"Hey." Maverick knuckled sleep from his eyes. Then his brows tightened in concern. "What's up?"

"I'm sorry." Nimah jabbed the sedation syringe into the side of his neck and his hands closed around her wrist in alarm. "I know you won't understand," she continued as the plunger depressed, pumping the drugs into his system. "By the time you wake up, it'll all be over and I'll be making my way back to you. But if something goes wrong . . . tell my grandmother . . . don't come for me."

His eyes flared with urgency and tears, his lips struggling to form words, but it was too late. He was already sinking into unconsciousness like an anchor dragging him to the darkness of the ocean floor.

The needle retracted and Nimah kissed his lips one last time. "I love you." And she could only hope he'd heard it. That it would somehow temper the hurt and rage when he awoke. She'd given him enough sedation to keep him down for at least three hours. After that, he'd undoubtedly rally the crew to come after her, but she had to trust it would be over before they reached her.

Because Nimah was not going to see him or anyone else she loved die for her sins.

Drawing on her jacket, Nimah slunk down to the engine room, where the massive pistons and cables and gears were washed in the shimmering blue light of the core powered with the remains of the stone sparrow. It hovered in the core tank. One-winged and with a cracked tail.

A broken bird somehow still capable of flight.

"Y'heard what Jono said." Dobs moved like a shadow from behind Nimah's left shoulder, one half of her face etched in glowing blue, the other swallowed in fathomless shadows. "Taking in elite makes you strong—but it also makes me *stronger*."

"I know." Nimah pressed her palm to the glass, gaze fixed on the sparrow. "But it's what I have to do." Opening the core panel, she reached inside and sighed as elite flowed through her.

Into her.

Potent and heady. Welcomed. Her body greedily drank in its power like it was starving, and took in all that she could hold. Supercharging herself for what was to come. And once every fiber and cell in her body was saturated, Nimah released the sparrow and rubbed her fingers against her palms. The simple touch cascaded across her nerves and a hum vibrated along the base of her skull like the rumble of thunder before lightning split a storm-blackened sky.

Turning from the core, Nimah stopped by Chu's workstation where the matte black ball of a nova lay perched atop the battered surface. Like a true scrapper who'd spent twenty years collecting on Sahara9, Chu hadn't let an opportunity pass her by, and from what Nimah's inexperienced eye could see, she'd removed its gravitational detonator—which is why she'd been able to hoist it aboard the *Stormchaser*—and installed a manual activation switch instead. Clever. How she'd managed to find the time to snip one amid all the chaos, Nimah didn't know, but right now she was grateful.

Because not only did she have a purpose, she had a plan.

Dobs puffed a cloud of smoke and the bright burn of tobacco and chemicals seared Nimah's nostrils—sharper than ever before. "Hope you know what you're doing, kid."

"I do." Nimah flattened her palm and played with the shocks of elite firing across her naked skin. And smiled. "Let's burn this motherfucker to the ground."

CHAPTER TWENTY-FOUR

The nova might be little bigger than a soccer ball, but the damn thing weighed about half as much as Boomer. Nimah adjusted the rucksack across her protesting shoulders with a grimace as she stepped out of the rover and into the swarming streets of the lower RIM—drawing the trench tighter around her waist, careful to conceal her flight suit. Smoke and steam billowed from vents and pipes, carrying the scent of fire-roasted meat, burning trash cubes, and the damp musk of air scrubbers clearing debris and buildup from oxygen filters. But none of that compared to the ripe smell of unwashed bodies.

Water was far too precious on the RIM to waste it on frequent bathing. Perhaps when the atmo-netting was upgraded, they could harvest trapped water particles into rainfall. *Soon.* She imagined a lot of such changes were to come once the accord was finalized and the people received their long-awaited reparations.

"You really think SIGA is gonna hand over four *quadrillion* credits?" Dobs chuckled. She hadn't left Nimah's side since powering up on the *Stormchaser*, and she was saturated in such astounding clarity it was almost easy to forget Dobs wasn't as solid as the RIMers flowing around her.

"Naïve ain't a cute look, kid."

"They won't have much choice," Nimah grumbled when a tug on the hem of her trench had her meeting the gaze of a frail woman. Her hand stretched up in yearning and cheeks streaked with tears long since dried into the filth worn into her skin. Given the thinness of her fingers and wrists, Nimah would guess she hadn't eaten much in close to three weeks. And she was not the worst of them.

Men. Women. Children. There were so many in need and very little she could offer to help, but she could do this much, at least. Withdrawing a half-finished roll of chips leftover from what she'd accepted from Liselle back on Corlys, she pressed the stack of plastic coins into the woman's hand and smiled before walking away.

Dobs whistled low, keeping tight at Nimah's side. "Gave her all you had?"

Nimah set her jaw. "Why not?" Fifty credits wasn't much, but it would get her a sleeping pad and a small sack of purple rice that could stretch for a month if she ate once a day.

"What happens when the next hand yanks your ankle? What you gonna give then?"

Nimah shot searing eyes to Dobs. "I get that I'm stuck with you until Jono figures out how to pry you from my skull, but in case I wasn't clear before—let me be so now." The toes of her boots bumped against the ghost of Dobs, somehow making contact with an entity that wasn't even there. "I'm not afraid of you anymore."

"That so?" Dobs clicked her tongue. "Guess I've gotta up the ante."

"You do that."

Dobs answered Nimah's dark grin with one of her own, the pinpoints of her irises glimmering with the barest flash of laser-beam red. "Just might."

Nimah stalked away with a scoff, and didn't have to look back to know Dobs was gone. For now, at least. Drawing in a sobering breath, she willed her energy to calm, sealing her immediate thoughts away from Dobs and behind a fortified wall. Going into *BPRO* alone allowed no room for error—she had to keep her wits about her if she was going to get through this alive.

The RIM's armory had been built on the edge of the quay, and after scanning around her for patrols to make sure the way was clear, Nimah throttled her cutlass to its highest gauge. The blade's edge seared from deepest blue to brightest white, and with a quick slash she cut through the thick carbide lock as if it was made of air. Had this been an armory on an outpost or within the Inner Circle, she'd have never been able to cut her way through without a clearance badge or retinal scanning. But on the RIM, security relied on more . . . tactile measures.

Turning off her cutlass, Nimah sheathed it back on her hip as she quickly disappeared inside. Made from scrap tin and reclaimed fiberboard, the armory ran in a single open rectangle a hundred yards long and half that in width. Flicking on the grid of lights that webbed across the ceiling, several rows of metal grated shelving were stacked in tight lines, each laden with crates and barrels and all conveniently labeled.

Bless Jono and his need for ruthless organization.

Based on her earlier flyby with Maverick, if she was going to infiltrate BPRO, then she'd need welding shears to cut through carbide steel, extended clips for her blasers in case she met with sentries, drones, or both, and a fresh power cell for the cutlass, leaving the energy she'd just siphoned from the elite aboard the *Stormchaser* as a backup if things went awry.

After twenty minutes of searching, Nimah was tossing the last of her supplies into the rucksack when a rough cough from a male throat caused her to nearly drop a crate on her foot.

"Stealing from us so soon?" Jono stood just behind her, his hands braced against shelving that ran on either side. The overhead glare reflecting off his lenses made it impossible to read his gaze.

"Jono—"

"Relax." He dropped his hands, his eyes coming into focus as he stepped out of the hot pool of light. "Whatever you're up to, I think I can ascertain you have good reason for it."

Nimah frowned. "So . . . you're not here to stop me?"

"Given all you've done for the RIM—and myself—letting you pillage our armory is the least I can do. Just wanted to make sure there isn't anything else you need before you . . . take off." He whisked a hand through the air, miming a ship breaking atmo. "Want to tell me what you're up to? Maybe I could offer assistance."

"Honestly, Jono, the less you know, the better. Trust me." She tightened the closure on her rucksack. "Actually," Nimah added before she turned away, "there is one thing you could do to help."

"Name it."

"Cover for me." Nimah shouldered each strap and adjusted the weight on her back. "Someone is going to look for me soon. Probably my grandmother. If you could buy me time—as much as you can—before anyone realizes I'm gone, I would be indebted."

Jono swayed his head in thought then nodded. "I'm about to head over to my lab. It's why I stopped in here to gather a couple replacement cables for—anyway, that doesn't matter. I can swing by the hospital first and let her think you're helping me with the excavation."

Nimah gave Jono a fast hug. "Thank you."

"Just come back in one piece." His arms closed tight around her. "Or else your grandmother will break my neck."

Breaking into *BPRO* was a lot like the night she broke into the Academy with Dobs. It should have been impossible. But apparently, much like SIGA, the lab had been built under the assumption that no one would be brazen enough to risk it even once—let alone circle back and climb the same fence twice.

Nimah slipped away on the shuttle that Maverick had left parked at the quay for recharging after their flyby. While the *Stormchaser* was powered by elite, the shuttles were older-gen models that had independent fuel cells that needed to be recharged by a grid. Lucky for her. Otherwise evading attention would have been exceedingly more difficult, if not impossible.

She parked the shuttle beyond the web of kraken eggs, then shot out into the void, her suit activated for personal flight mode. Using palm thrusters to steer herself through the security net, she launched for one of the service hatches used by site engineers to access the exterior for maintenance or routine inspections.

Three minutes of carving with the carbide shears and Nimah slipped inside, sealing the hatch until the systems pumped the hatch with oxygen. Nimah tapped the collar of her suit and her helm rolled back like a liquid veil. If they didn't know she was here before, they likely did now, but that couldn't be helped. Moving quickly meant she'd had to sacrifice stealth for agility, which was why she'd come armed and fully charged with elite.

Unholstering her blaser, Nimah released the safety and proceeded to jog through the engineering corridor, her senses on high alert as she swept for any possible movement or threat. She'd studied the schematics on the flight over, memorizing the route she planned to take along with a contingency exit should she get cornered or was forced to divert, depending on the response she received from what remained of their security.

By her guess, of the eight she'd ejected into the void, three were likely dead, the other five probably receiving treatment for injuries sustained in the venting. That would leave three or four at most for her to contend with. And, of course, the drones, but she'd come stocked with grenades this time.

At the end of the corridor, Nimah reached for the handle, took a slow, calming breath, and prayed for the strength to face whatever came next. Wrenching open the door, she leapt out into the main atrium, dropped low, and swung her twin blasers out on either side, prepared for assault. Confrontation.

Something.

Her eyes shifted warily from left to right. Silence. Not a single soul. No sound or movement. The once-blinding lights were cast to a low dim, as if the entire wing was emptied out. Holstering one of the blasers on her left hip, Nimah tapped the screen on her wristdeck, connecting to Ma's system via the shuttle and toggling her responses to text instead of audio.

"Ma. Are you able to access the interface and run a scan on biological heat signatures?"

/No, unfortunately, the signal is encrypted.
And with the Stormchaser out of range,
I am unable to boost the shuttle's system capabilities./

"Perfect." Nimah scanned the atrium. No personnel, but a few service bots sat idle, toggled to offline, otherwise they'd have stuttered awake at sensing her proximity. "What about transportation vehicles?" On their earlier trip, they'd counted close to thirty ships housed in the quay. "How many remain onsite?"

/Authorization requested to remote-pilot for line of sight./

"Granted." It took three minutes for Ma to circle back with a response. Just enough time for Nimah to cross the atrium.

/All registered transport vehicles are unaccounted for./

Nimah jolted to a hard stop at the base of a wide stairway that corkscrewed through the entirety of the lab. "*All* of them?"

/That is correct./

Twin pangs of relief and trepidation shot through her at the news. This facility would've taken considerable cost to build as well as maintain. Choosing to abandon such an investment after a breach, rather than fight to reinforce it, alluded to only one troubling conclusion.

This wasn't their only location.

Pushing her concerns aside, Nimah shot up the stairway, no longer bothering with stealth. She had to place the bomb at the central sphere for it to maximize impact. At the top of the stairs, Nimah slowed. Stopped as elite coiled in her belly, tightening like a snake sensing a threat. *There.* That ancient energy from earlier thrummed in a heady echo, only now she could almost see its resonance vibrating, if she narrowed her eyes and honed her vision just beyond it. The same silver hair-like threads slipping into the earth on the RIM shimmered in the air like floating threads of spider silk.

Searching. Reaching.

Whatever she'd felt earlier—*it* was still here.

She followed those threads to the central chamber that, unlike the rest of BPRO—which was made mostly of diamond glass—was solid carbide steel without a single viewport or vent hatch. Nimah hesitated at the start of the bridge leading to the open doorway. A black mouth in a wall of steel. The pull was immense now. Almost urgent. And the stronger it grew, the more afraid she became as that voice screeched deep inside her bones.

Free me.

Free me.

Free me!

Clamping down on her own source of elite, Nimah gathered her energy to shield herself from the ricocheting force of its cry vibrating against the enamel of her teeth. "Come on, let's get this over with." Gathering her nerve, Nimah pushed forward across the bridge and scanned the way ahead with her eyes trained down the barrel of her blaser.

Even if it appeared empty, she was not about to let up her guard, and slowed as she reached the open doorway, peeking left then right before proceeding inside. The lights lifted as she entered—a gentle rise that reached full saturation once she arrived at the center.

Nimah slowed. Stopped. And nearly dropped her blaser.

The room was staged like a historical building. The walls were covered in pixel sensors that, once the lights activated, would render the interior to the preferred settings, and this was designed to mimic a grand cathedral from Earth-Prior. Vaulted ceilings met with stone buttresses and stained-glass windows. Beneath the façade, the low thrum of lights and tech pulsed, feeding into overhead, surgical lights that cast a harsh unyielding glare, drawing her attention to the raised auditorium with a dozen staggered rows of observational seating. But it was the tanks lining the far wall that nearly stopped her heart cold.

Condensation fogged the glass, but it wasn't enough to conceal the grotesque shapes floating within of half-formed infantile bodies suspended in clear green viscous liquid. Ill-shaped, with limbs that jutted at impossible angles, and eyes—too many eyes—that stared blankly. There had to be nearly a hundred of them, varying in stages of development. Twisted amalgamations of flesh fused with metal, all stacked upon one another like a grotesque display of trophies.

Retrofitting was common within the Inner Circle. A procedure that many of the cadets at the Academy, including Liselle, had undergone as embryos, and those that successfully developed to maturity in their echo wombs saw an average of thirty percent enhanced performance capacity and cognitive capabilities above their natural-born peers.

But this—whatever these poor, misshapen creatures had endured—this wasn't retrofitting. This was monstrous.

The faint acrid scent of antiseptics and the sickly tang of something both alive and rotting laced every tense breath as Nimah scanned across the rest of the lab. She didn't have time to waste when Jono wouldn't be able to withstand a hard breeze any more than he could her grandmother's commanding glare. He'd collapse under the pressure, and even if he somehow managed to hold the lie, Maverick's sedation would soon wear off.

Removing her rucksack, Nimah fastened the blaser to her hip then dug out the disabled nova and got to work twisting together the spliced wires that had rendered it inactive. A single red dot appeared—a tiny and steady red sun within the cube's matte-black surface. Breathing slowly, Nimah set it down between her feet.

The remote Chu had rigged for it looked like it was short-range, putting it at probably twenty feet at max. While that wasn't much, it should, in theory, be enough to clear her of the immediate blast radius. Then, according to her wristdeck, while it took her nearly fifteen minutes to reach the core of the lab—she'd likely be able to halve that time if she sprinted for her literal life. Her only regret was that Doctor Doom wasn't here to go down with the foul remnants of their work.

"Hands up." The blunt end of a metal barrel tapped the side of Nimah's temple. "Nice and slow."

Nimah's heart shuddered in alarm as she looked up and into Vesper's cold, dark eyes. Either Vesper moved with the stealth of a ghost, or Nimah had let herself get distracted and sloppy in her haste.

"Saint." Vesper clicked her tongue. "To me." A soft growl answered her command from across the chamber, and Vesper's hunting hound—Saint—slowly closed in. Head low, teeth bared, and eyes gleaming. "She doesn't like it when my commands are not followed." And Saint's growl deepened, tongue flicking across the front of her teeth in warning. "Hands up."

Nimah raised her hands, nice and slow.

"Good girl."

Cool and smooth steel met the skin of Nimah's wrists, and the soft hiss of fastening locks let her know she was secured in cuffs, though not SIGA grade. She had a moment of relief that was quickly shocked away as she was wrenched around by Vesper to see they were not alone. A boy and girl were with her, maybe twenty, primeswords drawn but not activated.

Holy fuck . . . cybers.

"What are you doing here?" Nimah asked, finally finding her voice through the shock.

"What does it fucking look like? I'm collecting my bounty." Vesper grinned. "Couldn't risk moving on you while you were crewed up, so I figured the best time would be after you concluded your Reckoning—or whatever. Let everyone drop their guard and find a way to pick you off from the herd. But imagine my surprise when you had to go and make it extra easy for me by slipping the RIM all on your own?"

Nimah tightened her ankles around the box of the nova that Vesper had yet to notice. She wouldn't be able to get to the remote in her pocket, not with her hands bound. "Please, you don't understand—"

"Save it, Nimah." Vesper's grip tightened around Nimah's bicep with enough force to bruise. "I'm here to bring you into SIGA, and you'll go without a fuss. Or else we'll stop by the RIM on the way, and I'll let Saint have her fun with the Valkyries."

The clamor of voices drew them both to attention as sentries and lab assistants flowed in from the doorway, followed by a nightmare wrapped in a tailored lab coat seated proudly in a hoverchair about three generations ahead of Maverick's design. Her hair, an almost metallic shade of silver, was combed away from her severe face.

"The fuck is this?" Vesper snapped. "Chairwoman assured me I'd have the place cleared out."

"And it was, of all non-essential staff. I, myself, was not going to abandon my life's work," the woman in the chair replied. She spoke softly and unhurried, with the confidence of a woman accustomed to issuing orders and having them obeyed.

She rolled her chair closer, skeletal fingers working the controls, both hands replaced with robotics at the wrists without the guise of protoskyn. Her legs, also amputated below the knees, were little more than nubs pressing against the wings of her lab coat.

"Hello, Nimah. It's a pleasure to meet you at last."

"I . . . I recognize you . . ." Nimah shifted her weight as her mind peeled through years of memory. "Hillard. Samantha Hillard."

Though she was at least forty years older than the holograph in Nimah's textbook, her features wrinkled and cheeks sunken with the weight of jowls, it was her acknowledging smile that hadn't changed. Small teeth set in a wide mouth—she grinned like a velociraptor. Menacing and cold.

In her youth, Samantha Hillard had been a geneticist lauded by the Bioethics Commission and Medical Council. She stood at the pinnacle of biogenetic innovation, heralded as a visionary for pushing humanity beyond its evolutionary constraints, she forecasted a future unburdened by frailty, disease, and the limitations of flesh itself. A dream that was destroyed when a research assistant exposed her brutal methods during her study of limb regeneration to the BCMC.

She'd sought to alter DNA so that soldiers with arms or legs blown off in battle would be able to regrow their missing limbs in the field, significantly reducing military medical budgets while also improving garrison retention.

A week after her life sentencing, she disappeared off the grid and was never heard from again.

"I must admit, you're not quite what I expected." Hillard raised her chin, her thin-lipped smile as chilling as the steel encircling Nimah's wrists. "Then again, I'm sure you'd say the same about me."

Realization and dread churned within Nimah, as the gravity of her circumstances took root. If Samantha Hillard was the woman behind the mask of the monster she had sought to unveil, the only thing worse than death would be falling into her maniacal hands.

Fuck the remote. There was only one sure way to end this. Fear giving way to surrender, Nimah raised her foot.

And stepped on the mine.

CHAPTER TWENTY-FIVE

"You know what will happen to all of us if I press down."
Vesper's eyes dropped as the weight of Nimah's foot settled over a matte-black metal orb, not enough to trigger but certainly enough to threaten.

A nova. She was standing on a fucking nova like it was a voiddamn football, threatening to blow them all to hell. And while some might take her warning for a bluff, the cold look etched across her face canceled any doubt. She was a woman with nothing to lose and ready to risk it all at the slightest provocation.

Vesper had never witnessed a nova detonating, but she'd been told about it by a merc who'd survived a run that went south, when an idiot in his squad had bolted from position too soon and broken the trigger line. What followed hadn't been an explosion—the expanding violent blast of fire and pressure that tore through muscle with shrapnel and heat—but a terrifying inversion of reality folding into itself, swallowing all traces of life and light into a singularity-like void.

At this range? The best they could pray for was instantaneous disintegration.

Otherwise they'd be sucked into the agony of temporal distortion, where time slowed and sheer gravitational force tore apart molecular bonds—stretching their bodies toward the collapsing core, alive and aware and trapped in a state of ceaseless agony as seconds were drawn beyond what the laws of time or physics should allow. And when it was finally over? There would be no remains to recover.

A nova wasn't just death. It was absolute erasure.

Vesper ground her teeth, her mind furiously working through her options—from firing a shot between her eyes, charging Nimah like a linebacker, or signaling the cybers to cut her down with their primeswords. But all of that required precious seconds, and Nimah only needed a fraction of one to obliterate them all. This was *precisely* why she preferred to transport her marks deceased. Breathing ones caused no end of headaches.

Should've just snatched her at the quay and taken my chances with a rough exit. But that's what she got for thinking luck had played her a finer hand, leading Nimah all the way back to BPRO, where the Valkyries were unaware and no one around for thousands of parsecs to interfere.

"Dear girl." Doctor Hillard arched a bemused brow and a smug fucking grin. "We're a bit old for theatrics, aren't we?"

Vesper pressed her lips tight, barely repressing her snarling curse at the blithe taunt. What was she playing at? Clearly, she was deranged as fuck, and while Vesper wasn't against rolling the occasional dice to shake up the playing field when she found herself cornered, any fool with eyes could see Nimah was not fucking around.

"I don't make empty threats." Nimah's foot lowered by a hair and the soft hiss of a mechanism disengaging—the last warning to back away before it all blew to shit—sent a shocking burst of cold to wash through Vesper until she ran icy with genuine fear. An uncomfortable sensation she hadn't felt for quite some time.

"Pull back," Nimah barked. "All of you. Otherwise I'll take everyone with me."

The skeletal tips of Doctor Hillard's bionic fingers tapped against her armrest like the tick of a metronome, counting each pressurized beat of Vesper's heart. "No," she said at last. "I don't believe you will."

Nimah's chin lifted, high and proud. "I'm the granddaughter of Indira Roscoe. A Valkyrie of the *Stormchaser*. I fear no hell from you."

She stomped down on the nova and terror snatched the breath from Vesper's lungs before she could form the thought to scream. Her world pitched black and Vesper swung an arm over her face, bracing. But there was no snap of detonation, no violent suction or crushing force.

No pain . . .

Vesper peeked over the line of her forearm as Nimah cursed, her boot slamming down on the nova a second time. A third. And still—nothing.

"The nova can't rupture inside the facility," Doctor Hillard called out sweetly. "Part of our ingenious security. Sensors embedded within deactivated it the moment you brought it inside." She gestured toward Nimah blithely. "It's now little more than a very costly paperweight, I'm afraid."

"Why did you let me think it would work?" Nimah's voice cracked with something far greater than the blind terror Vesper had experienced only a moment ago.

"My dear, I am a scientist. I wanted to see how far you'd be willing to go, and apparently—quite far."

"That's enough!" Vesper snapped, her scathing words directed to Doctor Hillard, who grinned like she enjoyed toying with people's minds almost as much as she did taking them apart. "I don't know what sick games you get off on playing, but now that it's clear the threat has passed, I'd like to collect my mark and be on my way."

Her hand closed around Nimah's arm, hauling her forward, but the sentries only tightened their stance, making no attempts to clear her path.

"I said *stand aside*."

"I'm afraid I can't do that."

Vesper tucked Nimah behind her. "You realize you're interfering with directives from SIGA. I am required to bring Nimah Dabo-124 to Chairwoman Annelise. Alive. And *in person*."

"I am aware of your directives, but my work here supersedes them," Hillard answered, her tone pleasant but chilling. "Nimah is a prime specimen, one that I have waited a lifetime to acquire, and who is crucial to unlocking the next stages of my research. Therefore, she is not going anywhere."

Vesper scanned her surroundings, gauging her odds. While she was outgunned two to one, these were pencil-pushing mid-tier security grunts at best. It would take her maybe ten minutes to blast through them alone, but with two cybers?

Light work.

With only the barest of nods from Vesper, the cybers, beautiful killing machines that they were, reacted in perfect precision, swords raised—searing blue running along the lethal edge of honed steel. And at the click of Vesper's tongue, Saint, always on guard, bared her teeth in warning.

"I didn't plan on killing anyone today, but if you don't tell your men to stand down, things are going to get bloody, and quick." Vesper palmed her weapon. "Consider this your first and last warning."

"Honestly, such theatrics are hardly necessary." Hillard punched buttons on the armrest of her hoverchair, *tsk*ing under her breath. A holoscreen opened in a single pane before the old woman's face, cloaked for privacy.

A few tense moments later, the holo closed, and at that same moment, Vesper's wristdeck vibrated with an incoming urgent notification signaling that her contract was complete. She tapped the screen and a confirmation tag floated into view for the transfer of funds into a trust for Chance and Yasmin.

At her side, Nimah's mouth fell open at the staggering sum of three hundred and eighty billion credits. The regulation stamps and seals were unforgeable, certifying without question the transaction's legitimacy.

It was done. She'd won.

"I don't understand . . ."

"Quite frankly, my dear, you're not paid to understand. Only to deliver. But I think you're smart enough to deduce the obvious—or do I really need to spell it out?"

Vesper's eyes narrowed in thought. The only way the funds could have cleared into trust was from the chairwoman, which meant this psycho must be working for SIGA. Annelise had wanted Nimah captured alive but apparently not to lock her away in a cell or even have her quietly executed, but so she could be brought here—to this place. What remained unclear was why? This wasn't a prison or an interrogation cell. And given the wall of fucking deformed fetuses, it wasn't hard to imagine what went down here.

Vesper never cared about her marks. For the few she'd delivered still breathing, whatever happened to them once she was finished with her job was none of her damn business, but Nimah wasn't some ex-con or abusive alcoholic merc who enjoyed beating women and stealing from anyone too weak to stop him. She was just a normal girl who happened to fall on SIGA's bad side. And while Vesper hadn't expected kittens and rainbows for Nimah's future once she was in SIGA's custody, this? This felt fucking . . . deranged.

Hillard's grin stretched wider. "There. I can tell by the look on your face the dots have connected. Smart girl, after all."

Vesper's jaw tightened. "This isn't how I do business."

"It is now." Hillard linked her mechanical hands. "Now that we have that messiness behind us, come, come. I have much work to do."

In one smooth movement, Vesper pushed the charge as high as the blaser could go and took aim for Hillard. "I'm not bloodying my soul with this perverse shit. You want Nimah? Razor. Chairwoman Annelise can deliver her to you, herself. But I'm walking outta here with my mark and I'll drop anyone who tries to stop me."

Eyes following the line of her barrel, Vesper fixed on her target. Dead center of Hillard's unbothered face. "Move."

"Hold your positions," Hillard ordered. "They're not going anywhere."

"Just shut up and shoot her," Nimah grunted.

Ignoring Nimah, Vesper kept her focus on the doctor. Her grin cut cold. "You're in no position to stop me. Seven minimum-wage sentries against myself and two cybers? Even if I held back and just watched, Saint alone could chew her way through your men in under ten minutes. In fact—I might just let her. Bit of sport would do her good."

Saint snapped her teeth with a barking snarl as if begging for the chance.

Doctor Hillard inclined her chin and drew something from beneath the neckline of her blouse—a slender whistle crudely chiseled from a dark-gray clay or stone. She pressed the whistle to her lips, blew.

The sound was pitched too high for human ears, but Nimah recoiled with a sharp cry. And the cybers—they snapped straight. Arms, legs, and spines yanked impossibly rigid, like puppets drawn taut on their strings. Silent screams stretched their faces into a grotesque mask, eyes rolled back and mouths agape in breathless agony. Barely a second later, they eased, eyes rolling forward, their expressions flat and dull. Even for them.

"Brenon. Sasha." Vesper rasped their names under her breath and eased back a tremulous step. "You good?"

They looked to her in tandem. Grim. Vacant. And there was no mistaking it. Brenon and Sasha were gone, and what stared back at Vesper now were expressionless drones who only knew cold, hard duty.

"Disable and detain," Hillard commanded.

The cybers swung for Vesper, swords sharp as their intent—and Saint lunged between them, feral teeth bared to protect her owner.

Vesper screamed, the sound swallowed by the sharp hiss of laser-edged steel as it sliced through flesh and bone. Saint's body fell at Vesper's feet.

Her head followed.

CHAPTER TWENTY-SIX

"There, that should do it." Liselle finished knotting the wrap on the little girl's arm, all the wounds from the extracted tubes in her neck and arms neatly sewn shut.

Jono had gathered thirty-four staff alongside the Valkyrie crew and still there were far too few hands to tend to so many. They'd worked nonstop for hours, but at last the din of frightened children had lessened to a soft rumble of dreamy sighs, and the occasional snore.

Although the body was suspended in an induced sleep-state, waking from cryo was like coming out of a three-day hangover leaving your mouth dry as cotton and stomach twisted in knots. Therefore, administering fluids and pain management meds was an urgent priority, followed by a clear bone broth for their overly stimulated systems to easily digest.

"How does that feel?" Liselle asked, stroking a strand of brown hair away from the little girl's face.

"Gud," she answered around a thumb lodged in her mouth, and hugged a tattered bear tight to her chest.

"I used to have one similar to this." Liselle tapped its worn button nose. The youngest children had been given toys from the donation pile for comfort to distract them from the unfamiliar, clinical setting, and to let them know they were safe. "Have you thought of a name for it?"

The girl nodded. "Pow-duh."

"Powder." Liselle withheld her smirk. "Adorable."

The girl smiled wide, her teeth flared from frequent self-soothing.

"How about you?" Liselle shifted her attention to the adjacent bed, where a youth sat upright, his right arm bandaged from shoulder to wrist. He was one that Nimah and Liselle had brought down from the lab. The oldest of the bunch. Liselle would never forget the sight of him, or the others strung up as they were. Eyes rolled back into their skulls—showing only the brightest of whites—and mouths agape in silent screams.

His eyes were open now, a shade of brown so dark they were nearly black, and haunted by things Liselle could never hope to understand. They lifted to her, and the tense line of his jaw wavered.

"My name is Liselle." She sat facing him and held out a hand. "What's yours?"

"Emmet Poole," he answered, so low she had to strain to hear him.

"Emmet," she repeated. "I'm very pleased to meet you."

Looking past her, his eyes moved across the length of the room, a slow sweep before they flickered back to her. "Have you seen my brother?"

"Maybe. What's his name?"

"Elijah." Emmet sniffed. "He's a bit older but looks just like me. Folks often think we're twins."

"No, I'm sorry, I haven't seen him." Emmet's eyes watered at her response. "But that doesn't mean he isn't here." She took his hand, offering a reassuring squeeze. "There's so many of you. I'm sure he's fine and just resting."

"No. I don't think he is," he whispered. "They put something in me. I can still feel *it*."

Liselle frowned. "Feel what?"

"In here." He tapped his chest. "What they put inside."

Liselle settled closer. "What did they do?"

Emmet shook his head, turning away as something flowed over him, and his expression went slack. Empty.

Liselle waved her hand before his face. Snapped her fingers. Nothing. Pressing along the side of his neck, she found his pulse and his breathing steady, as if he was unconscious but with his eyes wide open, like a robot powered down.

"They do that," one of the nurses said from behind her. "Not sure why. But the ones who were . . . affected, they appear to be disassociating."

Liselle rose to her feet. "Have you seen anything like this before?"

The nurse shook her head. "I'll make a note in his log. Jono has asked that we carefully monitor these ones and document all behavior or interactions." Her pen whisked across her tablet. "What did he say?" she asked, pausing in her scribbles. "His precise words?"

"Uh . . ." Liselle shook her head clear, working back to their brief conversation. "He asked about his twin brother, Elijah, then he said something like . . . *they put something in me; I can still feel it—in here, what they put inside*," she repeated.

The nurse frowned. "Did he clarify what that was?"

"That's when he . . . disassociated."

"I see." The nurse hugged her tablet to her chest and shook blunt copper bangs away from her eyes. "Stew's ready. Go on and eat, I'll finish this row."

At the mention of food, her stomach gave a fierce rumble. After all that had happened, eating had been the least of her concerns, but now that the nurse mentioned food, she was seized with hunger. Liselle made her way to the short line outside the makeshift soup station, accepted a warm bowl, and took it out back to a set of short steps where she wolfed it down while it was still hot enough to scorch her throat.

The stew was overly salty and thick as glue, with mushy lumps of rehydrated potatoes and chunks of rubbery meat that were easier to swallow whole than chew, but the comforting fullness in her belly made her sigh in relief.

But once her hunger was satiated, her mind spun out to the urgent gnawing of anxiety, which is what pushed her to work herself to exhaustion in the hospital in the first place. Scanning through her notifications, there was no response as yet from Admiral Wallace to her wave, and frustration twisted with fear and stewed in her gut. What if Admiral Wallace refused to help? Or worse, what if there was nothing she could do and she was doomed to live the rest of her days as a fugitive?

"Mind if I join?" Zensha flopped down aside her with a sigh, her platinum goddess braids knotted in a tight bun so her fade and tattoos glimmered in the weak lamplight.

"Devere, how is he?" Liselle wiped her mouth clean on a microcloth then deposited it into her empty bowl. She'd barely left his side since they'd touched the RIM.

"Sleeping." Zensha stared into the steaming bowl of stew, untouched in her hands. "He asked for his mother. And his sister." Her features were stony but her eyes shone bright with misery. "I haven't the heart to tell him yet. Not yet."

"Best to let him rest and recover first," Liselle agreed. "He's faced enough for now." Setting her bowl between her feet, Liselle's gaze swung across the empty and cleared field to a barrel bonfire. People gathered around it, and instruments joined the din of voices bringing the lilt of music to soften the chill night. Some of the staff had gone to join the growing festivities, taking a break from the heavy hours of work for a moment of fresh air and laughter. Her eyes narrowed, peeling through them.

"She's not there."

"Who?"

"Who you keep swiveling that head on your shoulders for," Zensha answered with a tender smirk, and planted her elbows on her knees. "I was about your age when Ro and I first met. She'd traded her brass for salt little more than ten years before we crossed swords over a deal, and I remember thinking, soon as she had me disarmed and knocked flat on my back—this was a woman I would follow to the ends of the horizon."

"I've heard the old stories," Liselle said. "She was really something."

"There has never been another like Indira Roscoe." Zensha clicked her tongue. "And I'd never say it to her face, but not even I, all these years later, can carry the weight of her steel."

"What split you two apart?" Liselle arched her brow.

Zensha's smile fell away and her gaze darkened with memories. "Her daughter," she said after a weary stretch. "Unlike Ro and the rest of her crew, who chose piracy, I was born into it. Three generations to the bone." She raised the last three fingers on her left hand. "Little Zory had just turned ten when I met Ro. Bright as a star, she was. Silver-haired and the deepest golden eyes—like burnt honey. Fell in love with her almost as quickly as I had her mother. Ro may have a heart as vast as the void, but she isn't what you'd call maternal. Or one to be tied down in a relationship, true?" Zensha chuckled, shaking her head at some absent thought. "We had many starts and stops over the next twelve years, but after Zory's death is when it all came crashing down. Ro tried her best for a time to raise Nimah, and hold it all together, until finally, without word or warning, she stonewalled us all, crew and granddaughter, with a coldness I didn't know she possessed."

"Did you ask why?"

"Didn't need to." Zensha rubbed her palms together, calluses grating like grinding molars. "Three days before, something happened. An . . . awakening, I guess you could call it. Nimah was always a strange one, even as a youngin'. Saw things that weren't there, heard voices that never spoke, and after she turned three, that's when the dreams began. Dreams that often had her screaming into the pillow. Where I come from, we'd have vented her out of mercy. But what we didn't see was that something was reaching out to her."

"Elite," Liselle whispered.

Zensha nodded. "No one knew of her grandfather, though we all had our suspicions. I'd been told of the time they'd spent on some alien world that predated all we ever knew. I'd taken it for little more than a fancy until . . . one night I woke in Ro's cabin with such violence from sleep—like something yanked me back into me bones. Followed that feeling until I found Nimah alone in the hold, just floating there, her eyes searing blue. Whispering in a tongue that was more sounds than actual words." Zensha's voice softened. "Couldn't move. Couldn't speak. I just stood there as whatever it was holding onto her finally let go. When Nimah dropped, it was Ro who caught her, and clutched tight in her small hand was a sparrow. A little trinket of stone Ro had given Nimah's mother when she'd turned twenty. That was the first time I'd ever seen Ro afraid.

"And I knew, somehow, whatever I'd just witnessed was connected to what happened the night Zory died." Zensha stroked her mechanical arm and kneaded the musculature made from synthetic protoskyn and tubing.

Liselle's throat thickened. "You were there."

"Close." She flexed her fingers and stared at the lines of her manufactured palm made from an exact print of her right one. "But not close enough to save her."

"So that's why Indira shut you all out?" Liselle asked. "And walked away from Nimah?" Terrified that her granddaughter would follow in the disastrous footsteps of her mother, Ro had put parsecs between herself and Nimah and elite—a frantic bid to keep her safe. Alive.

"Carrying the knowledge of elite and what it could do . . . that burden of responsibility, I expect for a time she thought it was one she could manage, but Ro is not the sort to ask anyone for help. And I resented her for it. For a long, long time."

"I should have."

Both Liselle and Zensha turned as Ro's voice floated from the doorway behind them.

"I should have asked for help. And I'm sorry I didn't." Her voice cracked. A hard truth for the proud captain to admit.

Zensha rose from the step and raised a firm chin, though her eyes were molten with unshed tears. "You know how much I loved Zory. She was practically mine, and I would've have protected her child to the end of my days." Zensha climbed to the top of the steps and cupped a tender hand to the side of Ro's strong cheek. "There is no weight in this void that I would not have carried," she whispered, "if only you had trusted me enough to ask. If only you had let me in."

The women embraced with hushed whispers and tears, and Liselle quietly slipped away to give them both a moment of much-needed privacy. Disappearing around the side of the hospital, she followed the surge of voices and music gathered around the barrel-fire.

"Oh, hey." Jono rose from a row of seating made from empty crates.

"Hi." Liselle removed the band around her wrist and tied back her shoulder-length locs. "Didn't expect to find you here actually enjoying some fun."

"An important part of leadership, Ms. Namsara, is delegating. My team has the hospital well under control. I, on the other hand"—Jono gestured to his satchel—"needed to continue excavation efforts at my lab. Just passing through on my way back from the armory." He angled his head in careful assessment, and Liselle struggled to hold herself steady rather than wilt under his knowing gaze. "You alright? You don't look so good."

"Can I ask you something?" Liselle hugged her arms tight to her chest to ward against the chill of brooding emotions almost as sharp as the damp night breeze. Both cut to the bone.

Jono placed a concerned hand on her shoulder. "Of course."

"I always considered myself well traveled. Well schooled. But this"—she gestured around them—"this is the first time I'm seeing the RIM for myself. Not a training sim, or a field recording, but for real. With my own eyes."

Jono glanced down at her with a knowing smirk. "I get it. First time for me was a real kick in the groin, too."

"It's like I don't know anything or ever have." And admitting that truth ruptured her pristine little privileged bubble. Nothing was going to be the same for her ever again.

"We were raised to view life beyond the Inner Circle through a particular lens," Jono explained. "And that is something that is going to take some time to undo, but it starts with understanding that all that separates you and I from these people is luck. We were born into the right families and under the right circumstances, that's all. My father—his wealth arguably gave him more power than SIGA, a power I stood to inherit, but I gave it all up to live surrounded by squalor in what we were always told was the worst place to be. But look around you." He drew her aside and turned her to the crowd gathered in conversation or dancing around a roaring fire where musicians played and sang. "What do you see?"

What she saw was smiling and laughter. She saw people who knew profound hardship and yet through great struggle they'd created a kind of peace and community that she'd never seen or experienced before. The kind that was impossible to achieve within the imposing density of the megacities, where people were taught to stand apart from each other.

Within the Inner Circle, life flowed like an assembly line. Cold and robotic. But here, the people were free. And the more she sat back and took in, the harder it struck her how biased and narrow-minded she'd actually been. While Liselle had always known Nimah was a RIMer, the truth was she'd never viewed her as such. They'd met and lived together within the Academy, and aside from the brand on her wrist, it was easily forgotten once covered.

To her, Nimah had been just another cadet. Scrubbed, polished, and dressed in the same uniform as everyone else. But what made her different was her compassion and empathy. Her determination to succeed and to be perfect at all costs—not because she was competitive but because of the fear she lived with of being cast out to the RIM. Its homes and streets made from mounds of discarded trash cubes, millions of tons dropped daily, because that was what their government had decided was all these people were worth after displacing them from their home planets so they could claim the ripest and richest for themselves.

Suddenly her chest tightened with shame. She'd blamed Nimah for her current circumstances, when the awful truth was as impossible to ignore as the ripe stench of trash beneath her feet. When Nimah arrived on Corlys asking for help, no one had forced her arm. Liselle could have chosen not to get involved, but instead she had. The fact that she was on the run with the Valkyries was no one's fault but her own—and SIGA's, for committing this heinous crime in the first place.

Liselle's heart clenched at the sight of a couple of women across the barrel-fire sharing in laughter and beer. A sight that echoed Zensha and Ro reconciling after all the time they'd lost to far too many things too long left unsaid.

That was the cost of pride. And if she and Nimah didn't find a way to work through the damage done between them, they would be no different. Life and the complicated choices that came with it might have forced them to stand on different sides of the line, but the distance in between didn't have to be a mile when it could be an inch. Someone had to take the first step to close the gap.

So let it be me.

Liselle turned to Jono. "Have you seen Nimah? She's not in the hospital or out here. I need to apologize for being a complete iceberg."

"Oh, Nimah? Yes. In fact, I sent her to the armory to grab some cables." He pushed his glasses with a trembling finger, and they skipped up the bridge of his nose. "She's going to meet me at my lab to—ah—help with the excavation."

"I thought you said *you* just came back from there?"

Jono winced, his features twitching like a droid after a faulty upgrade. "Ah. Yes. Well."

Liselle narrowed her eyes. It was giving guilty conscience. "Where's Nimah?" She caught him by the collar and yanked him forward until she could see the rings of silver haloing his brown irises. "And before you think of lying, know that I am in a terrible mood and would *love* any excuse to set it loose."

Realizing he was impossibly caught between a rock and a hard place, Jono's throat bobbed in trepidation. "I can't . . . I just . . . she needs more time."

Liselle clenched her teeth. "Time for *what*?"

"Nimah's gone." Liselle panted against the cramp twisting her abdomen, knotted from her sprint for the hospital before racing over to the *Stormchaser* after being told the crew returned to the ship.

Ro dropped her boots from the edge of the communal table. "What do you mean, *gone*?"

Sucking air between her teeth, Liselle struggled to slow her breathing. "Snuck out. Lab." She splayed her hands, miming an explosion. "Boom!"

"Boom what now?" Chu scuttled from behind the kitchen counter, an open glass bottle of beer hanging between her hooked fingers.

"Ah . . ." Liselle hissed, leaning into her left. "Cramping."

"Take a breath." Ro grabbed Liselle by the shoulders and held her upright. "Then I'm going to need you to be clear. *Real* clear."

Liselle sucked in air, nodded. "Nimah stole shuttle. Doubled back to BPRO."

Ro's face slackened in horror. "When?"

"An hour. After council. Debrief."

"With me." Ro blazed through the doorway and down the corridor. Liselle and the crew hurried after her. "You"—Ro jabbed a finger at Liselle as they rushed onto the bridge—"try to reach her on comms. Gertrude, I want a pin on the shuttle. *Find her.* Maybe she hasn't anchored yet."

"On it!" Gertrude dropped behind her navigation console.

Liselle claimed the second flight chair and drew up comm tags for everyone tethered to the ship. "She's deactivated her link."

Ro punched her fist to hull metal.

"Let me try the shuttle." Liselle chewed on the edge of her thumbnail as the outgoing wave icon blinked on screen. "Come on, Nims, answer." But as one tense minute bled into two, it was clear Nimah was either ignoring them or no longer aboard the craft.

"On my mother's bones, soon as I know she's safe, I'll wring her neck for this." Ro braced the captain's console and rattled it with frustration. "Where is Maverick?"

"Found him sedated in the medbay," Chu called out, pushing Maverick's chair with a grunt across the threshold to the bridge. "Had to pump him with a booster."

"Nimah." Maverick's eyes skipped in his sockets, face pale with nausea and drugs. "She . . . she . . ."

"Calm yourself, we know she's gone." Ro dropped before him. "Catch your head. That booster needs to circulate, and then we need to fly. Fast."

Beyond them, Mumbles flapped her arms by the doorway, fingers snapping and eyes wide.

"What?" Boomer crossed to her. "What is it?"

Hopeful, she turned to him, her hands moving in a frantic rhythm Liselle recognized as a form of sign language.

"You sure 'bout that?"

Mumbles bobbed on her toes, her braids flapping as furiously as her arms had.

"She says we can ask Ma to tether to the shuttle." Boomer translated. "Says we can track Nimah's wristdeck if she's synced to it."

"Liselle," Ro ordered.

In less than five minutes they were tethered. "Captain." Liselle swiveled in her chair and met Ro's questioning gaze. "There's a . . . there's a video message marked for the crew."

"Play it," Ro demanded.

Downloading the transmission, Liselle swallowed a gasp as Nimah's stoic face filled the screen.

"If you're watching this—Jono either did a really terrible job of covering for me or . . ." Her shoulders swayed with a heavy breath. "I know my actions will anger the council, but I am prepared to face the consequences, no matter what." Nimah reached forward, about to kill the transmission link, when she hesitated. "If I don't make it back . . . keep to the code."

The video ended and silence fell around them, thick and impossibly dense. Broken only by the sharp intake of breath from Captain Roscoe.

"Keep to the code?" Liselle whispered. "What does that mean?"

"A pirate who falls behind is left behind," Gertrude answered softly. "She's telling us not to come for her."

"Fuck that. I'm going back for her," Maverick croaked, his voice grainy and rough but his features had regained focus as he transferred himself from his hoverchair into the pilot seat.

"We all are." Ro straightened and set her hands, knuckles already bruising, on her hips. "Ma, give us a live stream from the shuttle cameras. Feed it to the main screen. Expand one hundred and fifty percent."

The ship hummed as the system went to work processing Ro's orders.

<I'm sorry, Captain. Recording features aboard the shuttle are not responding.>

Gertrude slapped an aggrieved hand to the nav console. "It's interference from their cloaking tech."

"For fuc— Are there any analytics in the shuttle's system to give us insight as to what's happened with Nimah?" Ro demanded. "Give me something!"

<According to shuttle logs, Nimah synced her wristdeck before deboarding for solo flight within range of the unregistered station. Eighteen minutes after, she approved a request for the shuttle to autopilot and run a scan of all transport vessels still on site. It was documented that all vessels are gone.>

"So . . . it's abandoned?" Gertrude cast hopeful eyes to the rest of the crew. "Nimah is out there alone?"

<Data would suggest so, however, the last output of vitals received from her wristdeck indicated extreme distress.>

Ro set her teeth, muscles flaring around her jaw. "What do you mean *last output*?"

<Her wristdeck was removed twenty minutes ago.>

Grief punched Liselle low in her belly, and she rocked forward in her chair. If this was it—if Nimah was gone and the last words she'd ever spoken to her best friend were ones of misguided anger . . . She squeezed her eyes shut in dread. *Source be good, I'll never forgive myself.*

"Are you saying she's dead?" Ro asked hoarsely.

<Not definitive. The device is intact but no longer attached to her body.>

"Someone must've taken it off her," Liselle commented. "Which means she's not alone."

"Could be Vesper," Gertrude agreed. "Or worse."

"Alright, crew, gather around and listen close." Ro positioned herself at the captain's console, arms crossed and features severe. "Nimah's been gone for hours. If that hellhole is still standing, then we can only assume she's in danger, and it'll be hours yet before we can reach her. A lot can happen to her in that time—so every minute we spend preparing is crucial."

Liselle tried to settle the unease of her churning stomach as she tried not to envision her best friend suspended in anti-grav, riddled with wires and tubes.

"We'll have to proceed under the assumption that whoever has Nimah may have cleared the lab but possibly called in SIGA for reinforcements," Ro continued. "And those reinforcements could very well reach her ahead of us, which means we may have a hard fight in and an even harder fight out."

Zensha stood by Ro, her gaze darkening. "Then we need to bring as much heat as possible."

"What about the wardogs the council is sending?" Liselle flagged her hands, capturing attention. "They're not just ships—they're weapons. We can ask them for help. Nimah's a pirate. She's one of them!"

"Salvaging a lone pirate is not part of the code." Gertrude sighed. "Especially not one who got herself in deep water defying the council."

"And that ain't the only issue." Chu crossed spindly arms, her white, grease-splattered tank stretching taut across her flat chest. "I hate to pick at a thorn in a tender foot, but now that you done mention it—Tortuga made it real clear we ain't supposed to go kicking rocks at SIGA. If we don't want to raise flags, then we can't pull out 'til them wardogs burned off the RIM with them kids."

"How long till they reach us?" Ro demanded.

"Another six hours," Chu scratched her chin. "Maybe five."

"Nimah doesn't have that kind of time!" Maverick snapped.

"True enough," Chu agreed. "But the recovery team is gonna be some kinda sus if Ro ain't here for the handover. We wanna keep the council dark—then hate to say it, Cap, but you'll have to stay behind."

Utterly defeated, Ro sagged back against the console.

"What about Jono?" Liselle rose, needing movement to ground her energy and her thoughts. "What if we ask him to oversee the handover?"

"No. Chu's right," she whispered through the weight of tears. "I must stay behind."

Grief switched to fury and in a flash, Ro swung a punch to the bulkhead—the bones of her knuckles crunching against hull metal, splitting skin. "I *won't* leave her out there." The crew stiffened when she swung again. Bone crunching. Skin splitting. "Not again," she roared.

Guilt clung to those words like gravity, carrying the weight of blame Liselle understood all too well. Ro had failed Nimah once, a decision that left scars too deep for either grandmother or granddaughter to forget.

Zensha caught Ro's fist before she swung a third time. A blow that likely would've broken her hand. "I couldn't help you save Zoraida," she said gently, holding that bleeding and bruised fist between them as the muscles in Ro's arm strained against her grip. "Let me do this. *Trust me with this.*"

The proud line of Ro's chin wavered. "Bring her back to me, Zen."

The women embraced, and the vulnerable sight made Liselle's heart twist with greater urgency.

"Okay, here's what we'll do." Liselle swept a hand through her locs, her mind working over the math. "*Stormchaser* breaks for Nimah, Ro holds back to liaise with the recovery team from Tortuga. While she does that, Jono rallies a seasoned crew with two additional ships to flank us for auxiliary support."

"Yes," Ro agreed, brightening in hope. "I can board the support ships once the wardogs are gone, and come in behind to protect your flank in a surprise show of force they hopefully won't anticipate."

The crew huddled together, forming the final points of the plan when Liselle's wristdeck hummed with an incoming notification. Opening her inbox, she scrolled to the urgent message from Admiral Wallace's private channel.

/*I called in a favor and secured a hearing with the review board scheduled for the day after tomorrow. You have thirty-six hours to burn to me in haste so we can debrief and coordinate a prepared statement to clear your record.*

I cannot overemphasize the importance of swift action. Fail to make this hearing, and all doors will be closed. It's now or never, Agent./

The world slowed and something inside of her squeezed in sorrow. This was it, her life—the chance to go back and unravel the noose looped around her throat—it was here. All she had to do was reach out and take it.

From the first day they'd bunked together, Nimah and Liselle had been inseparable. No matter what trials had come their way, they'd always chosen each other, and Liselle was not about to change that now.

You don't give up on family.

She deleted the message.

CHAPTER TWENTY-SEVEN

Nimah's temples throbbed from the teeth-ringing pitch. The sound chiseled its way through enamel, drilling into the roots and through her skull, where it burrowed deep. Hammering a single word into the aching folds of her tender brain until she thought her head was going to explode.

Obey.

It reverberated through Nimah like instinct, dulling her mind until nothing else occupied her thoughts beyond that singular command and the mindless urgency to follow it when Vesper's scream—an agonized wail full of devastation and loss—sliced through the cotton haze.

Nimah barely had a moment to recalibrate when something thumped to the ground by her feet. A dog's head. The body lay on its side, blood sluggishly pouring from the cauterized stump of the animal's neck onto glossy panels of white steel, polished to a mirror finish so pristine Nimah's own horrified expression reflected in Saint's vacant eyes.

Vesper fired off two shots before the sentries battled her to her knees. One caught the male cyber in the right thigh. The other grazed his temple. It was then Nimah noticed the blood sizzling on the laser edge of his primesword, and despite the wounds Vesper had dealt, he remained still as a statue.

"We have disabled and disarmed," he reported, the wound in his leg oozing.

"Is there anything else you would command of us?" the female cyber asked.

"Thank you. Your service is complete. Upon your swords, if you will."

Both cybers snapped their heels in stiff salute. "Upon our swords," they answered in unison, then, guiding the tip of their blades to their sternum, they dropped to their knees.

Hilts slammed to the floor and blazing steel ripped up into their ribcage. Blood, a shade so dark it was nearly black, poured from their collapsed bodies and joined with that of Saint like two oceans colliding. The smell . . . a nauseating blend of smoke and sizzling flesh, punched bile into the back of Nimah's throat.

"What did you do?" Tears rolled down Vesper's cheeks as she glared at Hillard in furious accusation but also with the grief of someone who, in a matter of minutes, had lost everything she'd held dear.

"No cyber can strike their mother." Hillard swung the whistle like a pendulum before tucking it back within the lapel of her gray blouse. "A particularly delicious bit of genetic coding I was smart to withhold from SIGA."

"You created cybers?" Nimah panted, her mind struggling to find sense through the chaos.

"You could say I quite literally *birthed* them." Hillard's pewter hair glowed like molten silver beneath the surgical lights as she whisked her chair forward, drawing into the center of her lab. "Cybers are cloned from two embryos harvested from my own womb. I could have used donors, but I wanted to be the source, you see. They are, all of them, my children. And my failures." She gestured to the wall of twisted infants, her eyes sharp and unyielding as they flickered back to Nimah. Bright with untamed ambition. "I keep them close as a reminder of the work and its importance."

"Get your fucking hands off me!" Vesper snarled, struggling against the sentries twisting her arms behind her back. "Tell your guards to release me, you deranged bitch. You have Nimah, you've won."

"You had your chance to leave without issue. But your insubordination has led to rather fortuitous circumstances." Hillard's chilling smile was saccharine-sweet, but her eyes . . . her eyes were utterly soulless. "You see, every experiment needs a control subject—and here we are." She gestured between Nimah and Vesper. "The same sex, close enough in age, height, and weight . . . Honestly, I couldn't have asked for more favorable conditions than this."

"Control subject," Vesper repeated. Realization dawned a fraction of a second later. "Fuck you." She wrenched her shoulders, twisting from the waist in an effort to break their hold, but the sentries at her back had the advantage of leverage and used it to quell her struggles.

"Resistance won't do you any good." Hillard raised her skeletal fingers in a commanding wiggle as she ordered her men to haul both Nimah and Vesper onto the descending examining table.

Two gathered Nimah by the arms and, still bound at the wrist, one took hold of her feet in case she sought to fight or kick. But, unlike Vesper, she didn't. Fighting would only expend vital energy, and she was going to need all of it to get out of this mess.

Reaching inside of herself, elite tingled in her chest and coiled in a tight knot, but for some reason, she couldn't unravel it or draw the energy forward. Almost as if the sharp frequency of the whistle had stunned it into confused submission.

Dobs! Nimah's desperation shot through the corners of her bruised brain but she was met only with resounding silence. *Where are you? Dobs!*

"What are you going to do with us?" Nimah demanded as she and Vesper were strapped down. The exam tables were suspended on a magnetic base, allowing them to swivel and move in a full three-sixty despite gravity or weight.

"Oh, dear girl. Telling will only spoil the fun, but today is a day of celebration, so perhaps I will indulge you." Hillard tilted her head, studying Nimah like a specimen under a microscope instead of a breathing human being. "Is it true you bonded with elite in its raw and unadulterated form?"

Nimah's eyes flashed wide. "How do you—?"

"—know of elite and its origin?" Hillard finished. "That's an even longer story, I'm afraid, one that goes back over thirty years but what I can tell you is that its discovery is what led me to the development of the cybers program."

Beyond them, Nimah tracked the movement of the sentries that—once finished with strapping down Nimah and Vesper, they collected the slain bodies of the cybers, depositing them onto gurneys as though they were packing away reams of paper instead of corpses.

"When the scandal of my research broke the newscast, our government may have condemned me publicly, but they endorsed me in secret.

Offering resources and protection to continue my work—under the condition I created an army of cloneable super soldiers. And while I was successful in that endeavor, the program is not without its issues. Cybers degrade quickly, only living for five years before they collapse from burnout—two of which are spent training them. And the cost to preserve them far exceeds the cost to simply grow another." Lifting one of the cybers limp hands, she injected the syringe into a vein at the wrist and drew blood into the vial.

"SIGA believes the purpose of my study into elite—the Eidolon Project—is to perfect these super warriors," Hillard continued. "But really, they are little more than incubators. Their blood contains a variant serum I derived from elite and during their brief lifespan, they distill this variant into a more malleable form, but elite is shockingly aggressive on our bodies—even the cybers can't seem to endure its intensity for long. When they die, they're brought to me for disposal. I then extract the refined variant from their DNA until I find a strain I can then synthesize into the next batch, which is then injected into the newly decanted cybers. Each generation gets me a little closer, but progress has been stagnant. At least until now."

Hillard pressed a sequence of keys on her armrest and a large glass chamber descended from a compartment within the ceiling. "May I introduce you to Subject X01," she said, her voice tinged with pride, as it settled to the ground.

Inside was a petrified form that stood eight . . . maybe nine feet tall and was eerily reminiscent of the bodies Jonothan had exhumed on the RIM, but whole rather than skeletal. Solid as stone. *No, not stone*, she realized dully. Stone didn't sing like this. Only elite did. And the pull struck Nimah like a blow to the sternum but it softened with a kind of awareness, almost reverent, as if it sensed she was finally close and relieved that she'd come at last.

Free me.
Free me.
Free. Me!

"You feel it, don't you? It's why you had to come back. I *knew* you would."

Nimah wanted to deny the claim, but whatever Hillard saw in her expression appeared to be confirmation enough. So many questions clamored through her, the most urgent of them being *how*? If elite was only available on the RIM, how was so much of it here?

"This is a native of the world I am told your grandmother so poignantly named Valhalla." Hillard laughed, bright as the hot, white surgical lights. "Elite comprises almost a third of their physical body, which they can seal themselves within until they are naught but pure stone. A defense mechanism that once done appears permanent, leaving behind a lifeless shell." Her gaze lingered on the petrified figure, expression unreadable.

"Why are you doing this?" Nimah wrenched against her bonds when Hillard raised a syringe, the point of the needle glinting with a liquid bead that shimmered faintly with little flecks of iridescent blue. "If you don't want to create weapons for SIGA—what's the point?"

"Isn't it obvious?" She lowered the syringe in bemused wonder. "Humans are a weak and morally bankrupt species, Nimah, surely you must see that. We plundered our home planet into decay, yet through luck and sheer stupidity, miraculously escaped our own extinction. But instead of honoring that gift, we learned nothing and continue to perpetuate our harmful cycle onto thousands more. Spreading like mold across the stars. *Sickening*." She flexed her other hand, curling the mechanical fingers into a fist. "But with elite, I will create a species devoid of our flaws, unspoiled by anger, ego, envy, or pride. Perfection." Her voice rose, almost reverent. "An intelligent life-form that truly exists in equilibrium. Neither predator nor prey. Call them angels. Gods. The universe made flesh. Can you imagine such a glory?" Joyful tears sparkled in the fringe of her lashes and Hillard's gaze ran across Nimah, almost tender.

Maternal.

"But to create heaven, I must first walk through hell." Hillard leaned closer, her eyes darkening like open graves. "That creature is the lock guarding the answers to every question I've ever had, and you are the key that will open it." Her mechanical hand brushed over Nimah's head, fingers stroking through her curls. "I hope you know that your sacrifice will not be wasted. Or taken for granted."

"You're fucking insane!" Vesper barked, and Hillard jerked slightly, as if only now remembering she was even there.

"Innovation requires madness," Hillard answered tersely. "It's a fact far too many lack the stomach to understand, but I have sacrificed everything for this project. Even parts of myself." She gestured across her body in emphasis.

Fucking psycho. Dobs's voice echoed limply in her mind like she was coming awake from a drug-induced sleep. *Shoulda sacrificed her crazed head and spared us the drag.*

Relief swam through Nimah so swiftly she almost whimpered with it. *Fuck, Dobs, I never thought I'd be happy to hear your voice again.*

Fucking A, Dobs answered with a tense laugh. *Keep her talking, kid. Distract her.*

Right. Nimah switched her attention back to Hillard. "Why did you take the children?"

Hillard's smile returned, cold and clinical. "Adults break too easily. Our minds are unwilling to surrender control, but a child can be . . . persuaded. After all, it's in a child's nature to surrender to growth and change. Pain, however, is where most tend to flounder. A body can only handle so much before it shuts down permanently and this procedure is invasive, but pain has proven to be our best conduit for adhesion. Pain provides a powerful anchor. To memory. To feeling. To existence." Hillard guided the large syringe to the exposed side of Nimah's throat, where her pulse hammered wildly.

No! Nimah struggled against her restraints. *No, no, no. Dobs!* But it was too late, the sharp point of metal punctured skin, and the cool rush of fluid injected into the vein.

"Brace yourself, my dear, because you're going to scream. Very, very loudly."

CHAPTER TWENTY-EIGHT

Pain. It stretched time into a blur. Seconds became hours. Hours became days.

Nimah floated above herself, a ghost torn from the walls of her flesh and thrust into a spiral of light. Unable to feel or move, she watched the garish spectacle of her body, bound upon a table of steel. They'd cut off her flight suit with laser scalpels, and stripped it away from her body along with her wristdeck, leaving her only in her pair of compression shorts and tank top, before they'd jammed her with IV tubes and electroleads.

"You were right, Doctor." An attendant whisked through data on her holopad. "Early bloodwork indicates not only is Subject N uniquely bonded with elite, her genome will also yield an even more powerful variant. This is exactly what we needed to break through the plateau with the cybers."

"Excellent. And what of this one?" Hillard tapped Vesper's arm.

Sweat soaked Vesper's hair and pooled in the hollow of her straining throat as she raved and cursed through her gag. Her eyes, bloodshot around the irises, expanded to nearly to swallow the whites.

"Subject V is not acclimating."

"That's because she's resisting. But she's got spunk, and elite appears to appreciate those with spirit. Let's begin the next steps of integration."

A dial twisted, sending a bolt of nerve-shocking agony between Nimah's temples, and her body arced like a crescent moon, teeth clenched around a mouthguard to prevent them from cracking. Everything blazed searing white—and Nimah was catapulted from BPRO, across the dizzying chasm of the void like a ship launched into hardburn, until she slammed to a sudden, violent stop.

Surrounded by nothing but dark, Nimah crouched to her knees, jaw aching and head on fire, unable to see anything beyond her shaking hands until, slowly, light bloomed and brought focus to her surroundings. A rounded viewport laden with potted plants. A narrow cot wrapped in a mustard-yellow blanket before it tucked away into a sidewall. And Nimah, her weary and exhausted face blinking back at her from the other side of a mirror.

This was the shuttle the morning she awoke in Kesh3. *How . . .* Confusion shifted into horrified realization. All those episodes, the sudden and invasive presence tormenting her for days, were not hallucinations . . . they were memories. *It was me. It was always me.*

Nimah beat her fist against the other side of the glass, but even though she made contact, it held solid as stone. *I'm here. I'm right here!* She screamed, but no voice or sound was emitted from her throat.

The current ceased, and within the span of half a breath Nimah slammed back into her bones.

"You are quite the trouper." Hillard snapped fingers before Nimah's eyes until they sharpened into focus. "You've taken enough voltage to kill most, but already your vitals are stabilizing. Pulse is strong." She waved a penlight, and the glare pierced Nimah's cornea like steel pins.

"Please." The taste of blood coated her tongue from when she'd bitten it, and the wound throbbed in tandem with her pulse. "No more."

"Well, that depends on you." Hillard planted her forearm to the table, lowered so that she could peer down from her chair with ease. "Look *through* her." She pointed across to the second table where Vesper lay prone and far too still. "Tell me what you see?"

"Through her?" Exhausted, Nimah breathed slow and deep, the nerves in her teeth still screaming. "I don't know what the fuck you want from me."

"Those born into elite hold a unique capacity to not only access it, but each other as well. Almost like code in a network, and in theory my serum should allow you to ground yourself in those same skills inherent to your ancestry. So if you want this to stop—project yourself into her body. See through her eyes."

"I can't!"

"Try!" Hillard urged, pitiless.

"Give her what she wants, kid." Dobs's voice tickled the back of her mind.

That's your grand suggestion? Nimah's weary laugh climbed the sandpaper walls of her throat. *Surrender?*

"Far as I reckon its our best play." Dobs circled into view from the foot of the table, her expression almost pained as her eyes swept over Nimah and then shot back to meet her gaze. "Quit being so stubborn and give her a show. Let her think she's won."

Except if she did that then Hillard would in fact win, and there was no telling who would suffer next. No. The only way to win was not to play. Nimah set her jaw. "I'd rather die."

"Suit yourself," Hillard sighed, her chair passing through Dobs as she steered away from Nimah and over to Vesper.

From this angle, Nimah couldn't see Vesper's face, but the stillness of her body and the struggling lines of her vitals leaping across her holoscreen were not good.

"Leave her alone, she can't handle any more," Nimah croaked, and struggled against the bonds of her restraints. "You're killing her!"

"Perhaps," Hillard agreed, gesturing for her staff to continue.

"Listen to me." Dobs planted her hands on either side of Nimah, caging her head. "Much as it warms my coal-black heart to see you bounce like battered fish in fry oil—this body of yours happens to be mine too, and I like breathing."

"Shut up," Nimah whispered, a sudden burst of nausea sending her eyes to spin. "I'm the one being tortured. Not you."

"*Hey!*" Dobs captured her face and squeezed until Nimah's vision sharpened back into focus. "I'm serious, kid. I need you to rally."

Nimah's proud jaw wavered, and tears rolled down her temples into her sweat-soaked curls. "I don't have it in me." Not because she was too stubborn, but because she was standing at the edge of her breaking point. The pain was too much, and everything inside of her just wanted to lie down and never rise again.

Releasing her, Dobs sighed deeply. "Then let me."

Let me, the urgent stirrings of elite chimed in. A layered echo of voices all tangled within her. *Let us!* But before Nimah could find the words or the strength to answer, Hillard cranked the dial, and both Nimah and Vesper bowed through another violent surge that sent fire shooting through the roots of their teeth and pressure exploding from behind their eyes.

And instead of blasting Nimah back through space and time, something else latched onto her, anchoring her to the present.

"That's it!" Hillard's elated gasp permeated the blinding haze.

Pressure exploded, so great the bones of her skull threatened to crack apart. Nimah's screams tangled with Vesper, their anguish torn from the depths of their very souls, and blending into a single, shattering cry so that she couldn't tell where Vesper began and she ended.

"*Hold on*, kid," Dobs urged, her energy wrapped around Nimah like a fist. "I gotcha. Hold on!"

As if she had any other choice. If there was a way to let go, exhausted from sheer agony alone, Nimah would have done it by now. Her blood went hot, frothing like liquid fire in her veins, and somewhere beneath the storm of pain, something inside of her was drawn taut—a cord that snapped with tension and then began spooling her in. Vesper slid into Nimah like a glove. Fingers into fingers, toes into toes, and eyes behind eyes.

Memories poured into her. Bits of Vesper's childhood knit with slivers of her adolescence. Ill-formed fragments of Vesper's consciousness, improperly fused into a jumbled mess that crammed into the folds of Nimah's mind with rough edges, sharp as broken glass.

The current ebbed with a sudden flick and, sobbing, Nimah slumped against steel. Sweat pooled beneath her back and tears rained freely down her cheeks.

"Perfect equilibrium!" Hillard's piercing voice rang in Nimah's ears, almost as painful as the current of electricity. She hunched forward in her chair, utterly fixated on their vitals splayed on the dual holoscreen. "We have achieved tethering." She clapped her skeletal hands with a bright giggle. "Well done," she applauded. "You've done in hours what often took us weeks. Let's pray this link between you can be sustained."

Returning to Nimah's side, she fastened a syringe to the IV tube taped down against the back of Nimah's hand.

"It's you who should be praying." Nimah panted as Hillard removed the stopper from the end of the tube and blood shot into the narrow cylinder of the vial.

"Ah. I see." Hillard worked quickly, popping off the vial when it was near full and replacing it with a second, then a third. "You believe rescue is coming." Once the third vial was full, she twisted the vent shut and resealed the IV tube with the stopper.

"I know it." There was no force in the void that would hold her grandmother back. Or Maverick. They'd come for her. And Nimah let that assurance restore strength to her bones and fire to her blood. "You're alone. You're unprotected." She grinned. "And whatever you've done on your darkest of days will be a mercy compared to my grandmother's wrath when she gets here. It's not too late," Nimah wheezed. "You can still let us go."

"Such defiance and hope. I almost hate to break you of it." Hillard *tsk*ed, stroking the edge of her thumb across Nimah's damp brow. "I'm sure it's hard to sense—our systems are quite advanced—but listen. Listen very, very closely." She raised a finger, ear cocked. "There, can you hear it yet?"

It was subtle, barely perceptible. And with all that was going on, she'd been too distracted to really notice, at least until now. Inertia shifts.

The vibrations in the walls that Nimah had identified earlier as the hum of energy cables drawing power from the main generators were in fact from the gravity stabilizers recalibrating from course corrections and acceleration, creating the slightest pull or sway that resulted in micro-flexing of the hull.

BPRO wasn't a sedentary station—it was a ship, and that ship was currently in *flight*.

"We detached the moment you entered this auditorium." Hillard confirmed the sinking feeling in Nimah's gut. "By the time they reach our anchor coordinates, they'll find what appears to be remnants of a wreckage and, naturally, will assume the worst." She loomed over Nimah, blotting out the surgical lamp like a moon sliding across the sun. "So, you see? You're mine now, and we are going to achieve fine works together, you and I."

Hopelessness, a vicious bloom—all thorns and no petals—grew within Nimah and it took every ounce of her strength not to lose herself to despair. Whatever Samantha Hillard may think, Captain Indira Roscoe would not be swayed by a farce of scattered debris. She'd hunt for Nimah until her last breath.

At best, this slowed Nimah's chances for recovery from a few hours to days. At worst, Nimah would have to fight her own way free of this nightmare. She almost preferred the latter. If she had to die—let it be on her feet rather than fastened to a table like a gutted pig.

"Now you have earned a rest. I suggest you embrace it while you can. When I return, we will move on to the next round of study, and if you thought tethering was painful—" She shook her head mournfully. "The worst is yet to come."

Hillard whisked from the room, the soft whir of her hoverwheels vanishing behind the seal of the nanite doors with her retinue of lab assistants in tow.

"'Bout fucking time." Dobs sparked a cigarette. "You ready to get off that slab, or are you just gonna mope about until that deranged cunt is ready to carve off the top of your skull next?"

Nimah cut her an aggrieved glare. "I'm tied down, in case you haven't noticed." Restraints were fastened at the wrists, the crook of her elbows, and the joints of her knees and ankles, without an ounce of give.

"So? Get out of 'em."

"How?"

Blowing out a thick stream of spiced smoke, Dobs tapped the butt of her cigarette against her lower lip, eyes narrowed to slits. "Know how to pop a thumb outta joint?"

"What?" Nimah gasped. "No!" Not only was dislocation painful, it was also likely to cause nerve or ligament damage in the joint if reset incorrectly.

"Better a wrecked thumb than being that nutsack's pincushion," Dobs answered, reading her thoughts.

Nimah closed her fingers around the thumb on her nondominant hand. *Fuck.* "I don't think I can do it."

"I can. Just gotta give me a bit a wiggle in that head of yours."

"Like I'm really going to trust you with my brain."

Dobs shrugged. "Then break it yourself."

Nimah bounced the back of her head against the table with a curse. "Alright. Do it quick before I change my mind."

Perched over her, Dobs pressed her hand to Nimah's chest, and with a gradual push, it slithered through her, thick and slow. Pressure expanded through Nimah's ribs, uncomfortable but not unbearable, and sent a ripple of force to course through Nimah's left arm, weaving around sinew and bone.

Dobs clamped the cigarette between her teeth and straightened the digit, drawing it back as far as it could go until the nerves in the joint sparked in warning. "Ready?"

"No," Nimah whined, the tip of her thumb resting against the bony knot of her hip.

Dobs grinned, ash breaking from the tip of the cigarette, and with a hard bunt of pressure driving her hand down, bone cracked free from cartilage in a sickening pop. Nimah's curse arched into a sharp cry that Dobs managed to smother, trapping it in her throat.

"There." Dobs nodded, pleased at her literal handiwork. "That did it."

"I hate you," Nimah wheezed, her vision molten with tears. For such a small appendage, it fucking hurt and throbbed like it was swelling to thrice its size.

"C'mon, that hardly comes close to what that bitch put you through the last few hours. Now, quit mewling and shimmy your hand out from the cuff. Use your fingers to straighten the thumb and tuck it close as you wiggle. I said *tuck it*!"

"I'm trying, but it fucking hurts!" Nimah shouted back.

"Yeah, well, pain means you're still kicking, don't it? Okay, there, now wiggle. Too bad we can't cut your wrist and grease it a bit. Blood's pretty slick before it coagulates."

"Bet you'd love that," Nimah seethed, blinking against the spurts of pain as she focused on the task. The restraint was made from foam and plastic wrapped around a flat band of leather, so it clung to her skin with a stubborn grip.

Progress was maddeningly slow, and more than once Nimah feared she'd never wrest herself free—until finally her hand popped out. She exhaled in immediate relief before refocusing on threading her arm up and through the second loop of the restraint fastened around her elbow. Thankfully it wasn't quite as tight as the one around her wrist, but the process was impeded by her limited range of mobility and took nearly twice as long.

"What you stopping for? Get some grease on those gears," Dobs chided once she had her arm free of both loops. "Seen a corpse have more hustle than you."

"You really are a beacon of encouragement." Reaching across herself, Nimah unfastened her other arm, and made short work of it—even with her screaming thumb—before continuing down to her knees and ankles.

Once free, Nimah leapt off the table and savored that first moment of uninhibited movement. Her legs were stiff and the bones of her ribs whined with every breath, but aside from those grievances, she felt better than expected, given the hours of grueling torture.

Vesper, on the other hand, looked awful. Her skin was sickly gray, her eyes glassy and vacant. She lay as still as a cadaver, apart from the soft wheeze floating between her parted lips like a ruptured tire leaking air with every spin of the wheel.

"Vesper," Nimah gently shook her shoulders. "Come on, don't give up now. Stay with me." But there was nothing. Not a flicker of life or movement behind her bloodshot eyes.

Dobs wove around to the other side of the exam table, eyes fastened to Vesper's sluggish vitals.

"Why isn't she awake?" Nimah demanded. "What's wrong with her?"

"Going off the dome . . . synaptic response is failing and her neuro-electric patterns are erratic. See those rapid bursts?" Dobs tapped a finger against the holoscreen. "That's her mind trying to wake up—but it can't. On top of that, her heart's limping like a slug through salt, probably because she ain't sucking in enough air to properly oxygenate after being flooded with enough cortisol to flatline a grown bull."

"What does that all mean?"

"Means whatever that woman did to her, if she stays like this for much longer, there will be permanent cognitive decay. Mumbles will appear loquacious by comparison."

Nimah's shoulders drooped in defeat. "Is there nothing we can do?"

"Yeah. Forget her, kid."

"I'm not leaving her in this place with *that* woman," Nimah snarled. Vesper might be a killer for hire with questionable morals, but whatever her faults, she didn't deserve to be tortured to death by a maniac. "You're a field-trained medtech. Either tell me what to do or fuck off."

Dobs snapped the cap on the Zippo. "Got a booster?"

"She's been shocked to near death and now you want me to shock her *again*?"

"Her mind's like a stalled engine, heard?" Dobs bounced a knuckle against her temple. "Gotta pump fuel back into her cells and get those circuits firing again."

"Where am I going to find a neuro booster? This isn't a medbay!" Nimah scraped a frantic hand across her curls, mind reeling, when it struck her. "Fuel cells," she repeated.

Elite was essence and energy. Whatever Hillard had done to them with her injections and violent barrage of electroshocks, she and Vesper were connected in a way that Nimah didn't yet fully understand. But somewhere inside, she felt Vesper curled away in a dark corner. She was there. And if all she needed was something to draw her back to the surface, then . . .

"*I* can be her booster," Nimah finished the thought out loud.

Dobs dipped her chin. The one benefit of her squatting inside Nimah's head meant Dobs didn't require an explanation to catch up. She simply knew.

"Worth a shot," she agreed.

Nimah placed her hands tentatively on Vesper, one atop her head and the other above her heart. "I don't know what I'm doing," she confessed. "What if I make her worse?" She looked to Dobs, her brows drawn in panic. "What if I kill her?"

"Your instincts haven't been wrong yet, kid. Don't start doubting 'em now."

Nimah drew a steadying breath and closed her eyes. "Be with me," she whispered.

And reached out.

CHAPTER TWENTY-NINE

Instinct. Nimah surrendered to it like a smooth dive into clear water and let elite flow through her. Into her. The intuitive force of it guided Nimah to Vesper's heart, and deeper still to where the core of her life force was protected.

Her senses gathered those gleaming threads of Vesper's waning energy, and when she found those tentative tendrils, Nimah gave a gentle pull. Then another.

Come on. She tugged again a little more firmly, and this time Vesper finally answered. Just the barest ripple, limp but there. *There you are.*

Nimah drew from the primal energy of the elite in her system and let it flow through her and out, feeding it along that thread into an interwoven loop of energy spiraling out from Nimah, into Vesper, and back again. The bones under Nimah's skin warmed. Hummed. Her entire skeleton rang like a sounding rod.

Be with me.

Vesper snapped awake, life blooming color into her cheeks and light into her eyes.

"No way!" Nimah giggled, swaying as the thread between them snapped, breaking the connection. "It actually worked."

"What the fuck!" Vesper panted. "Felt like I fucking died."

"You nearly did." Nimah began unfastening her restraints. "We don't have a lot of time, so I'm going to let you out and you're going to promise that when I do, you won't attack me."

Vesper scowled. "Don't have much of a choice, do I?"

"No," Nimah agreed. "You don't. Not if we want to make it out of here alive."

Vesper sighed. Nodded. "Okay. I promise."

Once the last of the restraints was freed, Vesper barely touched her feet to the floor when she swung for Nimah—and almost collapsed beneath the weight of her own body.

"Seriously?" Nimah scoffed.

Vesper planted an arm to the table, holding herself on boneless legs. "Was worth a shot."

Arms crossed, Dobs barked a smoky laugh. "I like her."

"Get lost, Dobs, this is not the time."

"Who are you talking to?"

"Never mind." Nimah looped an arm around Vesper's waist. "We gotta go."

Vesper hooked her arm across Nimah's shoulders and had only just settled her weight against her when a sharp snap had them both drawing still. They looked in tandem to the figure of stone, shuddering like a pipping egg. Soft little vibrational movements that indicated life trapped within.

"Is . . . is that supposed to happen?"

"I don't think so," Nimah answered, but her words were lost in the loud crack of splitting stone and something—*something*—emerged.

Long-limbed and narrow in the torso of what Nimah guessed might be a female form. Humanoid but clearly . . . not. Hair flowed in palest white against lustrous skin, a shade merging from blue into deepest obsidian that refracted light like the curve of a black hole bending reality.

"Is that an alien?" Vesper croaked.

Nimah could only nod.

Whatever it was—it was awake. And its attention was fixed on them as it scuttled down from the base of the cylinder, hugging robes that flowed like vapor and mist to its emaciated form. Each shuddering breath crackled from its chest like a comms tag set to an unfamiliar frequency, pulsing in a temporal rhythm Nimah could almost feel echoing through her.

Its raised palms hovered before Nimah and Vesper, and every instinct inside Nimah shrieked to fall to her belly, like a wolf submitting to a creature more powerful.

More deadly. Ancient.

"What is it doing?" Vesper whispered.

"Reading us," Nimah answered, not quite sure how she knew.

Its eyes narrowed, luminous voids swirling with shifting bursts of light, as if it had drunk whole galaxies and trapped cosmic storms within its fathomless gaze. A third opened vertically above the flat bridge of its nose, and suddenly the glaring white walls of the lab slipped away until there was nothing but those endless pools of swirling stardust.

Deep within Nimah's chest, the elite gathered and purred like a contented kitten being stroked by the hand of its master.

Feeling it, the being snapped its hands back and recoiled from them. "Abomination."

Its booming voice reverberated, felt more than heard, and overlapped with the echoes of Nimah's memory. This was the force she'd felt on the *Stormchaser*. Crying out to her for help.

"No." Nimah stepped forward, but it recoiled further, like she carried a foul disease it didn't want to catch. "I was not made, I was born."

"What are you on about?" Vesper snapped.

"It thinks I'm one of Hillard's clones." *But I'm not*, her thoughts urged. *I'm not an experiment; I'm one of you.*

Advancing on Nimah, it sniffed at her, drawing in layers of her scent, then exhaled hard as if clearing her from its nose in disgust. "No right to claim."

The walls of Nimah's heart pinched tight with hurt and rejection. It knew who she was—what she was—and in the end, it had determined she was not only lacking but undeserving.

"I knew it!" Samantha Hillard surged into the room, frothing with joy, her bionic hands punching in triumph. "I knew you would do it!"

The being glowered and a shimmer of light rose in vibrating waves around its frame—a halo of energy stoked by its rage. But when it raised its hand, casting that halo to strike like a weapon, it staggered weakly, the halo suddenly dropping away.

"Subdue the Exo!" Hillard ordered. "Quick! Before it recedes from us, again!"

Sentries charged forward, bunting it with the pronged ends of their batons, shocking it until it collapsed onto its knees with keening screams. Too weak to deflect their assault.

Vesper gasped. "What's wrong with it?"

"It's . . . it's dying," Nimah answered, again uncertain exactly how she knew, but somehow her senses were capturing a frequency it emitted almost like sonar. The sound triggering a sudden download in her mind, depositing information and images she absorbed in the span of but a moment.

It was a ranger, drawn to a concerning output of energy that led it to BPRO—where it was subdued by Hillard's team and tortured for decades. Too far from its home, it was starved from the disconnection to its own source. Elite was life. Sustenance. Power and spirit. It was everything. And without it, the being was forced to shield itself in stone, preserving strength to emit a distress signal, calling for help.

As Nimah's connection to elite strengthened, she'd tangled herself in that signal, but it was her tethering to Vesper that had drawn it from its cocoon. Sensing what it thought was home. Awakening had depleted even more energy than it had to spare, and now it was on its last breaths.

This is what Hillard had wanted, Nimah realized in dull horror, and now her real work could begin. Anger and desperation surged inside Nimah like a dark wave, and she urged it to build and grow until it was a force too great for her body to contain or control—a storm poised to break.

"You'll want to stand back," Nimah warned, and whatever Vesper saw in her face had her drawing away, eyes widened with a fear she'd never shown before.

Nimah flexed her hands and violent shocks of energy rippled across her palms and between her fingers as the air itself seemed to recoil—humming with static and sharp with the biting scent of ozone.

It was the Exo who looked to Nimah first, bloodied and on its knees, its hollow gaze expanded in disbelief. The sentries turned at last, helmets snapping toward her and extendos raised. Behind their tinted visors Nimah saw the instant shock, terror, and disbelief gave way to dawning realization.

She was no longer weak and captured prey—but predator.

Nimah lunged. A blur of light and fury, her body and mind fused into a lethal dance. She caught the first sentry by the arm and snapped it with a brutal twist just as she slammed her heel into his visor with a burst of energy that punched glass and shocked energy into his eyes, dropping him like a puppet with cut strings. The second swung the crackling end of his extendo at her head, but she caught his arm mid-strike, twisted, and drove her elbow into his chest with another violent burst that sent him flying into the wall with bone-shattering strength.

The third tried to flank her, but Nimah swept his legs out from under him as her other hand clamped around his throat, throwing all her weight behind driving him into the ground. The floor warped upon impact, and she stepped over his convulsing body to face the fourth. He clutched his weapon, tight as a prayer, panic rippling off him like steam—she could see the shimmer of his energetic aura and it made whatever was in Nimah smile to behold. She grabbed the end of his extendo—electricity screamed against her palm but to her it was little more than a flutter of lashes.

"How . . . ?" he panted.

Nimah answered only with a grin, then shot her power into the weapon. A raw current overtook the extendo and it exploded in his hands. He screamed, staggering back with nothing but bloodied stumps and shreds of fleshy bone dangling from his wrists. She finished him with a brutal strike to the chest, and what was left of him crumpled at her feet.

"Nimah!" Vesper shouted, drawing her attention with a point of her arm toward the back of Hillard's whirring hoverchair, racing for the doorway.

Grabbing one of the discarded extendos, Nimah launched it like a spear for Hillard. It struck one of the vents on the chair and the fuel cells ruptured from the power surge. The chair toppled and Hillard struck the ground brow first, barely rolling in time to miss being crushed beneath the weight of her mobility aid.

Grunting, Hillard pushed herself back onto her arms and peered up at Nimah, eyes blown wide. Not in fear, as one would expect, but in awe.

"Nimah, please." She raised a hand, the mechanical fingers broken in an effort to catch her fall. "I know you think me a monster, but I beseech you. Surely you can set aside your basest, selfish emotions and appreciate the opportunity we have before us. Imagine what you and I can do together, with your noble gifts and my remarkable skills to harness them? Think of all that we could uncover. The secrets of the universe. The truth behind creation. No more hunger. No more disease. No more war." Tears streamed down her face, and she reached for Nimah as if in supplication. "You are the key to unlocking *everything* I have devoted a lifetime to understanding. It can't end like this. Not when I'm so close."

Power swelled inside Nimah, fueled by the fathomless depths of virulent anger as she thought of all those children she'd been unable to save in time. Families slaughtered. Thirty years of death and terror.

Nimah lowered before Hillard, bringing them level. "You want to see what elite can really do?" She caged the woman's head between the palms of her hands. "I'll *show* you."

And she set her fury loose.

Elite retained memory as well as essence, and there was nothing but pain soaked into the walls of BPRO. All those screams. Ghosts trapped within steel. Tens of thousands of innocents. Nimah drew them into her and flooded it all into the center of Samantha Hillard's black heart.

She let her see. She let her feel and experience—every death, every tear. Until every cell in her body was saturated in anguish, and still Nimah poured out more. Until Hillard's screams went bloody, until her eyes ruptured and her heart seized. Until all vestiges of life ran in a stream from every orifice her body possessed.

"Holy fuck," Vesper whispered, but Nimah was numb to her horror.

What was left of Doctor Samantha Hillard lay in a twisted ruin at her feet. The only fitting death for a woman who bore no soul. Or remorse. And yet somehow it wasn't enough. Not nearly enough.

Nimah wanted to revive her, only so she could kill her again. And again. A million times in a thousand different ways. For her screams to ring across a millennium, a celebration of justice and a warning to anyone who would ever dare try to pick up where she'd left off.

Hands caught Nimah by the shoulder and drew her away from the violence. The Exo swayed on its feet, and the sheen of its skin dimmed with waning strength. Cracks formed across the surface as if soon it would scatter like ashes to the wind.

It gestured to Hillard's twisted remains. "Wrong."

"I had to do that," Nimah protested.

The Exo gestured to her chest, where Nimah's heart gave a pained squeeze between every frantic beat as if denying her response. "Death."

"What does that mean? What is happening to me?"

The Exo reached for her, and the moment its finger contacted Nimah's brow, a white searing flash yanked her from her bones and into a vision. The same vision that had been haunting her for months, only so much clearer. The void on fire. Whole worlds collapsing into flames in a brutal chain reaction that could not be stopped. Nimah was at the center of it all, a demon that consumed all life. All hope. Crushing planets. Draining the stars. Until the void was nothing but a chasm of darkness.

And she was all that remained.

Nimah detached herself with a gasp. "No. I won't do that." She rubbed the heel of her palm across her heart, kneading away the swollen ache. "I could never do that."

"Death," the Exo repeated, before snatching Nimah by the throat. Long fingers curled tight, but not enough to stop her from breathing, only to hold her fast.

"Stop!" Vesper lunged for Nimah, but the Exo flung a hand and sent Vesper flying against the wall.

Nimah yanked at its wrist, but despite its emaciated state, she was unable to break its iron grip. And as the shimmer of an aura rippled from its skin like heat waves off stone, once again awareness flooded Nimah.

Weakened from maintaining its own defenses, its death was unavoidable, but before it faded with its last breath, it was going to put an end to the threat Samantha Hillard and her research presented not only against its home but all life across the stars.

Luminous eyes softened with something like an apology. "Must."

A violent shockwave burst into Nimah's chest, a force that twisted through flesh, veins, and marrow—tearing elite from every fiber and cell. It was starved for power, and it was taking all that she had without mercy.

Lost to the siphoning, Nimah's vision shuddered in dark pulses timed with the furious pull, her scope of view narrowing into a tunnel of collapsing stars as every nerve in her body screamed against the invasion.

When it was done, it released Nimah gently. Gratefully.

Shaken, Nimah sank to her knees, empty. Spent. Her stolen essence surged inside of the being, lighting up its core and shining like newborn suns in its eyes. The glowing veins that had been wan streaks beneath the surface layer of its skin now throbbed like violent bolts of lightning. Its body shuddered, every atom vibrating at an unstable frequency, as if holding itself together required every stolen ounce of her power.

Not enough, something inside of her whispered. It needed more.

Arms flung wide, tendrils of energy slithering from the being into the facility itself and suddenly the walls around them trembled, metal shuddering under the strain of its force.

"What is it doing?" Vesper grabbed Nimah by the arm to help her back onto her feet.

"Gathering energy."

"To what? Escape?"

"No." Nimah twisted as the lights overhead flickered then exploded, raining sparks. The displays on the holoscreens glitched and shattered. The power lines tucked behind the walls crackled in warning and fury. "It's going to explode."

CHAPTER THIRTY

Vesper thought she knew death, but before today, she'd only met its sunlit shadow.

At four years old, she was on her way home from preschool when the synth-driver, due to a failed update in its systems software, missed the air-traffic signals and drove the sedan head-on into a delivery tram. The vehicle compressed like a trash cube, and Vesper's skull cracked open like an eggshell split by the back of a spoon.

She hadn't felt pain. It had all happened far too quickly. But for three minutes and twenty-seven seconds, her heart stopped beating in the back of an emergency transport to a medbay. Vesper awoke three weeks later in a recovery pod, after she'd been sedated and submerged in saline infused with nanites that knit her back together like a tireless team of surgeons.

Their work was so precise all she had to show for the devastating accident was the faintest of scars about the size of a grain of rice hidden within her hairline. But the memory left a scar no nanite could erase. And for months afterward, she relived the dizzying spin of that collision. Felt the crush of steel and crunch of bone.

It should've molded her into a fearful little thing. Instead, she'd became an adrenaline junkie—chasing the thrill of racing and extreme sports. Anything that put her on the edge and added another streak of silver to her mother's dark hair. Because the more she brushed against the boundary of her own mortality, the less she feared it.

Until now.

She'd died on that table. Even if her heart had never stopped beating. And Vesper had never felt so truly small or helpless in all her life as the moment those drugs had dragged her kicking and screaming into the breathless expanse where souls were forged—or extinguished. Unsure which of those dark fates awaited her until Nimah's voice had pierced through the silence and terror, summoning Vesper back into her bones.

"Hey." Nimah slammed Vesper's back against the wall, her face closing in until all Vesper could see were golden-brown eyes and the glimmer of something burning behind them like light on an impossible horizon. One she could never hope to reach.

"I know you're still pretty disoriented, but you've got to keep your head."

"I'm trying." Vesper pressed the heels of her palms against her throbbing temples. "The fuck did she put in me?"

"Elite. Or whatever version of it that deranged bitch concocted." Nimah punched a button on a wall panel, and only then did Vesper realize they were standing inside the main lift and not Hillard's fucked-up torture chamber.

Fuck, when had they even moved? Her mind was a scattered mess, like a stack of playing cards—but the suits were all out of order. The only clear thought she could latch onto was the urgent need to flee.

"Are you hallucinating yet?"

The doors shut and the drop sent Vesper's tender stomach shooting into her throat. "I . . . I don't think so."

"You will." Nimah scanned her face. "It'll show you all kinds of crazy shit and draw you deep inside yourself where you don't want to go. Where it hurts the most. But you can't lose focus. This place is sinking fast, and we've got find a way out of here before it implodes."

Right. Vesper sucked in an urgent breath, grounding herself in the facts. *Exploding aliens.*

"My shuttle is out of range, and I can't autopilot it to get us without my wristdeck." Nimah rubbed her bare wrist. "Where's your ship?"

"Docked in their quay."

"Great." Nimah exhaled in relief. "When these doors open, let's hope there're no more sentries or drones." She braced the curved wall next to Vesper as the lift rattled from the violent throes of the station coming apart at the seams. "You think you'll be good to run for it?"

Vesper blinked cold sweat from her eyes. "Guess we'll find out."

The doors to the lift opened into chaos. The metal floor of the atrium rippled like water, distorted by the shockwaves of energy cleaving through steel.

"You seeing this?" Vesper gasped. "Or am I hallucinating?"

"No. That's very fucking real. Run!"

Together they bolted from the lift and out into the open atrium. Orb lights exploded, raining sparks that pressed hot kisses against Vesper's arms and cheeks. She swatted them from her eyes as she struggled on legs that wobbled with each stride. Nimah led the way but slowed just enough to keep Vesper close, neither of them stopping until they reached the quay.

The *empty* quay.

"I thought you said you had a ship?" Nimah shouted over the blare of alarms.

The muscle in Vesper's jaw flared in aggravation. "Bitch must've vented it."

"Fuck!"

Warning lights bathed everything in spinning pulses of red and amber followed by a crisp automated voice ringing through the intercom.

Attention crew and staff, nova activation detected in Sector Four. Emergency shields have been deployed, but system integrity is fifty-two percent and declining. You have fifteen minutes to station collapse. Please proceed to the quay and prepare for emergency evacuation.

Nimah bounced on her toes, when suddenly a hopeful grin brightened her features. "I have an idea!"

Vesper followed as Nimah jogged across the quay and folded over a long shipping container, limp with relief. No, not a shipping container. A cryopod. Dozens of them, in neat stacks and fastened with anchor cables to the wall.

Vesper planted her hands on her hips. "Picking out a coffin?"

"These are the empty cryopods used to transport the children from the slaughtered commune," Nimah explained. "Infinity Matrix model."

"And?"

"*And*, after the disaster of the Kaisaan Launch, SIGA mandated that all cryos be equipped with short-range navigation which could be pre-coded with coords to auto-launch to the nearest point of safety in the event of an emergency."

"How'd you know that?"

"The fallout from the Kaisaan Launch was a core argument for my fifth-year health and safety dissertation." Nimah patted the top of the cryopod for emphasis. "Point is, I can program these to get us to the RIM. Check that row." She gestured to the stack nearest Vesper. "We just need two pods with fuel cells at sixty percent capacity."

"Why sixty?" Vesper demanded.

"Because anything less and the auto-launch won't engage." Nimah wove from pod to pod, tapping the access screens and cursing along the way. They'd gone through almost all of them before they found two, and they dragged them over to rest by the sealed hatch doors.

Nimah dropped to her knees by the first one. "Go to the supply room and see if you can find any thermal suits," she ordered, pointing in the vague direction of a doorway near where they'd entered earlier. "And atmo-masks . . . in case. Well, in case!"

Vesper launched for the storeroom, every step sending a shock of disorientation to reverberate within her skull. Bracing a shelving unit, she struck a hand across her cheek and hissed against the sting.

"Thermal suits. Atmo-masks," she reminded herself, and rushed to the task, scanning through boxes and tossing down crates. All loaded with replacement parts for drones and lab tech, yards of tubing, and hundreds of syringes and vials. Chemicals by the liter, but whether they were meant for cleaning or chemistry, Vesper couldn't say. She'd never cared much for science and doubted any of it was useful to helping her and Nimah escape.

Frustrated, Vesper rounded a corner to the next set of shelves, when her foot caught against a lump wrapped in black plastic, nearly tripping her in her haste.

A body bag.

Time slowed. Vesper sank to her knees and peeled open the zipper with shaking hands. The ripe tang of blood slapped her first, and it brought forward an acrid gurgle of bile to swell in the back of her throat.

Saint. Brown eyes, rolled back into her head and a large gray tongue hung from her open mouth. Vesper curled her fingers in the coarse tri-colored fur still damp with blood, and a soft whimper of distress tore from her chest, and as the gruesome memory slashed through her mind like she was seeing it for the first time.

Saint lunging to her side to protect Vesper from the sweep of blasersteel. The sound it made as it sliced through her thick neck. The tumble of her head falling to the floor and the hot spurts of blood that shot from the stump the kill stroke left behind.

Attention crew and staff, emergency shields at twenty-two percent. You have ten minutes to station collapse. Please proceed to the quay for emergency evacuation.

Tears splattered her cheeks, and Vesper sniffed hard as her vision blurred with the anguish of heartbreak. Pain—the delicate fibers of her heart tore one by one until all she could feel was the brutal devastation of loss.

Not Saint. Not her Saint. She folded over the head and wept as a gut-wrenching sob shook through her bones.

For four years Saint had been her constant and only companion. A starved little sack of bones dumped in a trash compactor by some heartless bastard. Vesper nursed the weak pup by her own hand with round-the-clock feeds, until one day Saint rallied with such life it seemed almost a miracle. From that first moment until her last breath, Saint and Vesper had never been apart.

"I'm so sorry," she sobbed against blood-dampened fur. Fingers closing around the collar, Vesper hugged it to her chest, rocking back onto her knees.

Beside Saint's remains lay two more bags, and she peeled open those as well to reveal Brenon and Sasha. They looked even younger in death, eyes closed and lips slightly parted as if only asleep, the hilts of their primeswords tossed by their sides. Weapons that had been as much a part of them as their own limbs.

The pain in her chest swelled, threatening to split open her ribs. Vesper beat an aggrieved fist to the floor, pounding her helpless fury into steel as tears poured from her in a torrent for every scream she could not vent. But seeing the bodies of those she had grown to love and care for brought into sharper focus the far greater risk of all that she had yet to lose.

Chance and Yasmin.

Chairwoman Aramir had made it irrevocably clear what would happen to them if Vesper failed to capture Nimah. How long before she found out her secret enterprise was destroyed and Nimah had escaped into the void before she acted on that threat?

In the shadows of the storeroom, a figure moved. Snapped arms and bent legs, bones protruding from cold blue flesh. The head hung on a limp neck, face hidden behind a curtain of dark hair. Vesper turned, locked in horror, as that head lifted and hair parted to reveal the shattered face of her sister.

Ashleen.

No. This wasn't real. It couldn't be. This was just a fucking hallucination brought on by drugs that had practically melted her brain in her skull. Nimah had warned her as much, but knowing and understanding didn't stop the ghostly broken remnants of her sister from scuttling out of the corner.

The crick of split bones. The pants of rattling breaths. She stopped before Vesper, the struggling expansion of her lungs visible through the holes in her chest where ribs pierced through after her fall, and her once dark brown eyes, always alight with laughter, were now the filmy gray of a long-dead corpse.

"Vesper." Ashleen reached out with a gnarled hand that fished between the dead bodies of Brenon and Sasha and withdrew one of the primeswords. "You know what you have to do."

She accepted the weapon, and cool steel warmed against her palm, filling her with clarity and purpose. She'd failed Ashleen and Saint. She'd failed Brenon and Sasha, too.

Her string of failures ended here.

Vesper sparked the primesword, and the bright wash of blue light filled Ashleen's dead gaze. "Yes. I do."

Nimah bounced her fist against her left brow where the throbbing pain of a migraine was making it hard to focus, and right now she couldn't afford any mistakes with coord entry. A single number out of sequence, and instead of waking up on the RIM, they could be launched into a sun. Or lost to the void. Deep where no one would ever find them, until fuel cells ran dry and they suffocated in dreams.

Finished with the first pod, Nimah moved over to the second to repeat the process and winced when a fresh burst of pain shot across the back of her eyes. Being so violently drained of elite left her feeling like she'd been run over by a jetbike. Everything hurt, and her stomach twisted like it wanted to vent the contents of her stomach—what little there was—up into her throat.

Nimah shuddered in disgust as bile blistered her tongue. Cryo-sleep was starting to sound great right about now.

The heavy drum of Vesper's boots charging from the storeroom beat toward her as the blare of alarms wailed and the smooth system voice counted down the minutes they had left before total demise.

"Any luck with the thermal suits?" she called over her shoulder.

Vesper responded with blaserfire.

Nimah dove for cover behind the pod she'd been prepping, arms hugged across her head, only to realize Vesper wasn't shooting at her, but at the remaining pods. Control panels popped like fiery bubbles, until the stacks billowed with smoke and belched flames.

"What are you doing?" Nimah demanded, coughing behind her hand.

Vesper dropped the empty blaser and turned to her, a primesword in her other hand and face set in a stony mask. "I'm sorry, I don't have a choice." Tears glittered in her lashes, bright as crushed stars.

Weaponless, Nimah kept the pod between them as something pushed its way into her aching mind. Not quite a thought or a feeling, but an awareness that tempered Nimah's confusion.

Failed everyone, a soft voice uttered deep within Nimah's bones. *Cannot fail again.* Whatever her reasons, she'd never get through to Vesper. Not now.

"Your contract is closed, Vesper. SIGA can't touch them."

"I'm not taking the chance." Vesper slashed, a searing blow of sword to steel, and the cryopod Nimah hid behind burst into flame, forcing her into the open.

With nowhere to run, Nimah set her feet, bracing for assault. "I don't want to kill you."

"You won't." Vesper settled into her haunches, the primesword gripped tight with both hands. "I'll make it quick."

Vesper lunged, and with nothing but her fists, Nimah clashed to meet her, diving as she swung and rolled into a crouch—slamming her heel into the back of Vesper's knee. When Vesper dropped, Nimah caught the swing of her arm with both hands, one against her bicep and the other around her wrist, forcing the joint of her elbow against the flat of her thigh.

Vesper screamed and the primesword fell to the floor. Nimah kicked aside the searing blade and they tangled together in a twisting knot of thrown punches and grunting kicks. Each of them grappling for an arm, or a leg, or a throat to wrench the other into submission. But beneath the brutal hammer of Vesper's fists to Nimah's torso and face, she could feel the threads of elite cinching together ever tighter, fueled by the adrenaline and emotions pouring from Vesper like blood from a mortal wound and filling Nimah until she drowned.

The station spun, violent as the churning thoughts colliding within her skull, and reality slipped away into subspace, where every second stretched to the breathless width of a dying heartbeat.

The walls of the fracturing station melded into a viscous blur that became the RIM—the day Nimah's grandmother had hauled her by the hand into a boarding house before vanishing from her life for what felt like forever. Nimah's cries for her grandmother rang out loud as a gunshot.

The ground lurched into another heaving spin, and the RIM was replaced with a recovery tank in a medbay—Vesper, maybe twelve, fell to her knees by the glass and beat against it with the fists of an angry child begging for her father to wake up.

Reality spun again, flattening Nimah beneath the nausea-inducing twist of gravity, then settled into the soft orange glow of a sunrise that glistened on the tacky pool of drying blood haloing a crushed skull. One brown eye, popped free.

The world spun once more on its axis, and they tumbled with it, cast through sorrow and misery, on and on, as the bond between them burrowed deep, building pathways that bridged across the synapses in their minds. Ricocheting them between each other's fractured pasts until finally tossing them free from subspace back into the crumbling ruin of the station.

Face down, dust kicked up with Nimah's gasping breath as she pushed onto her hands with shaking arms. The ground might have stopped spinning, but everything inside her head still felt like it was churning with movement. So much death and loss and misery and trauma between them, she was shaken to the core from the punishing weight of all that she now held.

Vesper struggled to her side, blood seeping from the gash in her lips where Nimah had headbutted her during their skirmish.

"Ashleen." The name returned to Nimah both in memory from the hours of her own study into Vesper's past but also the innate knowing they now shared. "You didn't fail her, Vesper. You have to stop blaming yourself for her death."

"Fuck you," Vesper snarled, teeth clenched and eyes molten.

Eight minutes to collapse.

"Killing me won't protect Chance and Yasmin," Nimah argued. They struggled to their feet in tandem, fists raised and shoulders hunched. "But we can protect them. Together."

"I don't need your help!" Vesper roared into another punch. One that Nimah narrowly dodged. "I don't give a shit about you!" She swung again. "You're just a mark. A fucking RIM-rat!"

Although exertion weighed down Vesper's shoulders and made her punches sloppy, desperation gave her reserves of strength Nimah simply didn't have. Not after being so violently drained. If the ship had eight minutes before collapse, Nimah had maybe four.

"I think you're trying very hard to convince yourself I'm the enemy." Nimah grunted, sweat blooming across her chest and brow, the bones in her legs shaking as hard as the hull with the strain of effort it took to stand. "Because deep down, you know I'm not the one you should be fighting."

The tense line of Vesper's jaw rippled. "Doesn't matter what I believe, or what I feel."

"So be it," Nimah whispered.

When Vesper lunged into another punch, Nimah dropped beneath the swing of Vesper's arm. Air rushed across her head as she dove, closing her grip on the hilt of the discarded primesword. Nimah rolled onto her knees—arced up with the blade.

And ran Vesper through.

CHAPTER THIRTY-ONE

Vesper gasped, a line of blood trickling from between her lips and the weight of her torso skewered on the end of blazing steel.

Nimah blinked in horror—and now it was Sigourney dropping to her knees.

"No!" Nimah withdrew the blade and Vesper collapsed with a groan, her eyes glazed with pain. Rolling her onto her back, Nimah pressed down with both hands, leveraging all her weight over the gaping wound, three inches wide and to the left of Vesper's navel.

What have I done? "I told you I didn't want to hurt you." Blood seeped from the seam of Nimah's palms. "Why didn't you listen to me?"

"She's in a bad way." Dobs stooped to a knee at Nimah's side. "Best finish her, kid."

"No." Maybe it was the effects of tethering making Vesper far too human for Nimah to ignore, or maybe it was not wanting to be haunted by yet another ghost, but she couldn't bring herself to move.

The wound was devastating but not fatal if treated in time, but that was the rub. *Time.* BPRO was minutes from collapse, and there were no vessels to transport her to a medbay except . . . Nimah's eyes fell to the single pod, the only one left unscathed by Vesper's rampage.

"I need you to move. Come on." Nimah yanked Vesper screaming onto her feet. Once she had Vesper's weight braced against her side, Nimah opened the hatch on the cryopod and eased her inside. "I take it you *didn't* find any thermal blankets or atmo-masks, like I asked?"

"No." Vesper wheezed through clenched teeth, her features pinched tight in pain and cheeks far too pale. "Just. *Them.*"

Nimah's eyes fell to where Vesper clutched at a bloodstained collar fastened around her belt, and the ache in her chest constricted tighter as suddenly it all made sense. In search of blankets and supplies, Vesper had been confronted with the bodies of those she'd cared about deeply, reminding her of all that was left to lose. And if Nimah had found herself in Vesper's position, it wasn't hard to imagine she might have been similarly provoked.

What wouldn't she do for her grandmother? For Liselle or the Valkyrie crew?

"Right." Nimah shook her head clear. Minutes were counting down into seconds, and she couldn't afford to waste a fraction of them. "Stack your hands on the wound." As Vesper's bloody fingers pressed against the ragged hole, Nimah unfastened and removed her belt, looped it around her midriff, then notched it tight across the flat of Vesper's hand, drawing it as tight as it could go.

"Fuck!" Vesper sobbed against the sharp burst of agony.

It would hurt worse than the initial punch of the blade, but it was necessary or else she'd bleed out in transport.

"Listen to me—listen!" Nimah slapped her firmly across the cheek, drawing her focus. "Once you're at the RIM, ask for Jono. He runs the hospital out there." For good measure, Nimah wrote his name on the inner glass of the pod's lid in thick letters, inked with Vesper's blood. "Tell him I sent you. He'll know what to do."

Anchoring the harness over Vesper's shoulders and hips, Nimah connected the buckles with a soft snick and it adjusted automatically.

"You're going to be okay," Nimah assured her.

"Why are you helping me?" Vesper panted, her skin pale and damp with sweat. "I tried to . . . I almost . . ."

Nimah braced the lid. "Because I see you, Vesper," she said finally. Vesper may have been ruthless and cruel, but everything she did was to protect the people she loved the most, and Nimah was so damn tired of watching good people die.

Sealing the pod, Nimah punched the auto-launch and bolted for the bulkhead doors. Once its emergency protocol activated, it would slice through and breach the hull to drop itself into the void, making the quay unstable.

The bulkhead doors slammed shut within an instant of the breach, sealing off a third of the quay, and the rush of the vacuum nearly sucked away the breath she'd been about to take.

Nimah crossed to the viewport and watched as the cryopod shot from the station like a rocket toward the haze of a stardust horizon.

Five minutes to collapse.

"So that's it?" Dobs reclined against the glossy white wall, arms crossed. "You gonna stand here with your thumb up your ass?"

"There are no ships, no pods. No flight suits." Nimah planted her forearm to the viewport with a dry laugh. "So yeah, that's it." Acceptance flowed through her in a wave of exhaustion, so thick and heavy that she slumped against the weight of it. She reached for the handle of the hatch door.

One pull and it would all be over.

One pull.

Dobs tracked the movement. Dropped her arms. "C'mon, kid. I know I been pushing you something fierce, but that's no reason to go all sideways on me now. Where's your grit?"

Nimah set her teeth with a liquid sigh. "You remember what you said to me atop the wall at the RIM?" She closed her eyes, letting her thoughts carry her back to two of them perched on the compressed flatlands of trash cubes after scaling the wall and gazing up at the rippling spread of the voidnetting.

What do you say? I make the run, ditch the Shinoda boy, and then who knows, say I come get you and we sail off on our own somewhere. Hear the astral rings are pretty slick.

Dobs clicked her tongue, and something in her softened with regret. "I meant it, you know. For a moment I really thought fuck it, why not? Me and the kid, nothing but dreams and possibilities rolled out like a field of grass."

Nimah swiped away tears but more flowed in hot to replace them. "That was the happiest I remember being in a very long time. Even though I couldn't say yes—just believing that it was possible. Knowing that I was chosen . . . meant everything to me." She sniffed hard, unable to stop the trembling in her chin or the waver in her voice. "I really loved you, you know?"

"Ah." The whites of Dobs's eyes seared red and she dragged a knuckle across them, clearing away whatever had been about to spill forward. "Been in that head of yours too long. Got me all soft."

Nimah turned to her, needing to say it all. Finally. "I'm sorry I killed you."

"Hush. Wasn't never none your fault to carry. I made choices and earned the consequences, heard?" She bounced her thumb against her chest. "Healing ain't a line you cross, kid. It ain't even a straight path all decked out with balloons and a waving crowd cheering ya on when you reach the end. It's a maze you spin through alone in the dark. It's a wheel, and I tried to crush you under mine, because breaking you meant I wouldn't have to face me and all that I'd done. All that I . . . am." Dobs ran the point of her tongue across the edge of her lip with a resigned sigh. "But if I'm 'bout to die a second time, best I own that." Cool blue eyes flickered to Nimah and shimmered with something like pride. "You're true salt, Nimah. Steel, too. So don't go wasting tears over the likes of me."

One minute to collapse.

The ship shuddered violently, flattening Nimah against the hatch door.

"You really wanna go out that way?" Dobs nodded to the handle clutched in her white-knuckled grip.

Nimah released a steady breath, fogging the viewport. "I don't want to become nothing," she whispered. *To be unmade* . . . somehow that terrified her more than the prospect of dying. At least out there she'd be part of the void. As real and everlasting as those planets and stars. Like ashes scattered to the wind. And when she searched inside herself, the only regret she carried was there was no time for her to say goodbye to Maverick. Or her grandmother. Liselle and the crew. But it helped to know they were safe and alive, even if it meant she would have to face her death alone.

Dobs grinned. Nodded slowly. "Heard."

Nimah blinked at her in surprise. "You're staying?"

"Coulda left me when the moment came, but you didn't. You stood there as it happened. And I felt you. Your . . . anguish. Guess it's why you've been so torn up since. You've carried that inside you. You've carried me." White brows lowered in a stern line as Dobs assessed her gloved palm before curling her fingers into a fist that she pressed against her sternum. "Don't know if I'm real or just a piece of you gnawing on your innards . . . who's to say. But I'm here. And I'll stay." She rocked into Nimah, shoulder bumping to shoulder. "I told you before—we're gonna finish what we started together. So let's finish it."

Beyond the viewport, the glittering darkness of the void awaited her, streaked with the gleaming bodies of dancing negs leaving iridescent trails in their wake.

Nimah swiped a tear from the end of her nose. "To the void then," she whispered.

"To Valhalla." Dobs closed her hand overtop Nimah's, and with the gentle sweep of her thumb tracing against the back of Nimah's hand, together they pulled the latch.

The final wailing seconds of the countdown faded into sudden silence. The hatch yawned open and Nimah released a steady breath, arms spread wide, as the vacuum of space snatched her with greedy hands and yanked her into oblivion.

There was no sound. No pain. No fear. Only the calmness of certainty as Nimah embraced the void.

CHAPTER THIRTY-TWO

About an hour into their approach, they realized BPRO had thrown off its anchor, leaving behind the barest ion trail Maverick miraculously located despite the chaotic clash of energy from the burst web of kraken eggs that should've smothered all hope. But between his incredible flying and Gertrude's impossible navigation skills, they were closing in with remarkable speed. Hope rallied into determination. But when the *Stormchaser* reached the end of that ion trail, all they found was dust.

BPRO had shattered like a soap bubble devoured by what the *Stormchaser*'s systems estimated to be the blast force equivalent to a hundred ruptured novas. There were no twisted sheets of steel, no floating remains of skeletal wreckage or flying shards of shrapnel to slice across the void. Just the smallest of particles suspended in a glowing cloud of fading blue.

A violent stillness.

"We're too late." What was left of Liselle's hope spiraled into dismay. She was almost too scared to take the next breath, lest the sound that come from her be the guttural sob brewing in her belly.

Maverick slammed a fist against the console hard enough to rattle the bulkhead. "Ma," he ordered. "Run a radial scan. Go to maximum range."

Yes. Now was not the time to fall apart. If Nimah was out there . . . there had to be a pulse. A beacon. Something! Nimah was a survivor, and she'd have found a way to get clear before the station collapsed. She always found a way. *Please. Please. Please.*

<Unable to comply.>

"Why the fuck not?" Maverick roared.

<Energy surge detected. Close range. Unregistered frequency. Levels unstable. System—unstable.>

Ma's interface lit like a circuit board struck by lightning, her systems going haywire beneath the strain of pressure waves that rocked against the belly of the ship like turbulence.

"Something is overloading the sensors." Liselle gathered her locs in a fist at the back of her head. "What is that?" She gestured to the horizon, where a searing glow gathered. "Could it be residuals from the explosion that destroyed the station?"

But something inside of her already knew that couldn't be true. Nimah's plan was to weaponize the stolen nova, and novas ruptured like a silent scream—devouring everything caught in their gravity field. But this was a flash of violet light that twisted space on itself. Coiling tight into a blinding spiral before casting out waves of energy that rippled in slow, deliberate pulses. Almost like a solar flare with a heartbeat.

"We got an object up ahead." Boomer's voice crackled over the intercom from his perch in the gun cage below the bridge. "Closing in fast. Vector eight, sixty-three degrees. Port side."

"What is it?" Maverick demanded.

"Could be a lifeboat." Already on it, Gertrude ran the nav scans. "Single-person capacity. Whatever it is, it's small, but our system is choked by that surge. Can barely clock it."

Liselle leaned forward, brow furrowed as she tried to make out the streaking object in the far-left corner of the main viewport, strobing with the cold blink of emergency lights. Its single thruster shot in a blazing arc, veering away from where they were currently positioned. Another few seconds and they'd have missed it entirely. The fact Boomer had even caught sight of it was near to miraculous.

"It's a pod. Come around, hard to port," Liselle ordered. "Prepare to—"

"No," Maverick interrupted, eyes fixed on the horizon, on the expanding waves of searing blue light and tendrils of rippling energy coiling around a dense and vivid center. Brighter than any sun.

"Are you crazy? That could be Nimah! We have to—"

"She's not. That." He punched a finger toward that distant orb crackling like a storm gone wild. "That's my girl. And that's the only place I am going."

Liselle's fingers cinched tight into the cushioned headrest of Maverick's flight chair. "How do you know?"

"Because I just do." Maverick answered, resolute and unwavering.

Liselle's stomach tightened with apprehension. If they went to investigate the anomaly, they ran the risk of losing the pod, and with the ship's systems nearly fried, the pod was too small for them to track by line of sight. It would be like hunting for a speck of dust across the void.

"I can't lose that pod, and we can't be in two places at once." Not unless they split up. "Zen," Liselle called out. "Take Boomer and Chu and use the secondary shuttle to retrieve that pod." In case they were wrong. Source help them. "The rest of us will investigate the anomaly."

"Aye!" Zensha answered.

They charged from the bridge and Liselle returned to the second flight chair, strapping in aside Maverick. Not long after, the shuttle broke away from the *Stormchaser*.

"Hang on," Maverick warned, jaw set like stone as he maneuvered the ship forward against the waves of energy that blasted across the hull like a hurricane sea. The muscles in his arms strained, his fingers locked around the yoke in a fight to hold the nose steady.

"Please." Liselle's chest coiled tight with urgency as she whisked over flight keys, diverting power to alternating thrusters to keep them steady. "Please let it be her." She raised the shield on the viewport, dimming the glare from blinding to bearable as they dove into the waves of energy and light, driving toward the searing center.

A hard thump rocked the *Stormchaser*, swiftly followed by a second. A third.

"What is that?"

"Negs." Maverick adjusted the yoke, toggling hard to recenter them, but his smile was as bright as the tears of relief in his eyes. "They're swarming."

The negs came into view, more than Liselle had ever seen outside of a simulation. Dozens of elongated, opalescent creatures spiraling in the vivid epicenter, tails flicking in synchronous rhythm. They released a low, resonant hum that gathered into a chorus as others joined, and wove together in vibrations that could be felt through the hull of the *Stormchaser,* almost like voices gathered in song. Deeper than music and more intense than the light they channeled.

At the center of those sinuous, gliding creatures—floating amidst the swirling eye of the vortex—a body. Nimah. Her limbs hung suspended in the zero gravity with a single neg, smaller than the rest, cradling her in its embrace.

"Nimah . . ." Liselle gasped. "Are they singing to funnel energy to keep her alive? Or to get our attention?"

Maverick leaned back in the pilot's chair, fingers trembling where they clutched the yoke. "I think both."

Once they were within a yard of the smallest neg, Maverick held the nose steady until its opal eyes gleamed back at them, filled with intelligence. With a subtle bow, the neg swatted Nimah's body gently—just once—and sent her spiraling toward the *Stormchaser.*

"Open the hatch and get into position." Uncoupling her harness, Liselle spilled from her seat. "I'll retrieve Nimah from the airlock." She didn't wait for his response as she bolted from the bridge, but the shudder of the ship that sent her careening from wall to wall as she ran told Liselle that Maverick had thrown the reverse thrusters and was bringing them into alignment.

She crashed down the last step of the stairway and into the cargo hold just as the airlock doors sealed around Nimah, her body falling in the sudden grip of gravity. Flushing the airlock with oxygen, Liselle counted the tense seconds before the doors opened, and she rushed inside.

Dropping to her knees, Liselle touched Nimah with shaking hands and found her warm—*too* warm. Thin veins of light pulsed beneath the sickly gray surface of her skin, fused into her flesh like molten gold used to mend broken porcelain. But—even more impossible—Nimah's chest rose. Then fell.

Then rose again.

"*Liselle.*" Maverick's voice floated through the intercom. "*Talk to me! Do you have her? Is she okay?*"

"I have her," Liselle confirmed, her eyes burning with disbelief. "And she's alive!"

* * *

"Where's Jono!" Ro blazed with equal parts fury and panic as they burst into the hospital in a cyclone of movement and raw emotion. "Get him!"

During the race back, Liselle had tried to call ahead, but the comms on the shuttle were fried from the intense energy they'd flown through to recover Nimah. So when they touched ground, it was to find Ro awaiting them, her expression melting into horrified concern at the sight of Nimah, draped across Maverick's lap—gray-skinned and milky-eyed, half of her body coated in a substance that glistened like viscous mercury.

A nurse scampered off at her heart-wrenching roar, and barely a minute later, Jono burst from the twin doors.

"What is it? I was just completing sutures on a—" His voice fell away as his eyes landed on Nimah. "Oh my." Donning his glasses, he crouched beside the inert body cradled against Maverick's chest. "We need to get her into an operating room. This way. And explain to me what happened," he demanded.

Snapping at nurses on the floor, they worked swiftly, hauling Nimah onto a gurney and rushing her down the back corridor toward the operating wing. Liselle and Maverick launched into their full recount, covering the details of the last few hours as he led the way past the main surgical room, currently in use, and over to a second one on the opposite side.

"She was floating when we found her," Maverick finished as Ro closed the door behind them. "We don't know for sure how long she was exposed, but Nimah was breathing when Liselle pulled her in from the airlock."

"Her pulse started dropping about twenty minutes before we touched ground," Liselle added. "I administered compressions to keep her circulation steady." And her forearms were going to burn for days from the rigorous effort.

"Bring her to the table," Jono ordered as a nurse helped him into a fresh full-body medsuit. "And you should suit up before you touch her again," he cautioned as Ro closed in at Nimah's side.

"I'll be fine," Ro snapped. "Just move your ass and get over here." Her hands shook as she scooped Nimah under the arms; her expression overwhelmed with a million emotions and even more questions that she stoically held in.

"I've got her ankles." Liselle swept in to help. If there was any risk to health, she'd been exposed already. Together they moved Nimah off the gurney and over to the prepped table covered in a sterilization sheet.

Jono pulled on gloves that covered him to the elbow then joined them at the table. He blinked at both Maverick and Liselle in shock. "You said she was floating? There's no exposure damage to her epidermis. Her capillaries are clear. No sign of expansion or rupture . . ."

"The negs were protecting her somehow," Maverick answered, struggling to hold himself where he sat. If his legs were functional, he'd have been wearing tracks around the room.

Jono hunched over Nimah's still form. "Not just the negs, it would seem." His gloved fingers probed the metallic silvery surface coating most of her. It yielded slightly to his touch but showed no blemish to the mirrored surface when he drew away. "I'll need to take a sample for study. Determine the makeup of its structure and whether or not—"

"Jono!" Ro set her teeth, fists tight at her sides as if resisting the urge to throttle him. "Spare us the narration and just *do whatever you must*. Quickly. Please!"

Jono cleared his throat. "Right." Using a small, sharp medical tool, he scraped some of it onto a slide, and a second sample into a vial, then handed both to the nurse assisting him—a slender older woman hidden behind a sterile face mask and large, dark examination goggles able to see through Nimah's skin to her bones and connective tissue.

"Run those samples through the sequencer," he instructed while adjusting the overhead light to shine across Nimah, highlighting her gray-washed skin. Lips a deep shade of blue. "She's oxygen deprived. Nurse, get me an O_2 mask, full saturation, please."

It was hard to keep quiet. To stand there and watch, helpless, as Jono and the nurse flowed through a variety of checks and scans. Fastening sensors, wires, and IV tubes into the back of Nimah's limp hands.

"She's alive," Jono said after what felt like an eternity.

A hard breath whooshed out of Liselle and her knees threatened to buckle, but she locked them underneath her, bracing the foot of the table to keep herself steady. "How bad is it?"

"I can't say for certain without further diagnostics." Jono removed his gloves, lips pursed and brows drawn. "I've done everything I can, but her vitals are thready and declining."

"What's wrong with her can't be fixed with all of this."

They all turned to the source of the interrupting voice and Liselle gasped. Vesper stood in the doorway of the operation room, one arm banded around her stomach, wrapped beneath surgical gauze.

"Hey—you're not supposed to be on your feet!" Jono called out. "Those sutures are barely set."

Ignoring him, Vesper staggered forward, and, jolted into action, Maverick and Liselle drew their blasers, aiming for the threat.

"Come any closer to Nimah and I'll pop those sutures myself," Liselle warned.

"Hold," Ro cautioned.

To her credit, or perhaps stupidity, Vesper merely raised her chin as the fearsome captain braced herself between the injured bounty hunter and her granddaughter. One hand poised over the coiled whip hung on her left hip.

"Are we going to have a problem?"

Vesper's face morphed into a sardonic grin as she raised her hands high and spun in a slow, wincing circle, a clear show that she was unarmed and not in much condition to put up a fight. "Look, I know I'm not winning any awards for popularity—fair." She stopped before Ro, dropping an arm across her waist. "But I'm not here to kick the nest. I want to help."

"You're going to have to give me more than that if you expect me to let you near her." Ro tossed her braid over her shoulder.

Vesper set her chin with a sigh. "Nimah wasn't the only one being held by that fucking nutjob. I was, too. SIGA threw me to her like scraps off a dinner plate. Don't ask me to explain what she did to us, because I can't. All I know is she's running low and I can use whatever that bitch put inside me to help Nimah before it's too late."

"Why should we even trust you?" Maverick demanded. "Maybe what you really want is to finish the job. You'd never leave this room alive, but I'm guessing you'd prefer a quick death at our hand than at SIGA's for failing to complete your contract."

His accusation hung in the air, and the whir of primed blasers escalated as Liselle's finger tightened on her trigger. Yet Vesper remained unruffled—standing her ground with a casual defiance that belied her battered state.

"Ask your doc, here. I'm held together with grafts, some surgical mesh, and probably a hundred stitches." She tapped a gentle hand to her bandaged abdomen. "I try anything stupid, grandma will have my guts for a new whip in under ten seconds."

"Bet your ass," Ro growled between clenched teeth.

Behind them, Nimah's vitals dipped in a sluggish decline that had Jono cursing in distress. "We're losing her!"

"Come on!" Vesper snapped, eyes widening in aggrieved worry. "Don't trust me. Keep those blasers hot and at my head, whatever, I don't care. But I'm only alive right now because Nimah saved me when she could've just saved herself. Means I owe her a debt—one I intend to pay."

"You said she's running low." Jono spoke up, pulling focus back to where it needed to be. On Nimah. "Running low on what?"

Vesper's gaze fell to Nimah, stretched on the table beneath hot white lights, and a flicker of concern softened the edge of her mouth. "Everything."

If Liselle didn't know any better, she'd almost guess Vesper *cared*.

Scanning the room, Vesper's gaze landed on Liselle, and a sudden, almost imperceptible flicker passed through her expression. Recognition that went deeper than their brief encounter on Corlys. "You don't give up on family," she murmured.

Liselle's eyes widened at hearing the echo of words she'd said to Nimah the day she'd been expelled from the Academy. "What did you say?"

"She's running out of time." Vesper pointed to Nimah. "Let. Me. Help. Her."

Liselle turned to Nimah, torn between love and uncertainty. But it was the soft blip of Nimah's pulse, the way it skipped and slowed, that had Liselle lowering her weapon. Whatever her doubts, someone had to take a leap of faith.

Liselle took Ro by the arm, urging her to stand aside. "You heard Jono—she's barely clinging to life. What do we have to lose?"

Reluctantly, hearts heavy with risk, Ro stepped back. And Maverick lowered his weapon.

Vesper approached the table. Only the very soft and subtle rise and fall of her chest indicated Nimah had not yet succumbed to death, but those breaths were stretching too far apart. And every time her chest sank, Liselle grew more terrified it wouldn't rise again.

Vesper cupped one hand gently at the crown of Nimah's head while the other pressed against her sternum. In a voice barely louder than a whisper, she murmured, "Be with me."

For a moment the room seemed to hold its breath, and Liselle could almost feel the weight of those words—a plea or a command—stir in the air. Thickening it until it pulsed. The sound of breath and blood reverberated like an echo in the mind, rattled against the walls. Bulbs wrapped in mesh flickered and dimmed as a force gathered within the room. A tangible charge that moved strong and unseen, but it prickled against Liselle's skin and crackled behind her eyes.

Light—a sudden surge as everything gathered in a violent, searing flame. So sudden, so sharp, the weight squeezed against Liselle's corneas until she was forced to look away. They all were.

Liselle pressed her hands across her face, overwhelmed by its soldering heat. The glare drove through her palms and into her skull, hot enough to score to the bone, and for a fractured heartbeat, time blurred into nothing but pure, unbridled power.

An awakening gasp shuddered through the chaos of energy, the sound of someone battling for air, and Liselle drew her hands away, willing to risk her sight to behold Nimah's body as it arched sharply on the table. Energy surged, igniting along every nerve—as Vesper held Nimah steady.

It was only a matter of seconds, then the surge dissipated and the room plunged into a sudden darkness quickly chased away by the emergency lighting that activated to replace the broken surgical lamps with a softer glow.

No one seemed to breathe save for Nimah. She released a sigh-like shudder. And those eyes that, only moments ago, had been lifeless and lost—fluttered *open*!

CHAPTER THIRTY-THREE

Nimah's hand closed on the back of a lattice chair, warmed by the late afternoon sun. "Mind if I sit down?"

"Please do."

Shucking her arms out of her weathered trench, Nimah folded it across the chair before sitting across from Annelise Aramir.

The chairwoman sat with her hands folded in her lap and one leg elegantly crossed. Her buttery white slacks—real cotton, without question—were loose and flowing, a robin's-egg blue blouse tucked in the waist, capped with ivory buttons that matched the rope of pearls laced around her slender neck. Her tawny hair, twisted into an elegantly messy bun at the nape, was held in place by a golden hairpin.

Until now, Nimah had never seen Annelise in anything other than her tailored navy suits but even here, so casually dressed in the relaxed environment of her palatial home, she exuded the unmistakable aura of a woman not to be crossed.

"Nimah Dabo-124," Annelise said after a lengthy sweep of her eyes that took in every detail about Nimah, from her shoulder-length curls to the toes of her scarred leather boots. "It's good that we finally have the chance to meet."

"Long overdue." Nimah settled closer to the wrought-iron table painted as white as the flowers assembled in the short glass vase.

Their dense petals hugged vivid yellow centers atop thick stalks covered in a downy fuzz. Next to it, a steaming porcelain teapot, two saucers and teacups with ridiculously tiny silver spoons. The setup was only half as pretentious as the surrounding gardens. Grooming drones hummed dutifully as they trimmed the lawn, snipped shrubs, and plucked wilted leaves off trees.

"Great to see our public levies being put to fine use."

Annelise's lips pursed ever so slightly, the barest ripple of irritation. "Any public audit would show my housing is self-sustained through my own *personal* accounts."

"Of course." Nimah winked. "But in all seriousness, let's not waste each other's time with lies or half-truths, Chairwoman. I've come a long way, and we both know that everything we say here is cloaked." She gestured to the gardens around them. "Gray-rocking, I believe it's called. Yes? Pretty advanced programming. Ingenious."

Ingenious, because unlike standard cloaks, this one was seamless and nearly undetectable.

Standard cloaks muted everything in the surrounding environment and flattened your voice so that each syllable sounded muddy, like speaking underwater. Whereas here, sitting in the chairwoman's cloistered terrace, every sound was as smooth and clear as sunlight filtering through water in a glass, yet any attempts to record within its parameters would be captured only as senseless static.

Annelise angled her wristdeck and tapped twice behind her left ear for comms. "Stanley, run a scan of our networks, particularly security. Yes, I'm aware. Run them again. Notify me when complete."

"You're not tapped," Nimah assured her. She had tried, of course, but the chairwoman's network was unfortunately too sophisticated even for Mumbles to break through. Yet. The trade-off, though, was that Nimah hoped she could prod Annelise to drop her guard and give some real truths for once.

"One can never be too careful." Annelise straightened in her seat, planting forearms to the table. "It appears you are extraordinarily well informed. Very few, outside of the board and my skilled onsite technicians, know about gray-rocking."

"Interesting. As it's the same tech that was used to cloak BPRO, I'd have expected it to be common knowledge across the board."

Annelise's eyes sharpened. "I wouldn't know about that."

Nimah smiled sweetly. "Of course not."

"Either way," Annelise continued, brushing off the veiled slight. "I see now that waving Vesper directly was an egregious mistake on my part. Granted, I didn't expect her to be so easily coerced in revealing my personal coords, considering all that's at stake. The terms of her contract were quite generous."

"You did allow a deranged psycho to torture her to death—can't say I'm surprised she tossed professional loyalty out the window for the sake of getting even."

"Hm. So she is dead then?"

"Put her out of her misery myself."

Taking a moment, Annelise drummed her clear-polished nails to the side of her teacup, ringing porcelain. "Perhaps that's for the best. If Vesper were still alive, there would be swift consequences for her treachery. Consequences some might suggest her poor niece and nephew be forced to remit."

"By executing a clawback of the Shinoda assets?"

"Just so. Trusts can be broken, as Vesper has so adequately demonstrated." Annelise smiled as sweetly as a shark—all teeth, heralding the promise of drawing blood. "And it would take our chief legal counsel less time to flush a toilet, but with election season commencing next quarter, I'd prefer to avoid the risk of blowback."

"That's good to hear." Nimah angled her head, her hands resting casually in her lap. "But in case you later change your mind, I think you should know that the trust is gone."

Annelise slanted her gaze. "Gone?"

"As of an hour ago. *Poof!*" Nimah flicked her fingers like a magician conjuring an illusion. "You can call Stanley to corroborate that, too, if you'd like."

Perfectly timed, Annelise's wristdeck chimed twice and she swiveled her gaze down to the "all clear" notification. "And *how*, exactly, did you manage to do that?"

Nimah offered only a bemused lift of her brow and enjoyed the slow simmer of irritation that wavered along the edge of Annelise's narrow jaw. Another crack split the surface of her poised mask. One more and Nimah might finally get her first real look at the monster lurking within.

"Before she died, I promised Vesper I'd keep her niece and nephew safe from reprisals, so I made good on that promise. That's all you need to know."

"I didn't realize you two were so *close*."

Nimah's smile thinned. "Shared trauma can often create allies of foes."

"Oh dear. Tea's getting cold. Allow me." Raising the pot gently and with both hands, Annelise poured a steaming amber brew into the waiting teacups. "Do you take sugar?"

"Yes, please. Two spoons."

"A woman after my own heart." Annelise added finely ground white sugar into each and gave them a quick stir before setting one before Nimah. "There you go."

Nimah raised the cup to her lips.

"Is it to your liking?" Annelise said after she'd taken a steady sip.

Dabbing a napkin against her mouth, Nimah returned the teacup to the saucer. Shrugged. "I prefer coffee."

"As do I, but it doesn't quite prefer me these days. And you're right." Annelise waved a breezy hand, her teacup untouched. "Let's be candid with one another, shall we? I'll ask the first question."

"Naturally."

"Elite." Annelise rested a clenched fist atop the table, and though she tried to appear relaxed, the edges of her knuckles shone on the verge of white against her already pale skin. "Is it true it's bonded with you?"

Nimah scored her teeth across her bottom lip, weighing the pros and cons before she answered. "Yes."

The shock of surprise at her unflinching honesty made Annelise's mouth tumble open. Some would have counseled Nimah to downplay the truth with misdirection, but all she'd done was only confirm what Annelise already knew.

Academy training had schooled her in the art of interrogation, and Nimah recognized the beautiful and casual atmosphere of the terrace and its gardens, even the offering of food and drink—were all carefully employed tactics to lull her into complacency. Building trust by making her feel safe and unthreatened. Even the way Annelise was dressed—like a woman who had spent a leisurely afternoon gardening instead of as a powerhouse seated at the helm of an intergalactic board—was a sleight of hand to misdirect from the true threat simmering beneath the polished surface in a low-pitched frequency only an animal could hear.

But Nimah heard it. And she emitted one right back.

"Why?" Annelise's voice was breathless with urgency. "Why you?"

"Genetics. My mother is a descendant from the planet of its origin, so I carry some affinity for it as well."

"Hm." Annelise nodded, her brows narrowing in thought. "We'd been given reports of your mother and the potential connection she had. Can it be replicated with someone who *doesn't* share your ancestry?"

"Far as I know, Hillard tried a hundred times over and failed." A truth to shield the lie, because if Annelise had any indication Dr. Hillard had succeeded—nothing would stop her from seeking Vesper out, if only to confirm she was in fact deceased.

"Hm." Annelise wiggled her jaw as if chewing on something she didn't care for the taste of. "I knew it was a sore point, but she'd seemed so certain this time it would . . . and I had hoped . . ." The fist atop the table tightened a degree further before relaxing.

"My turn." Nimah traced the arc of the handle on her teacup with the stroke of her finger. "Samantha Hillard's research into elite and the development of the cyber program was a cover to create a superior lifeform. She was willing to torture and kill tens if not hundreds of thousands, children included, in pursuit of that goal. My question to you is—what was your angle? What was so important to you that merited such evil?"

"I'm afraid I'm about as clichéd as Cormack Shinoda. Immortality." Annelise spread her hands with a self-deprecating grin. "At present, I've held office for the third longest tenure in our history, and as I prepare to run for my fourth term, my team has advised that this will be my last before I am forced to cede to a new chair and retire from the board."

"I'm guessing you're not interested in relinquishing control?"

Annelise's thumb scored across her tight knuckles. "I've worked too hard, Nimah, and sacrificed too much. A change of leadership always comes with a change of vision. Ideals. Which means everything I've established will be undone. Every thread unwoven, so that some new asshole can piss all over my legacy for no reason other than ego."

Not quite seeing her point, Nimah squinted. "And?"

"And it's disruptive. Counterproductive," Annelise snapped. "The Inner Circle needs continuity and consistency of leadership, which can only be achieved through a singular, cohesive vision." She raised both her hands and laced her fingers together, pressing palm to palm. "Strength through unity is the way we not only survive but thrive."

"So you want to take power away from the hands of the people—what *little* power remains to them—and allocate it all to yourself by steering us from a democratic system over to an imperial regime." Nimah leaned back as she took it all in. "Being a tyrannical dictator isn't enough, you have to be an immortal one, too?"

"Hard to argue with someone who can't be killed." Annelise raised her chin, shoulders drawn and eyes proud, as if she were already crowned. "SIGA governs fifteen hundred planets and moons. Almost thrice that in spacities. Our overall general population has grown so vast it borders on unwieldy. Something our forebearers understood and clearly exemplified in the ancient histories is that the true strength and resilience of empires cannot be outmatched. We lose so much time in the tedium of endless debating and politicking. Concentrics, Loyalists, Redemptioners—with every political shift we create further opportunity for destabilization and corruption. It's highly inefficient. Uniformity is the only assurance of not only our continued progress but our very survival. I can provide that consistency of leadership, and through my reign, herald an age of humanity without collapse or end. The stars are infinite—and with the power of elite, we could own them all."

Elbow planted to her armrest, Nimah propped her cheek against the tripod of her fingertips and barely managed not to roll her eyes. If there was one thing she was growing increasingly tired of, it was the privileged and their insatiable lust for longevity and power.

"Oh my." Annelise relaxed against the back of her chair with a soft giggle. "I can't recall the last time I could say any of this out loud. It's refreshing, even if only for a moment. I must also thank you for doing me the favor of cleaning up that mess Samantha Hillard created. Couldn't have wiped the slate cleaner if I tried."

Irritation hammered in the pulse point of Nimah's temple. "If by *mess* you mean saving most of the poor children she was torturing through her experiments, sure. Cleaned that right up. And gave Hillard a taste of her own medicine."

Perfectly timed, the whirl of a bot approached, its mono-wheel carving across the lawn with a platter hovering over the stump of its mechanical arm.

"Mistress." Its synth voice flowed from the grate of its mouth speaker as it deposited a clear disc from the platter onto the table by her hand.

Annelise looked to Nimah. "What is this?" she asked without reaching for it.

"We destroyed all of Dr. Hillard's sinister research and reports on her experimentation, but we made sure to keep everything else that could prove of its existence—including not only what she was doing, but who was involved." That, combined with the logs from the flight-box recorder seized from the sunken ship, the documents stolen from Lennox's console, and a copy of the contract issued to Vesper . . . Annelise's head tilted as if tracing all the unspoken dots Nimah laid out between them forming a single, damning picture. "Forget winning the election—I could have you locked away in a cell right next to Cormack."

Annelise's eyes twitched with ominous fury. "If that were true, you wouldn't be here. This would be blasted across every major newscast in the Inner Circle. But no." She cupped a hand around the shell of her ear. "I don't hear the wail of sirens or the stomp of boots from agents rushing in to arrest me." She dropped her hand and linked her fingers casually in her lap. "Instead, I'm sitting on my terrace at home, sipping tea and basking in the warmth of an amplified sun."

Nimah shrugged. "The newscasts are owned by SIGA and operated under its purview. It would be suppressed immediately, and the target on my back would only grow bigger out of desperation."

"Is that why you came here, then? Were you hoping to trick me into a confession as you had with Cormack?" Annelise *tsk*ed. "How disappointing to come all this way only to realize that's also impossible."

"I'm not here to trick you." Nimah smiled. "Cormack had an ego the size of the void, it was easy to get him to trip over his own arrogance. I knew you'd be smarter than that."

Annelise gestured back to the disc. "So what is the purpose of this, then?"

"An olive branch." Nimah set her teeth in a menacing grin. "I wanted you to know I have a smoking gun, but I'm prepared to toss it into the sea instead of pulling the trigger."

"Why?"

"Ejecting you from office won't resolve the greater issue. Cormack was a single man, but you are part of a hydra. I cut off your head, half a dozen more will sprout after you. The beast only grows." Nimah drummed the point of her finger to the edge of the table. "We have a long, long game ahead of us, Chairwoman, and for now I prefer to contend with the devil I know rather than the one I don't."

"Perhaps not as long as you think." Annelise's eyes glimmered with malignant humor. "I assume, then, you want something from me in exchange for . . . this."

"I do." Legs crossed, Nimah spread her hands wide as her grin. "We pirates like to call this *parlay*. In exchange for this disc, and my assurances that what remains of it will be buried, I propose the following terms."

"I am *breathless* with anticipation." Annelise sighed along with a roll of her eyes.

"Liselle Namsara is to be reinstated without issue."

"Surely you're joking."

"Not even in the slightest." Nimah lowered her chin. "On top of that, you're going to decommission the entire cybergenic program, effective immediately. Any cybers currently activated will be allowed to live out their short lives as they see fit, and the remaining embryos on ice will be destroyed. You will harm no more children."

"Our cybers are integral to our core security across both the Inner Circle *and* Fringe. Pulling them from active duty will severely compromise our operations."

"Hire more cadets. Commission more droids." Nimah shrugged a dismissive shoulder. "Personally, I don't care what you do so long as you honor the terms."

"And who are you to set such terms?" Annelise scoffed darkly. "You really think you're in a position to make demands?"

"Yes. And just so we're clear, this isn't a negotiation. I'm not asking. Fail to comply with these requirements and it won't be only me you'll answer to, but the queen of Tortuga herself."

"Queen?" Annelise arched a bemused brow. "And who is the new successor to the crossbone throne—*you*?"

"Indira Roscoe. You may have heard of her." Nimah had the deep satisfaction of seeing Annelise's smug expression flicker with the first real hint of wary apprehension at the mention of her grandmother's name.

I wear the crown, but Ro is our true queen. It is she they have always feared.

Sigourney apparently hadn't been wrong in that assessment. And now, in addition to the power of fear, Ro had command over a fleet that could put SIGA in a chokehold and few would have the stomach to reckon with.

Annelise's eyes narrowed, simmering with both rage and frustration at being so neatly backed into a corner. "The last war between pirates and SIGA did not end well. For anyone."

"No. But they also didn't have my grandmother at the helm."

"You think this is enough to cow me?" Annelise tossed the disc aside and it clattered against porcelain, sloshing the tea in the chairwoman's cup, which she was careful to avoid. "You may call yourself pirate, but you're still nothing more than a naïve child."

Nimah rose slowly from the seat of her chair, drawing every ounce of authority and confidence into her spine, as she had witnessed her grandmother do countless times before.

"In three days, I toppled a major corporation whose wealth and power surpasses even that of your own, Chairwoman. In less than five days I've destroyed decades of top-secret research, putting an end to your aspirations of achieving engineered immortality. Imagine what I could do in a month. A year. *Child*?" Pressing her palms to the table, Nimah leaned in close, letting the weight of her words settle between them. "Underestimate me at your own peril. *I dare you.*"

The chiseled line of Annelise's shoulders wavered under the effort it took for her to contain her barely leashed rage, and eventually it bubbled to the surface, too vast for her to contain. Not in the violent fits of cursing one would have expected, but in laughter.

"I'm afraid it's you who have underestimated me." The chairwoman's smile was so wide it was almost manic. "The effects are subtle, but you'll feel it soon. A tickle in your throat. An itch behind your eyes." She nodded toward the tea faintly steaming between them in Nimah's half-finished cup. "After that, the poison escalates quite quickly, and it's rather gruesome. A horrible, bloody spectacle that would turn even the staunchest of stomachs." She reclined languidly, as if reciting poetry instead of a death sentence. "Unfortunately, I have a bit of a weak one myself, but I think I shall actually enjoy watching you die. Very much so, in fact."

Nimah stared down Annelise's cold grin and unleashed her own. Reaching for her teacup, she brought it to hover at her lips. "Cheers." Nimah tipped it back. Tea flowed into her mouth, through her chest and belly, to rain down the side of her leg.

Annelise's look of triumph rapidly morphed into astonished disbelief as liquid splattered onto the stone tiles at Nimah's feet.

"And that is precisely the look I had on my face when Maverick pulled the wool on me the day I collared him on Tor12." Dropping her empty cup back to her saucer, Nimah plucked up her trench from the back of her chair.

"I don't understand."

"What can I say, Chairwoman." Nimah shoved her right arm into the sleeve, then followed with the left. "You're not the only one in possession of impressive off-market tech. Fully saturated projections are tricky. You can move objects under five pounds. This chair, for instance. Or a teacup. But liquids"—she clicked her tongue—"pass right through, I'm afraid."

Annelise's eyes fell once again to the small puddle between Nimah's boots.

"Thank you for hosting me in your beautiful home, but it's time to see myself out."

"Nimah," Annelise called out before she turned away. Her fingers curled into a trembling fist like a leaf withering on a vine. "If you were smart, you'd want me to be your friend." She lifted cold blue eyes. "Not your enemy."

"I don't need friends." Nimah tapped her fingers in salute against her brow, a signal for Liselle, standing nearby, to end the transmission. "I have crew."

CHAPTER THIRTY-FOUR

"Deep breaths." Liselle stooped in front of Nimah and handed her a water flask.

"Oh fuck. Maverick wasn't joking. That really hurts."

"Sorry, I timed the extraction sequence for twenty-three minutes, but you ripped out of there ahead of the buffer."

They'd been warned more than once by Maverick that ending a full-density projection without a proper shutdown was like running straight into a wall. Right now, Nimah looked like she'd been thrown through it headfirst.

"How many fingers?" Liselle raised two, flickered to three, and then back to two as Nimah extended her jaw and wiggled it sharply.

Nimah gave her a smirking shove. "Two fingers." She tossed her camo-mask into her rucksack. "And one asshole."

"Visual acuity, check. Sense of humor, questionable." Liselle capped the canteen when Nimah was done taking a long, deep guzzle. "How did it go?"

"Oh, you know. The usual posturing, and an attempt on my life."

"Butter knife?"

"Poison."

Liselle whistled low. "I thought those scones looked suspicious." The dry rumble of Nimah's answering laugh made her own smile stretch wide. "Good to know Vesper was right, and despite the chairwoman's ruthlessness, she is fallibly predictable. We should get moving before she notices we're close enough for her to trip over."

Running a full-body projection, they'd had to be within line of sight for it to hold saturation with the depth of clarity required to convince Annelise that Nimah was there in the flesh. Vesper had provided the estate's coords she'd retrieved from her call log, and based on the property specs Mumbles was able to draw up, it was decided that Liselle should situate herself at the southeast wall flanking Annelise's primary garden.

Even though it meant they were now crouched on the side of a street beneath the shade of a flowering magnolia. Thankfully the roadways on Opalus were shockingly empty of anything other than service droids and maintenance drones too busy catering to the wealthy families who lived there to care.

Known as the world of perpetual spring with trees always in bloom, limestone structures sun-washed to palest white and inlaid with hanging foliage and panels of thick moss, it was one of the eighty-eight "crown jewel" planets. Home only to celebrities, prestigious members of the government, and high-ranking members of society descended from the *founding families* who ran some of the most profitable businesses in the void and could afford residency among them. Anyone who lived here couldn't spend money fast enough to ever run out of it.

There were no poverty districts in the crown jewels. No rodents or pests. No roaring air traffic or dizzying haze of holoverts. Just absolute wealth and privilege nestled in warm sunlight, and a soft breeze that smelled sweetly of toasted honey and *real* vanilla from the perfume pods fed into the vents, misting the breeze every few minutes.

The contrast between this place and the RIM couldn't be more shockingly apparent, and Liselle barely managed to choke down the nauseating waves of disgust.

"Help me up." Nimah waved a hand, drawing Liselle out of her spinning thoughts. "My legs are numb."

"Such a baby. Okay, I've got you." Scooping an arm around Nimah's waist, Liselle hoisted her onto her feet and startled when an ivory and chrome sedan stopped at the curb.

The door lifted like the spread of a wing, and a man stepped out into the gilded sunlight.

"Daddy . . ." Her world narrowed to a funnel, squeezing tight as the ventricles of her heart.

Lennox Namsara wore a gray suit that was expertly tailored in temperature-regulating silk, lightweight and designed to adjust to the environs. His hair groomed into a low fade with silver winging above his ears.

Although it had only been days since she'd last seen him, they'd felt impossibly long. Every hour dense with worry if she'd ever see him again. And suddenly everything inside of Liselle began to tremble.

Lennox opened his arms wide, eyes glassy with knowing. "My sweet girl," he whispered against her brow after she rushed into them. "I'm so unimaginably proud of you."

Liselle burrowed deeper against the strong wall of his chest. The scent of spiced musk and sweet lemongrass engulfed her in the tender warmth of comfort and familiarity. It was the cologne she'd gifted him for his birthday when she was eight years old. She and her mom had gone to a skilled perfumery and Liselle had devoted nearly three weeks, returning countless times, to perfect the layers of fragrances and spices until she'd found the perfect balance of scents she thought would most please him.

He'd worn it every day until only the smallest drop remained, which he'd promised to save for a particularly special moment. She'd expected it for perhaps a major promotion, or even a milestone anniversary. But the fact that he'd chosen this one—this moment of reunification after the last tumultuous few days, filled with so much danger and uncertainty—told Liselle far louder than words ever could how terrified he must have been for her safety.

And how deeply relieved he was to be holding her again.

Drawing back, Lennox stroked a thumb across Liselle's damp cheek. "Get in," he said to both Liselle and Nimah. "I'll give you a lift to the quay. As always, there's much to discuss and we regrettably do not have much time."

"Is everything okay?" Liselle asked as Nimah didn't hesitate to leap into the back seat of the waiting sedan.

"It will be." Lennox gave her a gentle nudge toward the vehicle.

Tucked inside, Liselle gripped Nimah's hand, checking her features for reassurance as her father sat across from them, and the door winged down to seal them inside a lush interior of ivory leather upholstery and the cooling whisper of air conditioning.

"We can speak freely." Lennox cupped his hands in his lap as the sedan idled away from the curb. "The vehicle has been cloaked for privacy, and I hold sole access credentials."

"Perks of being SIGA's right-hand man," Liselle muttered, and at her side, Nimah's shoulders tensed at the unexpected snap of her harsh words.

But now that she was seated, giddy relief rolled away almost as briskly as the sedan flowing smoothly down the flawlessly paved road and a cold, trembling sort of anger began to bubble deep in her gut.

A flicker of regret deepened his steady gaze. "I'd be surprised if you didn't mistrust me after all you've now seen and uncovered. It's hard to look at you both. I can only imagine what you must think of me."

"Do you have any idea what I've been through?" Liselle demanded, her voice a harsh whisper. "I had to run for my life, Daddy. My life! Because you were going to turn me in for questioning?"

"I know how it all looks." Lennox flagged his hands.

"How it all looks?" The only thing holding her tears from falling was the searing heat of her incandescent rage. But tears would come. Oh, they would come. And when they did, she'd drown. "How do I know an ambush isn't waiting for me and Nimah when we get to the quay?"

"You don't." He set his hand over his heart and shifted his eyes from Nimah to Liselle and back. "But hopefully I can assuage your doubts by offering the truth."

"And I'm waiting for an explanation." Liselle folded her arms to hide the tremble of her hands. "All these years I worshipped you, and Momma, but I was a foolish child, unable to see what was really happening out there." She pointed to the tinted windows and the blur of the opulent city whizzing by, soft and hazy as strokes of water paint on a stretched canvas. "But you're an adult. You should know better. As a man who holds a prominent position, wielding great power and influence, what have you done with it?" She arched a brow. "You should be doing *something*."

"And I have been. Who do you think suggested Annelise contact Vesper from her personal line?" He inclined his head in gentle challenge.

Liselle's eyes whisked from left to right, thrown by his shift in argument. "What does that have to do with anything?"

"Everything, sweetheart. Part of my job as an attorney is knowing who I'm dealing with. And Vesper . . ." Lennox shrugged, the barest lift of his shoulder. "I believed she was the sort who would take the contract but ultimately reevaluate and shift her priorities along the way. If not, I trusted that once confronted by her, somehow you and Nimah would glean the information of the chairwoman's involvement as well as her personal location for potential leverage. Either path would lead you to where you are right now."

Whatever argument she'd had brewing died on her tongue, and Liselle slumped back against the cool ivory upholstery with a "*Huh*."

"Navigating the law is more than just understanding codes and legislation," Lennox went on. "It's advanced risk assessment and strategic evaluation. I have to understand the mindsets of complicated individuals and the various anchors of motivation that drive their actions so that I can position myself to intercede or outmaneuver. For instance." He gestured to Liselle. "Do you honestly think you could break into my office without me knowing?"

"You knew?"

"Sweetheart, I let you in. Just as I released the draft warrant early so that Wallace could warn you."

"How could you have known she'd do that? Or that I would even approach her to begin with?"

"Because the new admiral has already shown a shift in her allegiances. She is not the stalwart soldier she once was. Like you, she has seen and knows too much," Lennox explained. "I had strong reason to hope she would act, and she did not disappoint. I hoped you would find your way to Nimah—and together, the truth."

Liselle drew in a tight breath. All this time. The risks he'd taken and the consequences that might yet still follow, should SIGA ever find out. "You've put yourself in so much danger."

"The board was less than pleased," Lennox agreed. "But any decent lawyer with my depth of experience knows how to turn an argument on its head. For now I am indispensable, and so long as I remain that way, I can continue to exert my influence wherever possible. Which is why I am here now with the both of you." Lennox clasped his hands, shoulders rounded with the weight of the responsibility he'd carried in secret for far too long. "I'm not proud of the things I've done or been part of. The greater the life of privilege—the more it demands of your soul . . ." He drummed his foot against the inside of the sedan door.

A ceaseless beat.

Liselle swallowed hard. She'd never seen her father anxious a day in his life, but this man, seated across from her, was a bundle of nerves wrapped in an expensive suit.

"With SIGA . . . once you're in, there are only two ways you leave: retirement, after a lifetime of loyal service. Or in a body bag," Lennox continued. "You don't quit. You don't *resign*." His cool brown eyes hardened, as if seeing something beyond them. "You endure. And you wait."

"So what's changed?" Nimah broke the silence after a moment of reflection. "That's why you're here now, isn't it?"

"To answer that we would have to be somewhere far more secure. All I can share is that, with the RIM Accord hanging on the edge, there are those of us who are gathering in preparation and I want you at my side for what comes next." He reached for Liselle. "If you agree, then I will have you reassigned as part of my auxiliary staff. You will be as in as it gets, Liselle, and together . . . together we can make the impossible *possible*."

"How?" Liselle blinked. "SIGA knows of my connection to Nimah . . . they'd never trust me now to be so close to where they're most vulnerable."

"There are ways. If you trust me."

The sedan slowed to an easy stop and the door to her left clicked before smoothly whisking open. Lennox nodded to the open door and waited for both girls to exit before he followed them out onto the stone walkway leading toward the entry gate of the departure quay.

Reaching into the breast pocket of his suit jacket, Lennox withdrew a folded card and handed it to Nimah. "This permit has been authenticated to my office. They'll assume it's my junior associate returning after our check-in with the chairwoman, carefully timed ahead of your arrival in her gardens." He winked to Nimah. "No one will follow you. Or you." He looked to Liselle. "If you elect to decline my offer and leave with Nimah. Whatever you decide—whatever your path forward—I will support you."

Liselle drew in a slow breath to stabilize the intense emotions colliding inside of her. "I'm sorry I doubted you, daddy."

"Don't be sorry." He hooked a finger beneath her chin, keeping it high and proud. "I raised you to be fierce and independent. A free thinker. And you've done me proud. So proud." He looked to Nimah and then Liselle. And in his eyes, she saw equal love. Equal tenderness. "My girls," he whispered.

Reaching for them both, Lennox drew them into a hug so tight the shudder of soft sobs rattling from the hard wall of his chest rocked Liselle straight to the core.

Tucked at her side, she felt Nimah melt into him, her eyes pinched tight against the surge of emotion that made Liselle's own heart ache and tears form. Her parents had been the closest Nimah had to experiencing familial love. As much as Liselle knew Nimah had feared losing their friendship, sisters born of choice instead of blood, she must have been equally bereft over the loss of them as well.

Drawing back, Lennox knuckled his eyes clear. "I'll give you both a moment. But it'll have to be brief," he cautioned. "My clearance permit expires in five minutes."

"Nimah—" Liselle's watery voice snagged in her throat. All she ever wanted was to do good, and here was a chance to do far more than she'd ever imagined. Standing by her father's side, she could be a force for change from within. But to do so meant once again she'd have to lose the one person she had never imagined living without. And that . . . that tore her soul in two.

"Don't," Nimah interrupted, as if already knowing what she was about to say. "I want this for you. You deserve this, Lis."

Liselle's lips twisted into a teasing smile. "Guess it wouldn't hurt to have that inside man again, eh?"

"Oh, fuck that," Nimah laughed. "I won't trouble you a third time. I learned my lesson."

"But I want you to." Liselle captured her hand, and her attention. "Trouble me." She gave it an urgent squeeze. "Whatever you need. Anything . . . Please."

"Okay." Nimah squeezed back.

And Liselle's smile wavered with a fresh surge of despair. "I'm so sorry, Nimah." She wept, unable to hold it all in anymore. "It took me a long time to see the world as it *really* is, instead of what I'd been raised to see. And I'm ashamed of myself for it."

"None of us are perfect, Lis. We all have bags to unpack, but one thing that has always remained true is you are the best person I know." Nimah gathered her face and brushed away tears from her cheeks. "You inspire me to be strong. And brave. And good. Thank you for being not only my friend but my family." Her own watery smile cut across her face, bright as sunlight. "I wouldn't have made it without you."

They fell into each other's embrace, another tear-drenched goodbye before they drew apart. And as Nimah walked away, Liselle's chest bloomed bright with hope instead of the ache of sorrow. There was something in her friend she hadn't seen until this moment. A strength of self rooted in purpose.

Nimah wasn't a lost little girl anymore, abandoned and spiraling in the dark. She was a leader. A pirate. And Liselle's best friend.

CHAPTER THIRTY-FIVE

"Vitals are stable. All in all, you appear to be rebounding nicely." Jono removed biosensors from Nimah's chest, and deposited them onto the floating tray.

"Well, that's a relief." Nimah flexed her fingers, pushing feeling back into her hand. She hated being prodded like a pin cushion, but for now it was necessary to give Jono all that he needed. "I've been sleeping better. Almost too good."

Jono tapped the glass screen of his pad, bringing up his exam notes from their last three check-ins. "That's great to hear, but before we celebrate, let's talk about Dobs." Dropping to the wheeled stool, he pushed his glasses up the bridge of his slender nose. "Any further encounters?"

"None." Nimah swung her legs over the side of the table. "It's been a solid week." And the passing seconds were shockingly empty without the hounding pressure of Dobs beating against her temples at all hours of the day and night. She'd nearly forgotten what it felt like. *Normal.*

Jono angled his head. "You almost sound saddened by that?"

"I kinda am." A bitter smile twisted across her lips. "Dobs was . . . important to me, and I never really knew how to feel about her death. I think that's why my mind got so messed up. I wanted to keep her alive, and with me. I didn't want to let go." But in those final moments before releasing the hatch—she finally had.

She'd let go.

Lips pursed, Jono nodded thoughtfully. "Well, after spending the last week trying to make sense of Dr. Hillard's research notes, along with my own studies into elite—I have a theory." Jono scooted to the console, wheels skidding over uneven flooring as he settled behind the curved holoscreen. "Comparing diagnostics from today to when I first examined you, there's already a marked improvement. Your heart is still strained—don't get me wrong—but the significant drop-off supports my earlier hypothesis that Dobs was in fact an energetic parasite driving your system into overload."

Nimah frowned, trying to make sense of the intricate graph of her diagnostics—but it might as well be a whole other language. "Any idea how that is even possible?"

"I'm *so glad* you asked." Jono swivelled on his stool, hands clasped like he was gracing a podium about to give a lecture on his latest discovery. "When Dobs was about to die after you fought—what went through your head?"

Nimah rolled her bottom lip between her teeth. "At first, I felt justified. She'd killed Sigourney and I wanted to make her pay." More than that, she'd wanted Dobs to hurt as deeply as Nimah had been by her betrayal. But as the primefire countdown drew closer to venting, righteous wrath had yielded to heartbroken regret. "A split second before the vent released, I wanted to stop it. I wanted to save her." And the utter helplessness, knowing it was too late as she'd witnessed the awful, violent end, had birthed a hell Nimah spent three months struggling to claw her way out of.

"Exactly!" Jono snapped his fingers, face bright with eager excitement. "I believe the shift in your intentions compelled the elite to react. Following that emotional pathway, it latched onto Dobs—her soul—and pulled a fragment of her into you to keep alive. Then as the weeks went on, that fragment grew, feeding off you, her consciousness began to take up more bandwidth in your mind. Eventually, I think it would've either taken over your body, or killed you." He shrugged. "Most likely the latter."

Nimah shook a dazed head. A few weeks ago, she might have struggled to understand any of this, but since her tethering with Vesper, whatever connection they'd forged in that lab, there was an awareness inside of her now that hadn't been there before—almost like a sixth sense. Elite was a mystery that couldn't be quantified through research and study. Only experienced.

"One hole in that theory, if it was my intention that bound Dobs to me"—Nimah frowned—"why didn't it do the same for Siggy?"

"My guess?" Jono swayed his head in thought. "Because she didn't want to. Sigourney was a warrior, and warrior's are often proud to face their death. But Dobs I doubt was quite so eager, therefore I think it's fair to hypothesize that she'd have bolted for the smallest crack if it meant a chance at living. You offered that crack. She took it."

A soft, sad smile etched across Nimah's lips. "Sounds about right."

"If you want me to go a bit deeper into my analysis," Jono rubbed his palms together, "I think the transference of energetic consciousness requires a two-way handshake. You needed Dobs as much as she needed you."

Nimah frowned. "You're losing me again."

His grin flashed. "Believe me, my head's been spinning off my shoulders for days with all that I'm learning, but hear me out—I don't think elite just gives you what you want. It brings you to what you need. The first time you truly connected to it, what did it do?"

"It brought me back to the *Avenger*."

Jono nodded. "To a period of your deepest trauma, which you had to overcome in order to establish the first layer of that bond."

And once she had, that was when elite fused to her. "Okay." Nimah nodded. "Keep going."

"This connection it created between you and Dobs was another journey into healing these deep, inner wounds you carry. In your final moment together, from what you described, you quite literally released your demons, Nimah, which has allowed your bond with elite to further progress. It's no longer resisting you. It's embraced you."

Nimah sat back with a soft, "Huh."

"Can I ask you something?" Jono asked after Nimah climbed down from the exam table. "Why didn't you tell anyone about what was happening to you?"

"I didn't want them to lose faith in me. I didn't want to lose faith in myself."

"And now that it's behind you?" Jono raised a brow. "Don't you think it might be a good time to open up?"

Nimah mulled the question for a moment. Shrugged. "Dobs is gone, so . . . doesn't matter anymore, does it?"

"No," Jono agreed, but his brows tightened in doubt. "I guess it doesn't."

Leaving Jono's study, Nimah stepped out into the crisp afternoon air. The RIM's voidnetting spread like an overcast sky—pale gray, soft as smoke from a campfire. There was no sunshine on the RIM, no warmth of golden light. As a child, she'd thought it bleak and oppressive, but now it soothed her like the weight of a fuzzy blanket. She cast her eyes to that stark sky and let them roll shut. The whisper of a smile rose to her lips.

Dobs was gone, but that didn't mean she was free of ghosts, or that elite was through with testing her. As Dobs had said, healing wasn't linear, it was cyclical. There would always be a Dobs in the back of her mind wanting to tear her down, but Nimah could choose to make her own voice stronger. Louder.

And if the time came, when old wounds resurfaced and scars tore viciously open, she would face them with newfound strength and awareness.

Nimah followed her feet toward the quay and entered the roiling Rusty Screw cantina packed with more bodies than tables. The Valkyrie crew gathered around the largest one, its open surface made from an old door fastened to a cable spool. Bots swung through the crowd, depositing frothing mugs of beer to join the trays laden with smoked turkey legs, fried pupusas topped with pickled cabbage, fragrant jollof rice, and suya beef. Nimah's stomach grumbled at the sight. Life on the RIM, though humble, boasted a richness of diversity, of people and spices and culture.

Blackfyre's crew had docked the day before last and joined in the celebration as well. Tomorrow, they would all leave for Tortuga for the ascension of Indira Roscoe. Their new queen.

Ro hooked her arm around Nimah's shoulder when she appeared at her side. "There you are."

Nimah gazed up at her grandmother, cheeks flushed from laughter and booze. "I think you're drunk."

"I am." Ro winked, teasing a laugh out of Nimah.

It made her happy to see that her grandmother had come to embrace the council's decision, prepared to do her duty and support their community, even though it also saddened her to know that with this new step forward their paths would once again be forced to diverge.

"Here." Ro plunked a fresh mug of chilled beer in front of Nimah. "Start drinking and wipe that sorrowful look off your face."

"I'm not sad." Nimah's fingers closed around the cold glass, slick with condensation. "Not really," she amended. "I'm proud of you."

Something like modesty deepened the pink of Ro's cheeks.

"Sparra!" Zensha's booming voice followed with the smash of her stein to Nimah's. "There you be, at last."

"Hey." Nimah shook sloshed beer off her hand with a grin. "I take it the meeting with the ambassadors went well?"

"Oh, we sailed through the fairest of winds," Zensha answered, rippling her hand through the air like it was a kite dancing in the sky. "The ambassadors have accepted my proposal, and I have you to thank for the fine idea."

Nimah's cheeks warmed with a blush that deepened when she caught her grandmother's watchful and proud gaze. "Ah—well, I'm just glad I could help." She'd been stretched flat on her back while Jono prodded her in examination—utterly bored—when the idea struck her.

Solvanis was an empty unregistered planet; and it seemed an unbelievable waste to let such a gift remain empty when there were one hundred and fifty billion RIMers in desperate need of resettlement. Especially while the RIM Accord remained in flux.

"You did more than help." Zensha clapped a hand to Nimah's shoulder. "You've changed lives, Sparra. Solvanis would've been left to rot like an open grave, but now it will know the sound of laughter and taste the sweat of toil, once more. But I'd expect no less of the granddaughter of La Voz, our soon to be queen!"

Zensha raised her stein in salute, Ro joined her, and Nimah clinked her glass to both in cheers before taking a hearty swallow.

Reshaping a planet into a thriving homebase would demand immense effort and considerable resources to build whole cities vast enough to house all who wanted to resettle, but the RIM was forged on the impossible—and boasted some of the most ingenious engineers and brilliant minds. Along with Zensha's cached wealth from her payout for guarding the unregistered planet, Solvanis would soon become a haven. And for the rescued children it meant more than shelter, but a return to their beloved home where they would be guided and protected by Zensha and the Blackfyre crew.

"I was also thinking . . ." Nimah dragged out a chair and they sat down, leaning close to her grandmother as the music of the cantina swelled—joined by the gathering voices of the patrons. "Mumbles should stay with you in Tortuga. That way she can receive the care and support she needs, as well as further her exploration into gadgetry with greater access to tech and resources."

Ro nodded thoughtfully, taking Nimah's proposal into consideration.

As second, it was Nimah's job to support her captain with any decisions requiring administrative oversight. And whoever her grandmother appointed to take over as captain, she would continue to do so with the same devotion and diligence. Probably Gertrude, if Nimah had to guess, as it made the most sense to choose a successor with a few solid years under their belt, while she continued to grow into her pirate boots. Boots that felt a lot more snug and steady these days. Nimah swigged from her beer with a grin.

"Crew will need to hunt for another onboard tech," Ro pointed out.

"Boomer's surprisingly handy and has learned a thing or two from Mumbles." Nimah wiped foam from her upper lip. "I think we should see how he does. Give him a chance to cut his teeth."

A proud grin split her grandmother's face. "Nurturing and fostering talent among your own crew is the hallmark of great leadership." Before Nimah could respond, Ro raised her hands, calling for a hush, and the noise within the cantina hushed to hear the great La Voz speak. "Today marks my last as captain of the *Stormchaser*. I've known no greater honor than that of leading these fine women, seated before me."

Hands beat to tables; boots stomped to floor.

"I never saw myself as someone worthy of a crown," Ro continued, and again the cheers fell away so all could hear her words. "Leadership is a profound weight. One I hope to carry well as I prepare to do my duty to our people. But piracy is for the young. I've had my days of glory, and now it's time to pass the mantle to the next generation." She turned to Nimah and crooked a summoning finger.

"To your feet, Cadet." Maverick kissed her shoulder, then nudged her to stand. Thankfully, Nimah's legs held true.

"Nimah Dabo-124, I darsay there are few in this here room, or on all of the RIM, who have not heard your name or respect its weight. I name you captain, and bequeath you my mantle and ship, not because you are my blood—but because you've earned it. What say you?"

"Aye," Nimah answered, breathless with disbelief. The roar of cheers and beating of fists hammered almost as loud as her staggering heart.

"You are young. So was I when I assumed captaincy." Ro held her shoulders. "But you have been tried and tested more than most, and proven you are steel and salt to the bone. Not yet twenty-three, and already you are carving out a legacy to rival the best of us. Crew who call themselves Valkyrie, I present your new captain. What say you?"

"Aye!" Chu and Gertrude bellowed

"Aye!" Boomer threw up a fist.

Maverick cupped his hands to his mouth with a sharp whistle, his proud *aye!* carrying over the din as the patrons echoed in support.

"Well done, little bird." Gertrude hugged Nimah tight, eyes dewy.

"Are you sure you aren't upset it's not you?" she asked gently.

"Darling, the *c* in captain stands for cortisol, innit, and this face?" She waved a freshly manicured finger with two-inch-long knifepoint nails in shocking orange, at herself. "Go puffy with stress? Spare me the drag."

"The *Stormchaser* is a fine vessel, but as her new captain, you must also give her a new name." Zensha winked after giving Nimah a celebratory hug. "What will you call her?"

The name came to her as quick as an easy breath. Nimah looked to her grandmother. "Someone wise once told me that death is a storm few have the courage to sail into. So I will call her *Stormbreaker*," she said confidently for all to hear. "Let her name serve as a warning to those who challenge the strength of her hull, or resilience of her crew."

Ro's grin stretched bold and fierce. "A fine name."

"*Stormbreaker!*" Chu punched a roaring fist.

"*Stormbreaker!*" the rest of the Valkyrie crew echoed.

Reaching for her granddaughter, Ro cupped Nimah's cheek, as music and laughter and celebration resumed. "I may soon be queen, but before that, I was La Voz. The voice of the people. Now they will have you to stand for them, not only those here with us, but all who were silenced. So be loud, Nimah, be bold and true and let the ferocity of your voice strike to the hearts of those who seek to oppress and destroy. Strike, until the black of the void and the light of the stars tremble in respect of your name."

More rallying cries rattled the walls, and she soaked in this moment of triumph and belonging. Captaincy was a huge responsibility, but for the first time, Nimah believed she was strong enough to carry it.

"To the void!" Nimah raised her beer.

"To Valhalla!" All in the cantina roared back.

Finished with celebrating, Nimah decided to leave ahead of the crew, allowing them a moment alone to part ways with their now former captain. The *Stormbreaker's* airlock cycled open with a low hiss, spilling warm, recycled air out of the hold, and her boots clanked against the grated flooring as she entered.

Vesper stood at the sound of her entry and leaned against the rail at the base of the stairway, one boot planted to the step and arms folded.

"You're leaving?" Nimah nodded to the packed gear-bag sitting by her feet.

"'Bout that time. Got a clean bill of health, for the most part." She patted her stomach, where the sword wound was near to fully healed, leaving only the barest pink scar against the sidewall of her abs.

"I'm surprised you waited until I got back."

"Almost didn't," Vesper admitted. "I . . . uh, don't do goodbyes."

"Me too." Nimah swallowed past the knot in her throat. Her eyes winged up to the track lights casting long shadows across the stacked crates and lines of exposed cables overhead. "Listen. We've got room on the crew—on *my* crew," she amended, still struggling to take in the fact this was all hers now. "You've earned a berth. If you want it."

"On this geriatric heap?" Vesper's lip curled in a wry grin and she uncrossed her arms, flicking a hand at the ship. "Thanks, but I prefer boats that don't reek of burnt thruster oil and stale sweat."

The *Stormbreaker* rumbled—a deep, growling tremor that made the overhead lights flicker and the gantry sway-locks rattle. As if the ship itself bristled at her insult.

"Careful," Nimah teased. "I think you pissed off Ma."

"It's a ship." Vesper scoffed, tucking her hands into her back pockets. "You can't piss off a ship."

The intercom speakers crackled overhead, and Ma's low—and unmistakably menacing—voice clipped: <*Unregistered passenger, Vesper Crole, please be advised that any further disparaging remarks regarding performance and sanitation of the* Stormbreaker *may result in immediate venting, or oxygen siphoning from your allocated cabin during stasis, should you choose to remain onboard.*>

"Apparently you can." Nimah laughed. "And did."

Vesper glared at the intercom speaker, as if lasers might suddenly descend from the rafters to fillet her on the spot. "Good thing I'm getting off this boat, then."

Nimah's heart gave a tender squeeze. "Where are you headed?"

Vesper peered out at the bustling sprawl of the quay visible from the open hatch of the airlock. "It's a big void out there. Time I find my own corner. I'll have to lay low, but if there's anything I'm good at—it's disappearing." She met Nimah's eyes, and something passed between them, familiar and aching.

It was strange. Nimah had known Vesper only a scant few days, most of it spent as enemies and in that short time, bonded through blood and trauma, they'd become something that felt almost as deep and sacred as family.

The laughing voices of the crew flowed into the hatch seconds before they entered the ship, passing by Nimah and Vesper through the hold and up the stairways leading to cabins and bridge.

"That's my cue." Vesper gave a half smile—one part regret, two parts steel. "See you around, Captain." Tossing her gear-bag over her shoulder, Vesper disappeared down the gangway with a soft clank of boots and was swept away in the dusty churn of the bustling quay.

"*Attention all crew,*" Maverick's voice floated through the intercom. "*Detaching from quay, prepare for thrusters to engage. We have ten minutes to burn.*"

Nimah sealed the airlock, and the *Stormbreaker*'s thrusters ignited with a rumble that shook through hull metal and up into her feet. Pressing her palm to the cool hull, she could feel the engine's heartbeat thrumming through cables and beams like blood through veins. Eyes closed, she let the subtle tremor underfoot guide her stance as the ship peeled away from the dock ring. The torque tugged behind her knees—once, it would've sent her sprawling, but now she leaned into it. Steady and confident against the waves of a storming sea.

"Where to, Captain?" Maverick asked once Nimah reached the bridge.

Bracing the console, she gazed out at the viewport overlooking the arched expanse of the RIM, and beyond it to the deep recesses of the sprawling void. A tapestry of gauzy nebula clouds spread in vivid violet and gold, starbursts that pulsed like distant lanterns and long, shimmering traffic lanes of incoming cargo freighters and outbound vessels that blitzed across it like streaking comets.

The void wasn't an empty abyss. It was alive. Thrumming with infinite hope and endless possibility for fortune and adventure—all hers for the taking.

Nimah settled into the co-seat and grinned at Maverick. "Bring me to the horizon."

ABOUT THE AUTHOR

Fallon DeMornay is the author of *Stiletto Sisterhood* and *Flight of the Sparrow*. Known for writing about powerful girls smashing the patriarchy with swords or stilettos, she was a finalist in Harlequin's "So You Think You Can Write" contest, and her work has been featured on Cosmopolitan.com and reviewed by RT Book Reviews. Affection4ately referred to as Wonder Woman by her own real-life Sisterhood, DeMornay can be found tearing up the dancefloor to salsa or bachata when she isn't writing. She currently resides in North York, Canada.

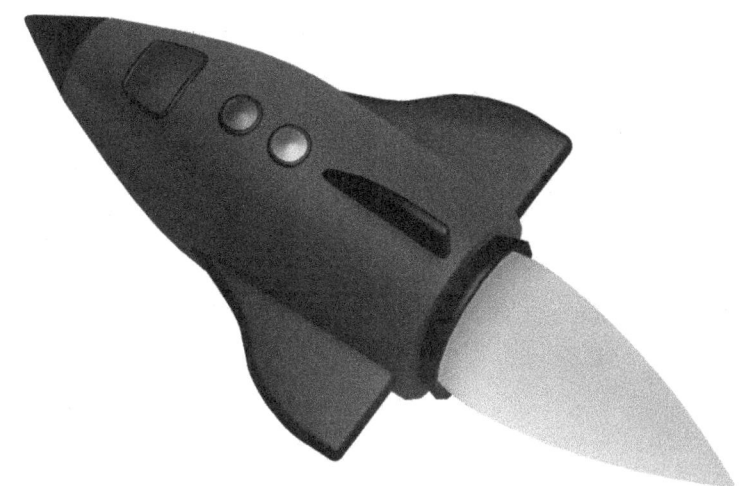

STELLAR CONTENT AWAITS
follow us on our socials

 podiumentertainment.com

 @podiumentertainment

 /podiumentertainment

 @podium_ent

 @podiumentertainment